accolades of wolves

accolades of wolves

toni mobley

ISBN: 979-8-8878500-0-9 (Paperback)
ISBN: 979-8-8878500-1-6 (Hardcover)

Library of Congress Control Number: 2022943988

Any references to historical events, real people, or real places are used fictitiously. Names, characters, and places are products of the author's imagination.

Howling wolf image by Freepik.
Book design by Allison Chernutan.

Printed in the United States of America.

First printing edition 2022.

emily@fracturedmirrorpublishing.com
Fractured Mirror Publishing
Knoxville, Tennessee

www.fracturedmirrorpublishing.com

Dear Dad,

Dreams do come true.

1960-2003

♥

CHAPTER
ONE

The moment I closed that door, I knew it was over. That didn't discourage me as much as I thought it would. Even after the click of the latch reverberated through my skull like the ringing of a gong. His face bore the tattoo of a broken man. But it was what was best for both of us. This relationship had run its course long ago, and it was as simple to me as driving a rusty nail through a deteriorating coffin. The dust would settle quickly.

"Phoebe."

His shattered voice reached out through the door, saying my name like it was the only thing he could hold on to, and in the frosted glass his shadow loomed nearby, waiting for me. If I stayed any longer, I would cave. I knew me, and I knew him. I owed it to both of us, as I turned on my heels, and walked away. My shoes clattered against the stone, and I resisted the urge to cast a glance over my shoulder.

His neighbours peeked out from behind the curtains of their windows, nosey nobodies whose only hobby was gossiping. In this small town, news would travel fast, and within the hour my phone would buzz alive with phone calls and text messages.

I took the liberty of turning it off now.

I didn't owe anyone an explanation, my reasonings were just that, my own. Liam knew why it had to happen, and I entitled no one else to such an explanation.

Crossing the street, I loitered in the park where I had spent my entire teenage life with the boy whose heart I just broke. Right there on the swings where a mother and child played was where we went after our first date. For hours we'd kick up off the ground and share our innermost secrets with one another. If your innermost secrets included a round of a hundred questions such as your favorite color, food, and breed of dog.

Red, chocolate, and huskies.

'Why a husky?' he had asked, as if it were a weird thing to say.

'It's the closest to a wolf I could ever own,' I had said.

"Mommy, higher!" the little girl cried, her pigtails waving in the breeze as her mother pushed her with an exuberance my mother once exhibited when I was a child. Their matching smiles were infectious. If I had come here under different circumstances, I would have found the courage to smile in response.

Glancing at my watch out of habit more than anything else, I cursed under my breath, picking up my pace. I was hoping this conversation would be quick. At this rate, however, I would be late to work.

Luckily, the moment my feet hit the sidewalk, the bus that would take me back into the city loomed into view. It eased to a squeaking stop before me. With one last glance at Liam's door, where he still stood, eyes on me, I boarded. Even as we pulled away, the park and homes disappearing behind us, I couldn't pull my eyes from him.

Pushing away the urge to check my phone, I let my mind wander among the emerald fields with its scattered spots of grazing brown cows. The grey-scale shingles on the roofs of the houses that fleeted by outside the bus cast a solemn mood everywhere I looked.

It was Edinburgh, after all, and yet I was finding the near constant shifting of the grey clouds across the sky insufferable.

It was all I had known my entire life, and yet, part of me yearned for more. Everything around me was cut and paste, never falling outside the realm of what I expected of it.

My life was simple, safe. And I needed a change, soon. Part of me thought dumping Liam would speed up that process, but all I felt now was discontent, even though I didn't regret my actions. I knew it was what was best for both of us.

The bus jolted to a stop, the driver calling out, "Edinburgh Zoo!"

Hesitating at the door, with my foot on the step, something pattered against the stones right outside. A gentle rain had risen, and with it a breeze that twirled the leaves around the feet of people who walked past.

"Miss, are you okay?"

I glanced up at the driver. "Yes, sorry."

Get a grip on yourself, Phoebe.

The doors shut the moment my feet hit the pavement; a breeze of cold, wet air smacked me in the face. I pulled the hood of my sports jacket over my head, shivering in the predictability of an Edinburgh morning. The glass-domed awning of the bus stop did little to spare me from the chill.

I stared listlessly at the flashing display on the billboard nearby, more for an excuse not to move or feel anything. A bear was roaring defiantly at the sky, an advertisement for the zoo's temporary European Brown Bear exhibit.

A girl with auburn-dyed curls barely contained in a polka dotted scarf bounded out from behind a row of trees to greet me, umbrella held tightly in her gloved hand.

"Phoebe, you mad dog!" She cackled, throwing her free arm around me, hugging me close.

My arms wrapped around her, my shoulders sagging as I tried to choke back a sob.

"Come on, none of that," she whispered.

Sighing as tears slipped free, I disentangled myself from her embrace. "Lucy, you didn't need to come."

She scoffed. "As if I wouldn't be here to support my best

friend in her time of need."

I offered her a weak smile.

"Besides, what crazy bird breaks up with her boyfriend and then goes to work like nothing happened. You're nuts!"

"I need the money." Not exactly true, and she knew that.

She rolled her eyes. "You can afford one day off."

Shrugging, we walked side by side, her umbrella fighting off the gentle mist of the morning rain as we made our way up the hill. Hordes of tourists rushed past us, their voices breaking the silence as they sprinted from the hotel to the zoo next door.

I was lucky that my best friend worked next door to me, whereas she entertained herself with mucking out stalls of exotic creatures, I did paperwork and drew blood from sick and injured people. It was an interesting location, having the hospital right next to the hotel and the zoo. It certainly made my lunch breaks entertaining, listening to the calls of the animals from the bottom of the hill.

It felt as if in the blink of an eye we had scaled the hill, finding ourselves standing before the doors of the hospital. Her foot tapped in rhythm to a song that played from the radio of a car waiting in the lot, the driver face deep in a packet of crisps.

"Call me on your break?" She asked, noticing the time on the clock hanging above the entrance.

I nodded. "Sure."

She rushed forward, planting a kiss on my cheek, before twirling on her heel. "Bye, love!" she called, humming the tune of that song.

"Bye, Lucy," I said in return, my voice feeling hollow and weak.

Retreating, she skipped along the road, her curls bouncing in time to the tune.

I envied that bouncy, merry soul of hers. She was always in the highest of spirits. Nothing could dampen the light she carried. I couldn't imagine living a life without her.

"Phoebe, you're late," called a voice from the foyer.

Shit.

Darting across the foyer, I strode forward, giving the woman a tight hug.

"Fancy meeting you here," I remarked.

She laughed, a throaty sound that told me she had been on her smoke break.

"Still sucking down those death sticks, I see."

Eyebrows raised, she smirked. "Ah. Yes, well…"

"You'd think a nurse would know better."

She huffed at me; her face reddening. "Come now child, that any way to speak to your mother?"

I gave her hand a squeeze, my eyes catching sight of the clock on the wall.

"Shit," I breathed.

"What's wrong?"

Shutting my eyes tightly, I groaned. "I'm gonna get in so much shit with Edgar."

"You're lucky your boss was in a fender bender this morning, otherwise he'd be chewing your ear off right now."

I nudged her with my elbow. "What a horrible thing to say."

She coughed, disguising it poorly with a throaty chuckle. "If it works in your favor, who cares?"

Groaning, I made a scene of stomping to the staff room with her hot on my heels. Hanging my jacket on one of the hooks by the door, I slipped into my scrubs, not caring who saw me throw them over my leggings and camisole.

My mother pressed a clipboard into my hands.

"Probably should get started with replenishing the storeroom." She winked.

Sure enough, my name was scribbled hastily right under the 'assisting with clinic work' section.

"Just you wait and see, I'm going to stack that toilet paper so good!" I said sarcastically, hanging the clipboard back up on the corkboard.

My mother coughed again, rubbing her chest in discomfort, her brows furrowing.

"What's wrong?"

Clearing her throat, she waved me off. "It's nothing dear. I've just had this horrid cough since this morning."

"Why don't you chill on the cigarettes for a day." I knew my words would go in one ear and out the other. Asking a pack-a-day smoker to shelve their habit was like begging a lion to eat grass.

"Yeah, yeah, yeah," she said, throwing the door open before disappearing into the hall.

There was nothing else to do but get on with my shift and hope no one outed me to Edgar when he got in. Or at the very least, my work ethic would be enough to calm the beast within.

The day dragged on though, and soon enough my lunch break loomed before me, and I was throwing on my jacket and heading out the door to wander the grounds. Ignoring the countless missed calls and texts, I thumbed through my phone until I saw Lucy's name in my contacts.

"Hello!" her voice sang after a single ring.

I smirked. "You were waiting, huh?"

"Of course, I was, girl! I need that juicy gossip, it feeds me!"

"Oh Lucy, what would I do without you?"

I could hear the laughter in her voice as she said, "Probably shrivel up and die."

"Wonderful descriptive prose as always, Lucy. I look forward to what you have in store for me next."

"First things first though, I gotta know—did he cry?"

My heart lurched at how excited she sounded at the prospect of Liam in tears. He wasn't a bad boyfriend, and our four years together were not always fraught with tension.

"It's over, Lucy. That's all. I went over to his house and told him and then I left for work."

There was a crackling over the phone as Lucy replied with a simple, "Oh."

"Yeah, sorry. Nothing juicy."

"Well, I'm sure you have the most delicious text messages

piling up on your phone."

I sighed. "Yeah, you're not wrong."

"From his sisters, right?"

I nodded to no one. "Yeah." I didn't need to check the names on those messages to know who sent them.

"Didn't think they'd let you get away unscathed."

"They never did like me, did they?" I giggled.

"They were probably just jealous you got something they couldn't have. Some forbidden fruit action if you catch my drift." I could practically hear the wink in her voice.

"Gross, Lucy!" I made a face, and two nurses sitting at a bench nearby glanced up at me.

She laughed; a hearty noise that helped fight off the chill of the misty rain that insisted on clinging to every inch of me.

"So, what does the great Phoebe Wood have planned now?"

"You know, I've always wanted to go gallivanting through the fjords of Norway."

"Norway! Why can't you be normal and go somewhere like Paris, or Milan, or shit…even New York? I'd go to New York with you."

"I know." She'd been begging me for years to go on a two-week girls' trip to the States, and so far, I had managed to hold her back with the best excuses. I had school, a new job, a boy-friend, bills. But now I'd lost one of my reasons.

An annoying ding sounded in my ear, and I glanced at the mystery call waiting to be answered.

"What was that?" Lucy's voice called out.

I ignored it. "I don't know, some random number."

It kept coming though, like a broken record player. Whoever was on the other line was annoyingly insistent. *That's one way to get me not to answer*, I thought sourly.

"Is it Liam?" Her voice held an edge of concern to it. "They seem rather persistent."

"I don't think so. If it were important though, they wouldn't be trying to hide their number."

"That's very true," she said.

I could hear a commotion in the background, just beyond that incessant second call waiting notification. "What's going on over there?"

"Oh my god, Phoebe, okay—so, we got this new—"

Lucy's voice was drowned out by the slapping of shoes on the concrete behind me. Turning, I heard my name called.

"One second, Lucy," I said.

One of the nurses who assisted my mother was staring back at me, hair wild, eyes wide.

"Barbara?"

She took a deep breath, steadying herself. "Phoebe, you need to come."

I frowned. "What?" I glanced at my watch. "I still have fifteen minutes."

Barbara wasn't listening to my words, her hands kept beckoning me to follow.

"Did Edgar get in or something? If so, I'll just talk to him after—"

"It's your mother, Phoebe," she said.

The blood in my veins chilled, my heart thudding loudly in my ears. Something was wrong. "What?"

I closed the space between us slowly, as if time stood still.

Barbara looked me in the eyes. "I tried calling you, we all tried…"

"What's going on?" I growled, my body shaking.

She swallowed, her eyes rimmed red with tears. "She's dead, Phoebe."

CHAPTER
TWO

The world around me was a silent, endless void. Nothing else existed, except the silence that I struggled through. It sucked at me, like mud in a swamp, that quicksand deathtrap threatening to pull me under. The staff parted before me like the Red Sea, pity marked their faces, their lips moved, mouthing the same dribble.

I couldn't hear them though, I couldn't hear anyone, or anything, except the pounding of my heart. Those cursed double doors of plastic loomed before me. The annoying neon lights shouted at me.

Emergency Room.

Shoving them aside, I strode straight into the first room, not caring who saw me. It didn't matter anyway because no one tried to stop me. I knew what was under that bleached white sheet, sitting stiffly on the metal stretcher. I was prepared for it, and yet when my trembling hand pulled back the sheet, my body went cold, numb. As cold and as numb as hers.

I cried out, my voice hoarse, but no noise came out. That didn't stop me, my chest heaving as sobs wracked my body, slumping me to the floor. Hands patted my back, voices tried to soothe me with sweet nothings. I still heard nothing.

The doors opened, and a squat man with a balding head and wiry beard waddled in. His arm was in a sling, his left eye a sharp shade of ebony, almost matching what little hair he had left on his head.

"Miss Wood." His voice was slurred, like his tongue was swollen.

I suppose he wasn't in a simple fender bender.

"Phoebe." He was more insistent now, but I couldn't tear my eyes from her.

I had just seen her, just spoken to her. She was right there, she just had a cough, that was all. But the rosy cheeks she always bore were now cold, the pallidity of her skin sickened me with its yellowing cast. Those emerald eyes were shuttered against the too bright fluorescent bulbs. Even as my hand grasped hers, I could feel that it was far too late. The warmth of her had seeped away. All that lay before me was a husk, the light had long gone.

"Please."

He placed one of his pudgy-fingered hands on my shoulder, the warmth of his sweaty palm awakening a rage from within me.

"What, Edgar?" I snapped.

He removed his hand from my shoulder. "Doctor Kerr."

Really?

You're correcting me, right now, right this moment, in front of my mother's barely cold corpse?

"Fuck you," I spat.

"Now Miss Wood, I know you're hurting, but there's no reason for that language. We need to follow protocol here and—"

"Get the fuck out of my sight before I hit you." I growled, my hands balled into fists at my side, tears blazing a trail of warmth over my cold cheeks.

The head nurse held out her hand, urging Edgar to follow her out. "She needs space Doctor Kerr."

"Mrs. Khumalo, we have strict—"

She waved him on, "Yes, yes, I'll see to it. I think it's best we leave, now."

Mercifully they departed, the other nurses in the room following their lead, leaving me to wallow in the pain that was threatening to swallow me whole. Rising on shaking legs, I pulled the sheet further from her. The bed creaked as I crawled in beside her.

"M-mom," I cried, the word broken—almost as broken as I felt.

I heard the doors open behind me, footsteps crossing the threshold. As I strained my eyes against the painfully bright lights, it was to behold a shaggy-haired man three years older than me, with eyes as emerald as the woman whose body I hugged.

"Feebs," he said.

I nodded in acknowledgement, too shattered to speak.

Without another word, he tossed the sheet off the bed, easing himself into the spare space on the other side of our mother. His eyes bore into mine, red-rimmed, but he wouldn't cry. He was the strong one. Besides, I cried enough for the both of us.

Hours turned into days, which passed into weeks. I felt nothing but the void within me, an emptiness that was all-consuming. I would stare for hours at nothing. The television, the radio, whenever they were on, were mere ambience to my perpetual state of nothingness.

"Are we leaving the house today?"

Luckily, I had enough leave to take months off if I needed to. My brother understood this, too. And since that night, I had spent every night with him at his flat in Sighthill. But he seemed to have recovered far quicker than me.

I glared at him, too tired to give him any more of a response.

"What about speak? Or is that too much effort, too?" He glanced into the fridge, shutting it with a disgruntled moan.

"Piss off, Finn," I grumbled, looking up at him from the fort

I had constructed myself of pillows and blankets on the couch.

He leaned over the kitchen counter, glaring at me. "You need to get your shit together, Fee. She's gone."

"Not everyone can not give a shit twenty-four seven like you can. Heaven forbid I need more time to fucking grieve." I don't know when I had grabbed the remote, all I knew was when it left my hand it went thumping against the counter beside him.

"Come off it, Feebs." The sound of his hand slapping the kitchen counter startled me, the remote fell, striking the tiles, and brought the television to life. Wolves began howling in the background, as a lady in a sapphire peacoat announced plans for the re-introduction of wolves to select reserves in the United Kingdom.

I sighed; he was tiring of the pity party I had set for myself. I couldn't blame him: he hadn't let our mother's passing, or her depressing funeral, set him into a downward spiral.

The doorbell rang, interrupting our staring contest. Sighing, he disappeared down the hall, leaving me to my memories.

"You have company." He returned, rifling through the fridge once more.

Contents haven't changed in the last ten minutes, Finn.

Heels clacked against the tile in the hallway a moment later. A woman with curly auburn hair set with a blue and green tie-dyed bandana strolled in. She threw a clump of papers on the table beside me, her eyebrows raised.

"Let's go," she commanded.

My brows furrowed. Go? *Where?*

Exasperated, she unfolded the papers, placing one with bold letters right in front of my face. I could avoid my brother's nagging, but Lucy was relentless. She wouldn't give in until she accomplished what she came for.

Taking a deep breath, I took the paper from her hands, reading it over. It was a pamphlet of a river hugged by sloping mountains. In bold letters over the landscape was a single word.

Norway.

"I don't get it." My voice didn't sound right. Probably because I'd barely said anything in three days.

Lucy rolled her eyes, taking another paper from the pile and shoving it into my hands.

My mind reeled as my eyes skipped across the oddly rectangular piece of paper. I knew exactly what this was, even though I had never been outside the United Kingdom before. It was a plane ticket.

"The fuck is this?"

Lucy smirked. "You said you wanted to go to Norway. You're fucking going to Norway."

My brother called from the kitchen, "Hey, if you're just handing out plane tickets, can I get one to Ibiza?"

"Shut up, Finn," she called, rolling her eyes.

Her amicability was admirable, considering they had dated for two years. It never bothered me; in fact, I would have been thrilled to call my best friend my sister-in-law instead.

"I can't go to Norway, Lucy."

She laughed, but not in an amused way. More in that way she does when she is trying to bite her tongue but knows she must do something.

"Besides, I thought you wanted to go to New York. What happened with that?"

Kneeling beside me, the scent of her lavender soap drifted towards me. "You need Norway more than I need New York."

I couldn't fight her. I knew that she could push harder than me, and if I said no too many times, I'd wake up at the airport with her by my side.

"Fine, whatever."

Squealing, she clapped her hands excitedly. I caught sight of a second plane ticket in the pile of papers. My heart swelled, if just a fraction. At least I wouldn't endure the crushing loneliness while hiking the fjords.

"When do we leave?"

I didn't miss the knowing glance exchanged between her and Finn, or the way his lips mouthed the words *thank you*.

Her eyes twinkled. "Tomorrow morning."

Edinburgh airport was packed with more people than I had seen since my mother's funeral. I suppose however that was to be expected in December. The holidays made people do crazy things.

Like jump on a plane to Norway in the middle of winter?

Lucy handled everything for us, in fact, I think I could count on one hand how many times I spoke to a random person from the moment we entered Edinburgh to the moment we were within sight of the jagged ice-capped coast of Norway. The entire plane ride was a blur, and Lucy was more than happy to let me lose myself in the view from the window seat.

"Where are we anyway?" Any information she had told me went through one ear and out the other. I was still in a trance, still hurt, still broken.

Lucy pulled her hood tighter around her face, glancing up at the clear blue sky above. We were lucky today. Yesterday the skies had grounded the planes. The bone-biting chill of winter lingered in the air, but so far it was tolerable.

"Bergen," she said.

My wide-eyed stare must have clued her in to my lack of recognition.

"Like a seven-hour drive west of Oslo."

She said it as if I knew where either of those places were. I knew Oslo was the capital; I knew it was in Norway, but if you threw a map at me and told me to point to it, I'd be lost. As much as I wanted to visit Norway, I knew very little about the country itself.

"Well, let's get a bite to eat first. It's only eight in the morning, so we have plenty of time to ourselves," she suggested.

I merely followed, like an obedient puppy, wagging my tail, just happy to be going on a journey. We stood at the car rental kiosk longer than I would have preferred, but Lucy couldn't help but flirt with the attendant. I didn't blame her though. With his flowing golden hair and dreamy sapphire eyes, he should have been a magazine model, not an employee at a car rental service.

"This is our first time in Bergen, do you have any suggestions on where we could grab some breakfast?" She twirled a strand of hair in her hand that way she did when she was hoping to get something for free.

He pursed his lips, more for show than anything else. "If you want to drive into Bergen, there's a lot of nice cafés on the main street."

Having been privy to their entire conversation, it was rather impressive how precise and clear his English was. Considering he had never been out of Norway, or so he claimed. He began scribbling down what I presumed were the names of his recommendations on a piece of paper. Pulling out a map, he circled several places, including our hotel, which Lucy was quick to emphasize.

"Good choice," he winked, handing her the keys.

Pressing the button on the keys, the lights on a nearby sedan flickered. Taking my cue, I relinquished her of our suitcases, dragging them to the car. Loading them up, I sat in the passenger seat, my eyes straying to where she stood.

Curling her hair around her finger, she offered him a smile as he hastily scribbled something down on a piece of paper. Waving him goodbye, she sat down in the driver's seat beside me.

Her eyes glittered with mischief.

"Did you get his number?"

She rolled her eyes, turning on the ignition. "Of course, I did."

The drive from the airport into Bergen was nothing short of magical, unlike the dreariness of a rain-smothered Scotland, Norway was a fairytale. And we haven't even seen the fjords yet.

For the first time in a long time, I was excited.

"Your new boyfriend has good tastes," I remarked, my stomach grumbling for more of the honey and syrup-coated waffles.

Lucy groaned. "Not my boyfriend! At least…not yet." She smirked, setting down her cup of coffee.

One of the waitresses walked by, pausing at our table. "Is there anything else I can help you with?"

"You know what, I think there is," she said, pulling out the map the car rental guy had given her. "The harda—uh, hardanger…"

"Hardangervidda," she offered. "The national park."

"Yes, that place, how do we get there?"

"It's about a two-and-a-half-hour drive east of here. If you follow the E16 to the E13, you couldn't miss the signs. However," she looked us over, "I recommend you seek a change of clothes."

"What's wrong with our clothes?" She glanced down at the frilly coat she wore, adorned with fluffy pom-poms.

"Nothing wrong, I adore your coat, miss, but…the weather out there can be unpredictable, and this time of year, it's extremely cold."

Lucy nodded her head, but I could see she was disappointed.

"Do you have a recommendation?" I asked.

The woman smiled. "If you want to hike or kayak and the like, Outdoor Bergen and the Norrona Concept Store are your best bets." She pointed to a cluster of stores on our map.

"Thank you," I said, as we wrapped up our breakfast and headed to the mall.

Lucy's good mood returned the moment her eyes caught sight of the frills and puffs and loud colors that the stores had to offer.

"Thank god I don't have to sacrifice my individuality to not freeze to death!" she said gleefully, handing over her credit card to the teller.

I smiled at her, my eyes widening at the price tag of her newfound wardrobe. Mine didn't fare much better, but I needed this break, I needed to get out there, to see the fjords, and distract myself. I could afford it, at least for now.

"Well," she said, arms laden with bags. "Hotel?"

Our hotel was the height of Nordic architecture, with multi-story glass windows and wide-open spaces with simple wooden furniture and minimalist decorations. It gave me a sense of freedom. And the moment I laid my head against the goose feather pillows, I never wanted to leave.

"Come on lazy, change and let's get going," Lucy said, going through the bags as she held clothing up against her body in front of the mirror.

I mimicked her, layering thermals over my underwear, then pants and a long sleeve shirt, and then a sweater, then one of those puffy vests, and to top it off, a thick coat. Lucy tossed me my gloves, hat, and scarf.

As I stared at myself in the mirror, I couldn't help but compare myself to a penguin.

"Well, I can tell you one thing for certain," she said, standing beside me. "I don't hold weight very well."

"Oh, shut up," I smirked.

She playfully nudged me. "Okay, I think we're ready. Let's go!"

"Yeah, yeah, yeah, one second." Pulling my phone from my pocket, I ignored the missed calls and texts from Liam and my co-workers. I loathed the fact that he found out the same day what happened to my mother.

"Ah, that's right. You promised to give Finn a little itinerary of what you were doing every day."

I nodded.

"Couldn't you have just given him this, I don't know, the day we left?"

"Would have worked if you didn't want to play every day by ear." I muttered, reading the text over.

Hey Finn, it's your favorite pain in the arse. We're headed to some national park outside Bergen. Something about Hardanger-something-rather. I'm sure it'll be fine. If not, can you remember to water my plants? Luv ya! Xo Ps I'm sorry for being a bitch, hope your counter is okay.

The moment I hit send, Lucy's hand grasped mine and dragged me from the room. She was as impatient as always, but luckily that didn't translate over to her driving skills. On the road, I always joked how she was slower than a turtle.

We did as the waitress recommended, taking the E16 east out of Bergen. It was a leisurely drive, void of distractions. The roads were clear, but the snow had piled up on either side, coating the landscape in a wintry blanket.

"Wow, would you look at that view," she whispered.

My eyes followed hers. Yawning before us was a silver bridge crossing a twinkling azure ribbon that cut through a landscape of ice and snow.

"This is what all those Hallmark movies are always going on about," I said, my eyes lost in the beauty of the snowcapped mountains and laden pines.

The world was untouched outside the confines of our car, as if we were the first humans to ever venture this way. At least, for today. There were no other tire marks on the road, no evidence of adventure except our own.

"There it is," Lucy said, pointing to a sign leading us into Kinsarvik, the last town on the way to Hardangervidda.

The world rose around us, the town replaced by rocky plateaus blanketed in hardened snow. The trees around us grew thinner, more spread out, giving way to bushes and stones covered in moss and lichen. Lucy rolled our car to a stop on the side of the road. A few other cars were here, and footprints in the snow lead out into the National Park. Clouds had formed on the peaks, grey over grey.

"Let's begin, shall we?" She grasped my hand, leading me along a rocky trail into the unknown.

CHAPTER
THREE

Although the trails were clearly marked, and people had trudged through recently creating easily navigable paths, our movement was slow. More than once either Lucy or I ended up with our knees in the snow. We rose higher and higher, pausing at a rocky outcropping that encompassed uninterrupted views of the town below us, and the snaking river beyond.

A chilly breeze had arisen in the hour since we left the car and try as I might to warm my face with my scarf, it found some way beneath my many layers.

"I guess that woman was right," Lucy breathed.

"What?"

She smiled. "About us needing better clothes. I would have frozen to death before we peaked the hill."

Lucky us.

"What's the chance that we disappear in the wilds of Norway and no one can find us?" I knew I was being dramatic, but it was hard to be positive when my heart was still in turmoil.

She paused, her feet kicking loose stones in our way to tumble down the path we had come. "Don't be silly." I could almost see the gears turning in her head though as she bit her lip.

"What?"

"You don't remember that English girl who disappeared in Germany?"

I shook my head.

"A few months ago, it was all over the news."

No wonder I missed it. I was too preoccupied with my own woes; I didn't have time for anyone else's.

"Anyway, she went for a wedding in Bavaria and just straight up vanished." She cleared her throat. "But she was alone and apparently had never gone hiking before. We'll be fine."

As much as I was sure we'd be fine, part of me didn't care if we got lost and never returned. I made a mental note of talking to a therapist when we got back to Edinburgh.

Another hour passed. Overhead a cry pierced the veil of grey, shattering the silence that we had comfortably settled into. Gazing skyward, Lucy and I watched as a brown speckled eagle with ivory tail feathers circled overhead. Distracted by the majestic beast, we didn't notice that we were no longer alone.

A group of five hikers had come upon us suddenly around the turn, their eyes widening as they looked us up and down. One of them stopped, an older woman with curly blonde hair. She held her hand out, stopping us in our path.

We looked up at her expectantly, eyebrows raised. She babbled on, her voice muffled, and obviously not in English.

"Oh, I'm sorry. I…uh…" Lucy looked to me for help.

"*Jeg kan ikke snakke norsk,*" I intervened. I'd rehearsed the words over and over in my head, mentally thanking the hotel for providing a quick guide on easy phrases.

"English?" she asked, and I nodded.

She looked to her companions, before addressing us in a thick Norwegian accent. "Where are you headed?"

I shrugged. "I didn't really have a particular place in mind. We just wanted to hike through the National Park."

"You haven't seen the warning?" She had an edge of concern in her voice.

Lucy and I looked to each other and shook our heads in unison.

"There's a blizzard coming, you best head back now."

Our eyes rose to the grey clouds twirling above. Indeed, they were far more menacing than when we had left the car. What used to be fluffy and light was now sharp, angry, and dark.

"We won't tarry long," Lucy said. "Thank you for the warning."

The woman looked at her companions, but took our word for it, following them back down the trail we had come.

"What was that?" Lucy breathed, eyes wide.

"What was what?"

"You can speak Norwegian?"

I laughed at her. "No, that's why I told her I couldn't speak it."

She groaned at me, watching the group of hikers disappear down the trail.

"So, what should we do?" She nibbled on her bottom lip.

What was this? Was Lucy…*worried?* My, my, I always thought it'd be a cold day in hell when that happened. A cold day in Norway would have to suffice.

She noticed that look on my face, her eyes squinting. "I'm not scared if that's what you're thinking. But neither you nor I have any experience with hiking in extreme weather."

"Snowdon doesn't count?"

She rolled her eyes. "The highest mountain in Wales during a little bit of a downpour, compared to a blizzard on a mountain in Norway."

I waited.

"No, Phoebe." She turned around. "Let's go back, we can hang out at the mall or something."

I don't know what prompted me to dig my heels into the ground, but I did, staring her down.

"Phoebe?" Her voice rose a little.

Shaking my head, I turned from her, continuing my ascent.

Her footsteps sounded behind me as her auburn-colored curls bounced into view.

"Damn it, Phoebe, you're going to be the death of me."

I smiled. "Nothing stopping you from turning back now."

"Yeah, well. If I'm going to die in a blizzard, I'd rather it be with my best friend."

The further we traveled, the less clear our path became. Somewhere between that fallen log we'd passed an hour ago and the rock that vaguely resembled a bear, the trail had disappeared. I could tell Lucy was becoming more unnerved as time went on, as the chill on the breeze became biting, as a gentle snowfall began settling around us. So faint at first, I thought I was imagining it.

Lucy had stopped just ahead of me, focused on something at her feet.

"What is it?" I stood at her shoulder, staring down at a rock.

Except it wasn't an ordinary rock. Flat on three sides, symbols had been carved into it, straight lines that were obviously not natural. They were manmade.

"What are they?" Lucy asked, cocking her head sideways.

Brushing away the snow that had piled up atop of it. The carvings were accentuated with ochre paint that had faded over the years. I knew what it was.

"It's a runestone."

I'd heard of them, read about them in books. England had a few, but I'd never had the pleasure of seeing a real one. It was surreal. And seeing a real one was like experiencing a myth come to life. My gloved fingers grazed the stone, catching in the grooves.

"Okay, we've been hiking for over two hours, Phoebe. We should really turn back now."

The clouds descended upon the mountain, setting the world alight in shades of grey. Silence had settled around us, the snow sheltering the noises of the world from one another. Lucy was right, it'd take two hours to get back to the car from here, but the way this storm had picked up in so short a time had me doubting we'd outrun it. We'd have to take shelter in the town and wait for it to pass if we turned back now.

"Maybe you're right," I breathed.

Lucy began her retreat down the haphazardly carved trail we had blazed through the snow earlier. We were far slower on the descent than the ascent, and the storm roiled around us. In a matter of moments our sight was shortened to just a few feet on either side. A roar had risen on the wind, snowflakes flurrying around us.

"Phoebe!" Lucy called out.

I grasped her hand, squinting against the blinding light. "I can't see shit!"

She laughed. "Yeah, you're not kidding. Just don't let go okay, if we hug the cliff here, I think it'll lead us back to the car."

I know she was trying to put on a brave face, because if she admitted we were lost, panic would set in. Panic got you killed in the wilds. We edged along the cliff, following it downwards, hoping that every placement of our boots would find sturdy ground beneath, and not plunge us over the cliffside.

Slow and steady we moved across the cliff until the edges of the world disappeared on either side. We stood on a rocky outcropping, gazing over the edge of the plateau. Squinting into the storm, we searched desperately for the town, for the farms, even just evidence of humanity.

Nothing but snow and rock spanned before us. Even the shiny sapphire ribbon that snaked through the mountains was nowhere to be seen. This wasn't the way we had come.

She tugged on my arm, her face looming before me. "I think we're lost," she cried over the blizzard.

Lost.

"We just have to go down, that's all." The words didn't even sound convincing to me, and yet I said them anyway, knowing she wouldn't believe it.

But we needed something to cling onto, and hope was a motivator that would keep us going.

"Over there," she said, pointing to a ledge that seemed to spiral downwards.

Hefting our backpacks, we tightened the straps, our hands grasping rocks and limbs and roots that jutted out from the rocky dirt to keep our balance. The wind blasted us against the cliff, threatening to pull us into the frozen ravine below. But we soldiered on.

My thighs ached, my hands ached, my eyes ached. Every part of me yearned to stop, even just for a moment. Lucy struggled too, I could see it in the sagging of her shoulders, the misplacement of her feet, and the huffing and puffing that she tried to hide.

We were tiring, we both knew it, and yet we couldn't stop. We also both knew that if we did, we wouldn't make it back to the car. Rocks tumbled loose beneath our feet, clattering to the ravine below. My heart lurched as I pushed away the images of our bodies tumbling after.

"Lucy!" I called into the storm.

She glanced back at me, her eyes dark.

"We can't keep going."

She thought for a moment, ideas swirling behind those big brown eyes of hers. "I reckon if we get down to the ravine, we can find some shelter."

I nodded, letting her lead.

Several moments later, her voice called out to me. "Lucky for you I'm black, otherwise you'd be hard-pressed to find me in this storm."

"Is that so?" I called.

She laughed. "Yup!"

She was trying to distract me, to distract herself. My heart warmed at her attempt.

"So how is it you haven't lost me, yet?"

She faced me. "Shit, I wonder why." Her eyes immediately went to the tendrils of hair that were escaping from beneath my beanie.

"You're not far from being hard to miss yourself," I remarked.

She told me the reason she dyed the tips of her obsidian hair auburn was because her mother disapproved, but it didn't matter what she said. I had it on good authority that she was a real fan of my locks.

"You mean, because I'm black?" she smirked.

God damn it, Lucy.

"No, dipshit, the hair," I said.

She laughed, "Yeah, yeah, I know. Just wanted to stir the pot."

"Ugh, you shit stirrer," I groaned.

Her laughter was eaten away by the storm, but I didn't miss the extra effort she had to put into it. We had exerted too much effort, too fast. This was a mistake, one giant horrible mess I wanted to pretend never happened. But, silver lining, I hadn't thought about my mother once, until just now.

"My mother would have hated this." I don't know why I brought it up, why I even had to think about it.

"Your mother was a hoot," Lucy said. "Woman liked the idea of snow, but the actual thing? Hah!"

I huffed, my breath forming a cloud that dissipated almost instantly, lost to the wild winds. "Yeah."

"Remember that one year we went for a road trip to the Scottish Highlands?"

"Cairngorms?" I did, I remembered it fondly.

"Yeah, that's the one. Your mother insisted on a girls' trip." She scoffed. "That woman, I swear. I told her it was snowing, I told her it was going to be cold, and what did she do?"

My heart ached, but my smile was genuine. "Remember when we got there? She opened her door—"

Lucy laughed. "And then immediately closed it again, didn't even step out!"

"She did roll down the window though for that damn cigarette." My voice was tight.

Lucy noticed. "You know, when we get back to the hotel, you should probably go see a movie or grab a bite to eat, whatever will keep you busy for about an hour."

I frowned. "Why?"

"Because I'm going to call that boy and fuck his brains out." She howled with laughter at the expression on my face.

"Oh my god, Lucy. You are vulgar!"

She waved off my disapproval with a flick of her wrist. "You should find yourself one too, I hear these Norwegian boys are wild. You know that Viking blood and all."

I groaned. "Maybe I will."

"Hopefully, then we can have a foursome!"

In the blink of an eye, so fast the world slowed enough for me to catch it, but not slow enough for me to react, I found myself falling. My right foot had fallen through snow, held by branches, with no world beneath them. It gave away instantly, my grip on Lucy broke, as I fell from the cliffside.

I fell and fell, a world of white passing me by. Rocks and roots and limbs reached out, lashing at me, but I felt none of it as I contemplated the moment I was going to die. I could see Lucy's face above me, through the whirling snow, the panic and fear on her face. I had never seen such an expression before, and it only worsened as I felt my back collide with the ground.

Stars swam in my vision, mixing with the snowflakes that flurried around me like fireflies. I wheezed, desperate to bring air back into my lungs, my chest heaving, my shoulders shuddering, as I rolled onto my stomach.

I could hear her cries over the storm. "Phoebe!"

Weakly, I raised my fist into the air, hoping it'd be enough to settle the anxious state she had run herself into. Breathing in and out, slowly and with precision, I let the cold air inside me, relaxing my body. Everything ached, and as my eyes reviewed the world around me, I knew this pain was only the beginning. I sat at the bottom of the ravine, at least six feet of snow having broken my fall. A frozen stream was nearby, the water somehow still trickling below the ice.

"Phoebe!" she called.

With knees shaking, I rose to my feet, staring up at where I could just make out Lucy on the cliff above. "I'm okay, Lucy!"

As I called to her though, I could feel the pinch in my side, pain when I called out or breathed too deeply. I had bruised something, or at least, I hoped it was only a bruise.

"What should we do?" She was frantic.

I glanced around us. But there was no way out or into this ravine, without her falling too. I knew my survival was pure luck, however, as sharp rocks and pointy sticks stuck up out of the surrounding snow. I could have died, and the chance of Lucy dying was much higher than I was comfortable with.

"Is there a way up that you can see from there?"

"I thought I saw it narrow further down, let's meet there!" She called, pointing to the other side of the ravine ahead of us where it disappeared around a bend.

Hefting one foot in front of the other, I held back the cry of pain as I fumbled through the snowy ravine. Sometimes I could just catch a glance of a baby pink jacket, or a strand of an auburn curl through the snow above me. She didn't call out to me again. We both knew we needed to preserve our strength. One, or both of us, was in for a climb at the end of this ravine.

The wind picked up, vicious, lashing out like a snake. It was unmerciful, closing in around us. Lucy would have it worse on the edge of the cliff, with the elements pounding her against the rocks. My footsteps were unsure; my feet plunged through ice and snow, my socks filled with the cold.

"Well, at least we'll be seeing my mother soon!" I called.

The howling wind was all that answered. My heart sunk into my stomach, a vile taste at the back of my throat as I frantically searched the cliffs above and ahead of me. Lucy was nowhere to be seen.

"Lucy!" I cried, my voice lost to the winds.

I called her name, again and again, my pace picking up as I charged through the ravine like one of those cattle during the running of the bulls in Spain. I crashed through the underbrush, shoving aside bushes and trees, calling for her.

She never answered though, and I never caught sight, even as the ravine opened before me, the stream feeding into a larger river of ice. I couldn't see anything beyond the few feet in front of me, the world had been devoured by the monstrosity that kept my best friend from me.

The wind buffeted me, forcing me to turn from the river. I followed the rocky shore, still intent on tending to our decision. Lucy had said to meet at the end of the ravine, and that was where we would meet. But I was already here, and she was not.

"Lucy!"

It was useless. Wherever she was, it was not here; it was not where we agreed to meet. Tears welled in my eyes, the warmth burning, melting the snowflakes and icicles that had formed on my lashes.

Fuck.

I didn't know what I could do. There was no signal on my phone, no way for me to call for help. The storm held no signs of abating. If I couldn't find shelter soon, I'd freeze to death long before I'd find Lucy.

"Forgive me," I mumbled, following the rocky shore to the cliff face.

Just as my patience was running thin, my body slowing to a point where I wondered if maybe I wasn't already dead, I saw it. Pits in the cliff ahead, boulders jutting out like spikes, guarding gaping holes of darkness. They were caves.

CHAPTER

FOUR

I was lost. Hopelessly, utterly lost. Lucy could be just around the bend, or miles away by now. I had no way of knowing. The blizzard raged outside, nature in all her glory threatening to take me down if I took one step outside this cave.

There were no sticks, no stones, nothing to build a fire with or block the entrance. I would have to suffer, waiting out the storm in silence, alone. Fishing my phone out of my pocket, desperately trying to get a signal. I knew it was hopeless, and yet I sent off a string of texts, anyway. To my brother, to Lucy, and even one to my boss. None of them went through.

"Fuck," I seethed, my heart pounding in my chest.

Lucy was right, she always was. I should have listened to her; I should have turned around right then and there when the hikers had warned us. But no, I was so lost in myself I wanted to keep going, riding that high of exploration to distract myself from the endless void that had swallowed me.

I should have told her why I persisted. That the reason wasn't as simple as I was enjoying the hike. Truth be told, it was the only thing keeping me sane. All these months, I didn't feel real, or alive, until I set foot here. In this surreal landscape of sloping mountains and endless snow, this world of endless myths.

Slinging my backpack onto the ground, I rifled through it for my water bottle, taking a swig. I knew I needed to preserve as much as I could, who knows when I'd get the chance to drink or eat again, but all the water I could ever want was piling up right outside the cave.

Maybe I'll drown, I thought bitterly.

Shivering in the gathering darkness, my hands fumbled through the pack, grasping a long, cylindrical tube. Flicking the switch, the cave came alive around me. The camping store claimed the torch would stay on for ten hours straight on a single charge, then would need to sit in the sunlight for hours more. For now, though, it was my only company, and I used it to stuff my face with a trail bar. The crumbly oats and seeds were dry in my throat, but my stomach was grateful for the sacrifice my throat endured.

My eyes flickered to an ochre vein that seemed to cut across the cave wall in front of me. I shined the torch on it, and my mouth gaped like a fish. It wasn't a vein of gem or stone cutting through the wall. It was a painting. My hand reached out to touch it, and when I removed my fingers, a part of the ochre paint clung to the tips of my gloves.

Frowning, I raised my torch to the other side of the wall. There were more here, rich ochre paint manipulated into the shapes of boats and men and horses and trees and mountains. They covered the walls of this cave, over my head, and under my feet, everywhere I looked was covered in them.

The cave narrowed at the back, but with my torch I could see that it did not end here. There was a passageway strewn with lichen leading into the darkness. Shoving my bottle back in my backpack, I shoved it through the passage, squeezing myself through after it.

There was another cave beyond this one, my torch revealed walls of stacked stonework. It was unnatural, manmade, and carved into each individual stone was a scene. Some had boats,

some had people, or animals, just like the art in the cave before. But these were special, dictating events that had happened.
There was a crude carving of a woman lying on a bed, with a
swaddled baby nestled in her arms. A birth, perhaps. Another
showed a man sitting in a chair at the back of a large hall filled
with people. A crowning, maybe? But the one that drew my attention the most, the one that had me taking a sharp intake of
breath, was the one with the most real estate.

My fingers traced the carvings in this stone, my eyes not sure
what aspect to focus on first. There were three men, one with
short hair, one with a beard, and another with long hair. They
each wore a crown and held a weapon in their hand- a spear for
the short-haired king, an axe for the bearded king, and a sword
for the long-haired king. It was normal, something I'd expect to
see in Viking art.

What wasn't normal, however, was what seemed to rise behind each king. A sculpture that was emphasized far more than
the kings they adorned. The short-haired king who brandished
a spear had an eagle rise above him with spread wings. A mighty
bear shadowed the bearded king who held his axe aloft. The
long-haired king who held the sword beside him was overseen
by the head of a snarling wolf.

Compared to the other carvings, even the paintings, these
were intricate, the details sharp and precise. Great care was taken
in this stone, as if it were sacred. Runes surrounded it, telling
a story that I could never be privy to. If I made it out of this
storm alive, I'd have to remember to tell Lucy about this place.

My heart pained for a moment. Lucy was strong though, far
stronger than I ever was or could aspire to be. If anyone could
survive this, it was her. I just hoped she remembers what I said
the day after the funeral, when I held that urn that contained all
that was left of my mother.

'When I die, burn me, and spread what's left of me into the North Sea.'

'Alright, you crazy white girl, Don't have to tell me twice.' She had
laughed.

I had said that as we overlooked that stone bridge at the

battery in Dunbar, far east of Edinburgh. It was my mother's favorite place, where my father had proposed to her, and where we had spread his ashes when he died. I saw it fitting for our family to end where it all began.

My eyes strayed to a grey stone at the center of the cave, three faces, all carved with runes. Just like the one we had seen earlier. Except, this runestone was quite unlike the other one we had seen, for on each face, at the very top, was carved the representations of a wolf, a bear, and an eagle.

I couldn't help but reach my hand out and touch the runestone, I was drawn to it, called to it. Like a moth to a flame, I couldn't ignore it, my fingers grazing the stone. A fatigue had settled into me, accentuating the pain in my side. The storm raged outside; the wind was whistling through the caves. There was nothing more I could do today, I needed to rest, to recuperate, and tomorrow I would search for my friend.

"Good night, Lucy," I whispered, laying my head against the backpack I had placed against the runestone.

Nestling against it, my hand wandered back to the stone. Her face was the last thing I saw as I turned off my phone to conserve the battery. My eyes growing heavy, my body warm, I drifted into a restless sleep.

The stone was hard and cold beneath my back, all too similar to the weekend I had spent camping when I was a child, with Lucy in the sleeping bag beside me. Unlike then, however, my life, and hers, was at risk. I could still hear the whistling of the wind, the chill on the breeze that bit into my bones like a million tiny needles.

There was a peculiar noise that met my ears, not unlike the shuffling of feet. My eyes opened, and I jumped to my feet, surveying the surrounding cave. The noise came again, closer, louder. It was in the other half of the cave, on the other side of the passage. Straining my ears, I tried to place that shuffling, to discern its origins as animal…or human. My heart skipped a beat.

Lucy.

Startled, I abandoned all semblance of trying to be discreet, rushing through the passageway. Rocks skittered loose in my wake; my impatience evident in the aching of my side being crushed against the stone.

I didn't care though, if Lucy was on the other side of this cave, I needed to get to her. I had to apologize, to tell her it was all my fault. That I should have listened to her, that she was always right, that I didn't know why I fought her.

"Lucy," I breathed, squeezing out of the passage into the cave of ochre paintings.

There was an answering light. It flickered across the walls, bathing the cave in a shadowy orange hue.

My heart lurched when my eyes caught hold of the snaking flames held aloft by a stick of oozing tar. My words died as they left my mouth. "You're not Lucy."

The man was draped in layers of furs and leather, reminiscent of one of those actors at a renaissance festival. Except the sight of his face sent a chill down my spine, it was obscured by a scarf wrapped around his head, protection from the prevailing winds. What was placed over it, however, was an animal skull lined with sharp canines.

My stomach lurched as I tried to force my way back into the runestone cave, but the company I had found myself in sprinted forward, grabbing me around the wrist. His strength was absolute and I knew he hopelessly outmatched me as he yanked me forward, and I fell to the ground at his feet.

His gloved hand reached forward, pulling my hood back and snatching the hat from my head. My crimson hair tumbled free, cascading across my shoulders like a wave. Turquoise eyes glared at me through that skull mask, squinting, as if in confusion. His gaze drifted from me to the runestone room.

"Please, I'm lost, and injured. My friend is waiting for me," I rambled, hoping one of those would encourage him to aid me.

Those ice-blue eyes narrowed, and when he finally spoke, it was strange words that made no sense to me. Unlike the hiker that I had met earlier, I knew it wasn't Norse that he spoke. It was more guttural, fierce, like the wolf's skull upon his head.

He spoke again, his words had a sense of urgency to them, as his eyes swept the cave again. He seemed almost...*afraid*. Frowning, I stood on wobbly legs, yanking my hat from his hand.

"That is mine, thank you," I said, surprised that I managed to suppress my quivering just enough to put up this charade of bravery that I knew was only moments away from faltering.

Part of me thought that feigned confidence would be my salvation, my ticket to getting out of here. But I had no way of communicating with him, it was obvious he didn't understand me, and I him.

"I think I'll be leaving now," I said, the adrenaline pumping through me like a bodybuilder on steroids.

I turned abruptly, putting too much faith in throwing him off guard as I placed my back to him. I had to act while the adrenaline was high, suppressing the shivers of fear that wanted to wrack my body as I stomped towards the mouth of the cave.

"What the fuck..." I whispered, my eyes scanning the world just beyond.

A chilly breeze struck me, scattering tendrils of hair across my face, tickling my nose. But I was in shock, too much to raise my hand and pull the strands from my face. My eyes were wide, stinging in the bright light that pierced the cloud cover to bathe me.

The world I had left outside had transformed. I still stood on a rocky shore by the azure waters of the river, a cliff stretching far above me. That was where the similarities ended, because stretched out before me, taking up the entire mountainside, was a fortress of stone and wood rising to the top of the plateau. People garbed like the man in the cave milled about, lugging sacks and crates and jars and chests back and forth between boats moored in the ice by the river.

The man said something behind me, and I turned to him, no longer able to disguise the fear within me. It was written on my face for all to see.

"Where am I?" I whispered.

He replied, shaking his head, his hand pointing to the rune-stone room.

"I don't understand…" I said.

Exhaling in obvious frustration, he pointed to one of the paintings on the wall. Peeling back from the entrance, my eyes focused on the figure he was jabbing his finger at repeatedly. My blood chilled in my veins as the differences of this figure screamed out at me. It was a woman outlined in black, with flowing ochre hair that cascaded down her shoulders, a robe of white powder hugging her shapely form.

Pushing the thought from my mind, I laughed. A shaky, unconvincing noise. "What's your point?"

He seemed to understand that, pointing between me and the figure. At her feet was a three-sided stone, with the faces of an eagle, a bear, and a wolf.

"Superstitious nonsense," I muttered.

I didn't need to understand him to know what he was getting at. The woman had red hair, and I had red hair. She was at the runestone, and I had been at the runestone. That was it, a coincidence. I didn't belong here, that much was obvious, and I was tiring of whatever game was being played. It was a rather elaborate joke; I'll give him that. But I wasn't in the mood to play anymore.

Wherever I was, and whoever he was, I didn't care. I needed to get back to Bergen, to my hotel. Where I had no doubt, Lucy was waiting for me. Ignoring his words that meant nothing to me, I pried my backpack from where it lay stuck in the passage, checking my phone. No signal, no missed texts, no missed calls. Slinging it over my shoulder, I pushed past him, knowing that Bergen lay roughly west of the national park. If I followed the river, it should bring me to the E13 or E16, or at the very least, I'd find the bridge again, then I could follow it back to the hotel.

There was a commotion ahead of me, freezing me in my tracks. Two men had appeared at the entrance of the cave, their voices carrying on the breeze that wafted in. The moment their eyes caught sight of me, they froze. The man who stood behind me stirred to life, walking forward to address the men.

Their voices rose and fell, arguing about something. Their constant glances told me it was about me. It was more than that, though. The wayward glances, the squinting eyes that darted between me and the figure on the cave wall.

Before I could consider forming a plan or even contemplate what was happening, the new men rushed forward, their hands closing over my wrists as they attempted to drag me from the cave.

"Let me go!" I screamed, digging my feet into the rock.

Their skull masks glinted in the torch lights they held in their free hands, their eyes of emerald and sapphire stared down at me. My protests meant nothing to them, and I knew if I let them drag me from this cave, I would never return to Bergen, and I would never find Lucy.

The first man I had met stood in front of them, his voice rising over my struggling. They ignored him though, whatever he had to say was falling on deaf ears. I didn't want to know where they were taking me, or what they planned. I already knew it wasn't somewhere I wanted to be, my only chance was to stick to my original plan, and I needed to free myself for that to happen.

When I was in high school, my mother picked me and Lucy up after school one day, driving us to this building whose front wall was a pane of glass. Just beyond were men and women dressed in white, colorful belts secured around their waists, going through the motions of an ancient art form.

'You need to learn to protect yourself,' she had said.

When we scoffed at her, like any teenager being told what to do, asking why, she told us of a young woman she had treated earlier that day.

'I admitted her with blood pouring down her face, a broken rib, and with her voice shaking she said she had just fought off a man who had tried to rape her.'

The look on my mother's face scared me. I knew she was telling the truth, and right then and there Lucy and I started a six-year addiction to martial arts. I remembered all of it, and right now I eyed my route for escape.

I would have to hurry, not giving them a single moment to react. If I did, I'd lose my only chance at escape. I waited until their grips loosened at the mouth of the cave, as there was only room for one person to walk through at a time. The moment the first man walked through, I made my move.

My boot collided with the back of his knee, and he lurched forward, face first into the rocks, releasing me. The man behind him was stunned, unsure of what had happened, and I used his confusion against him, striking out with my free hand. My fist collided with his jaw, sending him staggering backwards. Not enough to knock him to the ground, but that wasn't my intention. My arm was no longer burdened by his grip, and I bolted.

I sprinted across the rocks, as fast as I could, hoping the sure-footedness that I exhibited in track back in high school was still with me. I could hear their wild calls behind me, the voices rising on the breeze. There was a city full of people there beyond the cave. If I stopped, if I tarried even slightly, I was done for. I just needed to follow the river west, that blue ribbon that sliced through the mountains.

The sun disappeared behind the cover of greying, snow-laden clouds; a flurry of snowflakes whipped to life around me. I didn't dare look behind me, focusing on the path before me. There was no behind, only forward. I jumped from one flat rock to the next, hugging the shore, just beyond the reach of the slick ice.

A slope appeared between the rocky shore and the cliff on my left, and I made the split-second decision to climb it upwards. My hands grasped whatever they could as I jumped from one rock to the next, emerging onto a cliff overlooking the shoreline.

With the cold air filling my lungs, I listened for the commotion on the shore below me. Taking a few steps back, I hid behind a bramble of bushes, watching as far more men than I had anticipated burst forth, running along the beach. Each one carried a weapon at their side, a blazing torch in their hands.

Slowing my haggard breathing, my heart pounding in my chest, I watched as they milled around the shore. As much as I knew I had to put distance between them and myself, I was afraid to move, afraid to even breathe. Any excuse for them to look up here could prove fatal for me, and I prayed in my head over and over that they would go straight.

What the hell is even going on? Is this some sort of cult? Am I dreaming? Have I been drugged? *What the fuck?*

My subconscious mind assaulted me with every question and likely scenario that was paraded before me. Nothing made any sense. It could be a cult, I could be dreaming, maybe I was in a drug-induced stupor or a coma at the hospital right now in Bergen. Maybe Lucy and Finn were at my side, tears in their eyes, begging me to wake up.

All those would be preferable to the situation before me. Because as much as I wanted to believe this wasn't real, the ache in my side, the biting cold on my skin, and the pounding in my head told me this was all too vivid to be a dream.

Luck was on my side for now. The men continued their search along the shore, disappearing from view. Breathing a sigh of relief, I stood, turning to survey the small clearing I had stumbled upon.

I saw the emerald eyes, hidden in the bones of a wolf skull, a moment too late. His hand reached out, striking me across the face. The world spun around me, fading at the edges as the shadows enveloped me. I disappeared into a world of darkness.

CHAPTER
FIVE

Warmth had enveloped me, smothered me in an embrace that I was desperate to cling to, even though I knew the moment my eyes opened the fallacy I was so desperate to hold onto would slip away. I knew the men had won, and I had lost. Wherever I was, it was not where I wanted to be.

The musky scent of smoking wood, the bitterness of crushed pine, and the tinge of salty sweat was enough to tell me I wasn't in a hospital bed. I was still here, wherever here may be. As reluctant as I was, I knew I couldn't find my way back home if I didn't open my eyes.

A flame was flickering above me, a metal sconce like a seashell was plastered to a wall of stone. The wall in front of me, at the foot of the bed of furs I lay in, held a window of stained glass. A mural of a howling wolf was lit by a stream of sunlight, setting beams of emerald and sapphire and crimson to blanket the edge of the bed in a rainbow.

The pounding in my head seemed to rattle my eyes in their sockets. It worsened as I sat myself upright, cradling my head in my hands. There was a stirring somewhere near me and when I opened my eyes, it was to behold a man garbed in a white robe, with light blue eyes.

"You again," I muttered, rolling my eyes.

He said something again, something I still couldn't understand. But I knew it could only be an apology, from the shuffling of his feet and the downcast eyes.

He was far different from when I had first met him in the cave. Although he wore a necklace of fangs around his throat, keeping with that Wildman vibe. Sighing, I tossed aside the blanket that they tucked me into, and a shiver ran up my spine.

I was draped in a dress I had never seen before. But as the realization dawned on me, it wasn't the fact that my clothes had changed. It was the fact that not only did a stranger see me naked, they had also removed my bra and underwear. I was naked beneath this dress, my nipples forming small peaks through the thin fabric.

Crossing my arms against my chest, a blush heated my cheeks, indignation raging through me.

"Y-you undressed me!" I huffed in anger.

He hung his head, his mouth twisting. It was obvious he wasn't happy about it either. But all I could think was, *then you shouldn't have done it.*

There was a knock at the door, and I watched as the stranger sprinted to the door, his boots slapping against the stone floor. He brushed past a table laden with papers and scrolls and tomes with leather and wooden covers. In fact, this entire room seemed to be a small study, the shelves on the walls heaving with more books and scrolls that the desk had no room for.

Another man met him at the door, speaking in a hushed tone. The light blue-eyed man glanced back at me, nodding solemnly. Something bad was about to happen to me, I knew it.

The door opened, and a man strode forward, a thick, darkly colored cloak in his hands. He shoved it into my hands, uttering a command. It didn't take a Yale degree to figure out he wanted me to wear it.

Wary of what was to come next, but knowing there wasn't

much I could do, I threw the cloak around my shoulders. The man pulled the hood over my head, buttoning it around my bosom, so I could only see the darkness of the cloak. It completely hid the ivory gown I had woken up in. He placed dirt-brown slippers at my feet, and I slipped my feet into them.

Waving me forward, I glanced back at the ocean-eyed man. His tight nod was the only thing he would give me, as I followed this fresh man out into the hall. I don't know why, but it was a relief to see him following at a distance behind us.

There was no time to think on it, however, as a small congregation of men formed a line behind us. Our footsteps slapped against the stone of the halls as the man lead me up and up, standing before a room of double doors guarded by men with wolf skulls adorning their heads, leather bandoliers hid the blades of many daggers.

Swallowing nervously, my heart sunk as the guards splayed their hands against the doors, and they creaked open. They ushered me into a wide stone hall. A vaulted ceiling yawned above me, adorned by chandeliers of twisted wood, alive with flickering candles. Stained-glass windows adorned the roof, casting rainbows across the room. Pillars of wood and stone rose to the rafters, delicately carved with depictions of wild, snarling beasts.

The room fell into silence; the men sitting on either side of the cleared walkway stood, their eyes watching as I walked in. Their faces were wild, hidden by the skulls of more than just wolves, some were adorned with fangs and claws, or splashed with paint in whorls and swirls.

They disappeared from my mind the instant I saw what stood at the end of the hall where I was being corralled. On a dais of stone, embedded with glittering gems as varied as the hues of the stained-glass windows above, were three thrones. All three were cast of stone, covered in fur and feathers. But at the head of each throne, was one thing that set them apart, a bone-white carving of the head of a wolf, eagle, and bear.

As I moved closer, my feet inches shy of the dais, I could see they weren't carvings at all. They were bone-white for a reason. They were skulls, the unnaturally massive skulls of a bear, an eagle, and a wolf, with the feathers and fur of the creature that once owned those skulls resting upon it.

Preoccupied by the sheer size of the creatures they belonged to, I gasped when something stirred on the throne. Three some-things, on three thrones. As the shadows shifted, men walked out of the audience to light giant braziers around the dais, cast-ing a menacing hue on the people who warmed the seats.

Three men, similar yet different, sat on those thrones, their eyes passively judging me. One with a beard, one with long hair, and one with short hair, with an axe, a sword, and a spear sitting against their respective thrones.

Three thrones. Three kings. Just like in the ochre paintings in that cave.

The king in the middle, with the sword against his wolf-head-ed throne, spoke, and the guy behind me answered. He thought for a moment, contemplating whatever he had said, his eyes turning to me. He said something, and once again it was mean-ingless to me. I could imagine the many questions these people had for me. Who are you? Where did you come from?

I also had many questions, but I doubted I would get answers.

One of the other kings, with the beard and axe against the throne, spoke up, his eyes squinting. I glanced nervously around me. The short-haired king on the eagle-headed throne addressed me next. A glare that could melt you on the spot accompanied his words. My nails dug into the flesh of my palm, to remind me I was still here, still in one piece.

The kings' expressions were an equal mix of irritation and displeasure.

Wary of incurring a wrath that I knew wouldn't bode well for me, I tried the only thing I knew how to do. I spoke in English.

"I don't understand." My voice was small, weak, and under any normal circumstances I would have thought it was unintelli-gible. The mutterings of a confused child.

But their reactions were not what I was expecting. Their

eyes widened, and they leaned forward on their thrones, talking amongst one another, occasionally casting me concerned glances. They must have agreed on something. As one, they leaned back in their thrones.

The long-haired king on the wolf-headed throne waved me forward.

A voice came to life in my head, an echo that whispered through my skull like a breeze. For the first time since I had woken up, I could understand the words. He spoke to me in English.

What are you?

It was deep, sultry, the voice of a hardened man who knew what he wanted and how to get it. The voice of a king.

I went to open my mouth, to respond, but the voice was quick to silence me.

Speak to me with your mind, child.

I looked up at the man sitting on the throne. A fire burned behind those golden eyes, a mischievousness I couldn't place. I'd have to be careful around him.

What is this? I couldn't be sure I wasn't dreaming, but I knew myself better than this, I didn't have the capacity for my dreams to be so vivid.

Careful of the games you want to play, my lady, my companions aren't as patient as I am.

I frowned. *Games?*

He leaned forward on his throne, looking me up and down. I was a mere ten feet from him, but now I knew what it was like for those animals at the zoo, locked behind bars and cages while people mere feet away scrutinized every aspect of them.

Interesting, he mused.

Okay, now I was getting annoyed. *What the hell is going on here?* I snapped.

That sultry voice chuckled, amusement crinkling the eyes of the long-haired king.

Who are you?

I glared at him. *None of your business.*

His chuckled echoed in my mind. *What are you?*

Excuse me? *What do you mean, what am I? What are you?*

He ignored me.

You're not of my kin, or of those that belong here. Where did you hail from?

Hail? What is this, the Renaissance? *I'm from Edinburgh if that's what you're asking.*

That wasn't the response he expected, his eyebrows raising.

Then you are what my shaman says you are.

And what would that be? I couldn't help the sarcasm that slithered in. Shaman. *Jeeze, I must be dreaming.*

He smirked. *A Traveler.*

Like the television series? Or someone who goes on adventures? Either way, I was sure I was neither of those things.

Okay, you've had your fun, can I go home now?

He regarded me for a moment. *No.*

I didn't care. Dream or not, I was leaving. If he wanted to stop me, he'd have to do so himself, or kill me. Either way, he would do me a favor.

Turning on my heels, I strode from the dais, and was immediately apprehended by the men who had brought me here. Their hands grasped the upper part of my arms, dragging me back towards the dais. Voices rose in the hall, whispers breaking the silence, as at once people began asking questions. The light blue-eyed guy whose room I had woken up in ran forward, his eyes wide with worry.

The long-haired king smirked. The men who held me addressed the king, their voices rising above one another's. He raised his hand, silencing them instantly. Standing from his throne, he strode towards us, standing on the edge of the dais, looking down the bridge of his nose at me like a cat would a mouse. Or rather, a king to a peasant. The other kings leaned forward on their thrones; their interests piqued. I guess it wasn't often a king left his comfy chair.

They're saying I should slay you, to set an example for my people. His words echoed in my head, sending a shiver running up my spine.

Wow, the blue-eyed guy would betray me like that. I thought we were *friend*s! I said sarcastically, forgetting for a moment that he had probably heard that.

The king raised an eyebrow. *His name is Leif, and I can assure you his loyalty rests with me, and me alone.*

I rolled my eyes. *Just kill me and get it over with.* I sighed, my eyes drifting to the stone floor beneath my feet.

His eyes narrowed, boots thudding against the stone as he descended from the dais, standing before me. My eyes instinctively rose to meet his, my heart fluttering as I found myself becoming lost in the golden depths.

A gloved hand rose, gently pulling the hood of the cloak from my head. Gasps rose around us, the murmuring intensifying until the king held up his hand for silence. His fingers hesitated by the side of my head, his eyes distracted by the unruly mess of my unbound hair, as if he'd never seen such a shade before. The cold leather of his gloves ran along the edge of my jaw, resting under my chin as he tilted my head upward.

No.

I frowned; he would not kill me.

Then let me go home. I pleaded; my eyes watering. This had to be a dream, right? Things like this didn't just happen to people, especially nobodies like me.

As soon as my plea resounded through my head, I already knew his answer. He answered me anyway, though.

No.

Before I could respond, his gaze encompassed the awaiting hall. His voice a moment later was deadly serious, an air of authority in it. Even though I didn't understand what he said, I knew that whatever it was would not bode well for me. The men, Leif, and the man who had escorted me here yanked on my arms, pulling me back towards the doorway.

"What's going on?" I growled, trying to free myself from their grasp, even though I knew it was in vain.

There was no reply. His eyes narrowed, his face betraying nothing, as he watched his henchmen drag me from the hall.

CHAPTER
SIX

I raged against their firm grasps, knowing that it was ultimately
futile, like a lamb corralled to the slaughter. But I was no lamb,
and I would not go quietly. There was no way I'd let his lackeys
do a job that he should have had the balls to do himself. Once I
got back to that room with the parchments and scrolls and walls
of books, I'd fight.

Except, when they dragged me from the hall, we didn't go
right to return to that room where I had awoken. Taking a sharp
left, they unceremoniously hauled me over the stone, my bare
feet slipping and sliding across its smooth surface.

"Stop!" I cried, but they wouldn't listen, and even if they
could understand me, it wouldn't have changed their course.

If I wanted something to happen, I'd have to do it myself,
and quickly. If any of those historical shows I'd binge watched
when I was in high school taught me anything, it's that I was
likely being lugged to the dungeon.

Guards stationed along the hallway peeled aside, letting us
through. My feet finally caught on the stone, and with a little
effort I made myself keep up with them. After a flight of stairs

and another dash through a hallway just like the one on the floor above, their grips lessened.

"Where are we going?" I whispered, watching the wooden doors fly by.

A few moments later they brought me to a stop before a set of wooden doors reinforced with iron. They opened with an uncomfortable ear-splitting creak, and dragged me inside. Guards assembled at their posts just outside, waiting. *That sealed any attempts at escaping. At least not that way.* The room we stood in was far smaller than the hall with the thrones, which made sense, I suppose, considering this drab room was filled with cots of patchwork linen. One wall was peppered with alcoves hoarded with cups and plates and bowls stacked haphazardly upon each other, another had hooks nailed into wooden beams along the top, where fur coats, hats, and woven scarves hung. It was clearly a room for the working class, the servants.

The door shut behind me with a slam, and I stood there in the stony silence, hugging the cloak tighter around me. The stones beneath my feet were painfully cold, forcing me to take shelter in the cot furthest from the door, my shivering fingers pulling the scratchy linen over my body. Drawing my knees to my chest, I waited for the shivering to subside.

This couldn't possibly be real.

I had to be dead, or in a coma, or something. Anything would make more sense than what was happening. Even though I could feel the coldness in my bones, taste the burning logs in the hearths nearby, smell the scent of sweat on the air, I couldn't admit this was real. Deep down, I knew exactly why. Because if I did, that meant something bad had happened to Lucy, and I just wasn't ready to accept the fact that I had lost someone else. Liam, my mother, and now Lucy? No…no, no, no, *no!*

There was a light rapping against the door. The squeal of it opening jolted me upright. A beam of light streaked across the floor, cutting the room in half. A man in a cloak strode forward, he had a confident gait that reminded me too much of a peacock. When he pulled the hood from his face, I could see why.

It was the long-haired king.

"What do you want?" I glared up at him, not bothering to leave the comfort of the cot.

He smirked. *Not going to rise for your king?*

You're not my king.

He stood at the edge of my cot, his head cocked sideways. *I am now.*

Excuse me?

You don't get to decide who belongs to you.

He laughed, a haughty sound that sent shivers up my spine. The cot opposite me groaned as he sat down, his golden eyes twinkling with amusement.

That is precisely what being a king means, my lady.

Reaching out with his gloved hand, his fingers went to touch my hair. The sound of my hand slapping away his was louder than the beating of my heart in the silence. I stood, blanket falling to the ground with a soft thud. I glared down at him, my hands balling into fists at my side.

Believe what you want, but I am no one's property.

I made to walk away, but his hand shot out like a viper, tightening around my wrist. He yanked me backwards, my back colliding with the mattress. He straddled my waist, his hands holding my wrists above my head.

"Let me go!" I screeched, fighting against him.

It was futile though; he was far stronger than the two men who had brought me here. Their grasps had a little give, but his was absolute. He wasn't giving me a chance to escape, and I resigned to glaring defiantly into his golden eyes. Part of me grasped onto the hope that he wouldn't harm me, after all, dreams don't hurt. Right?

As your king, I bestow upon you a gift.

Leaning forward, his lips grazed my forehead, and I shivered under his touch.

"How dare you!" I growled.

"Do you not enjoy my gift, my lady?" he crooned in that strange, guttural language of his.

The gasp escaped from my lips before I could stop it, and a shit-eating smirk spread across his face. He released me, standing up to smooth his clothing.

"How can I understand you?" It made no sense. Or, I suppose, it didn't make that much less sense than him communicating in my head. Or me waking up to a world filled with men wearing animal furs like barbarians.

"A gift, nothing more. If you're going to be a part of my household, you'll need the ability to communicate with the others."

The least of my problems right now. But this could come in handy.

I glowered at him. "I told you I don't belong to you."

"Consider what way you will, but you are here under my protection. If you choose not to accept such a thing, then I'm sure the barracks could use some new entertainment."

"How *dare* you?" I hissed.

There was a light knock at the door. The man who had first brought me before the kings popped in. "My Lord Ulfrik."

He scowled, tearing his gaze from me. "What, Ogden?"

The man, Ogden, simpered slightly. "My Lord, they're here."

Those sunlight eyes narrowed, his nostrils flaring. Whoever was here, he was less than pleased about it. He waved at Ogden dismissively, his eyes returning to me.

"My Lord—"

"I am coming," he snapped, his icy gaze setting me on edge. "May the gods forgive me for making my brother wait."

Ogden nodded, closing the door with more force than necessary, rattling the door frame. The king stared emptily at the door, distracted by whatever awaited him. He mumbled something, but the only words I could make out were enough to figure out that Ogden was an advisor to the king, and he was sometimes too good at his job.

"Ulfrik, huh?" I said, breaking him of the spell.

He turned that cold winter glare upon me. "Lord."

"Right, *Lord* Ulfrik," I said sarcastically.

His gloved hand gently grasped my chin, tilting my gaze

upwards. "It's clear that you do not know what you have gotten yourself into, *Traveler*."

"Stop calling me that." I wrenched my jaw from his grasp.

His eyebrows rose. "Then what should I call you?"

"I already told you, my answer hasn't changed."

"Feisty," he purred, before shrugging off my glares. "If you won't give me your name, then I simply know you as the Traveler."

I glowered. "You can have my name when you earn it."

Amusement crinkled his eyes as he strode for the door, hesitating briefly, his face obscured by the shadow of his hair. "Do yourself a favor."

"What?"

When he turned, there was a warning in his expression. "Don't leave this room until I return."

I scoffed, but he was not amused.

"I've already told you—"

"If you're a *king*, surely your men will obey your word," I taunted.

His gaze became distant. "In case you haven't noticed, I'm one of three."

Rolling my eyes, I turned my back to him. I was done with the conversation, I just wanted to be left alone. I could feel his eyes boring into my back, and I prayed that among his secret abilities, heat vision wasn't one of them.

"Don't leave this room," he demanded, the door squeaking shut almost instantly, leaving me in the cold silence.

I once again found myself in a prison, but unlike the one I had placed myself in at my brother's house, I wasn't content to sit here and die. Lucy needed me, Finn needed me, and if this was real, and not an elaborate dreamscape I had designed, I needed to leave. Tossing the scratchy blanket over my shoulders, I sprinted across the room, my hand grasping the handle.

With a firm yank, the door creaked open, the sound akin to nails on a chalkboard. But that wasn't what sent the shiver up my spine. Standing before me, arms laden with clothing, was that ocean-eyed man. A bulging bag hung from his shoulder; the toothed necklace glinted in the harsh yellow light of the sconces.

He groaned, pushing past me, kicking shut the door without saying a word. As it shut, though, I didn't miss the two guards waiting outside. Ushering me to take a seat on the nearest bed, I glared defiantly at him, standing by the door, ready to bolt. Irritation was written across his face like a book, and with a heavy sigh he placed that bundle of clothing on the bed closest to the door, standing by it with an expectant stare.

"I'm not playing this game," I growled, staring him down.

Startled, he looked taken aback, but quickly regained his composure, a smile on his lips.

I folded my arms. "What?"

"It's interesting that our lord has given you such a gift."

I rolled my eyes, crossing my arms. "How is this a gift? So, what, now I know what my captors are saying."

His audible sigh was grating. "Consider yourself special, my lady. We have not given this gift to many others. At least, not until they have earned it."

That piqued my interest. "There were others here that didn't understand you?"

He nodded slowly, as if trying to put the pieces together to what I was asking.

Let me spell it out for you.

"Others like me?" And since I came here, my heart soared. There was a chance. If others had come here, then there had to be a way back.

His eyes narrowed. "I'll warn you once and only once, my lady. You'd do well to heed the king's advice."

Did he overhear us?

"And I'll tell you the same thing I told him, I'm nobody's property."

An expression so fleeting I was almost sure I had imagined it crossed his face, a shadow that had the hair on my arms stand to attention. There was obviously more to what was going on than I was privy to. And it took me a whole ten seconds to decide I wanted no part of it. I would find my way home at all costs.

"I brought you a change of clothing." His eyes slithered to the bundle he had placed on the bed.

I ignored him. "Your name is Leaf, right?"

His lips curved upwards with amusement. "*Leif.*"

"Right, *Lay-f,*" I said, sounding it out. But as fun as it was to be learning my captors' names, I had far more pressing questions. "Do you know why he spared me?"

Eyebrows raised, "Spared?"

"Why didn't he kill me, like the people in that hall wanted him to?"

The internal fight in that brain of his was clear as day, written across his face like a book. It was obvious Leif knew exactly to what I was referring. He was debating what to tell me, or rather, whether to tell me.

A moment of silence passed until he broke it, clearing his throat.

"I suppose there is no harm in telling you before the official ceremony."

"Excuse me?" *Official ceremony?*

His expression gave nothing away, but the words that followed chilled me to the bone.

"You are the newest member of the Praell of the Wolf Clan." He said it as if I should feel honored. Or that I could never have hoped for anything better.

"What is a *praell?*" Something deep within me told me this arrangement did not benefit me in the slightest. That dark, primeval part of being human that warned you when something bad was about to happen. A premonition. Survival instinct. A prickle beneath the skin, a heightening of the senses.

"You work for King Ulfrik." He was so sure of himself, his tone so matter of fact, I almost felt sorry for him.

I certainly didn't miss the words he didn't say. "I'm a slave, you mean."

Here, *wherever here was,* had a very strict way of life that felt so natural, so complete to all those who lived it, that they couldn't consider any other way as being right. Slavery wasn't extinct back home, but we had made great strides to abolish it. But Leif thought he was doing me a favor. The *king* thought he was doing me a favor. Ice chilled in my veins as he stumbled for words. He could see I was unwilling to accept whatever excuse he was ready to throw my way. He resigned with a simple nod.

"You can't make me do anything, *Leaf*." My gaze flitted to the door. "I will escape."

With his head held high, Leif stared me down. "I would advise against that, my lady."

Such pretenses. "You basically shackled me but dare address me as '*my lady*,'" I spat at him.

"You still deserve to be addressed as such, regardless of your station."

"My *station*. You are the one that decided that, not me, and I can promise you that given the chance I will not hesitate to return home." All I could see before me was red, the world spinning as my heart beat like a drum in my chest.

"Winter is closing in, the passes through the mountains and across the sea have closed. You would die out there if you dared even attempt such a thing." He seemed amused by such a notion, as if everyone who was proclaimed a slave just sat down and accepted their fate.

I didn't care about the other slaves, though. Because I was me, Phoebe Wood, and I was a slave to no one.

"Get dressed, and you can leave the room." He strode from the room, that damned door squeaking shut.

Waiting for the click of the door, I glared at the clothing he had designated for me. There was no way these strips of cloth and fur would be warmer than what I had first come to this place wearing. But I did not know where my vest or jacket, or even my shoes were. I was draped in that thin ivory dress, and even this cloak did little to stave off the bite of winter. If what Leif said was true, and the storm that had brought me here had truly closed the mountain and sea off, I'd need warmer clothes than what I was wearing.

I'd need food and water, and supplies, too, if I were going to do what I had promised Leif I would do. Staging a breakout would be no easy feat, and for the meantime, he, and everyone else here, had to believe I was onboard with the ridiculous notion of being a slave.

Kind of ruined that by telling him exactly what you planned to do. I groaned at that damned internal voice.

A few moments after I had fastened the hook of the strap of my apron dress under the gaudy metal button shaped like a wolf's head, there was a knock at the door. I ignored it, too preoccupied with smoothing the wrinkles on this horrid outfit they had forced me to wear. I looked, and felt, like one of those people you see reenacting the crowd at a jousting tournament. I thought my whole situation would suit someone who enjoyed spending their free time at a Renaissance Faire. It was just layers of dresses, and I simply put them on in an order that I decided in that very moment, not caring if it was right.

The knock came again. This time, my eyes snapped up as the door creaked open, and Leif stood in the torchlight. On either side of him, guarding the door, were men with heads adorned by the ivory skulls of wolves, their eyes smeared in charcoal. If their existence was meant to intimidate, they were doing a good job. I caught myself swallowing a lump that had formed in my throat.

"What did you do?" He held back a snicker.

"What you *told* me to do." I might have played along, but that didn't stop me from expressing my disdain.

"What even is this?" The hook of the strap loosened, the button flinging across the room, landing at Leif's feet. He seemed unamused, no doubt debating if I were truly worth the trouble. He bent over and scooped the button up, pressing it into the palm of my hand.

"First things first, perhaps you need instructions on how to dress yourself."

I glowered, his tone grating on my nerves. He clearly thought I was inept, incapable of the most basic of human actions.

He ignored my annoyed expression, as he dived straight in to chastise my incompetence. "First off, its chemise, then over-dress, then apron, then bodice."

"You assume I know what any of those things are," I said pointedly.

"Apparently."

Throwing his hands up in exasperation, he jabbed his finger each of the layers that clung to my body. "One, two, three, four."

I shooed him away with my hands. "Okay, I get it."

"You have two minutes." The door clicked shut, the silence of my own thoughts deafening.

What did it matter if I had the layers wrong? I was a slave. Who cared how they were dressed? I was hesitant to draw any more attention though, as I'm sure Leif would dress me if I kept up any resistance. Or perhaps the king would return. He seemed to have no qualms about touching me. A shudder shook my shoulders, and I pushed the thought from my mind.

Once I had stripped myself and followed his instructions, I realized why there was a particular order to the layers. They flowed like a pair of doves in flight, in sync with one another as each layer rippled beneath my movements. Even if it were the clothing of a slave, of a *praell*, it was comfortable and felt, oddly enough, like it suited me. I was certain it had more to do with the colors, how the hue of a summer pine graced the mellowness of a dawning sunset as it sat on a bed of greying clouds. The contrast was far subtler than the teal jacket I had come here in, and as hesitant as I was to admit it, I grew more and more attached to this modest array of clothing.

As promised, Leif appeared only two minutes later, ushering me from the room like a shepherd chastising his wayward black sheep for finding itself in the tool shed again.

"It's an improvement from that hideous guise you arrived in," were the only words he spoke to me. I ignored it; my focus was on where we were going, on every doorway, on every window. Anything that could be used as an exit.

We walked the stone corridors, their twisting and winding

paths making it beyond difficult for me to remember which way led where. It was reminiscent of those madhouses at the county fairs with the walls of mirrors, or the twisting maze of cornstalks in the fall. I had no hope of memorizing the path, especially if I were under constant watch. I eyed the guards standing outside doors and patrolling the halls. There was little room for escape; it wasn't just guards I had to look out for. People littered the castle. Milling in the halls, in rooms with open doors, and of course the guards who stood diligently outside the locked doors. Temptation grew within me, but also despair, as I realized there were a lot more people here than I thought. Escape would be tricky.

Leif took a sharp right, leading me spiraling downwards into the darkness of a stairwell. Every couple of steps the wall on our right opened, a slit of beveled glass that looked out over a world of ice and swirling snow. The further we descended, the closer the obsidian-shingled roofs of the town below got, twinkling like scales in the early morning light.

The stairwell opened into a long room of tables and chairs, sagging under the weight of crates and leather-clad warriors. Our intrusion did not go unnoticed. More than once I witnessed a double take, as if they couldn't believe the sight before them. I know I would have, after all, you had, what I was suspecting was the best friend of the Wolf King, escorting some strange crimson-haired woman through their workspace. I had yet to see any other women, and a pit formed in my stomach, sitting low and heavy.

Some men wore skulls of wolves, the sharp ivory fangs glinting in the flickering torchlight. Some, though, were clearly wearing the hooked beak of a bird of prey, the skin around their eyes smeared in ochre paint. The men whose faces were hidden behind the skulls of what had to be bears were the most terrifying. They wore the fur of the creatures like a veil on the head, some macabre machination you would expect to see in a sordid pagan ritual for cannibals.

Leif had marched ahead of me, holding open the door to

the outside where the faintest of snowflakes drifted lazily on a gentle breeze. Stone and wood buildings crowded the streets just outside, and the smell of burning wood filled the air.

The moment my foot hit the threshold, Leif stood aside, a smile on his face.

"Welcome to the High Keep."

CHAPTER
SEVEN

Words drifted away from me like the snowflakes that flitted by on the breeze. That put a smugness on Leif's face which prickled my nerves. It was like he had planned this all along. Conspiring with the Wolf King to woo me with the grandeurs of this city. I could only see a fraction, but the similarities it shared with old Edinburgh entranced me.

"What is this?" The awe in my voice was hard to mask. I despised the image of a child's first visit to Disneyland that crept into my mind.

Leif led me through wide streets of grey stone laid out like bricks, edged with the hustle and bustle of people leading their daily lives. Every shop we passed had a name, a purpose, and Leif eagerly shared it with me. There was a cobbler, butcher, baker, blacksmith, chandler, potter, even a barber.

"These are only the shops in the High Keep, the other wards have their specifications tailored to the clan that owns them," he said, perusing a small table of colored soaps wrapped in cloth sleeves.

"Is there a marketplace?" If I feigned interest, perhaps he

would be less suspicious of my intentions.

"Not in the High Keep, but the Conjunction houses some of the finest wares you can lay your eyes on. But we'll save that for another day. I don't want to overwhelm you."

"Oh yeah, heaven forbid," I muttered.

I played along as the dutiful tourist, absorbing the layout of the city. It would be easier to make my escape if I knew where I could rummage for last-minute supplies. Not entirely sure where, or even what, the Conjunction was, I had to make do with a simple mental note to investigate further.

An exit from this staggering display of stone and wood was proving difficult to find. Imposing walls manned by armed militia surrounded the High Keep. Steep towers curled upwards into the grey sky, snow swirling around their cone tips. I had suspected that Leif's route was purposeful; he was expecting me to bolt when I had the chance. I couldn't prove it, of course, but I'd have to be on my guard or I would wake up to find myself chained to the bed.

Feigning interest, I smelt the soaps he held to my face, touched the fabrics he encouraged me to, and watched with enthusiasm as a stable boy paraded one of the High Keep's finest stallions past us. It was all a show that I found tedious. Not unlike gun shows or military parades. I took special note of where that stable boy led the stallion. A horse would come in handy later, I could cover twice as much ground. My shoulders slumped, and as the day dragged on, I found it harder to keep up the pretenses.

Leif noticed my lack of enthusiasm, commenting on my haggardness as we left the streets, returning to that room with the men in armour and tables laden with goods. We ascended the tower with a hastiness that made me suspicious. But I was too tired to say anything, plodding along behind him like a good little sheep. The door to the slave chambers creaked open, and I collapsed onto the bed, not caring about the look of disapproval Leif bore.

"I'll be right back." He shut the door behind him.

My mind reeled, desperate to grab onto what little information I had gleaned from our foray into the city. This place was like any city or town. Edinburgh, London, New York. There were people with jobs, happy smiling citizens or scowling disgruntled citizens that went about their work with either laziness or gusto. Albeit wasn't far from feeling like I was a character in a video game. Those too long glances in the room at the bottom of the spiraling stairwell told me this place wasn't too far off being some dystopian world, like Mad Max. There was still no sign of any other women, and that pit that had formed in my stomach earlier only grew.

I couldn't stay here, I knew that, and the tour Leif had given me only strengthened my resolve. There were others like me here, but that meant little without more information. They could have been wayward hikers caught in snowstorms, or they could be other people that are more like the ones that surrounded me now. That little voice whispered, like a cricket in the distance, *or maybe Lucy is here.*

"No," I said out loud, jumping to my feet.

There was no way to be sure how much time Leif was going to give me, so I needed to gather supplies now. Whatever guardian angel was looking down on me had blessed me. Even though they had secured me in the quarters for their workers, it provided everything I'd need. I wouldn't have to find the Conjunction, after all.

Running from one side of the room to the other, I gathered bits and bobs into a small pile on my bed. A blanket, a scarf, an overcoat, some rope, a waterskin bulging and gurgling with what I hoped was water. *Or alcohol.* Hidden under a bed nearby was a more comfortable pair of boots with thick insoles, lined with thick, brown fur much more suitable to the outside than the thin leather boots Leif had provided me.

There was a gnawing suspicion in my stomach though, knowing full well that this would not end well for me if that door were to open. A worker returning to gather some supplies, a guard grabbing a drink, Leif returning as promised. Or heaven forbid, the king himself. Panic built in me as I imagined losing what little freedom I had. A pressure pounded against my skull. There were ropes scattered throughout the room, and outside I had seen innumerable chains tied to posts and hanging from walls. If they had even an inkling of what I was up to I'd lose my advantage, and possibly my life.

I needed somewhere discreet to squirrel away my supplies until the time was right. The room provided many nooks and crannies, but none of them gave me the discretion I really needed. Hanging from one hook above a bed was a satchel. There was no opportunity for second guessing myself as I snatched it from the wall and stuffed it full of the supplies I had gathered on the bed.

Leaning against the windowsill, peering out into the darkening gloom, it was hard not to let my mind wander: to Lucy, sitting in a police station in Bergen, filling out a missing person's report; to Finn, in Edinburgh, disregarding Lucy's warning and getting on the first plane to Norway. If my phone worked, that was, if I could even find it, it would have been inundated with text messages and missed phone calls by now. A part of me wondered if my colleagues knew. Dr. Kerr would simper, assuming my disappearance was intentional. *'She probably flung herself from a mountain top.'* His voice echoed in my mind. Doctor Khumalo, though, sweet hearted woman that was built like an Amazonian warrior, she would have rallied the team together for some sort of fundraiser for the search and rescue efforts. It'd been a single day, and yet it felt like an aeon had passed. Maybe they weren't looking for me. Maybe not yet, maybe Lucy still held out for me to stroll through the hotel door.

It was difficult not to feel like I was already there, curled up on the spacious bed with my head cradled by the goose down pillows. The sound of traffic zipping past the window far below us, as Lucy flipped through the channels hoping to find a show in English.

I would give anything to be back there again, including the risk of a snapped neck by jumping from the second story room

I stood in. To get that far, I'd need to first find a place to hide the satchel. The underneath of the bed was an obvious choice, or it would be, if you couldn't see under all the beds from the front door. The bold move would be to leave it out in the open, right where I had grabbed it from, on the hook above the bed. High risk for such a high reward. None of the options before me were appealing and time was running out. *Leif could be back any second.*

In my frustration, my foot collided with the wooden boards that circled the bottom half of the walls like molding. I cried out in pain, biting my lip to stop any more sound from coming out. The board gave way under my boot, sinking inwards, revealing a hidden alcove. Lady Luck was on my side. I rammed the satchel into the crowded alcove, and my heart soared as it fit in perfectly. Fiddling with the board, my foot struggled with keeping it in its place. My heart beat against my ribs like an enraged animal against the bars at the zoo. If Leif saw me now, it was all over.

A familiar creaking broke apart the silence just as the wooden board snapped shut against the wall. I leaned against it with as much casualness as I could muster. I pretended I was distracted by something outside as the door clicked shut, and Leif strode across the room to stand on the other side of the bed from me. He plopped a new bundle on the bed.

The shimmer of emerald caught my eye. "What's this?"

His eyes glimmered like the dress; those sky-touched orbs framed by wispy tendrils of sunlight hair. Under better circumstances I would have allowed myself to consider him handsome, but all I felt right now was the chance of developing Stockholm Syndrome.

"Lord Ulfrik has requested your presence for dinner tonight."

A hollowness swelled within me, allowing the void that had consumed me after my mother's death to rear its ugly head. I didn't want to dine with the king; I would not play his game. Some women would have been okay with such a thing, paraded around like some prize.

"My Lady?"

Nodding my head, my fingers brushed the silken fabric. There was an ivory chemise beside it, and the snow-white fur of what I suspected was a wolf to grace my shoulders. It was of a much better quality than the russet brown one that I had worn today, and no doubt held some sort of significance for the king.

"Can I have a few moments to get ready?"

His heartwarming smile could've been infectious if I weren't a hostage. He was pleased that I wasn't putting up a fight. "Take your time, dinner isn't for another hour."

Now, to plan my escape.

The moment the door shut, my fingers were prying apart the wooden board; the bits and bobs I had collected in the satchel were slung across my shoulder. The dress was exquisite, as was the fur, but I had no use for either. Back home, I wouldn't need any of that.

Securing the cloak around my shoulders, my stiff fingers fumbled with the latch on the window. It slid open with little effort, the room accosted with a bone-chilling breeze. Night had settled fast. The town was alive and twinkling beyond the confines of this room. Craning my neck out the window, I saw my escape looked more and more promising. Directly below the room I was in sat a balcony with a winding staircase that lead into a garden below it.

There was no plan. My hands seemed to move of their own accord as I gathered all the coils of rope in the room. With little experience in how to make a decent knot, I double and triple tied the ends of each rope to one another. The itchy fibrous material stretched a lot longer than I needed, and if I were ambitious (and a risk taker) it could have lowered me to the garden below the balcony. But I was already taking enough risks, I didn't need to add broken legs to the list.

Securing one end of the rope around the wooden headboard, I shoved the bed against the wall under the windowsill. Crouching in the open window, ropes gathered in my arms, I cast them into the darkness. A moment later, the thud of the rope against the stone told me my plan had worked. Tugging on the end attached to the bed, I steeled myself.

This was it. It was now or never. If I gave myself any more time to think about it, I would chicken out. My legs were wobbly and my hands shaking as I gripped the rope and exposed my back to the world outside. Staring at the grey stone pebbled with erosion, I tried not to think about the twenty-foot drop as I put one hand below another, rappelling to the balcony below. My arms burned, and my thighs ached. Sweat beaded on my forehead and on my palms. It took everything I had to concentrate on not falling to my death. My mind still wandered, as it always did, to Lucy, to Finn, to my mother.

Tears stung my eyes; the warmth like tiny blades cut into the flesh as they rolled across my wind-exposed cheeks. My fingers, although cold, were coated in a thin layer of sweat now, and the rope dug into my flesh as I fought to keep my grip. I didn't dare peek to gauge how much further I had to go. It wasn't because I had a fear of heights; they didn't really bother me. It was more the fact that I knew from something my mother said when I was younger. She told me a story about how humans survive unscathed from falls if it were from below ten feet. My window to the balcony was double that.

I had to be close to the balcony. It couldn't be much further. At least, that's what I thought. It was only twenty feet below, and yet it felt like I had scaled an entire building. The only thing on my mind was how grateful I was that the rope held. Weight had never been a major concern in my life. I was lucky genetics were on my side. I was thankful that the last few months I had spent immobile in my brother's apartment doing nothing but wallowing in despair had done little ill to me.

Even as the thought crossed my mind, my arms turned to jelly. Seeming to wiggle of their own accord, like the tentacles of an octopus. Ignoring it, my pace quickened. There wasn't much time left. In the blink of an eye, it happened. My grip loosened, the rope sliding between my fingers. My arms gave way. My back collided with the cold stone of the balcony, the air rushing from my lungs. Desperate for air, sitting in the swirling snow, I gulped like a fish out of water, waiting for my heart to quiet.

I made it. The hard part was done with. It was easy coasting from here. Animated voices, full of frustration and urgency, rose from behind me. My curiosity was eating away at me. It was risky to investigate. The right thing to do would be to stick to my plan, go through the garden, and out into the woods to find the runestone cave. It was by the water, there were docks nearby, that's all I remembered. How hard could it be to find?

The deeper voice called out to his companion, followed by the thud of something heavy hitting the wall. Flattening myself against the stone, edging myself beside the archway with its billowing curtains and stained glass, my eyes surveyed the room.

It was fancier than the one I was in, that was for sure. But it was clear from the wooden poster bed swathed in luxurious curtains against the far wall, the ottoman of leather at its foot, and the solid wooden tables and chairs against the opposite wall, this room belonged to no mere slave.

My suspicions were confirmed a moment later when a shadow moved on a fur-laden couch in a corner. A man was languishing across it like a drunkard, his face puffy and blushed. Another man paced beside him, pinching the bridge of his nose. The hooked nose and beady emerald eyes were on full display. His wolf's skull mask hung from his neck as he paced, exposing his mousey brown hair. The other had short hair and a hand that was taut around a silver sword. He was hard to forget.

It was the Eagle King and Ogden. My brows furrowed in confusion. I thought Ogden was the advisor to Ulfrik. Odd that he would be in a very heated conversation with the Eagle King in what I presumed were his private quarters. Shaking my head, I peeled myself away from the wall to the stairs, but my eyes kept creeping to the archway.

It's none of your concern, Phoebe. Besides, Ulfrik reminded you he was one of three *kings.*

My inner voice made sense, and that was all I needed to hear. Why should I even care? My feet skipped along the stone steps, every bounce reminding me of the bruise that was forming on my backside from the fall. It didn't matter. Hours from now

I would be back where I belonged, in that cozy hotel bed in Bergen. Lucy would be there, too, nagging me for having the audacity to worry her like I have.

There was no erasing the smile from my face, and the moment my feet hit the dirt of the garden, it only got wider. Trellises and tunnels of wood suspended above gravelly dirt paths, swollen with purple and pink and yellow flowers of varying shapes and sizes. It amazed me that they somehow still bloomed under the crushing weight of the hardening snow. I wish I knew their names, but I was never a green thumb. The dying stems of the potted ferns that sat scattered around my apartment were the extent of my knowledge.

Although time was of the essence, and Leif would discover me missing soon, alerting the entire High Keep, my hasty escape turned into a meandering stroll through the garden. There was a disturbing blanket of ease settling on my shoulders, which only hardened my resolve. At the far end of the garden was a tunnel that opened into the small, enclosed courtyard of a sprawling stone mansion. Hidden from the hustle and bustle of the common folk outside its high walls, this estate could only serve as the residence for one of the kings. Its design was impressive, with a grand curved staircase leading to stone columns and a double door entry guarded by two giant birds of prey. One with its beak open, the other closed. There was no doubting to whom this property belonged.

Taking a deep breath, I darted across the courtyard with the speed of Usain Bolt. Or at least, it felt that way. My lungs burned as they sucked in the cold air, the bruise on my back keeping me at attention.

A harsh snort tore my focus from the house. Opposite the mansion was an extensive building hedged by a row of thick bushes. They provided the cover I needed to sneak into the stable. I ran for it, the door shutting behind me with a thud. It would have been pitch black, if not for the few missing slats of wood on each of the stalls, letting scattered beams of moonlight shine on the horses within.

Unlike the stallion that was paraded before me earlier, these horses were sleek, agile. Their purpose was for speed and stamina, not looks. A muscular charcoal black horse regarded me for a moment, curiosity alive in its hazelnut eyes. Its head stretched out as far as the door on the stall allowed, steam rising from its whiskered muzzle.

My hand hovered by its face, before the horse thrust its cheek against my palm.

"Alright, I guess you're coming with me then," I said.

On the wall space opposite the stalls were rows of tack lined neatly: saddles and bridles, and warm clothes. Everything I'd need. Now I only needed to know exactly how to put them on the horse.

It wasn't the first time I'd ridden a horse; I was confident enough to guess my way through the motions. Now dressing the horse in its equipment? That was a whole new ballgame. The bridle went on the head; I knew that. But holding the many pieces of leather straps in my hands sent a quiver of panic through me. I hadn't the slightest idea which part went where, and time had me debating throwing it haphazardly on the animal and making it up as I went along.

The shuffling of boots on the stone outside snapped me out of the panic that had been building, my hands dropping the bridle. Someone was outside. Tossing it back onto the wall, I ran the length of the stables, past every stall. Some horses whinnied or snorted, alerting whoever was outside. His grunt was enough to tell me I had little time. I'd have to abandon the idea of taking a horse and risk it all on foot. The door I had come through slid open the moment I darted into an empty stall, as the horse in the stall next door eyed me suspiciously.

"What's all the complaining about?" the guy asked.

His boots shifted the dirt by the first stall, and a moment later I heard the clinking of the metal parts of the bridle on the wall.

"Who put this away?" His voice teetered off as my mind imagined his gaze sweeping the stables.

"I know you're in here!" he called out, boots stomping through the dirt as he passed by every stall. "You hiding anyone in there, Egg?" he whispered a few stalls down, the rustling of hay met my ears.

Shit. If I stayed here, he'd catch me, and then all of this would be for nothing, and I'd wake up chained to a wall in the dungeon. I didn't even know if they had a dungeon, but I wasn't willing to find out.

A coldness gripped me. My eyes followed a snowflake as it drifted past, landing at my feet. It was perfect, every fractal detailed, a shine of ivory in the dirt. Snowflakes… —*the window!* It took everything in me not to shoot to my feet, to give whoever was here a reason to quicken their pace. Like the other stalls, a window sat above me, secured with wooden slats, of which one was open. Moonlight filtered through, and with it, a breeze that carried a flurry of snowflakes to rest on the front of my long-sleeved dress.

Hooking my shaking fingers around the slats, I pulled and they gave with little force. Either side had dowels at the end, and with little persuasion I could remove each slat from the window, placing them on the straw-covered ground. The shuffling of boots got closer, only one stall away. Without a second thought, I gripped the windowsill, hauling myself over and out. Bushes grew high around me, obscuring me from the view of the window. Behind them was the stone wall; I pressed myself against it.

A moment later, a head popped up at the window I had just climbed through. A young man, not much older than I, with shaggy hair and a face, marred by days spent in the sun, peeked out. His brows furrowed as he muttered something under his breath, and disappeared. He must have known the slats hadn't been like that before. Help would be on the way soon. Scouring the wall, I followed its length, letting the bushes hide me from the glass windows of the mansion. Everything was the same, same bricks, same bushes, same dirt and woodchips littering the ground covered in snow. Except, just ahead, where the bushes thinned just slightly, the bottom part of the wall bowed inward.

My heart skipped a beat as I contemplated what stood before me. Iron spokes in the shape of a tree sat in the hole, snow drifting lazily just beyond it, like a scene from National Geographic.

Did my eyes betray me, or was there a grate in that wall, leading to a snow-covered forest outside?

Shaking with excitement, my feet skidded in the soft snow beside the grate, my hands hooked into the holes. Tensing my muscles, with my feet placed firmly on the wall on either side of the grate, I pulled with all my strength.

It gave way, narrowly missing my face as I teetered backwards. My eyes shot to the windows of the mansion and the flickering golden light within. No shadows stirred; no voices called out.

Now was as good a time as any, and freedom beckoned. Without a backward glance, I eased myself through the hole in the wall. It was barely big enough for me to crawl through on my stomach. The moment I emerged into the clearing on the other side, my heart soared.

I had done it. A forest, old and dark, creaking under the pressure of snow and unforgiving wind stretched out before me. There was a vague calling to turn right, to follow the forest along the length of the outer wall. The docks couldn't be far off, and if I found them, then I would find the cave, and the runestone.

Home was within reach.

CHAPTER
EIGHT

This was truly a road less traveled. The snow lay undisturbed, hampering my progress. Every step I took plunged me into the depths, brushing the tops of my thighs. I wasn't prepared for this; I didn't think it through at all. I saw my first chance at leaving, and I took it. Damned be the consequences.

It didn't matter though; I didn't regret my actions. This wall would bring me to the wharf, and from there, to the cave.

I'm almost there, Lucy.

If it weren't for the moonlight trickling through the growing cloud cover and occasional flickering of the torches on the walls, I would be in absolute darkness. My shivering had intensified, even though I huffed and puffed like I hadn't walked a day in my life. Even though I wore several layers, the bite of the outside still seeped through. Time was of the essence, but there was no increasing my stride. The snow was unforgiving, reminding me of the field of mud I had played in as a kid when it had sucked at my shoes, and every move I made was like wearing ankle weights.

The moonlight was disappearing; the wind roared louder as a

frenzy of snowflakes whipped around me. A storm had brewed fast, not unlike the one that trapped me when I had found that cave the first time.

Maybe it was a sign. Or maybe I was going to freeze to death out here, and no one would know what happened to me. I still had to try though; there was no turning back. I didn't belong here, in this strange world where people thought it was normal to adorn their bodies with the corpses and skins of creatures.

Hours passed, and the wall didn't end. There was no feeling in my toes or in my fingers now as darkness settled around me. My lips were raw and chapped, my muscles were becoming rigid. Time was running out.

The storm had increased in its ferocity, and my mind began to abandon the thoughts of finding the wharf, let alone the cave. What I needed to find was shelter, and quick. The dangers of frostbite, all the warnings in the pamphlets at the hotel in Bergen, were coming back to haunt me. The howling wind accompanied my every move, the deathly whisperings like daggers to my mind.

Nothing changed, no indication that I was any closer to the frozen waters that hugged the wharf. A forest stretched to my left, and the wall to my right. As far as I could see to the horizon, it was unchanging.

You really fucked up this time, didn't you, Phoebe.

I glowered.

At least you had a bed, clothes, warmth, food. You threw that all away, like some petulant child upset they got the wrong colored toy for Christmas.

"Shut up," I breathed, the tendrils of my breath curling into the air like the plume from a tiny smokestack.

She was persistent though, lashing out like a vine covered in thorns.

You're going to die out here.

Each lash was closer to ripping me to shreds.

No one will save you.

The snow began to crunch underneath my feet, the powder that was fresh hours ago hardening as the storm consumed me. The numbness had travelled from my fingers and toes to my hands and feet, which were now stiff and unfeeling. The darkness thickened just like the snow, my situation becoming dire with every passing breath.

It's all your fault.

"T-tell me s-something I don't know." My throat was dry, parched, frozen. Licking my lips did nothing, except highlight the chapped ridges.

You're useless.

What a revelation! Sixteen-year-old me would've felt so validated. The voice was relentless, her assault quickening. And my heart couldn't handle what she said next.

It was because of you that your mother died.

"Shut the fuck up!" I screeched, holding my hands to my face.

When I withdrew them, it was to see that the forest had managed to overwhelm me. Pines crowded every space available, their branches heavy with the snow. There was no avoiding it, no reprieve from those tiny white specks of cold.

My hand lashed out, weak and without any real purpose. The branch before me shuddered, dumping the load it had gathered at my feet. The world beneath me shifted. The tree disappeared as I tumbled down an unseen ravine, plunging me into the cold darkness of a bottomless snowbank.

If I wasn't cold before, I was now. The snow was everywhere, nestling between every layer of clothing, packed in nice and tight. Digging myself free, I exposed my head to the icy winds and screamed into the night. Even in the freezing conditions the tears still formed in my eyes, rolling hot, stinging trails across my cheeks.

I didn't believe that last comment. I knew my mother's death wasn't my fault. And yet, the pain was unbearable at the mere idea. She was all I had, the only family left. My dad died when I was a baby, a voiceless, faceless entity that meant nothing to me. According to my mother, he wasn't worth it anyway.

Only once did my mother ever mention him to me, one Father's Day when I was thirteen. Teenage Phoebe was a force to be reckoned with, and that day was the only day I had ever seen my mother angry. Truly, angry. Her face was puffy and red-hot with rage, clenched fists held tightly at her side as she bit back saying more than what was necessary.

'I'll say this once, and only once. Your father was a fool, a drunken idiot who doesn't deserve our love or our pity. He chose alcohol over his family, and it led to his death.' She had sighed, taking my hand in hers, and I could feel the slight tremor. She was remembering something she wished she hadn't. *'Never ask about him again, please.'*

'I promise, mum.' I had made her a lot of promises over the years, and I had broken a lot, too. But never this one.

She was my stone, as much as I was hers. I became a nurse because of her. The inspiration to try new things, to never say no to an opportunity, was all because of her. One time I even dabbled in veganism, just for her. She was the perfect mother. But those damn cigarettes.

Phoebe.

It was almost as if I could hear her, that unique rasp in her voice. She was eccentric in her greetings, the way she said my name, as if I were the star in her otherwise bleak sky.

"Phoebe."

My head snapped up like a dog at the ballpark. That voice wasn't in my mind, it was near to me, and it was familiar.

"H-hello?"

That's when I saw her, the voice that accompanied the body. A few steps beyond my ice-coated lashes.

"It can't be…" My mind reeled at the possibility. "How?" My hand reached out, but she stayed out of reach.

The golden bob grazed her jaw, highlighting her soft emerald eyes, and high-set cheekbones. The sparkle in her demeanor when her eyes caught sight of me, the luminosity of her freckled skin. It was her; it was my mother.

"Mum," I croaked.

Her thin lips curved upwards, eyes crinkling. There was no care for anything else as I pulled myself from the snowbank, barreling through it like a bull. Her smile widened, before she turned her back to me, walking away.

"Wait! Come back!"

The gap stayed the same between us, even as the snowbank disappeared beneath my feet, giving way to a rocky shore peppered in snow. My pace quickened, unhindered, and yet, she stayed out of reach. I just wanted to have her in my arms again, the scent of her cigarettes poorly hidden by the cheap perfume she was fond of. I even missed the headaches her synthetic rose scent fed, and how much harder it made my ten-hour shifts. I would trade anything to have that back, to have her back.

She stopped to face me, closer than she had ever been while we were walking. An empty prairie yawned before us, the snow only accentuating her features.

"Mother," I whimpered, the crow's feet crinkled around her eyes, amusement swirling in the emerald depths.

"Phoebe." Her voice was a whisper, a croaky noise that sliced at the wounds that had barely begun to heal.

My vision blurred significantly since we left the safety of the forest, the icicles that were once my eyelashes were heavy, begging me to shutter my eyes. The fight against that urge was weak, and the grandeur of drifting to sleep knowing my mother was right there beside me was irresistible.

Sensing what I was so desperate to have, my mother held her arms out before her, beckoning me into her embrace. There was no hesitation, my shoes slipped on the ice as I closed that annoying gap between us. Her yellowed teeth from decades of fervent tea sipping was a stark contrast to the snow and ice around us.

Wait…ice?

There was a crackling noise, heralded by the boom of something shifting beneath my feet. A second was all I needed to realize my folly. I wasn't standing in a prairie coated in snow. I stood on a frozen lake, that was breaking under my weight.

It was too late, I knew that, as the ice cracked and my legs buckled. As I plunged into the icy depths, I was eager for just one last look, to know she was still there. But there was nothing before me as the current swallowed me whole. There was only cold, and water, and darkness.

I should have known it was a trick of the mind. Desperation had soured me, polluting me like the plague. I was consumed, distraught at her death, and now my mind had betrayed me. It would be all over soon, and for that, I was thankful. The hard part was over, the struggle. There was nothing but endless cold, and no pain.

I was floating endlessly in a void, the blue ice above me streaked with ivory, like a marble countertop. It was surreal, even knowing this beauty meant the end of me, it was such a beautiful sight. The current was gentle, rocking me like a baby in a cradle. The cold waters had filled my lungs, and although I was sad I would never get the chance to see Lucy or Finn again, I was thankful my mind was kind enough to give me that last image of my mother, warm and alive.

My crimson hair streamed out before me, unburdened, like seaweed in the surf. Far above me, the storm must have abated, letting moonlight touch the ice. The ice seemed to crack and splinter, like a mirror, the light becoming brighter and brighter.

It shattered, chunks of ice sucked away into the void, never to be seen again. The light above me was blinding now, unavoidable, as it bathed me. Maybe this is what everyone was talking about when they were on their deathbeds. That tunnel of light. All I had to do was go towards it, accept it, and this would be over. I could be reunited with my mother.

This light was different than the stories I'd read. Inside of it stood a figure, something I couldn't quite make out. It approached me in the blink of an eye, my fingers reaching out. It had to be my mother. *She was waiting for me!* Pain erupted in my arm a second later, a piercing sensation that sent shivers of electricity running through my body. This wasn't supposed to hurt. *No one said this would hurt.* It was supposed to be peaceful, like drifting off to sleep. The water rushed by me, refusing to let me go as I was pulled into the light.

Wind assaulted my face, stabbing my skin like needles, my body convulsing in the snow. I wasn't in the lake anymore. A shadow loomed over me. My eyes barely opened as a massive, shaggy brown wolf regarded me with eyes that were reminiscent of the golden light I had been bathed in. It growled, deep and low, a guttural noise that was full of anger.

If this was heaven, it was unlike any I had ever read about. Heaven didn't have pain and cold. There were no feelings of fear or regret. I was supposed to feel content, happy, and at peace. Maybe I didn't deserve heaven, and this was my own personal hell.

My eyes were too heavy. My body was too cold, and the water in my lungs too much. I wanted the void, and I yielded to it.

CHAPTER
NINE

Hell was a far more viable outcome. The moment I was wrested free of the deep, solid sleep I had succumbed to, I knew I was still alive. Heaven wouldn't smell like wet dog, sweat, and burnt papers. There also wouldn't be an itch on my back that I couldn't quite scratch, or a pulsating pain in my arm. But perhaps hell was still an option, although I kind of expected a little more suffering.

There was warmth on one side, cold, unyielding stone on the other. There was a pounding in my head, a parchedness in my throat, and every muscle ached. There were bruises in places I didn't think were possible, and a multitude of cuts to accompany them. I didn't need to open my eyes to know I was coddled by a swath of blankets, furs, and pillows, but I did anyway.

My sight was blurry at first, an intensity of light and warmth assaulting me. Flames devoured hunks of wood and paper and tinder in a stone hearth less than a foot from my face. I was right about the furs, blankets, and pillows. They snuggled me, keeping me warm and comfy; safe, like a baby bird in a nest.

There was the inexplicable pull to close my eyes and relinquish myself to the tantalizing tendrils of sleep. But I couldn't, and curiosity demanded me to find out where I was. Stirring beneath the covers, it took more strength than I was comfortable with to prop myself up on my elbow. A nest was the most accurate description for what I lay in, the bundles set on stone before a roaring hearth. There was a shadow in the corner of my eye, and when I faced it, I understood the wet dog smell. Lying beside me, with its head resting on giant paws, was a dog that looked more like a wolf than a dog. A husky had nothing on this majestic creature. Its ears flicked forward when its eyes caught sight of me.

Easing myself into the best sitting position I could muster, I squinted in the dimly lit room. Save for the fire beside me, it was pitch black, and the outlines of furniture told me nothing except it was more than likely a bedroom.

Moaning at the sharp pain in my arm, I threw back the covers, trying to gather my feet below me. The wolfdog's head snapped up, lips pulled back, teeth barred. A snarl erupted from that darkened muzzle, sending me into a panic.

Screaming, I flinched further into the nest.

"Quiet," came a voice from the darkness.

"W-who's there?" I cried, my voice a whimper.

An impatient huff answered me, followed by a stirring of a shadow in the darkness. Whoever, whatever was there, remained silent.

"Am I dead?" My voice was raspy, with little substance to it. I was weak, unable to muster enough energy to speak and stay upwards. Swaying uneasily, I collapsed back onto the bundle of furs and blankets and pillows.

Boots shuffled along the stone floor and a familiar face loomed above me.

"Is that what you desire? Because I could have granted you a far cleaner death than the one you had attempted." He was furious. I could see it in the flaring of his nostrils, the furrowing of his brow, the clenched fists, the way his chiseled chest heaved in the firelight.

"Oh, it's just you," I grumbled, squinting up at the Wolf King.

The careful mask of neutrality he usually kept was long gone, replaced by a scowl.

"Is that what you wanted?"

My eyes drifted to the smoking wood in the hearth. "I wanted to be with her." Tears gathered in my eyes, but I had no energy to hold back the tide or wipe them away. I hated this feeling, the situation it placed me in. I didn't want to die, I wanted to return home. To Lucy, to Finn, to my stupid potted ferns that were probably already dead. Dead like me.

"Who?" Out of the corner of my eye it was clear that his tone matched his expression. Rigid, and fraught with controlled anger.

My throat was thick, the tears sliding unburdened across my face. "My mother."

The rigidity vanished, replaced with a knowing expression, one that echoed my own. He knew loss, had felt it before, had been exposed to those tendrils that loved ones leave behind.

"Phoebe." His voice was soft. His shadow teetering when he knelt beside me.

The wolfdog beside me had calmed down, ears relaxed, its head once again resting on its paws.

"Is that who saved me?" It was smaller, and lighter colored, than the wolf that had plucked me from the inky depths of the frozen lake. In the final throes of death, my view of the world would have been distorted, a version that was far from reality.

There was a smirk in his voice. "I saved you."

I shook my head. "What? No…I saw a wolf…"

A gentle hand gripped my shoulder. "You're exhausted. You need more time to recuperate."

Sleep gnawed at my vision. He was right, I did need rest. I had the answer I awoke for; I wasn't in heaven or hell. I wasn't home either, I was here, in this world with three kings in a fortress of stone. And my mother was still dead.

"Whatever," I grumbled, rolling onto my side. Ulfrik's hand was warmer than the hearth, a comforting presence as I floated in that emptiness of the world one went to when one fell asleep.

A light rasping of knuckles against wood awoke me, and the door swung open a moment later. Familiar golden hair and blue eyes greeted me, but they held no signs of amusement in them. His expression was cold, annoyed even.

"Leif," I whispered. He placed a tray filled with bowls and plates of heaping food on the floor beside me. Shifting, a bag slid off his shoulder, and he placed it beside the tray, turning to leave. "Wait!"

"What?" The hesitation in his voice led me to believe he didn't want to leave, but also didn't know what to say.

"I'm sorry." It was clear that my disappearance weighed heavily on him, even though I couldn't quite fathom why.

"I was meant to protect you, to keep you safe. That was my charge, and because of me, you almost died." He wouldn't face me, addressing the door instead. His shoulders were rigid, hands slack at his sides.

Wait, did that mean…

"Did you get in trouble because of me?" My voice wavered.

A sigh. "You're safe now, and that's what matters."

"Leif, I didn't mean for you to get in trouble."

He held up a hand. "It doesn't matter."

It did. My actions had consequences, and the one person who had been nice to me this entire time was being punished, because of me.

"Do you remember that day you met me, in the cave?"

A tight nod, his gaze shifting to me over his shoulder.

Leif gestured to the space beside me, hesitating only a moment before closing the gap between us. He didn't sit beside me like I thought he would. Instead he sat on an ottoman that hugged the end of a poster bed swathed in maroon curtains.

My fingers grazed the array of salted meats and sauteed vegetables, my stomach gurgling loudly in response. I hadn't eaten in days, and it no doubt was responsible for the pounding headache behind my eyes. I was starving.

"Will you eat with me?" Truth be told, I didn't want to be alone, even though a cursory glance behind me told me I wasn't.

The wolfdog still lay by the fire, its eyes wide as it regarded Leif and me.

He didn't react, staring listlessly at the fire consuming fresh logs in the hearth. Taking one of the least loaded plates, I put a little bit of everything on it before passing it to him. Leif ignored me at first, but I wasn't going to take no for an answer. His eyes narrowed, and after a moment of contemplation he reluctantly took the plate from me. I offered him a smile, trying to ease whatever wound I had caused.

"Why do you ask about the cave?" he finally spoke up, only after I had shoved some shredded salted fish into my mouth.

Swallowing the lump that had formed in my throat, I fought for the words to use.

"You're lucky, you know." There was an edge of darkness there, a hidden warning.

"What do you mean?" Luck had nothing to do with my being trapped here.

A shadow crossed his face. "Most do not survive the journey you have."

The blood in my veins chilled, the realization dawning on me. "Are you saying…"

He nodded.

I could have died, maybe I should have died. I pushed those dark thoughts aside.

"You said once before I wasn't the only one, and now you've said it again. Where are the others?"

He pondered for a moment. "Here and there. You may meet them eventually."

My heart soared, if only for a moment. There were other issues that needed to be addressed before I let my emotions get the better of me. Again.

"Does anyone ever leave?" The most pertinent of information he could ever give me. Knowing I wasn't alone was a good start, but knowing if it were possible for me, even us, to return home, was far more important.

"None that I have known of." My expression must have been

clear as day, as he quickly added, "But there are myths, legends of a world that exists at the other end of the bridge. As a shaman I have had fleeting glimpses of worlds beyond our own."

"If this…bridge, can bring people here, surely it could be reversed, right?"

He shrugged. "Theoretically, I suppose."

"Has anyone ever tried?"

"No."

That surprised me. Of all the people on Earth to stumble upon this place, none had tried to return home.

"Why not?" I hadn't noticed I'd been absentmindedly pushing the food across my plate and forced myself to take another bite at the rumbling insistence from my stomach.

Another shrug. "They like it here."

"How do you know that?" There was a bite to my words, anger simmering within me. "Have you ever asked them what they want?" I highly doubt everyone was content with being relegated a slave to a king who meant nothing to them.

"They've told me as much."

I frowned. "They've told you, personally?"

He rolled his eyes. "I'm Chief Shaman to the Wolf King, and that cave I met you in, is mine. It has been in my family for generations, and will continue to be so, passed down to my children and my children's children." He toyed with a strip of dried meat. "I was there when each of them walked across this bridge."

Everyone before me had touched that runestone, had sheltered or stumbled upon the cave then.

Wait…he had said *this* bridge. My heart was hammering in my chest as my brain ran full steam ahead. "Does that mean, there are others?"

"Other what?" He frowned.

I threw my hands up in front of me, startling the wolfdog into raising its head. "Shamans with caves and runestones."

It took a moment before he seemed to be on the same page as me. "Yes."

"Does everyone only come through your cave?" There was a roar in my ears.

"The majority do, but occasionally someone stumbles upon one of the others."

Lucy could be here, it was possible. She had disappeared suddenly on that ridge, without a noise. Maybe she had stumbled upon a cave, or a runestone.

"Have you seen a girl about my age, maroon-colored hair and dark skin?" There was a chance.

But Leif shook his head, and with each shake my hope diminished. That was that then. If she wasn't here, then I needed to return to Norway, to Bergen. The silence between us stretched, broken only by the occasional pop of cracking wood in the hearth.

"Can you open the bridge?" He was a shaman, and if he could sometimes catch glimpses of these worlds, possibly even my world, maybe he could help me to see my friends and family again, and eventually return to them.

He hesitated. "It's possible."

"Please, Leif…" I begged.

His eyes softened. "Long ago, our shamans used to travel this path, we were called world walkers back then. Such a skill used to be passed down each generation and took decades to master fully."

"Do you know how?" My future was getting a little brighter with each word he said. Maybe home was still on the horizon for me.

Once again, my hope died with a shake of his head. "I don't know how to world walk, but I can delve into the archives."

"Archives?"

He nodded. "There's a mausoleum beneath the High Keep that stores the records and artifacts of our people. It stretches back thousands of years."

"Please Leif, I'm begging you. Can you check them for me?"

He released a deep, heavy sigh, his eyes thoughtful as he gazed at the sleeping wolfdog. There were many emotions and shadows I could not put a name to that crossed his face. After some time though his lips pursed, and he cleared his throat.

"I will make you a deal." I perked up, curious to what sort of deal I would have to indenture myself into to ensure my passage home. I was already a slave after all, a praell, what more could he ask of me. "If you promise to behave, no more running away, no more stealing, no more fighting, I will help you return home."

The stubborn part of me was fighting for control, wanting to disagree with such a request, but the logical part of me won. It knew he was right. If I wanted to return home, I needed to do as I was told. I needed to blend in.

I thrust my hand out at him, palm shaking. "We have a deal."

He regarded my open palm like a dog would a new toy.

"You shake it. Like this." I took his hand in mine, shaking twice.

"An odd gesture." He remarked, my hand releasing his.

I shrugged. "I read somewhere it had something to do with showing someone your hand was free of a weapon, and you meant no harm."

"You can read?" He seemed to ignore everything I had said, zeroing on what I considered the most boring part of my statement.

"Of course, I can." I groaned inwardly, don't tell me this was some medieval world where women weren't allowed to read or write or own property or have any sort of opinion or rights. I sighed, as an awkward silence settled between us. "What happens to me now?"

This was a question that brought a flicker of joy to his face. "Ulfrik has decided that the High Keep is no place for you."

Why would that bring joy to his face? "Is that…bad?"

He offered me a smile. "We will be returning to the Forest City."

Forest City?

He knelt beside me, rearranging the plates and bowls on the tray. The bowl was dead center, with three plates circling it. "This bowl represents the High Keep, after the winter solstice the clans gather together under one roof until the eve of Disting. I believe there is a reason you have come to us before such a precious occasion." The name meant nothing to me, a holiday I couldn't even fathom. As far as I could recall, there was no holiday at the end of January or beginning of February. At least, not for an atheist living in Edinburgh. There were a host of religious holidays whose names I couldn't remember, but somehow, I doubted they had anything to do with this place.

He moved on before I could enquire into what he meant. He pointed to the top, right, and bottom plates that surrounded the bowl representing the High Keep. "The north encompasses the Cliff City, home of the Eagle clan; the south is the Cave City, the livelihood of the Bear Clan; and the east is that of the Forest City, home to the Wolf Clan."

"When do we leave?" It was an odd thing to consider. A city that wasn't a city, divided in three distinct parts, each one led by someone different.

"Tomorrow."

So soon…

"You should take the rest of the day to rest, I'll come for you in the morning." The door clicked closed behind him, noticeably quieter than the door of the slave quarters. The wolfdog didn't bat an eyelid at his leaving. Although I was sure if it were me, he would be up and ready to tackle me to the ground.

I'd have to remember to ask Leif whose room this was, and whose dog. There was no artwork on the walls, no statues on the tables, and no collar around the creature's throat. Nothing to give away whoever resided here. I was sure if I checked the drawers, they would all be empty, just like the rooms of a display home.

There was no energy to spare on investigating, and I had promised Leif I would behave in return for him helping me. My hands were tied, my fate sealed. I resigned myself to doing what I was told—resting until Leif came for me in the morning.

CHAPTER
TEN

When Leif said morning, he meant before even a hint of the sun had awoken. The world was pitch black, the air icy cold and still. The animals still slumbered, waiting for their cue to arise and have their voices mingle with the day.

I was in the same mindset, my mouth shut tightly, my body and mind still numb from the days before. There was a soreness in every muscle of mine, bruises and superfluous cuts splotched my skin. The most energy I could muster was in observing everyone else. Wagons laden with goods, pulled by thick, shaggy horses littered the streets. Everywhere I looked people had segregated themselves into their clan, the skulls and feathers and fur of their tribe obvious as they mingled among one another.

Leif had escorted me to one of the wagons, leaving me to absorb the scene as the men toiled around me. Part of me ached, and part wished I could offer some assistance. But my new shaman friend was adamant that I do no such thing, and if I did offer such support, I would either be laughed at or denied. I would only get in the way anyway, I had no idea what I was doing, or even what they were doing. Somehow, with little communication, they knew where each crate and barrel and chest and bag was meant to go.

"Alright, good to go," Leif said.

It felt like hours had passed, but there was no real way of knowing. The sun was still behind the horizon, the streets lit only by the flickering torches and sconces. Poking his head into the wagon, Leif looked me up and down. Content with whatever was going through his mind he disappeared, leaving the flap to wave in the gentle breeze. His return was heralded by the sound of hooves. I poked my head out through the flap, eyeing him curiously.

"You're not riding in the wagon?" I asked.

He scoffed, as if such an idea was preposterous. "No."

With a flourish that was more dramatic than necessary, Leif maneuvered the horse to stand at the back of the wagon. It threw back its head, snorting, tendrils of its warm breath snaking into the air.

"Settle, Egg," Leif whispered, patting the horse's neck.

Egg. I knew that name, and the blackness of its coat, the hazelnut of its eyes. It was the horse from the stable, the one who had greeted me. The one I was going to steal.

"I hear you two have met."

Reaching out my hand, Egg thrusted his muzzle into my palm. The warmth of his breath tickling me.

"And here I thought I was subtle."

He smirked. "Unfortunately for you, Asger is exceptional at his charge."

"Was he the stableboy?" The mystery man who forced me to abandon the plan of sequestering a ride to the wharf. If I had been more bitter, I would perhaps blame him for what had followed. But I knew it wasn't his fault, it wasn't Leif or Ulfrik's fault either, it was mine.

His eyes widened as he bit back a smile. "I wouldn't say that to his face."

A horn sounded nearby; a deep bellowing filled the air with a presence of its own. Leif pulled Egg back, allowing me an uninterrupted view of the High Keep's portcullis, and the procession that was emptying from it.

The guard was first, men who wore the same ensemble as the ones who stood outside the room with the thrones. Following close behind were the three kings. They were embellished with shiny metals and gems, highlighting the flare of the skulls and furs that adorned them. Ulfrik was first, flanked by two wolf-dogs which bore quite the resemblance to the one that had accompanied me by the hearth. The one that had disappeared the moment Leif had awoken me to bathe and prepare for today's events. Ulfrik looked every bit the king he was supposed to be, adorned with gold and silver jewelry, the necklace of a wolf sat front and center above the cuirass where a painted face of the regal canid was displayed. Even the pauldrons were in the shape of wolves, the teeth sharp and glistening in the torchlight.

His golden eyes locked with mine; a brief smile played on his lips. Nodding in acknowledgement was enough for him. He turned his attention to the crowd that had gathered at the gate.

The other two kings rode side by side, their expressions bland, giving nothing away. They were dressed as impressively as Ulfrik, but it was clear which king was in charge. Whether the Bear and Eagle King were fond of this arrangement was unclear, but the rigidity of the man adorned in feathers told me perhaps not.

With a wave of Ulfrik's gloved hand, another horn sounded, and the procession began to move. The wagon I was in lurched forward, I heard a man speaking in the driver's seat, urging the horse to move along. Leif followed closely behind the wagon, Egg danced nervously, no doubt eager to do what he was born to do—run.

"What are their names?" I asked when I was sure there was no one else within earshot.

Leif frowned. "Who?"

"The other kings."

His nervous glance around told me it was an awkward question to ask, but if I was going to do what I promised Leif properly, I needed to know more about this place. Or at least, enough for me to fake it. Egg tossed his head up as Leif urged him closer to the wagon, waiting until the two guards who were straggling behind passed us by.

When he spoke, his voice was low. "Ulfrik is the High King, leader of the Wolf Clan. He commands not just the Forest City, but also the High Keep. But I suspect you knew that much." My encouraging nod bid him to continue. "The Bear Clan's leader is the King of the Cave City; his name is Bjorn. Stern fellow, he lives and dies for tradition. Loyalty and honor are the trademark of his clan. But his people have not been High Kings for hundreds of years."

The man with the beard and axe, he seemed to fit that description very well.

"And the other king?" The one with the glint in his eyes.

Leif's expression twisted as he pursed his lips. He didn't seem too fond of the last king.

"Arne of the Eagle Clan, he is King of the Cliff City." He hesitated, fighting for careful wordplay. "A cunning man, he revels in the spoils of the world."

The words left unsaid told me as much as I needed. As such was confirmed when I got sight of the Eagle King ahead of us at a fork in the road. He was being doted upon by droves of women. My heart skipped a beat upon seeing them. I wasn't the only woman, there were others. But these women weren't like me, their role in life was clear. Around their necks were iron collars, a stark contrast to the bright beaded and laced dresses they wore. Swallowing the lump that had formed in my throat, I could only pray that my designation of praell did not force me into that kind of servitude. I wouldn't keep my promise to Leif if that was the case.

I needed a distraction.

"What makes someone a High King?" I asked once we had passed Arne.

What's the point of three heads on a snake?

Leif's brow furrowed, as if the answer was obvious. My

silence prompted a response that had his mouth twisting. "Trial by combat."

I blanched. "They murder each other?"

"There's no honor in senseless violence, upon the death of the High King the heads of the clan are brought to the arena. Cunning, guile, and humility are the weapons that determine a winner. It's a tradition that has served our kingdom for centuries, and it is fair. The strongest of us should lead." It sounded barbaric and vile to me, but the expression on Leif's face told me he was supportive of such a savage way of life.

"If Ulfrik dies, who becomes head of the Wolf Clan?"

He tried to hide it, but there was no missing the eye roll. "Ogden. Ulfrik's hand."

"What about you?"

He smirked. "I am the Chief Shaman for the Wolf Clan."

"Yes, I remember you telling me that but…does that mean you can never be king?"

He mused it over a moment. "I suppose if Ulfrik and Ogden were to die at the same time, then I could become the king for our clan, and if I won in the arena, I could become High King."

Another horn bellowed ahead, the procession ground to a halt as horses and wagons peeled apart, disappearing down other streets and alleys.

"What's going on?" People meandered past the wagon, carrying, and dragging supplies. Stalls were scattered haphazardly around, heaving under the weight of goods. There were plates and trays of foods, barrels of liquids which smelt faintly of alcohol, bundles of furs and cloths were piled high next to strips of leather stretched taut over wooden racks, some even had salted fish or plucked birds carcasses hanging next to them.

Leif smiled. "We're at the Conjunction."

The Conjunction. Leif told me there was a market here. There would have been no way for me to get to this place without being noticed.

The steep walls that surrounded the High Keep met with three other towering walls, forming a circular courtyard. There were four towers along the walls heavy with patrols, guarding portcullises of iron, marked by stone gargoyles with the heads of a bear, a wolf, and an eagle. The last one, where we had just come from, had a shield above it, split into thirds, with a respective animal in each part.

Our wagon didn't tarry long enough for me to discern the other stalls, lurching forward I teetered at the edge of a crate, my knee plunging into the hard wood. Leif leaned forward, grasping my arm, allowing me to regain my balance.

"Thank you," I breathed, leaning back in the seat I had created for myself between two crates of what I suspected were vegetables.

When we passed under the tower of the wolf the scenery changed dramatically. Gone was the grand stonework of the High Keep, replaced with towering pines, haughty spruce, and the ivory striped bark of thin birches. My heart lurched, as if someone had gripped it in their palm. The memories of hiking such forests with Lucy only days earlier clouded my mind of anything else. I became lost in those memories, grasping at what I had left. I had nothing to remember her by, nothing to remember my brother by, or my mother. My backpack had been taken from me, my phone was probably dead by now, a pinnacle of human engineering, now a decorative brick. If I kept shoving those memories aside, hiding them until I could feel nothing, I would forget them.

I would forget the springy curls on my best friend's head, and the way they bounced when she cackled like a dolphin. She could have been bald for all I cared, though. It was that infectious determination and no-nonsense attitude that had me looking up to her since we were children. The first time I had met her was in elementary school. I was eating my peanut butter and jelly sandwich alone at a too-wide table, the cafeteria abuzz with people who had quickly formed friendships, but it was the fourth week, and I still had no one.

It didn't bother me back then too much, after all, I had lost myself in imaginary worlds of talking lions, treasure hoarding dragons, and children not much older than me saving the world. This girl, with bushy pigtails and braces waltzed up to me, sliding her identical peanut butter and jelly sandwich next to mine and proclaimed, *'You're my friend now!'* We were inseparable, until I fell down a ravine and let her disappear from my sight.

It wasn't just the memories I forged with her that would disappear with the passage of time. I let the memories of others override hers, afraid to be drawn toward that inescapable darkness that had smothered me after my mother passed. In that darkness, there were two faint lights that tried to keep my head above it. One was Lucy, and the other was my brother.

Finnegan Wood. My brother, bane of my existence. I graced his life with my existence when he was three years old, and I'd been a pain in the butt since then. I was your stereotypical little sister, I wanted everything he had, to go everywhere he did, to be friends with all of his friends.

I'd forget my brother's awful attempt to grow a moustache, the sparse hair on his upper lip brought a shine to his eyes. He didn't care that his students had an endless barrel of jokes at his expense, he was proud of it.

And my mother, if I didn't have that video I took of her during Christmas, struggling to open a box of crackers with her shiny new reindeer-themed nails, would I forget her? Would I forget that distinct raspy voice, or the abruptness of her character? The way she constantly adjusted the glasses on her face because they were far too big for her, after she had proudly lost fifteen kilos.

"Phoebe," Leif said, breaking me of my reverie.

Hardening my resolve, I offered him a weak smile.

"We're here."

The wagon had stopped, Egg had stopped. Voices rose with excitement, met with the hurried footsteps of the procession. Leif dismounted, offering me his hand. My legs wobbled when they hit the dirt, my eyes squinted against the glare of the sun on the snow. Dispersed in unusual harmony with the trees that towered above us sprang buildings of wood.

They were built with the trees in mind, open floor plans that let the trees grow through roofs and act as supporting walls and beams. Nature was in harmony with the architecture, as if not a single bush or tree was worth being sacrificed. It was something I had always dreamed would happen back home. The forests were disappearing at an alarming rate, and no matter the age or size of a tree, if it were in the way, it was coming down. Humanity's need to conquer was still in full swing today, no matter how hard we tried to pretend otherwise.

A smile lit my face as I reached out to stroke the smooth bark of a nearby birch.

"Welcome to the Forest City," Leif said.

My mouth gaped as he led me through the throngs of warriors happy to return to their families. Children ran forward to hug fathers, wives jumped at the chance to embrace their husbands, and mothers burdened with age hobbled across the dirt to welcome their sons home. There were tears and laughter and a sense of infectious happiness that was hard to ignore.

Most infectious of all was the smile on their King's face as he knelt beside them. When the children flexed at him, he feigned terror, when they tried to arm wrestle him, he pretended to lose, and when they remarked on his long hair, he ruffled theirs in response. He was gentle and kind to the children that flocked to him. Their eyes wide with excitement, like they were meeting their favorite superhero. Or their father after being away for a while.

"Are those his?" My voice wavered, and I bit my tongue, willing myself some control. I don't know why him having children would affect me in the slightest. After all, he was king—High King, and he needed successors.

Leif laughed. "No. The High King has yet to choose his mate. Ulfrik is just fond of children."

"*Mate* is a weird word for a queen," I remarked.

"I suppose our worlds aren't so much alike." That was an understatement. He ignored the look I gave him. "There are no queens, at least not here."

I frowned. "Then what are the wives of a king called?"

"You don't know?" His eyes were wide with disbelief, but before I could respond a young man strode before us.

"Leif, the King is asking for you."

Leif waved him off. "I'll be back in a bit, don't get into any trouble."

"Yeah, I'll think about it," I offered.

Although it was a warning, I could see the smile dancing on his lips. He trusted me, and the bargain we had struck. I watched him stride towards the king, who was now preoccupied with letters and paperwork at the foot of a double-doored house. I settled in, prepared to wait for him to return.

After everyone had been greeted, and the wagons had been unloaded, and the horses turned out to pasture, Leif returned to where I had sat watching the commotion. I was certain the steps I was on led to a storehouse of sorts, at least, that seemed to be where many of the crates and barrels and bags were being brought. No one spoke to me, but my hair received several second glances. I was used to it, not just here, but in Edinburgh too. Although redheads were far more common in Ireland and Scotland, that didn't stop people from gawking at you like some show pony. Here, however, I had yet to see anyone with the same hair as me.

"Thanks for not running," he said, helping me to my feet.

I rolled my eyes. "Because that worked out so well for me the first time."

An expression, so fleeting I thought I had imagined it, crossed his face. He was quick to compose himself, plastering a smile across his face. Tossing his gold hair across his shoulder, he led me through courtyards, under archways, and around doors to a garden ringed with walls formed from latticed roots of bushes and trees.

It was filled with women and children hanging wreaths of wheat and vines of flower on the boughs of large, gnarled trees that saved the courtyard from everything but a slight dusting of snow.

"What kind of trees are those?" If it weren't a pine, palm, or maple, I wouldn't be able to identify it. Same with plants and bushes and flowers. I never found the need to know such things, after all, I had lived my whole life within the urban sprawl of Edinburgh.

"The most sacred kind of trees," he said. "Ash."

A woman approached us, the smile vanishing from her face the moment her eyes drifted downwards to where Leif still held my hand.

"Shaman, how good to see you again. Have you brought us company?" Her voice was delicate, a façade I could see through like glass.

Releasing my hand, he splayed his palm against my back, nudging me forward. "This is Phoebe. Lord Ulfrik hopes you will help her acclimate to her new role here in the Forest City."

"What role would that be?"

Another woman walked forward. "She's the chosen mate of our Lord, is she not?"

I blanched.

CHAPTER

ELEVEN

"When you said I was to accompany the Wolf Clan to their ward for a ceremony, I didn't think I'd be coming here to be a whore," I seethed.

Leif grabbed my arm, pulling me out of earshot of the woman who watched us curiously, as if my reaction was unusual.

How could you be so stupid, Phoebe!

"You're not a whore, Phoebe."

"Slave, sex slave, how is this any different Leif?" I raged against his grip. "All bets are off if you think I'm going to sit here and let myself be abused!" I had heard stories of pagan holidays rife with fornication in forests under full moons, but I never intended to be a part of one, especially without my consent.

Leif leaned in, his face mere inches from mine. The scent of pine and cedarwood wafted to greet my flared nostrils.

"You're not opening your legs for anyone," he hissed.

I answered him with a defiant glare.

"At least, not without your permission," he added softly, his eyes searching mine. "You are a praell, and as such you will assist the women with preparation for Disting. This is a celebration of rebirth, and of our women. You are an honored guest, Phoebe."

Our noses were touching now, my breath mingling with his in the frigid air. "Then why is she under the assumption I am the mate of *your* king."

Leif glowered. "*Our* king, and because he himself chose you when he decided to spare your miserable life—twice!"

That caught me off guard. I tried not to think about it, that day when death had clutched me tightly with her tendrils. I didn't like death, after becoming so close and personal with it; I was adamant to stay on the side of the living for as long as I could.

"What are you saying, Leif?" He needed to say the words, say them outright.

He glowered. "We had an agreement Phoebe, do as you're told, and I'll help you get home."

"Tell me what my role is here, Leif. You're tiptoeing around the issue like a frightened dog!"

"Watch your tone with me, child." His voice was low, a controlled anger building heat across his cheeks.

Coward.

"Come with me...?" The lady stood before us now, no doubt overhearing my cries of indignation.

"Phoebe," Leif offered after a moment.

"What a lovely name!" she exclaimed, grasping my hand. Hers was soft, delicate, the hands of someone who did not toil in the dirt all day.

Dragging me from Leif, she whispered under her breath. "Let's not do anything crazy, at least not yet."

"What?" My rage was still white-hot, my head confused and jumbled, not quite sure what she was referring to.

"Angering the shaman or the king is not the way to go about it. I can tell you're not happy about your predicament, but if you stay with me, I can make this easier for you." These were not the honeyed words of someone complacent with the world around them. These were the words of someone with guile, someone whose intelligence could be a boon to me. But, if I weren't careful, could also prove to be a hindrance.

She led me to the gathering of shadows beneath the boughs of the ash trees, far from the earshot of the shaman who stood under the archway, a scowl spreading across his face.

"Forgive my eavesdropping, but it's sort of my job. My name is Eldrid, and I am the Teacher."

"Teacher?"

She gestured to the children and younger women gathered around the garden.

"These are my charges," she said with pride. "My job is to prepare them for life as members of the Wolf Clan."

I frowned. You need a teacher for that?

"Wait, are these people praells as well?"

She smirked. "You catch on quickly, Phoebe. Yes, the children and young women gathered here are praells of the Wolf Clan. Born, raised, or even pledged, those gathered here today will be under my guidance as they prepare and are eventually assigned a grand role in the world that Ulfrik envisions."

How…noble. At least that's what they thought they were going for. It made me feel uneasy.

"They don't get a say?"

Eldrid smiled. "It is a grand honor. Most of these children are orphans, and most of the women come from poverty, or kingdoms far off. If it weren't for the High King giving them this opportunity to become members of his own clan, they would be begging on the streets."

"Is that my purpose too, then?" Did Ulfrik think he was doing me a favor?

She regarded me, cocking her head sideways. "You may be called a praell, but I, and Leif, and even the kings do not regard you as such."

"What do you mean?"

Her mouth twisted. "Only time will tell."

"Another fancy word for a slave." Cool.

She held up her hands, the bangles on her wrists clacking together. "Oh no, the praells could certainly be considered as such. But no, my child, you are no slave."

"I can't go where I want, do what I want. How am I not a slave?" This conversation was getting old. I was tired of being told the same thing over and over, the clarifications held no meaning. At the end of the day my fate was still the same.

"You do not realize what you are capable of, what you truly are." There was a glint in her eyes.

Her cryptic words sent a shiver up my spine, but we were quickly overwhelmed by a gaggle of rowdy children. Eldrid held a finger to her mouth, promising to continue our conversation later. She led me and the children and the young maidens around the garden beneath the boughs of the trees, procuring knotted wreaths to hang on the branches above and beaded ropes with colorfully stained glass beside them. Everything seemed to have a purpose, a place; this was a routine that everyone here was familiar, and seemingly, fond of.

I was the only one who stood off to the side, silent as the grave, waiting with wreaths and colored ropes in hand, to be told where to go and what to do. The other adults were quick and efficient in their movement, dashing from branch to branch, tree to tree, hanging the wreaths and beaded ropes with a twinkle of excitement in their eyes. Whereas the adults knew where each wreath and rope went, the children found it to be a sort of game. They'd try to remember placements of those that belonged on higher branches, the ones they could never hope to do themselves. I wasn't that tall, but at five foot six I was a giant compared to the children, who couldn't have been older than seven or eight.

"Miss?" squeaked a young girl with braided hair, her hand pulling gently on my sleeve.

I knelt beside her, offering a smile. "Yes?"

"Can you help me reach that one?" she asked, pointing to a sparse branch above our heads.

Nodding, I slid my hands under her arms, hoisting her to the branch. She tied the rope with a precision that had me a little green with envy, bidding me to place her back on the ground.

"That was fun!" she squealed with delight. "Again?"

I opened my mouth to reply, and a voice cut the air between us.

"I think our guest would like to help with the food now, isn't that right, Phoebe?" Eldrid winked, earning me a repose from what would have ended up being an arduous task.

The moment my back turned, another woman took my place, her back bent from obliging the requests of the children for hours upon hours. It seems I was spared from ending the night in agony.

"What are we making?" I asked as my foot brushed the threshold of an open-spaced kitchen area.

Its build implied a communal space, with several brick ovens against one wall, open fire pits filled with pots and pans on the other, and a long wooden table in the middle. The table was laden with sacks and crates of vegetables, fruits, eggs, and flour. Women toiled within, cutting, and dicing, and rolling. No one was sitting, relaxing, it was nothing but honest, good work.

"Anything and everything! Breads, soups, stews, pastries… -the list goes on. Disting is a celebration, and admittedly, a time to take advantage of food that will soon begin to spoil." Eldrid had her eye on a loaf of bread that sat on the table, the crust was impeccable, golden and speckled with seeds.

"What did you need me to do?" I asked, and the hunger in her eye caused my stomach to rumble in response.

"I have a peculiar request for you," she said, leading me past the table. Some of the women raised their heads, greeting Eldrid with a smile or offering kind words.

It was obvious she was well loved by the community here, and I could understand why. She had a cunning about her, hidden underneath the layer of warmth she exuded to everyone she walked past.

At the end of the kitchen was a row of benches before a metal pit, not unlike a trough. It was filled with peelings and skins, and it was then I noticed the sacks sitting under the benches, filled with potatoes and carrots and squash and gods know what else.

Taking a seat on the bench, she patted the space beside her.

"I suppose you know what comes next," she said, a smirk on her face.

I offered her a sincere smile, taking my seat beside her, and brandishing one of the knives that sat at the lip of the trough. "Yeah, I know what comes next."

We spent hours peeling and skinning fruits and vegetables, only stopping when the light outside had vanished. The women in the kitchen began cleaning up, emptying their refuse into the troughs at my and Eldrid's feet.

"Only thing left to do is bring this to the pens." She said, hands on her hips, back arched as she fought to undo a knot in it.

Although the kitchens were warmed constantly by the fires in the pits and ovens, my hands were numb and aching by the time we were done. My back was sore, my butt, too, but I was not eager to express or show any discomfort. After all, I was a nurse back home, I was used to ten hour or more shifts on my feet, constantly bending or moving heavy objects, or people.

Eldrid slipped through a nearby doorway which I'd occasionally seen women darting in and out of, emerging moments later with wooden buckets in her hands. Placing one at my feet she nodded at the scraps in the troughs.

"At the end of every day the kitchen staff bring the scraps to the animals. The pigs are obsessed with the potato skins. Sometimes we'd keep them to make a sort of pancake."

A pancake made of potato skins… "My people have a name for those, hash browns."

Her lips pursed. "Hash browns, what an odd name, I kind of like it."

"Eldrid!" called an older woman by the door, waving frantically. "Bodil ripped her dress, again."

"Was she climbing that damn tree again?" Eldrid sighed, "You've got this, right?"

I nodded. What's not to get? Fill the bucket, find the pen, empty the bucket. The sounds of Eldrid's shoes slapping against the wooden floorboards as she retreated were the only noise to fill the air as the kitchen was plunged into silence. I was the only one left, everyone having left after the sun departed.

Both the buckets were heaving by the time I managed to squeeze myself out into the cool fresh air beyond the stuffy confines of the kitchens. No longer was my nose assaulted and stuffed with the smoke of burning wood and raw starch. A wind had risen, dark clouds hugged the horizon, threatening to smother the world in another storm.

I stood there like a deer in headlights; Eldrid had forgotten to mention the location of the pens. Lucky for me (and thanks to the gossip of the kitchen staff before they departed) I had the vaguest idea of the pens being north of the kitchens in a glen devoid of trees. Unlike the divide I was used to between the urban sprawl and rural areas of the United Kingdom, the Forest City had no divide between where they kept their animals and agriculture, and their homes.

The pens were where I thought them to be, with walls of latticed roots and vines used to keep and separate the different species from one another, not unlike a zoo. Surrounding them were homes, and light from flickering torches and sconces twinkled in the twilight.

Pigs snorted, goats bleated, chickens clucked, and cows lowed. Everyone crowded around the troughs, eager for the scraps, barely waiting for me to dump the bucket before shoving their heads into the troughs. Eldrid was right, the pigs really did enjoy the potato skins, fighting one another for even the tiniest pieces.

Eldrid appeared at my shoulder. "I'm sure this is nothing like what you're used to."

I snorted. "That's an understatement."

"Where are you from?" Her eyes glinted in the twilight as she watched the pigs beg us for more.

"A place called Edinburgh." I didn't have the energy, or heart, to lie to her. What good would it do me, anyway, why would I need to hide such a thing. I was already different.

Her reply was barely a whisper, and for a split second, I was certain I had misheard.

"I'm sorry, what did you say?" My throat was dry, my heart beating out of rhythm.

She smiled, reading the trepidation on my face with a mischievous and coy expression. "I haven't been there in so long."

"What?" I breathed, taking a step back.

"I'm a Traveler, just like you my dear."

"What gave it away?"

"Aside from the hair?" she laughed. "The way Leif and Ulfrik dote on you, and exchanged some tepid words, I knew you must have been like me."

"I don't know what you mean."

"You think just anyone who appears here gets a personal audience with the High King?"

Personal audience? I was dragged before him without my consent. I didn't get a choice in the matter.

"We're special, you and I, and the others like us. We can do something, without any training, that used to take their shamans decades to learn. A skill they have forgotten, a ritual that we don't understand, and yet we have mastered."

"Have you never wanted to return home?"

She scoffed. "This is my home."

We watched as the animals abandoned their begging stance before us, huddling together under the trees, preparing for the night. Once we were caressed by a wind that seeped into our very bones, Eldrid turned to me.

"I suppose I should show you to your house."

House?

Sure enough, it meant what I thought it meant. Meandering through the tunnels and archways and interconnecting platforms of the Forest City, Eldrid led me before a wide home of wood and beveled glass. It was identical to the ones beside it, and yet as she pressed the iron key into my palm, I knew it was special.

Built of the forest itself, the home was spacious, letting full grown trees sprout through it, engulfing it in an air of tranquility.

Walls did not separate rooms, instead the spaces were made with latticed wood denoting a living space and guest area. A sunken bed and dresser occupied the living space, with tables and chairs in the guest area. There were even bookshelves filled with pottery and extra linen, and chests that Eldrid told me held additional coats and blankets, as the winters became quite brutal. A sliding door at the back of the living area opened to a covered courtyard of boulders circling a pool of simmering water.

"The Forest City was built around these springs; every house has one. It's a bit of a ritual, to soak away one's fear and doubt at the end of every day," Eldrid said. "I'll leave you to it, there's fresh food on the table, enjoy the rest of your evening."

"Eldrid?" I called after her.

She turned, hand on the front door.

"Thank you."

She smiled. "Sleep well, Phoebe. It was nice meeting you."

The door shut with a click, and I was left alone in my house.

"My house." I said the words aloud, not quite believing them. I had never hoped to be able to afford my own home on my meager salary, and yet here, I was handed one. For no reason. There was no way I deserved this kindness, they had to expect something of me in return. But Eldrid was happy…could I be, too?

My head was swimming and my body aching. Such questions could wait, as the pool of hot water was beckoning me like a siren, and I was more than happy to answer her call. Eldrid told me to enjoy my evening. I planned to do just that.

CHAPTER

TWELVE

It wasn't Eldrid's face that greeted me bright and early the next morning. A sliver of dawn on the horizon lit Leif's golden hair, the halo of light drawing attention to his high cheekbones and sturdy jaw. I'd never taken much time to look at him, but if it weren't for the Stockholm Syndrome setting in, I wouldn't have given him the second glance. Except it was hard not to admit he was handsome.

"I thought we'd try something different today," he said, a smirk playing on his lips.

I grumbled incoherent nonsense; exhaustion still gripped me. My muscles screamed from the abuse I had put them through yesterday, and I wasn't eager to spend the rest of my day peeling vegetables on a hard wooden bench in a stuffy, poorly ventilated kitchen. Even the hours of soaking in the hot spring did little to alleviate my pain. At the time, I felt like I was floating on air. All good things must come to an end, though.

Swathed in layers like I was on an adventure across the Siberian Tundra, I followed Leif through the city. Although I had only awoken a short time ago, most people were awake, out

111

and about performing various tasks. It had snowed overnight, leaving a fresh, glittering blanket over the land. The satisfying crunch beneath my boots brought out a childish giddiness I hadn't felt since I was young. We walked past the kitchens and animal pens, stopping at a wooden building adjacent to a corral coated in churned snow and dirt.

"Eldrid is preparing an outfit for you tonight," he said, throwing open the door to the stables.

Oh right, the ceremony.

Egg thrust his head out of the stall, whinnying at the sight of Leif, who pulled a carrot from his hand to let him devour. They had built this stable like the one in the mansion's courtyard where I had first met Egg, with stalls on one side, opening to the corrals, and a wall on the other with hooks holding reins, saddles, and blankets. Pulling the reins from the hook opposite Egg, Leif nodded at the stall next to him.

"That one is for you."

Frowning, I peeked into the next stall, and was greeted by the warm nuzzle of a chestnut horse, coat as fiery as the hair on my head.

"His name is Dancer."

Egg, Dancer, what creative names. "Why is he named that?"

He chuckled. "You'll see."

"What are we doing?" Dancer pressed his mouth against the palm of my hand.

"Going for a ride."

I was woefully ignorant of my ability to ride a horse. After all, Hollywood made it seem so easy and glamorous. My experience was far from that. Just mounting the damn creature took more tries than I was comfortable admitting to myself, and eventually, after laughing himself hoarse, Leif had stood behind me, his warm hands gripped my hips and thrust me upwards into the saddle.

"Hey! I didn't ask for help!" I huffed, a blush spreading across my face.

"For someone who seemed to scale the side of a castle with no problem, I wouldn't have expected you to be defeated by mounting a horse." His eyes were alight with amusement, but all I could do was scowl and hope the blush would disappear before he noticed.

If he did notice, he gave nothing away, mounting Egg with ease. Tossing his head with impatience, Leif pat his neck, soothing him. "Soon, we have to make sure this one doesn't fall off before we leave the city."

"Those are fighting words," I threatened.

He howled with laughter as Egg stomped his hooves in protest. "If you want to fight me, you'll have to catch me." Before I could reply, he yanked on Egg's reins, urging him into a gallop.

"Wait!" I cried, my heels tapping Dancer's sides.

Lucky for me he seemed to understand what I requested and broke into a gallop. It took everything I had to stay on his back, my hands balled into fists around the reins, his mane, the pommel. Fear coursed through me, but so did exhilaration. Once I was sure I would not find myself eating dirt, I allowed myself a reprieve to remember how to breathe, and to open my eyes.

Leif and Egg weren't too far ahead of me now, the rays of the rising sun catching in his golden hair. Dancer was smooth beneath me, like a rocking horse, and I felt myself slowly relax against him. If he led, I could follow. Just like dancing.

Before us the trees grew thinner and farther apart, and our exuberant ride came to a meandering halt. A meadow coated in fresh, undisturbed snow stretched before us, hedged by bushes desperate to escape the touch of winter.

Leif dismounted with ease, leading Egg back towards where Dancer and I sat.

"Need some help?" he asked, palm extended.

I balked at him. "I'm good."

I didn't think I could ride a horse, and I managed just fine. Dismounting should be cakewalk compared to that. Mimicking Leif's movements, I gripped the reins, throwing one leg over, and slid off Dancer's back. Except unlike Leif, my legs buckled, sending me into the snow.

Dancer snorted, tossing his head. He might have been disturbed by my lack of grace, but it had Leif howling with laughter.

"Shut up," I grumbled, ignoring his offer of help once again as I stood up.

My legs threatened to buckle, and I couldn't help comparing myself to a newborn lamb.

"I take it you don't ride much?" The sarcasm was alive in his tone, eyes glinting in amusement.

I rolled my eyes. "My talents lie elsewhere."

Strands of his long hair fell across his face, his gloved hand casually tucking it back behind his ear. "Do tell."

Ignoring the bait, I wobbled into the middle of the meadow. Déjà vu sent shivers up my spine. I'd done something just like this once, in a place not so different. Back then, though, it was with my ex-boyfriend, on the side of the road during a trip to Loch Lomond. Not with a stranger in a place whose name I still didn't know. There were also cars, and cell phones, and I wasn't being held against my will.

Kneeling, I scooped all the snow in front of me, molding it into the best ball shape I could manage. There was plenty of snow to work with, and as it hardened it became easier to mold. What I thought would take half an hour took only a few brief minutes.

Boots crunched the snow underfoot behind me as his shadow loomed over my creation. "What are you doing?"

Leaning back from my masterpiece, I searched the snow for the flattest pebbles I could find. "Help me find some pebbles."

"Pebbles?"

"Flat, preferably. Like the ones you find by rivers," I said, rummaging through the snow.

I'm sure his feeling was one of bemusement, if not confusion, but if so, he didn't express it. We searched the meadow, and within a few minutes we gathered what we had found.

"Will these do?" he asked, placing a handful of perfect, flat pebbles at my feet.

Unable to contain my excitement, I squealed with joy, placing the stones right where they belonged. "Yes, these will do."

The longer I stared though, the longer I knew something wasn't right.

"It's missing something…" I mused, gazing around the snowy landscape.

Then I saw it, just a few feet from me, sticking up from the snow like it was begging me to use it. Grasping the stick, I yanked it from where it rested, plunging that perfect piece of wood into the center of the head of my creation.

"It's perfect," I whispered, clasping my interfolded hands against my chest. I was like an artist reminiscing over their finished work.

Leif cocked his head. "What is it?"

I balked. "What?"

He shrugged. "I don't understand what you did. Is this a custom from your homeland?"

I hadn't even considered the fact that what I had did was unique. To Edinburgh, or to my own time.

"It's a snowman."

He circled the snowman, observing it from all angles. "Well, I suppose it could pass for a man made from snow."

Rolling my eyes, I bent down, scooping a handful of snow into my gloved hands and fashioned it into a ball shape. Maybe he didn't know what a snowman was, but I knew without a doubt he'd recognize a snowball.

"Don't you dare," he growled, eyes narrowing.

It whistled through the air, colliding with his boot. Leif's eyes widened, as he bent down to create a snowball of his own.

"Go ahead, do it again," he threatened, eyeing the second one I had prepared as soon as I loosed the first.

"This next one won't miss," I smirked.

His fingers curled, beckoning me. "Try it, then."

Without a second thought I hurled it through the air, watching as it flew past him, disappearing into the snowy meadow behind him.

"My turn," he smirked, cocking his arm back to lob the snowball at my thigh. It exploded into dust, coating me.

"Wow!" I said, in feigned indignation. Before he could react, I gathered a snowball, running towards him with every intent to lob it at his pretty face.

He bolted for me, closing the distance quicker than I could have anticipated. The snow was a burden for me, but for him, he seemed to almost dance across it. Like he was born of it. In my panic my feet stumbled in the snow. The carefully crafted snowballs fell to the ground with me.

Leif gathered me in his arms, sparing me from the ground as he collapsed onto his back, with me atop him. The gasp that escaped my lips brightened the blush that was forming across my face. I could feel the electricity that seemed to run through him to me, the intensity of his gaze seemed to slow the air around us; time stood still.

"Phoebe," he whispered, the struggle all too apparent on his face.

Rife with embarrassment, I struggled to free myself from his grasp. My attempt was slow and half-assed. I knew all too well I wanted the opposite.

"I'm sorry," I whispered, falling off him onto my back in the snow. I lay there, reminding myself how to breathe. The snow chilled me, the common sense rushing back into my head.

Leif sat beside me, staring at Dancer and Egg digging hopelessly in the snow for something to eat.

"We should head back soon," he said, watching the sun break free over the canopy.

I nodded.

Taking his extended hand, I let him lead me to the horses, my eyes widening as I looked around for something to help myself back up onto the horse. There was nothing but snow and thin trees around us, none of which would provide the leverage I needed to hoist myself up onto Dancer's back.

"Perhaps I should teach you how to ride."

Rolling my eyes, I groaned. "In case you haven't noticed, I managed quite fine!"

A smirk. "Hanging on for dear life is not the same thing as riding."

He did have a point, and since the only vehicles happened to be attached to beasts of burden, it wouldn't hurt for me to learn.

"Just help me up." I wouldn't admit he was right. At least, not yet.

There was no hesitation as his warm hands gripped my waist, hoisting me up to crawl across the saddle. Settling in, I grabbed the reins, giving a tight nod to Leif. One of these days I'd be able to do it on my own, but for now, I'd have to accept his help, and the help of others. At least, until he could secure the path back home.

The ride back to the Forest City was calmer than the ride to the glen, as the horses maintained a steady walk. The wispy puffs that curled upwards from their muzzle was a distracting sight. More than once, I caught myself drifting off to memories of cups of hot tea during the winter and the jacuzzi in Liam's home in Newbridge. Memories I had tried to block, knowing full well they did nothing for me, at least not here. Dwelling on what I had lost would only serve to drown me in despair and I feared the Phoebe I had become during those long, dark months after my mother had passed.

"Everything alright?" Leif had pulled Egg beside me, calming him with a pat against the neck as he tossed his head in defiance.

My face was so cold, bitten by the morning chill I hadn't realized the tears that burned lines down them. There was little point to hiding the evidence, but I wiped at them anyway.

"I'm fine."

He pursed his lips. "I doubt that."

We walked side by side in silence, Egg calming to the point where the only evidence of his annoyance was the occasional harsh flicks of his tail.

"Before all this, before I ended up here, I had a rough couple of months." What was I even saying, he wouldn't want to hear this? The nonsensical drivel of a child is what it was, yet, I couldn't help but continue. The words spilled out of my mouth like an avalanche, rushed and with little adherence to cohesiveness.

"I broke up with my boyfriend and then the same day, the same exact day, she died. I was right there, I had just said good morning to her. I had felt the warmth of her hug, smelt the ciggies on her clothes and the coffee on her breath. I can still remember the yellow tint of her teeth from her love of tea, the way her hair grazed her chin, the same way it had for as long as I had known her, because she loved the way it made her jaw look thinner and her hair thicker. I mean... —fuck." The tears were flowing freely now, the dam bursting. "I was laughing and joking around with my best friend, while literally feet away my mother was taking her last breath, and I ignored every phone call and text message I received because I thought it was some ploy by Liam to get us back together."

"Phoebe…" He sounded as lost as I felt.

"She died alone, Leif!" I wailed, hands balling into fists, held tight against my eyes.

Our knees touched as Leif bridged the gap between us, pulling me into his arms. At least, the best he could manage without toppling me from my horse. The warmth of his embrace spread quickly, breathing life back into my shattered soul.

I felt safe and warm, and as if someone genuinely cared. Like that day in the hospital when I lay beside my mother, my tears the only warmth between my cheek and hers. Until Finn had shown up. Much like then, Leif was there for me now, just like Finn had been. In a world where I was convinced I had no one, I was beginning to believe I had at least something to look forward to in the gloom.

CHAPTER
THIRTEEN

The city was a frenzy of activity when we arrived. People darted to and from, carrying an assortment of wreaths, and flowers, and candles. Every inch of space was decorated with fresh fruits and vegetables. Leif reassured me that the display was how the ceremony began, with thanking the farmers who toiled in the fields, the women who slaved over the stoves, and the gods and goddesses that had blessed the families with the bounties that saw them through the darkest and longest nights.

"Your people have a pantheon?" It seemed a difficult concept to wrap my head around, even though I knew certain cultures still celebrated having multiple deities. I came from a Scottish family, and we weren't overly religious, but growing up, like all my friends around me, we attended church and were baptized. We were a stereotype, but it was my life, our life. Until we were old enough to choose what we wanted, and my mother was more than happy to surrender the charade. Finn and I were not immune to the knowledge that her opinions changed dramatically after our grandmother died.

Leif watched a baker with a basket of fresh bread scurry

across the road in front of our horses to the other side. "Of course. They watch over and protect us, grant us strength and vitality, and most importantly keep us honest and true."

Made sense. "Who does this celebration honor?"

"Ah, this festival is more to honor our ancestors, namely the women who had long since passed. They watch over us, and because of their knowledge and sacrifice every year we toast to their spirits." He gazed off into the distance. "But sometimes something odd will happen during Disting. A cat will appear in the boughs of a nearby tree, but as soon as it appears it disappears again. Many of us like to think it is Frigga, the goddess of motherhood, come to bless us."

"Interesting," I said, distracted by a group of women giggling over a loaf of bread that had caved inwards.

Eldrid strode forward like a woman on a mission, our horses skidding to a halt before her. Egg tossed his head with impatience.

"Where have you been hiding her, Leif?" she grumbled, hands on hips.

He threw his hands up in defense. "I returned her in one piece."

Her eyes narrowed. "Play time is over, the women must prepare for tonight." She nodded to me. "Follow me. Leif will take care of your horse for you."

Leif dismounted quickly, helping me from Dancer's back. When she was sure I would obey her, Eldrid strode off to a nearby house.

When I was sure she was out of earshot I whispered, "She sure is bossy."

He huffed. "You don't know the half of it."

I made to move, but Leif's hand grasped my upper arm.

"Are you okay?" he asked.

Frowning, "Yes, I'm fine."

He didn't seem convinced. "I'll have to take your word for it."

A breeze ruffled his hair, the shadows on his face grew as I said, "Once in a while you just need to…let everything out. I'm fine now, I swear."

This seemed to please him, or at least be more acceptable than a simple yes. He released me, nodding in the direction Eldrid had disappeared. "I'll see you tonight at the feast."

Grasping the reins of Dancer and Egg in his gloved hands, he turned to leave.

"Leif," I called out.

He paused.

"Thank you."

A smile and curt nod followed before I watched him lead the horses away.

Eldrid awaited me in a house whose walls were covered in cupboards, shelves, and dressers bursting at the seam with an assortment of gowns and coats. Every available space was occupied, as if the sole purpose of this residence was to hold the clothing of the entire city. Or at least, any clothing related to public festivities.

The moment my foot passed the threshold Eldrid was tossing clothes and shoes and undergarments at me, instructing me to try everything on. It was easier said than done, I didn't know the purpose of half the garments, and like earlier when Leif first presented me with clothing, I had no idea which were supposed to go on first.

"What even is this?" I held up a stiff piece of fabric that somewhat resembled one of the dozen exercise bands I had impulsively bought and then left to sit in a box in my closet.

She rolled her eyes. "It's a brassiere."

"What?"

"A bra. You know, a prison for your ladies." She pointed to her breasts for emphasis.

"No way," I whispered in feigned horror. It felt like the most uncomfortable thing in the world, and bras were already uncomfortable. I gently placed it on the pile of clothes Eldrid had designated as 'not working for me'.

"This." She handed me a white gown that didn't seem any

different than the other white gowns she had already handed me. She pointed to other gowns that were piled at my feet, "You layer that one first, like a chemise, then that one and that one. Obviously, the vest goes on last—you know what, here."

She dropped what she was doing and strode over to help. Luckily, I didn't care much about the indecency of dressing in front of a total stranger, because as she was helping to layer the outfit, several other women came in. They spoke of mundane things like children and food and laundry, sifting through the clothing through sheer obligation. What seemed to have taken us half an hour took them only a few minutes. They departed almost as soon as they arrived.

Tugging at sashes and belts and over garments, Eldrid split her time between showing me how to wear whatever this outfit was supposed to be and doing her own. She looked much better than I did.

"What are we supposed to be?" My reflection in the mirror was haunting. I looked like a ghost.

She laughed. "I'll admit it was weird for me the first time too."

"No one has told me anything, I have to be truthful. I'm not entirely sure what we're celebrating, or whom." My entire time spent here so far was non-stop me questioning what was going on. "What is Disting? Why is it being held at night?"

She gave me an apologetic smile.

"It actually began this morning. But that was the men's work, not ours. They begin by furrowing the fields, breathing life back into the farms." I glanced out the window at the snow that smothered the landscape, sometimes feet deep beneath windowsills where no one had bothered to remove it. Eldrid noticed my cursory glance. "Yes, well. It's been working for them for centuries, why change what's not broken? Besides, there is some truth in the equinoxes influencing agriculture. This was a sort of, awakening, to the vernal equinox."

"Vernal equinox?" I knew of the equinoxes and solstices, but I didn't know their dates, or even what influences they could have. After all, in suburban Edinburgh it meant very little to me.

"Yes. It's usually in mid-March, that's a bigger celebration, this one is smaller, a mere nod to the presence of these ancient beings who the citizens of the High Keep believe influence their livelihoods."

"And what do you believe?" She came from my world, my time. Surely the influences of growing up in a world of technology and conveniences shadowed the simplicity of such a culture.

Threading the sash at my waist through a corset of bone and leather, she mused over my question. "I came from a place of privilege. The daughter of a wealthy Portuguese broker and an Irish mother who spoke four languages and worked at embassies around the world—my future was decided for me long before I was born. Catholicism was as much a part of me as my love for art and propensity for my mother's soda bread."

She stared longingly out the window as the torches of the city came to life.

"God was a major part of my upbringing too, and sometimes, I thought He was the only thing out there for me. But after spending the last fifteen years here, the things I've seen and done, I know for a fact He isn't. That's not to say I don't believe in Him anymore, but I don't believe He's the only thing."

"What do you mean?"

She shrugged. "There are no words to describe what I've experienced here, that is a journey you must make on your own."

Delving into her past seemed to be making her nostalgic, her gaze wavering on the flickering flames of the sconces. As fast as she had disappeared into a memory, she danced right back.

"Wait, the finishing touches!" Plucking at the strands of my hair, she freed it of the hasty half-up do I had arranged earlier. My hair tumbled across my shoulders, poking out from under the cowl like a red wave in a field of snow. "Perfect."

We stood before the mirror, looking our outfits over and smoothing creases.

"I look like less of a ghost now, maybe a corpse bride."

She laughed. "Well then I did my job well."

"Is that what I'm supposed to be?" I blanched.

Her teeth grazed her bottom lip as she smiled. "Sort of. The festival relies on pleasing the female goddesses, and they seem to have a particular way they like their female worshippers to look."

I bit my tongue. I didn't have to agree with this, or even like it. I just needed to put up with it and hope that Leif would do what he promised to do. Biding my time by playing along was the minimum amount of effort I could afford to extend, and if I were being honest with myself, I didn't mind that time if it was spent with Eldrid. *Or Leif.*

"Let's not keep them waiting," she said, offering me her hand.

I placed mine in hers. "Lead on."

The women walked shoulder to shoulder, the swishing of their ivory cloaks as their boots trudged through the snow was greeted by silence. In the middle of the Forest City surrounded by the wooden walls of homes, was a crater. Occupied by a sunken villa of crumbling stone and pillars, the closer we got the more I realized what it was. It was a temple.

Women stood by the entrance, a torch held aloft in one hand, a book in the other. Their faces were covered by a thin veil of lace. At the entrance, tucked in an alcove, was a basket of lace veils. Following the cue of those ahead of us, Eldrid and I placed the veils over our own faces. Further inside, past the archway where we had entered, which was supported by pillars of intricately carved stone, stood more women, their voices mingling with the others who had entered. A chant had arisen, vibrating the air around us. Their words were oddly hypnotic, and even though Ulfrik and Leif had made a big deal of me understanding their language now, I couldn't understand anything these women said.

Eldrid squeezed my hand, the skin around her eyes crinkling. Glancing around, I noticed all the women were dressed the same, one by one lending their voices to the chorus. There was a single wide room within where we stood, open to the sky above. Pillars reached for the heavens, supporting a roof that no longer existed. The women had gathered closely to one side. I was going to question Eldrid, until the women with the torches and books at the entrance joined the throng, standing at the front of our side of the room. A moment later, a line of men filtered in, same as the women had. They were clothed in white, their faces obscured, but not by veils like us. They were adorned by the skulls of wolves, the pelts gracing their shoulders. One by one, their voices rose to meet the women's. The chant rose and rose, and soon I noticed that even Eldrid had joined in.

I would like to say I've never felt more left out of something before, but that would've been a lie. Every sports team in high school, every clique in middle school, every work function that always ended at a pub. I didn't care though, I was enthralled, entranced, like a baby watching fireworks for the first time.

I had no idea when the instruments had started, they could have been there the entire time, but I was none the wiser. The rising beat of drums and the melodical whispers of the lyre, mingled with the serious notes of a stringed instrument whose origin I could not place.

The chanting rose into a crescendo, and then suddenly, silence. Like the breaking of the wave, the music and voices stopped. The men and women faced one another, bowing deeply, and within the same breath the groups collided. The music began again, but this time it was wispy, like the music you'd find in some tavern during a Dungeons & Dragons game.

"What's going on?" I whispered.

Eldrid gave me a playful nudge. "It is time to find a partner."

"Partner?"

She giggled. "I believe you have a suitor already arranged." With a wink she disappeared into the throng, leaving me standing awkwardly in the middle of the floor.

Our eyes met at the same time, the intensity of the gold stunned me to silence—and I did nothing but watch him stride towards me. Even though no one cast him a second glance, the crowd seemed to part, giving Ulfrik a clear path. His stride was confident, almost arrogant, so sure of himself.

But of course, he was a king. High King. Even though his outfit was the same as everyone else, there was no mistaking the crown adorning the wolf skull on his head and the strut in his gait.

Readying the words on my tongue, shoulders squared, chin raised, I waited for him. The satisfaction of denying what he was going to ask tickled me pink. I didn't care if he was king, he couldn't have whatever—or whomever, he wanted. I had no doubt this society was similar to how most cultures hundreds of years ago were. Women had little say or power in matters. Marriage was rarely about love. And slavery was a lucrative trade.

A puzzled expression marred his face as a little girl stood her ground before him, blocking his path. I remembered her from the courtyard where I had first met Eldrid. Wavering slightly, he bent over so the little girl could whisper in his ear. He placed his palm outwards, and she gripped it with tangible excitement. Offering me a polite smile, the king led the girl into the mass of dancers, weaving in and out with her balanced delicately at the lengths of his arms.

Their matching smiles were infectious, as he twirled her around and around, her giggling easy to hear over the parading of feet and beats of the music. It was hard not to admit to the jealousy that oozed over my skin like sludge. There was an uneasiness settling into my stomach, sitting low and heavy like a rock in a pond.

This wasn't the Ulfrik I knew. Or at least, not the one I thought I knew. He was the High King, leader of the Wolf Clan, and yet since leaving the High Keep, he had shown no disdain for those who were unequal to him. Men, women, children—everyone was equal in his eyes. He abandoned a dance with me because a little girl, a praell, had asked him to dance.

The nails on my fingers bit into the flesh of my palm as I squeezed my fists tighter. I wanted to feel anything except what I was feeling right now. This ancient warrior, riddled with bulging muscles from years of fighting, was more akin to a miniature poodle than a wolf. He wasn't a tinman, a mercenary who upheld the virtues of bloodlust, there was a heart under the façade he had borne in the throne room. This man was someone else entirely.

Several other children crowded around the king, begging for their turn. He said something I couldn't quite hear, and the children joined hands around him, dancing in a circle like kids did in elementary school.

There was a stirring within me, a flutter, a feeling that soared and soared and I couldn't even put a name to. I'd never felt this before; my throat threatened to close, my palms were sweating, and the world began to spin around me faster than the dancers. I needed out, I needed fresh air, and I needed it now.

Not caring who saw, and knowing full well they were distracted anyway, I made a beeline for one of the archways, the drizzling snow outside beckoned me. The air against my skin was freezing, and yet the freshness of it was warmer than when I had been inside with the others.

What is wrong with you?

I wish I knew. There was no logical explanation, at least not one that I could find, in my feeling that way. To allow my emotions to smother me like that. The closest I could even compare it to were the feelings I had in those months after my mother had passed. But this was different, this was foreign, this was scary. Panic was taking control, at the helm of my already shattered mind.

I just needed to be alone, a space all my own. Except, I wasn't alone. The moment I heard the boots scuffing the stones beside me, my muscles tensed. There was no need to look up to know who was there, but I did anyway. I owed him the least amount of courtesy he was due. After all, standing before me, was the king.

"Are you not enjoying yourself, my lady?" Although the words were serious, it was edged with sarcasm.

"I needed a breath of fresh air was all." Not a lie, the moment I burst into the quiet stillness outside, the bubbling emotions within me began to settle.

"Ah, so what you're saying is you couldn't find a partner?"

My glare was met by bemusement, which only further annoyed me. My expressions must have been clear as day to him, a frown marred those perfect features as he closed the gap between us.

"Your absence will be noticed, *my lord.*"

The space I was desperate for was being choked as Ulfrik towered over me. My back met the cold, unyielding stone. I gazed up into those mesmerizing eyes. The fluttering intensified, my head swam with emotions so fleeting I didn't dare try to understand them. There was no settling, no release of the tension within. It intensified with each breath I took, inhaling the scent of fresh snow with the musky breeze that rolled off him.

My head swam, my heart beat louder than the drums that echoed from within the temple. Although he towered over me, our faces were inches from one another, the curling of our breathes mingling in the suspended air between us.

Boots slapped the stones to our left, our heads swiveling to meet the unapproving beady emerald eyes of the king's right hand. Ogden looked us up and down, clearing his throat.

"My lord, perhaps you would be more comfortable inside?" It wasn't a question.

Ulfrik huffed. "A king will do as he pleases."

Ogden's eyes narrowed, but he surrendered, giving a tight bow before disappearing.

"It seems you are right," he said, pulling back to extend his hand. "My lady. May I have this dance?"

Something about a king asking for permission made me giddy. It was so wrong and yet gave me a power I would never hope to wield back home. Sure of the ridiculous smile on my face, I placed my hand in his.

"You may."

CHAPTER

FOURTEEN

The temple was silent, still, as Ulfrik lead me into a waltz through the crowd that parted like a wave. The music did not falter, and neither did we. His movements were precise, his footing sure, as sure as he was of himself.

My heart soared with each step and I dared to let myself smile. Those feelings were still bubbling up within me, the fluttering getting stronger, like a swarm of butterflies threatening to break free of my chest. But now that I was here, his body pressed so close to mine, my head was distracted.

This wasn't the first time I'd danced. Aside from the forced recitals in high school, Liam was fond of attending lessons. Not that I was bad at it, but my heart had never been in it when I was with him twirling around in the studio or tavern or friend's backyard. The feelings I had felt back then were a stark contrast to what roiled beneath my skin and in my heart now. I didn't want to dwell on them; I didn't want to feed them. But I couldn't help but get carried away in the moment, I was allowed to feel happiness, to feel joy, even if it were only for a moment, and only as a mask.

A horn bellowed nearby, breaking our trance. The crowd moved, shuffling to make way for a row of tables and chairs that were aligned in the space we had just danced in. Everyone seemed to have a place, there was no confusion as to where they belonged. Eldrid had taken a seat at the end of the farthest table, along with the young girl who had danced with the king, and several of the maidens I remembered from the courtyard. Leif and Ogden sat at the first table closest to the door, their eyes on the entrance. Everyone had their place. Unlike me, who stood awkwardly to the side waiting.

Ulfrik cleared his throat. "Will you not take your seat, my lady?"

Following his gaze to the first table, at the head sat an empty seat, which I had no doubt belonged to the king. It was the empty seat on his left, beside Leif, that caught my attention. Was that for me?

Ogden, the Hand of the king sat on his right, and I, some nobody, on his left. It felt unnatural, and I wasn't the only one who felt it wasn't right, with most of the eyes of the hall on me. Especially Ogden's, which I was certain would burn me to a crisp if he had such an ability.

I was thankful for the distraction of boots on stone, and the clicking of hooves coming from the archways surrounding us. Heads swiveled as several robed women walked forward leading lambs and calves to surround the tables. A woman, bent with age, her knobby bone-white hands clutched around a rope heralding the biggest calf, stood at the end of the farthest table where a marble altar stood. It was curved, as if it served more as a shallow basin for water than as a tabletop for holding anything. At one end of the altar was a notch, the perfect height and length for the calf to place its head on comfortably.

"Offspring of the Wolf Clan, this day we pray to the Disir, and the mother souls of our ancestors to grace us with the proof of a dawn at the end of these most darkened days. Today, we have born not one calf or lamb, but six! The goddesses of the deep winter, the fresh harvest, the hearth, and fertility, have answered our prayers, and have provided evidence that we have secured their favor." Although frail looking, her visage was a stark contrast to the voice that bellowed so assuredly from her delicate frame. "And to prove our devotion and gratitude, we shall surrender our token of favor to reunite with the Disir."

The hall erupted into clapping and whooping as something glinted in the old lady's hand. My eyes narrowed as I tried to ascertain what was about to happen, and as I did, her hand jerked underneath the calf's throat, a crimson tide gushed outwards into the basin. My blood chilled, my heart skittered in my chest as bile rose in my throat. It was a sacrifice.

My chest heaved and I fought to keep myself under control as the calf struggled in the old lady's grasp. Its hooves struck the stones, skidding wildly. I bit my bottom lip so hard I was sure I would draw blood as my hands twisted in my lap.

A warmth embraced my folded hands and I tore my eyes from the bleeding calf to see Ulfrik offering me an apologetic gaze. He didn't remove his hand from mine, and I found the presence, however the smallest of gestures, oddly comforting. The queasiness subsided long enough for the roar in my ears to dissipate, and the chanting of the old woman to fill my head.

"I had not considered such a sight would be foreign to you. I apologize." I wanted to be angry, but the sincerity in his tone calmed the flames burning within me. I wasn't immune to the cruelties of the meals I was fond of back on Earth, which led to my abstaining of such delicacies of veal and foie gras. Not that there was much opportunity to partake of goose liver in Edinburgh, but I did try it once when meeting Liam's parents at a fine dining establishment that catered to French cuisine. His mother thought it was delightful to explain what I was eating after I had taken several bites, my reaction fueling a hearty chuckle that had nearby diners glaring at us.

"My lady?" Ulfrik asked.

The old lady was speaking to the quietened room, but her words didn't register, my mind drifting to a different time.

Ulfrik leaned in so only I could hear his words. "You may leave at any time if you're uncomfortable."

My heart stirred at how much he seemed to care, but I steeled it away before my emotions became clear as day on my face. "I am fine, thank you."

The other women led the rest of the lambs and calves away, and two men bent beside the altar to carry the dead calf by its legs outside. The old lady bowed before the tables; a smile spread across her face.

"Let the meal begin!" She clapped her bony hands together, the sound echoing like thunder through the halls.

A throng of women filtered into the room carrying trays filled with plates and bowls laden with scents that made me forget all about what had just happened. One by one they spaced the trays out on the table, filling the empty spaces. More women filed in, some carried jugs filled with liquids, while others carried more trays of food. There was a dazzling variety of food, from pickled and salted vegetables, to baked breads and desserts, and seared nuts and sugared berries. The drinks were just as varied, between milks, teas, and potently scented alcohol.

Everyone waited, their eyes on the king. Ulfrik released my hands, reaching forward to grasp a spoon that he then proceeded to scoop a pile of pickled parsnips and carrots onto his plate. The moment he placed the spoon back onto the tray, everyone moved to fill their plates.

I waited patiently, not sure what to grab. Leif was sure of everything he was placing on his plate, and it only served to make me feel more out of place. I knew what a carrot was, and parsnips and beans, and cabbage and onions, but I couldn't bring myself to lift my hand and grasp that spoon. Eldrid at the far end of the third table was laughing as she playfully ruffled the hair of the young girl from the courtyard, Bodil, I believed her name was.

When the conversation at the table around me shifted to the ploughing of the snow-covered fields and idle talk of taxation, I felt myself shrinking into the chair. At least, that's what I wanted to do. Ulfrik had no such plans, however, taking advantage of the distraction to lean towards me.

"My lady?"

"I'm fine." My voice was low, holding back the anguish that threatened to crush me.

We both knew I was lying. Ulfrik grabbed my plate, loading it with a little of everything. Vegetables, fruits, baked desserts, honeyed nuts, sugared berries. He did the same with my glass but summoned one of the women who held a tray over, asking her for more glasses. When she came back a moment later, he proceeded to pour something different into each glass, and arranged them before me.

"I'd advise trying the nuts with the bread and following it with a glass of this." He pointed to the steaming tea that smelt faintly of roses.

I didn't say a word as I carefully scooped some of the honeyed nuts onto the marbled bread. My throat was parched and my mouth didn't want to open. I knew I shouldn't have, but my eyes strayed to his. He smiled encouragingly, and I found myself unable to deny him. He was trying, he cared. I delicately took a bite and the explosion of flavour vanished all feelings of unease I had pent up like a volcano ready to blow. Instead, I became lost in the complexity of flavours and textures, distracted by how something so simple tasted better than anything I had before.

Until a woman arrived, heralding a tray of thinly cut strips of meat.

"Is that…" I couldn't bring myself to say it.

The table came alive with excitement, everyone eager to partake of that poor calf who was not even a day old. Everything was fine, perfect even, until they began to parade around that creature's seared flesh. I hated myself for salivating, or even thinking it smelt good. I liked to think in Edinburgh it was different, that the meat on my plate was from animals who didn't suffer, from ones that were treated well before they ended up on my dinner plate. And maybe they were, I went out of my way to support local and organic farmers, so I liked to believe that. But I knew this calf suffered, slitting its throat was not a fast death. No matter what the movies and television shows led you to believe.

Ulfrik whispered so only I could hear. "You do not have to partake."

I appreciated the gesture, but my limited knowledge of pagan rituals told me I didn't have a choice. You don't offend your hosts, and you don't offend the gods. It didn't matter that I doubted their existence, because I could feel their influence on these people and that was all that mattered.

"I do not want to offend my hosts or have anyone say anything." In all honesty, I just wanted to disappear in the background, be one of the expendable nameless actors drinking coffee in the corner of a scene.

"No one would dare." His gaze became cold.

At least, I thought only I could hear, until I saw the look of disapproval on Ogden's hawk-like face.

The woman placed the tray before Ulfrik, and like before, the tables waited for their king to take the first strip. Eldrid placed a calming hand on Bodil, who was preoccupied with devouring a slice of honeyed bread. She placed the mangled crumbly remains of the slice on her plate, following Eldrid's gaze to the king. Even a child seemed to understand the significance of such a gesture of tradition.

"My lady?" Ulfrik asked.

My heart swelled, the fluttering threatening to topple me over. He was asking my permission. The ball was in my court, and yet, I knew I could not refuse. I realized to be unseen, I had to fit in, and that required me to do what they did.

A simple nod was all it took for a beaming smile to spread across his face as he took a strip of beef, sitting it on his plate between a pile of peas and cabbage. Pushing the thought from my mind, and all too aware of the eyes on me, I mimicked his gesture. The moment it was on my plate the tables rejoiced, and the woman lifted the tray, bringing it around the tables so everyone could have a strip. Servants jumped at the opportunity to remove the empty trays from the table, refilling cups and answering questions.

I was aware of Ogden's pensive gaze on me as I pushed the

beef across my plate with my fork. There was no denying his contempt for me, it was clear as day. If I didn't do this, if I tried to prove a point, I would never be able to slip into the shadows, I would always be on the radar. If I was always on the radar, I could never return home.

With a deep, steadying breath, my fork ceased its endless wobbling in my shaky hand as I brought the steaming strip of thin meat to my mouth. There was no denying the juicy, savoury delight it brought to my tongue, but nothing would distract me from the fact that only an hour ago this newborn baby's hooves were dancing on the stones beneath my feet.

It was enough to convince Ogden to remove his gaze from me as he focused on his companion to his right, a sour looking man. I recognized him from the throne room. He had every earmark of a greedy politician, with beady eyes akin to Ogden's, but the rotundness of someone who has led a life of complacent luxury.

"Harvaldr."

I jumped at Leif's voice by my left shoulder, even though I knew he was there. So wrapped up in my own thoughts, I hadn't considered how obvious I was being. Clearing my throat, I took another bite of salted peas.

"I know you're curious, so I'll tell you now that you'll want to steer clear of him." His tone was icy.

Swallowing, I tried to hide the fear in my voice. "Why?"

Leif's gaze narrowed on his plate; his voice so low I had to focus to hear the words. "He does what is necessary to fuel his ambitions. Everyone is a pawn to him."

"You seem to know him very well," I mused. "Why does he sit beside the Hand?"

"He's my uncle."

I frowned. "He's a shaman?"

It was to be expected, of course. I assumed there were more shamans, perhaps even one for every city.

A wry smile. "He's the Chieftain."

What? "I thought Ulfrik was the leader?"

He considered how to reply. "Harvaldr is an interim leader when Ulfrik is in the High Keep. He does not lead the Wolf Clan."

"Why not?"

"Because Ulfrik won." He sipped absently on his mug, obviously not caring about the contents of his drink.

Our conversation was interrupted by the man on Leif's left, asking about upcoming ceremonies pertaining to his position as a shaman. I was desperate to lean in and listen, to learn, but soon their discussion meandered to things that made no sense. I found myself eating my food in silence, listening to those around me.

The night passed quickly from there, as the jugs of drink drained empty, and the plates of food were left with crumbs. No one dared leave the table, no matter how tired or cranky they were. The children at the far end fell asleep in their chairs or against their parents or caretakers. Eldrid was having difficulties holding herself upright, choosing to balance her heavy head on her palm. I, too, felt the heaviness of sleep tugging at my consciousness and wondered how long until I could feel the sweet embrace of my fur-covered bed.

The chair to my left scraped against the stones as Ulfrik rose. The tables snapped to attention, everyone sat on the edge of their seats. Ulfrik held an almost empty mug up in the air and drained it in one gulp. As he set the mug on the table, everyone rose. Not wanting to be on anyone's radar, I rose as well.

"The time has come; the Grandmother has made her presence known." And with that he strode from the room. Even bowed down from copious alcoholic beverages, his swagger was hard to miss.

Leif leaned over. "Now we may leave."

The room was filled with activity as everyone filed out, tired and disheveled, words were mere murmurs as they shuffled through the temple. I stood by my chair, watching as Eldrid and Bodil walked past, offering me smiles.

"Who's the grandmother?" I asked Leif as he moved aside to

let an elderly man limp past.

"A goddess of the night, she blesses us with sleep."

"Basically, a sandman, gotcha."

A yawn wracked my body, my shoulders slouching with the effort.

"Do you know your way back?" The temple was near empty now, a few stragglers mingled with the servants who were now furiously cleaning, desperate to return to their homes as well.

I nodded, mouthing a thank you that I wasn't entirely sure wasn't just said in my mind. It was hard to still imagine that I had a house here, a place all my own, and it was leagues from anything I could have hoped to have back in Edinburgh.

Leif followed the few who had lingered, disappearing back into the Forest City. I poked my head out of the doorway and was greeted by the High King.

"My lady." His voice was pleasant, if not a bit slurred.

Startled, I caught myself before taking a face full of snow. Eyebrows raised, he held back a laugh as he offered me his arm.

"I thought perhaps you would enjoy an escort?" I was too exhausted to rebuke such an offer, placing my hand on his arm.

He lead me out of the crater that housed that ancient temple, and we wandered with a slow and quiet grace through the courtyards and alleyways of the Forest City. Most of the lights in the houses had begun to disappear as people resigned to their beds. Here and there couples mingled on their porches, offering lingering kisses and touches that had me blushing and quickening my pace.

If Ulfrik were aware he gave no indication, steering me back to the front door of my humble abode without any issues. Here though, I lingered. I was sure there was a protocol to adhere to, perhaps I wasn't allowed to leave before the king did? Was I supposed to invite him? Wait for him to open my door for me? *No, that's absurd.*

I did wait, however, the snow falling around us as I held my cloak about myself. I was desperate to fight off the grip of a midnight's winter bite, but these clothes were ornamental and not made for comfort. Ulfrik shifted beside me as he placed the wolf hide from his shoulders onto my own. The lingering heat of his body seeped from the hide into my own flesh, the scent of musky pine drifted on that cold breeze, and I found myself drinking it in.

"Thank you," I breathed, the shivering lessening, the goosebumps less noticeable.

"You didn't have to eat it," he said.

It took me a moment to realize what he was talking about. "I was shocked, at first. That was all." I was hesitant to admit to him how good it tasted.

He stood so close, our bodies mere inches from one another as he whispered. "Never be afraid to be yourself."

I wavered, my eyes searching his. I'd never had the fortune to meet royalty before, in fact the closest I ever got was on a trip to London, where we drove past Buckingham Palace. I didn't even know if the royal family were there that day, but it would still end up being the closest I had ever gotten. From what I knew, in history books and television shows and period pieces, the way Ulfrik acted was nothing like what a king usually did.

Those feelings that threatened to overwhelm me during the dance began to rise, seeping to the surface like water in a bog.

Why was he so different? Why was he so *un-king-like?*

"Why do you care?" My voice trembled.

His gloved hand rose, pausing beside my cheek, not quite touching it. Tears warmed my eyes but did not fall. My expression was so easy to read and whatever he saw convinced him to place the back of his hand against my cheek.

"I want you to feel that you deserve happiness." His hand, although gloved, was intoxicatingly warm. "That you deserve a life worth living."

Although my body was chilled, his words warmed a part of me that I didn't think would spring back to life. I had told myself that before, almost those exact words. When I was convincing myself that breaking up with Liam was a good idea, a healthy idea. And when I allowed myself to smile after my mother's death.

Ulfrik was dangerous, but not in disposition or because of who he was. Ulfrik was dangerous because I knew myself. Right now, in the silence of the snowfall, our breaths mingling in the air between us, I wanted to kiss him.

He wanted it, too. His golden eyes swirled with longing, his lips slightly parted, his body tensed. We gradually closed that distance, until our noses were touching, and we breathed in the scent of one another. The alcohol was still rife on his tongue, and I'm sure mine smelt no different.

I waited with closed eyes, sure that if I took the first step, I would lose myself entirely. But the kiss never came, and when I opened my eyes, it was to a pained expression. His hand dropped from my face to run through his hair as he leaned away from me.

"Good night, Phoebe," he said, hesitating on the steps of my house.

The pain must have been just as clear on my face, as the warmth of his hand faded, he retreated into the night.

"Good night," I whispered after him.

CHAPTER

FIFTEEN

Eldrid interrupted me, my mouth full of bread I had hastily shoved in there the moment I heard her call my name at the front door. She barged in, and I tried to recall locking the door the night before.

"Good morning, sunshine," she remarked, looking me up and down.

I was a sight for sore eyes. Disheveled frizzy hair plastered to my unwashed face, sitting in a woolen smock that had me itching every couple of minutes. Almost everything was made from wool and although it did more to soften the bite of winter than the linen or silk, it was scratchy and wire-like and my hair was not a fan.

"Some vinegar will fix that right up," Eldrid remarked, eyes zeroing in on the red patches on my arm that I was furiously scratching like a leper.

I recoiled. "You want me to bathe in vinegar?"

She burst out laughing like it was the funniest thing she had ever heard. I glowered.

"No. The smock, dummy."

"That's not the kind of language I would expect of a teacher!" I taunted.

Taking the seat beside me at the table, she folded her arms. "I figured a fellow Traveler would be the ideal person for me to be my true self with."

True self…

She moved on, oblivious to the effect her words had on me, and what they reminded me of. I could almost still feel the ghostly warmth of his hand on my cheek.

"We have work to do, so get dressed." She paused, eyeing me up and down. "On second thought, I'm going to help you."

I groaned, giving in to her relentless plea to play dress-up.

I was happy I gave in to her demands because the clothing she picked proved warmer than what I was going to wear. Especially since she dragged me across the whole of Forest City, performing chores and offering a helping hand to all those who needed one. From dawn to dusk we busied ourselves gathering fresh berries and nuts from the woods nearby and firewood split by the lumberjacks to store in a shed to dry, hauling bags of freshly ground flour to the kitchens for the women to turn into delicious breads and desserts, dusting empty houses awaiting new families to move in, and mucking out the animal pens.

The most interesting of our chores brought us to a longhouse adorned in brightly woven cloth with twirling glass baubles hanging from the rafters. Within were women hard at work with blistered fingers, whom Eldrid informed me were hauling bags of wool and flax to be scrubbed clean. The women crowded within this place had formed a sort of assembly line. At one end, by the front door where a latrine of water emptied outside, were the women that held the shorn fleece, soaking and scrubbing the black and white and brown fibers. When they were done it was passed along a narrow table where women with metal tipped combs brushed and brushed and brushed, making the wool finer and finer. On the other side of the room sat the women who were preparing the long stems of flax in a similar fashion. Some of the stems were soaking in shallow trays of water, and others were being beaten with a wooden tool before a comb was passed through them.

Eldrid walked me past the women bent over, focused on their craft, to the back of the room. Here, the bundles and spools of fleece and yarn had been carefully bound, weighed down with sturdy stones from a loom of wood. The oldest women in the room sat here, their fingers deftly spinning and weaving the materials into what would become a dress, shirt, or blanket.

"Do you have any cloth ready for the dye?" Eldrid asked, her hand gently grasping one of the women.

She turned to her, squinting in the limited light from the dying sun. Her eyes drifted over me, narrowing.

"Saddled with babysitting duty, Eldrid?" she remarked, chewing on the stem of what I assumed was also flax.

"Careful, she's the chosen of our dear Ulfrik," snarked the woman next to her.

"I'd remind you to hold your tongues, Oili and Solvej, lest you forget whose company you currently entertain."

"She's a Traveler, is she not?" said the second woman, Solvej.

"We are doing you a favor which can easily be rescinded." Eldrid's gaze became icy.

Solvej rolled her eyes, nudging her friend. Oili sighed, pointing to two baskets in the corner of the room filled with neatly folded plain cloth.

"Turid is at the millhouse," she said dismissively, returning her focus to the loom before her.

An expression passed Solvej's face before she, too, returned her attention to her loom.

"Let's go." Eldrid shoved a basket into my hands, bidding me to follow her out.

"What was that?" I asked when we were no longer within earshot of the longhouse.

She hefted the basket onto her hip, turning to me. "That didn't upset you?"

I offered her an apologetic smile. "You know, normally it would have."

The snow crunched beneath our boots as we walked along a twisting path of gravel, Eldrid's voice carrying on the gentle breeze. "I'm sorry. I wish I could have not cared, but those two have been the bane of my existence since arriving here. They're not particularly fond of Travelers."

"How come?" The going was harder here, less snow had been cleared from the roads. Every step had to be calculated or I'd end up plunging my foot into a hole in the ground, as I had already done twice since leaving the longhouse.

"Well, as you know, you and I are not the only ones, and likely not the last, to come from our world to here."

"Of course."

She paused, placing her feet carefully on the road ahead, where a fresh layer of snow had gathered, undisturbed by even the wildlife. Snow was sprinkling down around us; the sky was dark and foreboding. I was eager not to show her how apprehensive I was, imagining being stuck outside again in a blizzard had my heart racing.

"There was this one girl, five years before I arrived. She, um… didn't take very well to the circumstances. She was pregnant when she ended up here, and miscarried." Eldrid paused, a shadow so fleeting, passed upon her face. "Anyway, it was to be expected. She was a newlywed, had a baby on the way…"

The road narrowed around a corner ahead, declining towards a stone building in the distance.

"When she lost the baby, she snapped. She lit several houses on fire, screaming that everyone here deserved this for killing her unborn babe." She shuddered. "But I don't think she intended for the outcome to be what it was."

"That's awful," I whispered.

She sighed. "Two of the houses she lit on fire belonged to Oili and Solvej, so I can understand their animosity. They lost more than their homes in the chaos. Now they busy themselves from dusk to dawn weaving and sewing to escape the families they had lost."

"I'm sorry," I muttered, unsure of what to say. What could really be said?

Something seemed…off. Then it occurred to me, everything I had heard and seen so far had suspicion growing in me like a weed. "Are they all women?"

She turned to me, the edges of her teeth gently grazing her bottom lip as she thought about my question. "You know, now that I think about it, all the Travelers I knew or have been told about were women."

"I wonder why that is." Such an occurrence couldn't have been a mere coincidence.

Shrugging, she used her free hand to gripped the wooden latticed wall that ran the length of a flight of stairs and deposited us along a slow, gurgling river of shattered ice. In the scattered sunlight that remained, it almost looked like the pieces of a broken mirror floating on the water. Mesmerizing, but dangerous.

A woman, easily in her forties, knelt by the edge of the river that snaked by the millhouse with its fast spinning wooden wheel. The pail in her hands was plunged into the freezing depths, revealing the white as snow linen cloths within.

"Turid!" Eldrid called, running to her side.

The women placed their pail and basket on the shore, embracing each other like long lost siblings.

"Eldrid! You bring me a friend!" she exclaimed, summoning me forward.

I didn't get to place the basket on the ground before she wrapped me in a fierce hug. Her embrace was warm, her voice sincere, as she pulled back. "You smell so good, like roses."

Blushing, I gave her a weak smile. She was adept; I had splashed rose infused water over my hair this morning. I was sure that it had faded long ago, replaced with the familiar scent of sweat and dirt.

"Phoebe, this is Turid, the famous dyer of Forest City!" Eldrid said with a flourish, causing the woman to blush. "And Turid, this is Phoebe."

"The Traveler?" she asked, eyes wide like a child at the zoo. At least that's what I felt like, the gawking was starting to bother me.

But then I noticed the way she held herself, at an angle, with layers and hair carefully placed. The slight movement of her bending to check the basket Eldrid had brought confirmed as much. She was a woman who was used to being gawked at. A pale scar, splashed with splotches of crimson spread from where the curtain of hair had parted along the left side of her jaw down the side of her neck where it peaked out from under a cozy, woolen scarf. I knew the moment I caught sight of it that it was no ordinary scar, caused by a cat scratch or an accident, it was the mottled work that only fire had on the flesh. I knew that look well; Finn had a similar mark on his leg where he had branded himself on the furnace when we were children.

"Poor thing, you must miss your family and friends—" Turid said, beckoning us towards the mill. "Come inside!"

Inside the mill were buckets of water filled with soaking scraps of cloths. Some were ochre or brown, green or yellow. Very few were brighter colors, such as blue or crimson. There were no purples.

Eldrid began sorting the cloths out, and I did the same, matching the different panels and bundles of fibers. Turid pulled out ceramic jars from a cupboard, sprinkling the contents into different buckets.

"What are you doing?" I asked.

Eldrid answered for her. "Unlike where we're from, the dyes from this world are organically produced."

"What do you mean?" My nose wrinkled when Turid popped open one jar, the distinctive scent of fresh walnuts was hard to forget. It reminded me of furniture polish, and also of the banger banana bread with walnuts Lucy made that I always looked forward to.

"If you want a red dress, you have to use beets. If you want yellow use yarrow, and if you want brown you use walnut shells. Makes a pretty nice ink, too," Eldrid clarified.

"It depends on the season, really. Everything I have here has been drying or fermenting for months, can't be wasting precious resources like beets or yarrow on having a pretty dress!" Turid exclaimed, gazing fondly at the single bucket of reddened water. "Besides, I have to share my ingredients with the herbalists and shaman. I don't get much to work with."

Eldrid's gaze swept the room to a corner where several colored dresses and scarves and blankets hung across a wooden beam by a window which would have been fed by the sun.

"You're doing a wonderful job with what you have at your disposal. No one else could have accomplished this," she said pointedly.

I wasn't going to disagree; it was hard to imagine that the layered golden overdress I wore was dyed from a simple flower. Eldrid was right though, the clothing and scraps of cloth that lay on that beam were beautiful.

"How did you come by our world?" Turid asked, using a long stick to stir the buckets, the swirling water bubbling under her vigorous motions.

I looked to Eldrid for support, she gave me a reassuring nod.

"There was this stone sitting in a cave…I don't know, I took refuge in it during a blizzard and when I woke up, I met Leif and next thing I know…" I shrugged.

Turid nodded her head thoughtfully. "The Cave City."

Eldrid must have recognized my expression. "I suppose no one has told you about the caves, or the stones."

"I don't know much about a lot of things." There was a pathetic, solemn note in my voice, I quickly recovered. "But I have all the time in the world to learn."

Eldrid clapped her hands together, the sound echoing. "And I'll be there for you every step of the way!" She shuffled along the wooden floorboards, peeking out the window where only a sliver of magenta on the horizon gave evidence of the sun. "Which reminds me, I think it's best we feed the animals before dinner. Are you good, Turid?"

Turid whipped her head up from where she had been nose deep in a jar, "I could dye sheets in my sleep!"

Eldrid laughed, opening her arms to embrace her friend. They exchanged a few pleasantries before a shadow loomed over me. Turid stood there with her arms wide open. I wasn't going to deny her request, after all, I was sure Turid and I could become very good friends. Her embrace was warm and tight, like one exchanged between best friends. Like the hugs I'd used to give and receive from Lucy.

Turid leaned in, a mischievous glint in her eyes. "You wouldn't happen to have any roses at your humble abode?"

"I think I have some rose petals in a jar?"

Her eyes widened. "You have *no* idea how hard it is to source roses for my dyes! I keep getting told there are none when I ask but then I find out they gave them all to the herbalist or apothecary, or to use in the hot springs."

I couldn't hold back a smile. "I'll sneak some out for you."

Satisfied that she would be receiving a harvest of hard to source goods, she waved Eldrid and me off. The rest of the night was quiet, our hands and minds occupied by feeding the animals in their pens before we swung by the kitchens. With a basket each filled with breads and pickled vegetables, we retired to our homes and prepared to do it all again the next day.

CHAPTER
SIXTEEN

Except the next day was far different, starting bright and early with Leif on my doorstep, the reins of Egg and Dancer in his hand.

"I thought perhaps I would give you some respite from Eldrid."

Raising an eyebrow, I leaned against the doorframe. "I hardly need a break from her company. I quite enjoy our time together."

He smirked. "Well, either you can earn some time in the saddle, or you can muck out the pens."

I grimaced. "Is that what I was supposed to do today?"

He merely raised Dancer's reins in response, jiggling the leather straps against the iron bit. I bounded across the porch, yanking them from his grasp.

"Let's go," I grumbled, struggling to keep the pout on my face.

We rode at a leisurely pace around the outskirts of the Forest City, the wide, spacious homes were lit with the sun's rays, highlighting the canopies of the trees that burst through them. It was still a difficult thing to accept, that the balance of nature and civilization was so delicate, and yet this seemingly primitive culture had managed something that my people could not. It was almost druidic.

Evidence of their love for the forest was everywhere I looked. In the latticed walls made of branches and roots carefully shaped and woven into one another from living, breathing plants nearby. In the reverence of the treatment of their animals, they weren't just beasts of burden. Although they lived in pens in the dirt and mud, the enclosures had trees and canvas canopies to protect them from the worst of weather, and they were fed fresh food daily, not just sloppy leftovers that had spent months maturing in barrels. Although I had yet to figure out the answer to question that had plagued me since I had arrived here. Where did the clans source the fur and skulls and bones of their namesake? I had yet to see any captive bears or eagles or wolves, and the closest I had come was the wolfdog that had kept me company in the High Keep.

"Are you listening?"

We had stopped at an archway that opened into a circular courtyard of dirt. There was shouting and grunting inside, as if a fight had broken out. Swinging my leg over the saddle I managed to hit the ground with as much grace as I had the first time I dismounted, but I didn't lose my footing, and I didn't need help from Leif.

Leaning against the latticed archway laden with prolific, blooming yellow flowers, I watched as two men wrestled in the dirt. Their breaths curled before them with each heave of their muscular chests, naked to the winter's light. Their skin red, their faces contorted, and yet I thought from my brief glance that they were sparring.

"Is that—?"

Leif appeared by my side, taking in the scene. "Even a king needs to practice."

Ulfrik had pinned his opponent's face in the dirt, having twisted the younger man's arm behind his back. I was surprised when he raised his eyes to stare at me, somehow knowing that he had an audience. Leif nodded his head in response, and Ulfrik showered us with a grin.

His cockiness allowed his opponent the brief respite he needed to wrest control from Ulfrik, startling him with a movement so slight I wasn't sure what happened. It ended with Ulfrik on his back in the dirt, his body shaking with a surprised laugh.

Leif strode to his king's side, with me hot on his heel.

"My lord," he said, offering him a hand.

Ulfrik smirked, clasping hands with his shaman. "I think our young cub is prepared."

Leif looked the man up and down. "What say you, Eske? Ready to join the pack?"

I hadn't noticed how young the man brushing dust from his pants was. From the sureness of his step and well-defined muscles I had thought he was in his twenties, but the man before me was no such thing, he was a boy who had barely left puberty. Yet he had the strength of a team of horses and the body of a god. I squirmed uncomfortably, knowing my mind lingered on a barely pubescent child.

Eske smirked. "Yes, shaman. My lord. I would be honored."

"Leif, escort the cub to the barracks," Ulfrik commanded with a twinkle in his eye.

Leif hesitated.

"I can manage without your presence," I whispered while Ulfrik was distracted by the small crowd of people that had engulfed him. Leif's mouth twisted, but he nodded, wrapping an arm around Eske as they left the courtyard.

Ulfrik noticed me standing by myself under an awning, not wanting to intrude. He waved the crowd away, beckoning me to a table where sat a single bowl of fresh blueberries. Taking our seats on opposite sides, he pushed the bowl towards me.

"My lady?" he offered, his chest still rising and falling with the adrenaline of battle, although he made an attempt to hide it.

My eyes couldn't help but roam over him. His skin glistened from the rigorous workout, the muscles moving under skin blemished by countless battles and skirmishes. A myriad of scars crisscrossed his body, forming a tapestry of pale streaks, like a marble countertop. My fingers itched in my lap, an impulse to reach out and trace the longest one, a jagged smooth ridge from the top of his ribs under his left breast to just above the curve of his pelvic bone. It was hard to ignore, and as my mind moved faster than my body, I raised my hand and was unable to place it back in my lap before he noticed.

"Curious?" he asked.

I nodded like a simpleton, not trusting the words that would pour from my mouth like a broken faucet.

He stood before me; the rays of the sun that had managed to escape a blanket of grey graced him in a beam. My lips parted, my heart raced, and I swallowed an uncomfortable lump in my throat. His chest was inches from me, the scar a shiny ribbon against his sun-kissed skin.

"Go ahead," he encouraged me.

My hand didn't wait for me to make up my mind, reaching out to trace the blemish from his ribs, I paused just as it dipped towards his pelvis.

Withdrawing my hand, my eyes caught his. "What happened?"

"I became king," he said.

"How does it work?" I'd only heard bits and pieces, and placing the puzzle together was becoming a chore.

"The High King before me was also a wolf. When he died, he left a hole in our clan that could only be filled by one of his bloodlines. Ogden, Harvaldr, and I were the only ones who could stake his claim. The winner could fight in the arena against the other clans, the losers…they could be a Hand or the Chieftain, or granted another high-ranking title."

My mouth twisted, that gave Ogden and Harvaldr a reason to be sour. "When the High King dies, the leaders of the clans fight in the arena to take his spot?"

He nodded.

"Who gave you that scar?" Ogden, Harvaldr, or someone else?

A breeze had picked up, heralding storm clouds on the horizon. The day had only begun, and yet, soon it would drive the citizens of Forest City inside.

His eyes darkened, as if the memory was still a fresh wound. "Arne, the Eagle King."

Ulfrik had made some powerful enemies, indeed. But the cordiality of this culture astounded me. The man had nearly killed him but could still take his place beside Ulfrik in the throne room like nothing had happened.

"How long have you been High King?"

Musing over my response, he stretched, raising his arms to the sky. "Almost a decade, a few more months will mark my tenth year."

Ten years he has been a king, a decade of sitting beside men who had almost killed him, pretending everything was fine. I suppose it wasn't pretend though, was it? It's worked. His kingdom was seemingly prosperous, his people happy. That was all you could ask for, a populace with heavy pockets, full bellies, and a grin from ear to ear. This was a paradise led by a leader who genuinely cared. A stark contrast from the capitalist hungry society I had left behind.

"Would you like to give it a go?" He waved his hand across the courtyard.

"What?"

"Sparring." A mischievous glint was in his eyes, like he knew a secret he was keeping from me.

Panic replaced the slight fluttering, "I don't think…"

"Nonsense. Come, I'll show you." He led me to the middle of the courtyard, a breeze ruffling a few petals from the lattice wall to brush across our path. Palms up, he held his hands outward. "Attack."

I shook my head, taking a step back. "I'm good."

He took a step forward. "Attack, or I will."

Hesitant, I took a few steps forward, and he took a few steps back. Sparring was a dance, and if my youthful years spent practicing karate with Lucy in the red-bricked dojo in downtown

Edinburgh taught me anything, it was that I was likely to lose this fight. Of course, it was possible for a smaller, less experienced fighter to take down a larger, more experienced opponent. But if you had to compare my hundred-and-thirty-pound self to this man who had spent his entire life fighting…I didn't have much of a chance.

He knew that, and yet, here he was, egging me on. In the blink of an eye he jumped forward, his fist narrowly missing my shoulder as I stutter stepped away from him.

"Really?" I gasped.

He smirked. "All is fair in love and war, my lady."

That shit-eating grin plastered across his face gave me the strength I needed to lash out, charging forward like a bull on a mission. My fist whooshed through the air, but never came close to hitting him. A boisterous laugh met my ears, and I growled, swinging again and again and again. Each punch missed. For someone who encapsulated your typical History Channel Viking warrior, he was as agile as a cat.

"Come now, my lady. We both know you're holding back."

My hands were already clenched, and yet, I squeezed them tighter.

"Maybe I should pit you against the children first, get you some practice," he taunted.

Enraged like a bull seeing a crimson flag, I charged at him, foregoing any thought and colliding with his solid chest. We tumbled into the dirt, stirring up a small storm of dust. He was quick to take back control, straddling my waist and pinning my wrists above my head.

"Admirable attempt," he smirked. "But you will have to try better."

Struggling was useless, his grasp was firm. He was in control.

"You got what you wanted," I muttered.

His expression faltered, as if wounded. "My lady, you mistake my intentions."

"Oh? Your intentions weren't to make me feel incompetent?" Years of karate practice down the drain. Lucy would have been howling with laughter if she ever caught wind of this. She had every right to since we were evenly matched during our practice. My heart skipped a beat at the thought of her, reminding me what this was all for.

Ulfrik stood, holding out his hand. With brows furrowed and lips pursed, I placed my hand in his. He pulled me in close, our bodies almost touching, as he whispered to me. "My intentions, if you were to allow it, was to show you what you are truly capable of."

I glowered. "What makes you so certain of me?"

He pondered my question for only a moment, the expressions on his face shifting so fast, so violently; there was a story somewhere there he had been struggling with for a very long time.

"You remind me of someone our clan lost long ago. Same rage, same fury, she knew what she wanted, but not what was needed to get it. I only want to give you the best options available. Only you know what is best for you."

He couldn't be talking about the girl Eldrid had mentioned? The Traveler who had set fire to the Forest City.

He shook his head, trying to pull himself from the memory. "It doesn't matter anyway; everything is different now. What matters is the present, not the past, and all we can do is learn from it."

His words moved me, clicking with something in my mind, like the gears that turned in a clock.

A small crowd of men and women had gathered under the awning of the building adjoining the courtyard, intent on the entertainment within. I paid them little heed, the muttering a mere whisper in the back of my mind.

Ulfrik made a move to address the crowd, or rather, a single person standing at its edge. Ogden's glare could melt butter, the sour look on his face curdled the milk in my belly from breakfast.

"My lord," I paused. "I would enjoy sparring with you again."

His face lit up, taking my palm in his to gently press his lips against the back of my hand. "I look forward to it."

I watched him retreat into the throng of people, Ogden's disappointing gaze lingered on me until his attention snapped to the king. There was something off about him. I could understand his animosity towards me. I was a stranger in his world, who has managed to get impossibly close to the king. I would be worried, too.

Leif appeared by my side as the crowd dissolved into the city.

"That was horrible," he said, poorly containing the laughter in his tone.

"Ugh," I groaned, shoving past him. "Can we get back to the horse riding lessons?"

We mounted Egg and Dancer, spurring them into a running trot. It still amazed me how sure footed these horses were in the snow, and the fact that they were smaller than any horse I had ridden. I would have been compelled to refer to them as ponies, except the one time I voiced my opinion Leif glared at me like I had cursed his family.

"They're horses," he reiterated, clearly not ready to let my accident slide.

"Okay, okay, they're horses," I said, pulling Dancer back. Unlike Egg who was happy to be out of the stables, Dancer was impatient, wanting to feel the wind in his mane.

"I'll be heading to the High Keep in the morning."

That means the horse-riding lessons would simmer for a while, and I'd once again be stuck playing housewife with Eldrid. *You still have Ulfrik.* I surprised myself with the smile that stretched across my face. I did still have the sparring to look forward to.

"I'm glad my absence makes you happy," Leif grumbled.

I raised my hands up defensively, pulling on Dancer's reins. He tossed his head in defiance, pulling my hands back down.

"Careful," Leif warned. "Some horses prefer a loose rein, Dancer is very particular about it and isn't afraid to let you know."

"Sorry," I whispered, patting the side of Dancer's neck. "It wasn't that, Leif. I just have a lot on my mind now." He searched for something in my eyes, and whatever he found must have pleased him. "Why are you going to the High Keep? Is everyone else going to?" It seemed odd that within a fortnight an entire population would uproot again. But tradition is tradition, and humans have done weirder things for weirder reasons.

He shook his head. "No, just me." He eyed an elderly couple walking past, hand in hand. Once we were out of earshot he whispered. "Besides, I promised you something."

The reins slipped from my fingers as I remembered our arrangement. If I behaved, tried to fit in, he would help secure me passage home. Or at least, he'd try. But now he was presenting me with a timeline.

"How long will it take?" My voice was barely audible to my own ears, and for a moment, I thought he hadn't heard me.

He cleared his throat. "There are a few archives that I suspect will herald an answer to the runestones."

"How *long?*" I stressed, my anxiety causing my hands to shake, my heart to do somersaults in my chest.

"Give me a month."

I blanched. "A month?"

His mouth twisted. "I'm hesitant to involve anyone else in our deal, Phoebe. Those archives span several floors, several buildings, and cover several centuries. The High Keep is old, our people are ancient."

I nodded. "I'm sorry, yes, that makes sense. I just…"

He offered me a smile. "It's all right. Just give me a month, okay?"

Reaching out, he handed my reins to me, his hand closing around mine briefly in a show of support. "Soon."

Soon I would be home. Finn, Lucy, that potted fern, soon I would be reunited with them all, and this would just be a dream.

CHAPTER
SEVENTEEN

True to his word, Leif was nowhere to be found the next morning. The windows of his home were shuttered and Egg's stall barren. The sun played on the horizon, just piercing the treetops of the Forest City, and I found myself alone with my thoughts.

Eldrid had yet to make her presence known, and I was eager to make use of my free time before I was burdened with peeling potatoes, mucking stalls, or hauling bags of goods from house to house like a milkman. Or a postman of the Royal Post, except instead of letters I gave people fresh baked bread, clean linen, or jars of sugar.

Remembering a promise I had made, I rushed home, filling a linen bag with as many rose petals as I could. I had no doubt that Turid would be thrilled that I had managed to secure a hefty source of pink dye for her.

The roads were already filled with people going about their day. Even the children were on a mission, collecting colorful stones, playing with their friends, or shadowing their parents to get a head start on becoming just like mom or dad. Several young girls were already outside the kitchens, kneading dough or sorting through wagons filled with vegetables. On the other side of the road, opposite the kitchens, was a butcher with a gaggle of young boys surrounding him as he taught them the right way to strip and salt beef to make it last.

This foray into the city on my own was stirring feelings within that I wasn't prepared to feel. This world was wholesome, rich and diverse with a culture that was much like the Scandinavia of old. Like the Scandinavia I had set foot in with Lucy…

"Are you lost?" asked a little girl, sidestepping into my path.

"Oh!" I exclaimed, clutching my hand to my heart in surprise. "I didn't see you there, sorry."

"Eldrid was looking for you," she said, folding her arms as if disappointed in me.

I guess Eldrid knew I was avoiding her.

"She was?" My tone was light, surprised, but I expected as much.

Bodil nodded. "She says she has an exciting job for the praell today at the pens."

"Alright, I just have an errand to run really quick." I held up the bag of rose petals.

She pursed her lips. "Eldrid says she needs you now."

Kneeling beside her I held the bag open for her to see, "Do you know Turid?" She nodded, a smile on her face. She must have been fond of her. "I promised her some petals for her dye."

Bodil's eyes lit up. "Pink! I finally get my dress!" She clapped her hands together in delight.

Cinching the bag tight, I stood. "I'll drop this off at the mill, then catch up, okay?"

I made to leave, Bodil's voice carrying after me. "Don't take forever! Eldrid doesn't like it when we're late."

Giving the animal pens a wide berth, I followed the river that cut through the city, knowing that upstream sat the mill. The snowfall had been wildly unpredictable as of late, the temperatures fluctuating around or below freezing. I was grateful for Eldrid's teachings, if not for her I would have had to amputate my toes and fingers from frostbite long ago.

The waters were still sluggish, choked by the fractured ice. It was no more chaotic than it was beautiful, and I found myself at the shore, mind wandering as my eyes lost focus in the floating shards. A rustle of feathers heralded by high-pitched whistles sounded above me, and my eyes soared with a mighty brown speckled eagle with tail feathers that matched the snow beneath my feet.

It circled above me and the river, eyes focused on something in the forest to my left. I followed its gaze, where just beyond the nearest pines was a latticed fence. It blended in so seamlessly with the trees and bushes I hadn't noticed it. There didn't seem to be any building attached as I navigated the deep snow to peer through the holes in the fence.

Voices met my ears as my eyes adjusted to the courtyard within. The circular yard was set with stone, and in the very center was a dais supporting a woman in a thin dress that hugged every curve in her body. Her mossy stone façade supported a vase. Even from here I could tell by the darkened stone at its spout that this statue was a fountain, once upon a time.

The statue slipped from my mind when I saw who gathered around it. A man and a woman, who I recognized instantly. If not for her voice alone, the pale scars that stretched from jaw to neck were unmistakable.

The man wore a hood and the mask of a wolf skull hiding his face, his voice was low and somehow familiar. But I couldn't place it. Turid fingered the hem of her flowery apron, her eyes avoiding his like a lovestruck teenager. A blush spread across her face as the man pulled her into an embrace, her head nestled against his chest.

What are you doing, Phoebe? Good question, conscience.

It seemed wrong for me to stand here, spying on something so personal. It was none of my business, and as much as I would have liked to see the smile on her face as I handed her the bag of rose petals, I knew I couldn't delay meeting up with Eldrid any longer. I'd just have to return to Turid later. I left her to that secret rendezvous in the courtyard, making my way back into the Forest City.

Avoiding the path I had taken along the river, I slipped in through the alleyways, following them past homes and shops. Most people were working, the houses dark and silent, except a large dome-shaped domicile on my left. Light twinkled within, the sconces struggling to stay alive as shadows moved in the windows.

As I rounded the corner of its inner courtyard, I was greeted by two men in wolf skull masks, armed with swords. They regarded me for a moment before their eyes returned to staring at the wall before them. I admired the dedication; the Swiss guard that stood outside Buckingham Palace had always fascinated me. I hadn't realized I never knew which home belonged to the king, and now that I did, I knew it wasn't just a normal house. It wasn't a castle either. The mere idea that crossed my mind had me giggling like a child. It reminded me of longboats flipped over and stacked atop one another. The spaces beneath each were supported by wooden beams. The walls were peppered with doors and archways and circular windows.

The opulence rivalled the ancient houses you'd see driving through The Grange or Dean Village in Edinburgh. My mother was fond of Dean Village and the West End, sometimes after school we'd go for a drive through the streets of the luxurious parts of Edinburgh and discuss (very adamantly sometimes) what we would have done differently for the houses we liked. Maybe a wooden gate over a wrought iron one, different stones for the walkway. One time we got into a heated argument about French doors. Almost as heated as the voices that argued behind a window that overlooked the alleyway I was making my way through. They caused me to pause because I knew one of those voices very well. It was Ulfrik, and whoever he was talking to, wasn't happy.

Shadows shifted in the window, and damn my curiosity, but I couldn't tear myself away. Peeking over the wall, careful not to draw the ire of the guards, who watched me from the corner of their eyes, I waited for the shadows to move again. The shadows shifted again, and this time, Ulfrik appeared in the window, wearing a mantle of wolf fur graced by his dark as night locks. Head held high, eyes narrowed, he pursed his lips as another man came into view. It was Arne, the Eagle King.

"Enough!" seethed Ulfrik.

Arne, face flustered and eyes ablaze, turned from his king, disappearing from the window. Ulfrik slammed his fist against the windowsill, catching sight of me, and his expression softened. There was still anger beneath those eyes, even from here, as he followed his fellow king.

A door slammed somewhere in the courtyard, and the guards out front hardened their resolve, shoulders back, chins up, eyes unwavering as they stared straight ahead. Boots thudded against the bricks laid out in the yard as Arne stormed out the gate, wrenching it back to have it clang against the wall.

His eyes met mine.

"What are you looking at?" he spat.

I lowered my gaze, mumbling an apology.

He disregarded me, disappearing down the alleyway, thronged by two guards who emerged from the shadows decorated in feathers and adorned by the skulls of birds of prey. Ulfrik emerged a moment later, waiting for Arne to disappear around the corner before addressing me.

"Enjoy that little debacle, did you?" His voice was tight, controlled.

I shrugged, walking to his side. "Looks like you could use a distraction."

Ulfrik groaned, running his hand through his hair. But his demeanor changed, a mischievous look spread across his face. "What did you have in mind?"

"Don't be gross," I glowered. "I thought perhaps you'd want to spar."

Even before the words left my lips, I felt a twang of guilt. I was supposed to meet up with Eldrid.

He rolled his eyes. "Better than nothing, I suppose."

I made to leave, but he pulled me back. "I don't feel like going out today. We'll practice in the courtyard."

The gate clanged shut behind me and Ulfrik turned, summoning me to attack with a curl of his fingers.

"I'm more of a defender-against-an-attacker sort of person," I said dumbly.

"You're not going to get very far with that mindset." He circled me, like a dog around a herd of sheep.

I realized too late that's what he was doing, herding me.

"Manipulation can be subtle, my lady. Sometimes you won't know someone has the high ground until it is too late."

In the blink of an eye, he had closed the distance between us, wrenching my arms behind my back.

"That's not fair!" I ground out, struggling in his grasp.

"War is not fair and fights certainly aren't. You can play by the book, and you will most certainly lose." There was a hidden meaning in those words, one I couldn't quite grasp, but the sight of his guards peeking through the holes of the iron gate told me not to dwell on it too much. It was meant for me to understand, not them.

CHAPTER

EIGHTEEN

My body felt like I had just finished a triathlon. I was covered in bruises, inside and out, bringing attention to the existence of muscles I didn't even know I had. Not that I had ever done a triathlon, but I was certain my body would feel like this afterwards. Ulfrik had been harsh on me last night, and no matter how hard I tried, or whatever fancy moves I attempted to come up with, he was always one step ahead. It was hard not to consider my years in the dojo as being useless, but I felt reassured in the knowledge that Lucy and I didn't join up to be fighters.

The hot, bubbling water of the spring in my home, however, did help to relieve some of the ache. My eyes wandered to the bag I left on the table, stuffed with the rose petals I had promised Turid. Although none of my business, my imagination couldn't help wandering, trying to discern the identity of her mystery acquaintance. One thing I was certain though, they were more than friends.

A knock sounded at my door, and before I could throw my robe on, the door creaked open and a woman stomped through the house. Her gaze hardened as she expelled a disapproving sigh.

"Eldrid! I'm bathing!" I cried, desperate to cover my naked-ness with a towel.

"It's not just me that's disappointed, Phoebe. Bodil is, too."

I frowned. "Why would she be upset?"

"You know how kids get." I was hesitant to correct her, but I knew nothing about children. "She thought she was in trouble, in tears the entire night until I convinced her otherwise."

"I'm sorry, Eldrid. I didn't plan on not showing up, just a lot of stuff happened. I didn't mean to upset you, or her."

Eldrid let out another sigh. "Where were you anyway?"

I froze, water streaming across my naked skin, leaving trails of warmth where the fresh air of dawn kissed me. Could I admit that I forgot? Or should I be honest and tell her I had spent the day wrangling with the king. Or rather, getting my ass handed to me by him. I'm sure the truth would tickle her fancy more than a lie. But just to be safe…

"I'm sorry, Eldrid. I'll make it up to you, I promise."

She cracked her knuckles. "Damn straight, because you'll be spending the entire day with me."

I wrapped the towel around my body. Like everything here, it lacked the softness of anything I had back home, especially the cotton towels Finn had bought me from his trip to Japan. It wasn't these people's fault though, as far as I could see cotton wasn't a well-known fabric. Wool and linen ruled here, and it was easy to see why. The clothing was warm and dry, perfect for the harsh temperatures in this Norwegian-like landscape.

"You mind if I get dressed first?" Water still trickled down my arms and legs, and my hair was a tangled mess. She'd have to drag me kicking and screaming right now if she wanted me to leave this house before I'd managed to run a comb through my hair at the very least.

She waved her hand at me dismissively, like one would shoo a pigeon trying to steal a French fry. "Hurry up then, but I'm not leaving." She parked herself on one of the chairs by the table, eyeing the bag sitting atop it.

Aware that I had little choice, I dried myself off, combed my hair, and began layering the many articles of clothing needed to stay warm out here. When I emerged, it was to find Eldrid snooping in the bag of petals.

"Whose been sneaking you extra flowers?" She fought to keep the jealous tone hidden, but it was as plain as day.

"Remember when Turid said she'd basically kill for some rose petals for her dye? I was thinking I'd just give her mine." It was the truth and yet, part of me thought that she didn't believe me.

"So dramatic," she dolled. "I kind of miss how dramatic our—*your*, world is. Never thought I'd say that, but everything is so formal here, so serious. Although down to earth, the colloquialisms of humanity that you brought with you is refreshing."

Now that she mentioned it, the atmosphere here was all too apparent. People seemed much more serious, their words carefully chosen. I'd need to be more careful; I could get in trouble just being myself. It was only for a little while longer, a month, and that golden-haired shaman would stride through my front door with news. Good or bad, it would set my future and determine where I went from here.

"Are you ready yet? We're losing daylight," she grumbled, her eyes fixated on the sliver of gold on the horizon.

I knew I wouldn't be able to escape her wrath, and I came prepared for every possibility. Eldrid escorted me across the city, watching me like a hawk. Scrubbing linen in the basin, chopping carrots in the kitchen, kneading dough at the bakery, mucking out the stalls at the stable. Even Dancer's enthusiastic whinny at my proximity did little to soften the ache I felt in my bones. I was beyond exhausted, and yet the sun was still high in the sky.

There were twenty stalls in the stable, and after what felt like an hour of work, I'd only made it to the fifth stall. Dancer's head had never disappeared from where it stretched to greet me in the third stall. Every time I made a move to shovel manure into the wheelbarrow at my side or toss a fresh serving of hay into the trough, he'd whinny until I made myself seen again. It reminded me of the stray cat that used to live outside Finn's apartment, crying for a pet from everyone that walked past.

Groaning under the weight of manure on my shovel, I heaved it into the wheelbarrow, then wiped the sweat from my brow with the back of my hand.

"What have we here, a damsel in distress?" a familiar voice taunted.

Although I was breathing heavily, I didn't attempt to disguise my discomfort. "I'm hardly a damsel in distress."

Ulfrik smirked. "Well in that case, I'll leave you to it."

I groaned, staring at the pile of manure, so fresh that steam curled from it. *Curse him.*

"Fine, but no sparring."

"I promise." He ushered me from the stables, running me right into Eldrid. She balanced a basket of fresh saddle blankets on her hip, a bag of carrots hung from her wrist like a shopping bag.

"My lord." She bowed.

"Lady Eldrid, I have need of your assistant today."

She wanted to fight it, to tell him that I was needed here, that it was punishment for abandoning my chores yesterday. But she didn't know that yesterday I missed out on chores because of the king as well. Her expression was vivid, but eventually she pointed her chin up.

"Of course, my lord," she said with obvious disappointment.

Ulfrik made to leave, and as I followed, I leaned over and whispered a simple 'sorry' to Eldrid. She rolled her eyes but gave me a wink before disappearing into the stables. No doubt she would be left to finish my chores, which I did feel guilty for. I'd have to make it up to her somehow.

As we turned the corner to follow the wall of the corral, two giant wolfdogs appeared.

"Are you frightened?" Ulfrik asked, eyebrows raised.

Cringing at how obvious I was being, I couldn't control the stutter. "N-no."

The grin on his face stretched ear to ear. "There is nothing to fear of Skoll and Hati. At least, not while you are by my side."

The wolfdogs whined as they approached him, tails between their legs, ears pinned back as they licked their lips. I didn't need to be an expert in animal behaviour to know they viewed him as leader of the pack. Ulfrik ran his hands along their heads, giving them a scratch behind the ears.

He noticed my gaze. "Do you want to pet them?"

I nodded dumbly.

The wolfdogs were sitting beside their king, watching me approach, no doubt ready to tear me to shreds on his command. Not that I thought they would, at least not right now. Flashbacks of those days I spent in the room by the fireplace with one of these dogs by my side rushed back and I paused.

"Which one guarded me that day?" They were near identical, grey pelts streaked with white and brown, with striking hazel eyes.

He nodded at the one on his left. "Skoll, she was the first-born of her litter."

My hand shook slightly as Skoll's eyes met mine. Ulfrik reached for my hand, guiding it to Skoll's head. The wolfdog arched her neck, urging for a scratch between the ears. It wasn't so bad, and her fur was impossibly soft, like a cashmere sweater.

"They're so big for wolfdogs." His eyebrows raised in response. "Where I come from, they're lanky. Do you breed them yourself?" Skoll rolled her head in my hand, encouraging me to rub her fur in a line from the top of her head to the back of her neck.

He laughed, startling me. "Oh, these are not dogs, my lady, these are wolves."

I snatched my hand back, my anxiety swelling inside me, threatening to spill over. I had been left alone, unconscious, with a *wolf*. They were wolves, real living wolves. An honest mistake to make, right? Considering only today was I confronted by the fact that I had never seen a wolf in my life that wasn't on the television.

Although I could see how much these wolves looked to Ulfrik like a god, I couldn't shake the uneasiness that settled in me. I wished I could just accept things for what they were, that my body wouldn't react in such a negative way to the smallest inconvenience as if it were the end of the world. I suppose that's what happens when you try to manage your undiagnosed anxiety on your own.

"Phoebe?" Ulfrik's golden eyes simmered with concern, and I shook myself from the pity party I was dissolving into.

I snapped myself out of it. "I'm sorry, I was just surprised is all." I started walking. "Shall we?"

The road outside the stables led us past a hall of windows filled with children sitting in circles on the floor with etched stones beside them. It took me longer than I would have liked to realize it was a school. The teacher would hold up a stone and the children would search through their piles for the same stone. Eldrid might have been there, somewhere further in the building, after all, she was a teacher as well.

It was only then I noticed the two men garbed in dark clothes, skulls shadowing their faces, walking behind us. When we stopped, they stopped, when we moved, they moved. My erratic glances did not go unnoticed by the king.

"Do not fret, they are my guards," Ulfrik whispered.

I gave them one last glance before focusing on the world ahead. I hadn't noticed his guards tailing us before. Or I hadn't considered the fact that, of course, a king—high king—would have guards.

We walked side by side through the city, answering the nods and smiles and welcoming greetings of the Wolf Clan with mirroring gestures. Every time a citizen's eyes met their king's, they would perk up, as if his presence invigorated them.

"To answer your question from before, I do not breed them."

I frowned. Did he go into the forest and steal the wolves?

"As per tradition, I must be found worthy of our ancestors."

That answered nothing, only alluded to more questions.

The wind ruffled the fur on his shoulders. "Whose pelt and skull do you wear then?"

"Their mother." Skoll and Hati sat on their haunches as we came to a stop. My eyes glanced between the living wolves and their dead parent draped over Ulfrik's shoulders like a trophy of war.

"I suppose in your world that is frowned upon?" He was always concerned by my reactions and my opinions, like he fought for my approval.

Did the wolves follow him by choice, or was it simply Stockholm Syndrome? I could ask myself the same question. I had an ulterior motive to playing along, and yet, I was slowly finding myself growing accustomed to this life, to these people, this world, and their king.

"Did you kill her?" I needed a distraction from the butterflies, and what better a distraction to imagine him as a monster undeserving of my love.

He reached down to scratch the wolves behind their ears. "No. Their mother had been injured, a hunting mishap I presume. I followed a trail of blood for days before she led me to the den. Inside were two tiny pups, curled together. Their mother wasn't going to survive much longer, her wounds were deep and infected. She had chosen me, waiting with each step for me to follow, as if she knew I would protect them."

The fluttering intensified, and tears gathered in my eyes. I wanted so badly to view him as a monster, and yet, at every chance he proved to me that my bias was unwarranted. He was an honest man, in an unforgiving world. My anger subsided instantly, like someone had removed a kettle from the stovetop, quieting the fumes.

"They're lucky you were there," I said quietly.

"Maybe, but I'm lucky they chose me. Skoll and Hati have saved my life more than once; I owe a debt to them that can never be repaid."

The wind had picked up, and once again a storm sat low and dark on the horizon. I had hoped we would've been safe from the blizzards by now. The wolves at his side sniffed at the air, their ears pinned back.

"Will you have dinner with me tonight?"

His question came out of the blue, and I found myself stammering.

"W-what?"

He held up a hand, "You can say no, my lady. I will never force you to do something you are not comfortable with."

I scoffed. In the beginning I would not have felt comfortable, I wouldn't have hesitated to say no. But now?

"Yes, I'll have dinner with you."

CHAPTER
NINETEEN

The moment Eldrid had caught wind of my invitation she was at my house with all manners of lavish ingredients loaded into bottles and vials. She forced me into the hot spring, insisting I forego my usual rose-scented water, presenting me with a ceramic vase filled with a silky white cream.

"What is this?" It was soft, sliding across my skin like the lotion I was used to back in Edinburgh. Although it didn't smell like jasmine and honey, it carried an earthy, waxy scent.

Eldrid was sorting through the clothing she had brought, lying it out across the table, matching colors and fabric. "Goat's milk. Made it myself."

I barely recoiled, instead reminding myself that this was probably fresher than anything I'd placed on my skin before. There was hesitation as I applied it to my skin now, but the way it smoothed and cooled my skin was heavenly.

"This isn't half-bad."

Eldrid offered me a smile before grabbing a small bag and rushing to my side with a comb. "Alright, I have this vision in my head." She tugged on my hairs, curling them over a handful of black cylinders in the small bag she carried at her wrist.

"Ow!" My fingers gingerly rubbed my scalp. "I'm not a doll, Eldrid."

"Hold still. I never got to play dress up with my daughter so you're going to have to do."

That startled me, my pain forgotten. "You have a daughter?"

She shrugged. "Well, I'm not sure whether to say have…or had."

"She didn't come through with you." It was hard enough having left my brother and best friend. I couldn't imagine having left my child behind.

She curled the last of my hair over the cylinders, standing back to admire her handiwork.

"Oh yes, that will do nicely." Her eyes lit up as she circled me like a hawk, smoothing stray strands against my head.

"Tell me about her."

Taking the seat beside me, she began crushing a few herbs in a mortar that she had brought with her. "Her name was Gabriela." Taking a square of wool, she dipped it into the powder before applying it to my face. "Bodil reminds me of her sometimes, or at least, what could have been." Her dabbing slowed as she perused the bottles and jars she had brought with her. "Sometimes I think I was lucky that I ended up here. It gave her a chance to grow up without worrying about the circumstances, about the fact that her mother was a sinner."

There were so many things I wanted to say, and yet, I found myself speechless for once.

"I had a very strict upbringing, my mother was Irish, my father Portuguese. We were Catholics, and as I'm sure you are aware sex outside of wedlock is a sin, as is becoming pregnant."

I knew where this was going. It's a story I had heard many times, and even experienced. My parents weren't strict Catholics, but growing up we did attend church. Finn and I were instilled with the knowledge of taboo subjects and how sins could lead us on a path that would exempt us from God's love. I was forever grateful that my mother had a different view, and as we got older, she told us that God would love us so long as we strived to be a better person every day. I didn't know if I believed in God, but sometimes I liked to believe there is someone out there watching over me, someone who cared about the choices I made.

Eldrid snorted, interrupting my jumble of thoughts. "Needless to say, I didn't pay much attention in Sunday school. I fell in love with a boy, thought it would be forever, and nine months later I was a single mother at the ripe old age of fifteen." Taking a wooden brush made of animal hairs, she swirled it in a red powder, dabbing it against my cheeks. "Parents weren't too happy about that, and the boy's parents weren't either. Of course, abortion was out of the question, so as soon as that child was born my parents sent me to live with my aunt in Oslo for a bit. We lived in a small town outside Evora, in Portugal, and my parents wanted me gone for a while so the rumours wouldn't spread."

"That's horrible, Eldrid. I don't think the word *sorry* conveys how deeply messed up that is." My stomach twisted. Here she sat dressing me up like nothing was wrong, and yet she carried this burden around with her.

"Thinking back on it, leaving them for my closeted gay aunt in Norway was the best thing that ever happened to me."

At least something good had come of it. "You never got to see her grow up, to see the woman she became."

She offered me a small smile. "Want to know how I found my way here? A letter arrived in the mail a few weeks after I had been living with my aunt. The mailman had ripped the letter, so I decided to take a peek. It was addressed to my aunt of course, from my parents. Inside they asked if my aunt would be willing to adopt my daughter as her own. I was distraught of course, but I knew my aunt wanted a daughter of her own someday and was looking into adoption agencies in Norway. She was single, earnt six figures a year, owned her own home. She had everything, and I had nothing." Placing the brush on the table, she leaned back. "I wrote her a letter, begging her to adopt Gabriela, and placed it next to my parents' letter on the kitchen table. Then I left, taking the first bus out of Oslo. I don't even know where it was meant to go, but I got off at one of the stops in this giant forest and just started walking. I found one of those stones and ended up here."

Her story softened my heart, and for the first time since coming here I had to reconsider why I wanted to return home. She had so much more to look forward to, and as much as I missed my brother and best friend and modern conveniences, if anyone deserved a trip back it was her. Even if it was only for a moment, so that she could see her daughter again.

"How long has it been?"

She motioned for me to stand, holding out the underskirt and dress for me to shimmy into. "About fifteen years."

If Leif managed to find a way back home, I'd have to involve Eldrid. I'd give her the first opportunity to return. She thought she had nothing, but she had everything.

"If you had the chance, you really think you'd never return?"

She pursed her lips. "I don't know, to be honest. This new life, even the name, suits me more than anything back in Portugal, or Oslo, did."

"Your name isn't Eldrid?"

She smiled. "My birth name was Sophia. I like Eldrid more."

"A new name for a new life."

"That's what I was thinking. Besides, I have Bodil now, and the other praell children. Most of them are orphans. Bodil's mother was one of my first friends when I got here."

"What happened to her?"

"There were complications when Bodil was born, I can't say for sure what happened, but I promised her I'd take care of her daughter. I named her after her mother."

She had experienced so much chaos in her life, and finally things are going well. I couldn't blame Eldrid for not wanted to return. She had a life here.

"Now hurry up, we're going to be late."

Eldrid's story humbled me, and as I let her help me dress, I couldn't help but question my motives.

"This dress is gorgeous." The silken ivory dress that went over my undergarments of wool was threaded with gold, embroidered into what could only be tiny stars around the lower half of the skirt. A lace bodice of gentle pink with buttons of gold cinched in my waist, giving my breasts the illusion of growing an extra two cup sizes.

"I was worried you might not like it." She seemed overly pleased, like she really was worried I'd fight her on it.

The world was nearly pitch-black outside. A howling wind trailed snow across the city, as the icy fingers of winter gripped us even under the dozens of layers that we had donned. By the time we made it to the king's residence, I couldn't feel my face or hands. Nodding to the guards at the gate, Eldrid guided me up the steps slick with fresh snow. A man at the door turned towards us, a pleasant smile on his face.

"Shall I take your coats, my ladies?" he offered.

Eldrid answered for me, helping to remove the scarves and coat and long-sleeved outerwear underneath. The man took our bundle without a word, hanging it on a rack on the wall.

"This way."

He led us through a hallway pregnant with oil canvases of people I had never seen. All of them were accompanied by a wolf, all of them bore stoic expressions. These had to have been the chieftains of the Wolf Clan who had come before Ulfrik. We passed several plain closed doors before coming to an oaken one carved into the likeness of a howling wolf. The man knocked once, twice, three times, before pushing the door open.

"This is where I leave you." Eldrid embraced me before distracting herself with the task of removing my hair from its careful bun. It fell over my shoulders like a fiery wave, lending a stark contrast to the ivory dress.

"Oh, by the way," she leaned in close. "That dress was a present from Ulfrik."

My eyes widened so much I thought they might pop from my head. "Oh my god, Eldrid. Why didn't you tell me? That's kind of important."

I couldn't help but be annoyed. Ulfrik had given me a gift, but it was far more complicated than that. I couldn't pretend to know the intricacies of life here, but I knew one thing for sure. Accepting this gift carried some sort of levity with it. For a king to do such a thing, especially to someone who carries the title of mate…

She laughed. "I thought you might fight me on wearing it."

"Eldrid. Things like this carry connotations…expectations!" My hands wandered over the soft fabric, my anxiety causing my heart to pound and my head to drift.

The man cleared his throat, eyes darting towards where he still held the door open.

"Yes, yes, she's going," Eldrid grumbled, ushering me through the door. "Remember which fork is which!"

Oh, no.

"Eldrid!"

It was too late. The door was already shut, and the sound of a chair sliding across wooden floorboards alerted me that I'd have to figure this out on my own. I turned to greet him, and froze, my heart hammering against my chest.

"My lady." He had crossed the space between us, towering over me like a god. A long-sleeved ebony tunic was cinched around his chest by a burgundy leather vest embroidered with silvery wolf heads. He wore dark pants that melted into the shadows that played off the burning hearth against the wall. Handsome was an understatement. I found myself lost for words.

"M-my lord." My anxiety forced me to say something, anything, and there was no preventing the stammering.

Extending a hand, which I took without hesitation, Ulfrik led me along the length of a table that had been carved from a massive tree, unfinished, as if to admire the beauty of it that nature had intended. Supported by thick blocks of wood that spiraled into branches at either end, it nearly filled the entire room. The accompanying chairs were just as impressive, carved from a single piece of wood, they reminded me of the impressive driftwood that collected on the beaches of the Pacific Northwest in the United States.

Ulfrik pulled out the chair on the right-hand side of the head of the table, and I took my seat, letting him play the perfect gentleman by pushing the chair in before taking his seat at the head of the table.

The man who greeted Eldrid and me at the front door appeared through a small door at the far end of the room, carrying a tray with two plates on it. He placed one before the king, and one before me, before bowing and retreating from whence he came.

Whatever he had prepared smelled heavenly, the wafts of rosemary and lemon lingering in the air. The door creaked open, and he presented us with mugs of a sour smelling liquid, tinged with honey.

"Anything else, my lord? My lady?" Ulfrik and I shook our heads, thanking him for the meal and he disappeared back through the doorway.

"Something wrong?" Ulfrik asked.

I shrugged. "Excuse me for my ignorance, but is this not the wrong chair for me to sit in?" I knew I sounded stupid, after all, my only knowledge of medieval etiquette came from television shows and movies and what limited history lessons from high school that I still remembered.

"Would you prefer to sit at the end of the table?" he challenged, eyebrows raised.

"It's not that. It's just…" I cleared my throat. What would be the point of holding back now? "Surely Ogden would oppose such a thing." I brought the mug to my lips. The sweetness of the drink was such a distinct contrast to its aroma that I was taken aback, coughing to clear the liquid from my throat.

"First time?" He ignored my bait, instead teasing me, swallowing his without issue.

Sniffing at the mystery liquid in my mug, my nose twisted. "What is this?"

He chuckled. "Mead."

I groaned, grabbing the fork farthest from me, gently prodding the roasted potatoes on my plate. "Apparently, I've never had mead before."

His face puckered, as if he was holding back a smile, but it wasn't at what I said. His eyes lingered on my plate. There was a hidden joke I wasn't aware of.

"What?"

He nodded at the fork in my hand. "You're using the wrong fork."

Damn it. Eldrid had warned me, and yet I had still failed to pay attention to what I was doing. If I had been slower in my eagerness to quell the grumbling in my stomach, and not been distracted by Ulfrik, I would have noticed the fork in my hand was smaller than the other one. Why didn't I just grab the closest fork?

Ulfrik laughed. "It's not an issue, my lady. I will forgive such a mistake."

"How merciful of you, *my lord.*" I dripped with sarcasm, but it only served to brighten the light in his eyes.

After I casually changed my fork unnoticed, we ate our meal in silence, stealing glances at one another. His expressions were fleeting, but the way his gaze lingered every time our eyes met had my heart racing.

"Tell me about yourself." He laid his fork and knife on the plate, folding his hands in his lap to stare at me. Giving me his full, undivided attention.

Swallowing nervously like one would before a speech, I distracted myself by pushing my carrots across the plate. "What do you want to know?"

"Everything. Where you come from, who you are, what you did. I want to know what it means to be you."

His tone was so genuine, his words so caring and full of wonder, and yet, I couldn't help but feel the pull of reality.

Cynical was the only feeling that settled onto me, a suffocating blanket. "Why would it matter now?"

He frowned.

"You kidnapped me, forced me into a life without my saying, proclaimed that I belong to you…and now you want to know more about the prize you have conquered?"

His eyes narrowed as he leaned his elbows on the table. "It's not like that."

"Isn't it?" There was poison on my tongue. I was desperate to lash out at him. I wanted to tell him everything I had lost, everything that I could never be. Because of him.

"There are things you do not understand, Phoebe."

I pushed my plate away, looking him in the eyes. "Then enlighten me."

"You're angry, I understand—"

Slamming my fork against the table, I jumped to my feet, staring him down. "I doubt you have *any* idea what I have lost!"

"Then tell me." He said it so calmly, I faltered.

As the anger receded, I took my seat once more, my eyes on my hands in my lap. "My name is Phoebe Wood, I'm twenty-three, I've lived in Edinburgh, Scotland, my entire life." I felt like I was filling out forms, my mind wandering to my endless days of filing and sorting at the hospital.

"Well, Phoebe Wood…this is a world of harsh realities, and although all you see before you is calm, it simmers beneath the surface, like an infection."

"Then why did you proclaim me your mate without even considering what I wanted?"

"If I hadn't done what I did, you would be dead." He had lost all emotion, and yet I knew there was more to be said.

Although the hearth crackled and spluttered, encompassing the room in a blanket of warmth, I couldn't resist the shiver that overcame me. He circled behind me, leaning over my shoulder so his breath tickled my ear.

"My name is Ulfrik Wulfson, I have lived to witness the passing of thirty winters, knowing only the world you see around you."

I mulled over what he had told me, knowing that even with-out an explanation, his words rang true. He had saved me, twice that I knew of, and even if he didn't explain why he did it, he'd been nothing short of accommodating. He never forced me to do anything that I could possibly consider bad or evil.

"Why did you save me?"

My gaze rose to meet his, and the moment our eyes locked my mind went blank. I became lost in the golden hues of his irises, questioning whether this man before me could give me something I had never considered myself worthy of, with Liam, or anyone.

"Some things are worth risking everything for."

Ulfrik's fingers grazed my cheek, leaving a trail of warmth across my jaw. I shuddered in response, locked in place, deciding if I wanted to stop him, and yet knowing, I longed for more. I rose to meet him, my lips trembling.

"Ulfrik…"

CHAPTER

TWENTY

"My lord," said a voice tight with controlled anger. I didn't have to turn to know who had intruded on a very private moment.

"What?" Ulfrik's eyes didn't leave mine, but his hand dropped from my face.

Ogden paused, choosing his words carefully. "Perhaps we should have this conversation elsewhere."

"Speak your concern, Ogden."

His eyes narrowed. "This is highly inappropriate, my lord."

"Last I checked, I was king, not you." Ulfrik's voice was cold, the expression on his face drastically different than it had been moments before. This was a side of him I hadn't been privy to.

Ogden's eyes widened only briefly, as if he couldn't believe his king would respond in such a way. He recovered quickly, a mask settling into the wrinkles of his face as his beady eyes darted my way.

"Is there anything else?" The king was clearly done with the conversation.

The Hand's mouth opened and closed, but whatever else

occupied his mind was left unsaid as he pursed his lips. "No, my lord."

"Then I advise you leave."

Ogden's answering glare could cut diamonds. With a sharp, barely distinguishable bow and a wrinkling of his nose he departed, leaving us to stare after him. I could hear nothing over the pounding of my heart and the crackling of the burning wood. I jumped when Ulfrik leaned over to ask me a question.

"Where did you go?" he asked, amused by my reaction.

I swatted him away like a bug. "Nowhere, let's finish our meal."

The wind howled outside, extinguishing the torches and sconces that lit the courtyard and porches. We ate in silence. The clinking of our silverware against the plates and the sound of the mugs being placed on the table occasionally broke the stillness.

"Can I ask a question?" My stomach was full, my mind clear, and the questions that I had pushed back until now were threatening to burst forth.

Ulfrik leaned back in his chair, his eyes on the far window, where speckles of white drifted chaotically outside. "Of course."

"What was that about?"

The stillness in the air was replaced by a smothering tension, and I regretted even asking. But Ulfrik wanted me to feel welcome here, like I belonged, like I was safe. Ogden's animosity caused me to feel anything but.

An uneasiness settled into his features; the shadows cast by the hearth gave him an edge I didn't recognize. He seemed older suddenly, as if he had seen too much, experienced too much, for someone who was only thirty.

"Ogden doesn't always agree with the decisions I make, and as Hand he has every right to make his displeasure known. But I am also not immune to the knowledge that at times he despises me and wishes that he or Harvaldr were king instead."

A power struggle simmered under the surface of this place, as did any government in the world. Although things seemed peaceful here, I couldn't imagine the type of world that would have met me on the other side of the runestone had Ogden or Harvaldr won in the arena.

"He doesn't seem to like me very much."

Ulfrik scoffed. "The man has never felt the touch of a woman, of course he would envy anyone else." He winked at me and I turned my head away, hiding my blush. "To be frank, however, he isn't fond of the knowledge that the High King seems to have chosen an outsider as his mate."

I perked up. "Seems?"

He sighed. "The moment you were presented to me, I knew what I had to do. Bjorn and Arne, even Ogden or the other members of the court, would have jumped at you like vultures. I had to save you from such a fate, even if it meant that for the meantime you would lose your freedom. I didn't think I'd be having this conversation with you just yet. I thought there'd still be time. But it's good that I can discuss this with you now, to be prepared for the long nights ahead."

Trying not to simmer at the prospect of losing my free will, I twisted at the fact that he had ultimately saved me once again. I was a perpetual damsel, with no real choices of my own, seemingly waiting to be saved.

My eyes narrowed. "What does this mean, though?" It didn't matter if I'd be forced to marry him, since I didn't expect to be here that long anyway. At least, I had hope. Leif said he would be back within a month. I just had to hold out.

"Typically speaking, you would become my bride. The chosen mate of the High King is an accolade and staking my claim so publicly sealed your fate." He said it so casually, with such little emotion, I found bile rising in my throat.

"And I don't get a say in this?"

His eyes softened. "You can deny my claim, but then my protection ends, and anyone can take you for their own."

The idea of Ogden, or Harvaldr, or any of the other kings having their way with me...I knew I had no choice.

"A praell has no rights." The chair slid against the floor as he stood behind me. "But I will not force you to do anything. Ever."

"Are there not certain expectations to be upheld? Surely I could not be allowed to walk around and do as I please forever." *Just a little longer, Phoebe.*

"Marry me, placate the court, and I will let you do anything your heart desires." His voice was dark, his face clouded in shadows.

I snorted and jumped to my feet to face him. "Was *that* a proposal?"

It wasn't like I was against the idea of marriage, to him, or anyone, but I certainly didn't imagine it would happen like this. Liam and I had discussed it. The whole shebang in fact, with a band and fog machine, white-robed tables lined with lanterns and placards of cursive gold-leaf names. Somehow, I doubted that something as grand would happen here, mainly because I was certain I didn't care enough to try. Back then I could imagine a wedding with a man I loved, but here in this strange place as a slave to a man who looked like a Viking warrior?

"I suppose in a way it was." He seemed amused.

My heart hammered the walls of my chest as his eyes searched mine.

He reached out to gather my hand in his, his golden eyes swirling. "I know this is not what you anticipated, and I suspect nothing like you wanted. But for the sake of keeping you safe, would you consider doing the honor of becoming more than just a symbol of my accolades by becoming my bride?"

"I need to go. I'm not feeling well," I said, pulling my hands from his as I stumbled across the room. I shoved the door open with little regard for anyone on the other side, even after I heard a stuttering yelp. I mouthed a half-assed apology as I stomped my way to the front door, startling the guards who stood just beyond it.

Immediately I was assaulted by the raging storm that was but a whistle from within the home. A gale surged, snow and poured from the heavens in a deathly sheet that hid everything from view. My heart sunk knowing I would never know how to return to my home if I couldn't see farther than a few feet in front of me.

"My lady, please, come inside!" called the man whose face I had just smashed with the door.

"Birger." He took a step back from the doorway for the king to appear, his expression sobering. I stared him down, daring him to stop me. "My lady, please. Come back inside." His concern bothered me, more fuel for the flames he had fanned earlier with his ridiculous notion.

"I'm going home." I turned on my heel, striding across the courtyard.

"Phoebe."

His tone caused me to still my hand on the gate, the guards shivering in the storm just beyond it, casting me curious glances. *No.* I hardened my resolve, throwing the gate open and bursting out into the alleyway, following the wall into the city. Ulfrik's ebony hair waving in the freezing wind was the last I saw of him as the world around me went white.

You know that eerie silence that snow carries with it? Even within a howling gale you can hear it, be smothered by it. A blinding blanket with a surprising heaviness that followed every step I took. I knew I had made a mistake, not so much leaving Ulfrik's cozy abode to jump headfirst into an active blizzard—I didn't quite regret that. What I regretted was leaving my coat and scarf behind, even the long-sleeved outerwear would have sufficed. As it was though, my face and bare shoulders and arms took the full force of the biting cold.

I'd never known anything as cold as this. It was far below freezing, and the snowflakes that floated by stuck to my eyelashes, coating my hair in a layer of ivory. I shivered uncontrollably, my chest heaving as I fought for a breath that didn't stab my lungs with an icy grip. My home couldn't be far off, but I knew I couldn't walk around aimlessly for long.

After a while though, the alleyways and houses all looked the same, at least, whatever I could make out through the deluge of snow that came down around me. I hugged myself, knowing full well how futile such a gesture would be as I wandered through the streets.

Everyone else had taken the hint. They were cozy and warm inside their homes, smoke curling from the chimneys. Time was running out, my breathing was now erratic and painful, my skin so cold it felt ablaze, and I was hopelessly lost. I didn't recognize anything around me, and not a soul was near enough for me to ask for help. Even the guards knew better, retreating behind closed doors to see out this storm. I knew it easily rivalled the one that Lucy and I had become lost in.

"God damn it, Phoebe," I growled into the silence.

I cursed my inability to think before I acted, once again finding myself in a predicament I was ill equipped to solve. For all the time I'd been stuck here, I had a vague idea of where everything was. I knew how to get from my house to the stables, or the kitchens and the animal pens, and how to follow the river to the millhouse. Outside of that, the vastness of the city with its twisting alleyways of stone and latticed wood were a labyrinth that meant nothing to me.

My body was stiff, my feet shuffling the snow beneath me. I left a trail in my wake, filling faster behind me than I would have liked with fresh snow. No one ever talked about how suffocating snow was as it came down from the heavens. There was a deadliness in the tranquility it offered, a promise of death. I was hyper aware of the dire mistake I had made, but a quick glance behind me told me there was no way for me to find my way back to Ulfrik. Not that I think I would—I couldn't handle the inevitable remark of a puppy returning home with its tail between its legs. I had too much pride for that.

Enough pride that you would rather die? I hated that inner voice of mine, even though she made sense. I was such a fool.

The shivering was second nature now, so much so I hardly noticed it. What I did notice though was the exhaustion that tugged at my mind and at my body. My feet were sluggish as they trudged a path through the snow; my eyes struggled to stay open in the blinding white.

It had to be around ten at night by now, although it was impossible to tell. In the middle of the blizzard everything was impossibly bright, and yet I struggled to see anything. There was an insatiable urge building within me, begging me to just walk up to the nearest porch.

I ignored the creaking wood as it groaned beneath my feet, settling myself against the door as my legs collapsed beneath me. Exhaustion came on quick; a dizziness lulling me towards the darkness as I shivered into a hazy dreamlike state.

Something moved in the blinding white, and even within my dream I could feel something out there. It watched, it waited, and then it crept closer, blocking the white of the world. My eyes struggled to open, the world fuzzy beyond them, but the softness beneath my fingertips invigorated me. My eyes crept open, as the glare of the frosted world beyond me was dimmed by the brown and grey creature that nuzzled up against me.

"You," I said in a voice that was but a squeak.

The wolf met my eyes, silently judging. It nuzzled against my hand. The warmth gave me enough stamina to tear myself from the nothingness I had crawled from.

I didn't know where I was, or whose house I had taken shelter under, but my hand crept to the doorknob twisting it sideways. The wind caught the door, smashing it wide open, and I stumbled across the threshold, the wolf hot on my heels.

From what I could see beneath snow-coated lashes, the house was laid out similarly to mine—a wide front room that led to a dining area that guarded a back courtyard of rocks caressing a simmering pool. Even under the deluge, the water was just hot enough to avoid snow piling around it.

I paid it little heed, stumbling across the wood to the bedroom on the left. There were no thoughts in my mind, nothing

I really cared for, except the promise of sleep. I didn't bother undressing, falling beneath the blankets as the wolf curled up against me.

"Interesting," came a voice from the darkness.

My eyes shot open as I jumped from the bed, blankets pooling across the floor. Standing before me was a man in riding leathers, his face obscured by a wolf skull, his shoulders bearing a wolf's pelt. Snow clung to him like Velcro, and every movement he made sent small tufts drifting to the floor.

"I-I'm sorry. I was lost in the blizzard; I couldn't find my way home—"

He held up a hand, a light chuckle filling the air as he removed the wolf skull from his face to place on the armoire.

"Leif?" Did my eyes deceive me? Had I gone mad?

"Of all the houses to take refuge at, you found mine," he said, eyebrows raised. "I see you brought a friend with you, too." His eyes darted between my face and the massive wolf taking up the other side of the bed.

"He wouldn't leave," I grumbled.

Leif hefted the bag on his shoulder, letting it slide to the floor as he struck a match, lighting the nearby sconces. The room came alive, heralding a scene reminiscent of my college days. Somehow, I had managed to remove my shoes, flung across opposite sides of the room where one had hit a bookcase, the wounded leatherbound books lying in a heap on the ground.

"You should consider yourself lucky, she doesn't usually like anyone. Except Ulfrik, of course." He seemed not to care for the destruction that I had caused in my wake, and in fact, he seemed to avoid as much eye contact as he could as his eyes swept the room.

My hand glided across the wolf's fur. "She?"
"Skoll."
The wolf perked to attention, eyeing Leif. He extended his

hand, letting her sniff at him before she issued a low guttural noise that had him take a few steps back.

Scooting across the bed to put distance between the wolf and me, I found the floor as I rose on shaky legs. "What was that?"

Leif shrugged as if it wasn't that big of an issue. "I told you, she doesn't take kindly to others."

His words sounded true, or at least, he believed what he had said. It didn't help to make me feel less wary, though.

"What makes me different, then?"

He began rifling through the armoire. "I couldn't tell you what goes through the minds of animals, but you can look at it this way, you have a new friend."

Indeed, once the wolf—Skoll—seemed certain that Leif would keep his distance, she laid her head back down on the bed, eyeing me.

There was an insatiable need for me to clarify things, and my mind was becoming restless from letting him assume what he wanted. "I didn't know this was your house, by the way."

Leif pulled a pair of tawny pants and a matching tunic from the armoire, thrusting them into my arms. "It's not my business to ask such things, but I would consider it common courtesy if you gave me an explanation."

Fidgeting under her poignant stare, I sighed. "I had dinner with Ulfrik last night, it…I don't know, things happened so fast. I had to leave, I needed to leave."

"So, you walked out into a blizzard?" He didn't believe me.

I groaned, tossing the pants and tunic on the bed to grasp the sides of my head in frustration. "I didn't think it would be that hard to find my house, and I was pretty sure I was suffering from hypothermia and I panicked. I passed out on your doorstep and then when I woke this—Skoll—was here."

Leif's face softened. "He cares about you, you know. It isn't just all business."

"It's going to end in tears for him, then."

His eyes lowered. "It is."

Although his demeanor darkened, mine perked up at the hidden meaning in his words.

"Does this mean…"

Leif nodded. "I found a way to get you home."

CHAPTER

TWENTY-ONE

After I changed, I sat opposite Leif at his dining table curled around my feet as the wind continued to howl. My mood had brightened considerably, and I knew it. How could I not be chipper? After all, soon I would be again. With Lucy and Finn and maybe I'd return to town right now I wouldn't even mind seeing my old boss. I'm

"Tell me what you found." A plate of salted fish and of steaming tea sat between us, and I sipped from my cup was playing catch-up with an old friend.

Leif flipped open the leatherbound book that had sitting in front of him for the past hour; every turn of pages exuded a cloud of dust across the table. It was was ancient—the threading had come undone, the spine in tatters, and the marks on many of the pages were so that, in the flickering candlelight, it was as if they had completely.

"In this chapter lies a single passage. There are no only drawings." He laid the book flat, pushing aside the of salted fish so I could see it more clearly. The drawings

191

like those in the cave, made of crimson ink that flowed like blood. It formed the shapes of the moon in all her phases as she danced across the night sky, as well as the passage of the sun, and a stone that pointed towards the sky, etched in markings. He flipped through the pages of the chapter, letting me drink in each drawing. Every one depicted the runestone, combined with different phases and conjunctions of the moon and sun and stars.

"How many books did you look through to find this?"

He leaned back in his chair, a shadow crossing his face. "Too many."

"What does this mean then?" I pointed to a drawing on one of the pages that had a full moon next to a blazing sun. The runestone sat in a field of blooming flowers, with what appeared to be lambs and cattle grazing with their babes beneath.

"From what I've gathered, the runestones become active during the equinoxes and the solstices."

I paused. "That doesn't make any sense though, I came through after the winter solstice."

His lips pursed. "It's possible they work differently on your side. But everything I had read leads me to believe that the next time the path will open is around Ostara."

"What's that?"

He tried to hide the frown, but it was not an easy thing to miss. "The spring equinox, the celebration of when day and night are equal. When the frost retreats and the world warms, when the gods have decided to show themselves once more."

I nodded dumbly.

"A month from now."

A *month*. My heart sank at his words. I was stuck here for another month playing dutiful citizen, while my friends and family mourned, thinking me dead. It was enough for tears to gather, and the sniffling to start.

"You miss your home." No shit.

He fidgeted with the book, carefully closing it before looking me in the eyes. "Listen Phoebe. You have a month left, that's all

I'm asking for. Do what is needed, and like I promised, I will get you home."

And what if what was needed was to marry the king?

"A deal is a deal." I said. That was a road I would cross when I got there—*if* I got there.

"In the meantime." He glanced under the table at Skoll sleeping atop my feet. "I think it's best you return Ulfrik's wolf."

Leaning back in my chair, I folded my hands in my lap, thinking of any excuse I could use not to have to see him again. At least, not so soon.

Leif's eyes narrowed. "Did something happen?"

I threw my hands up. "No, no…no! Nothing like that…it's fine…honestly. It's just me being…well, to put it frankly—childish."

He noticeably relaxed. "Would you like an escort back to your home, then?"

The chair scraped across the ground as I untangled my feet from the wolf and stood up. She stirred to life, eyeing me. "If you could just point me in the right direction, that'll be enough."

Leif smirked. "That works for me, besides, I'm sure Eldrid will find you soon enough."

Oh god, that's right. Eldrid.

"Let's get this over with," I muttered, letting him lead me into the gale that raged outside, snow piled high around the homes.

If only I had walked for another few minutes last night. My home was a straight shot from Leif's, following a latticed tunnel that edged a park of pines and bushes. Although in the aftermath of the blizzard, the world was nothing but white, snow piled high over everything and anything. Few people were brave enough to hazard the howling winds that seemed to turn the tunnel into a vortex.

Skoll plotted along beside me, the snow not seeming to bother her any. Whereas I sunk with every step I took, she seemed to float along the top, her hefty, wide paws serving as built-in snowshoes. My teeth chattered in my skull, but at least I was warmer than the first time I had attempted this. The shivering was tolerable.

By the time I strolled through my front door, I was burdened by a layer of fresh snow, the sight of me nearly unrecognizable in the mirror hanging in my bedroom. Shimmying out of the pants and tunic Leif had graciously loaned me, I dropped them to the floor with a wet plop. With little care in the world, I strode to the hot spring in the courtyard, easing myself into the bubbling waters, letting them soothe and caress me. The wolf curled up at the lip of the hot spring, eyes closing, no doubt content that I would not be going anywhere any time soon.

Now that I had a single moment to myself, my mind raced. I couldn't wait to be back in my own bed, with electricity, and central heating, and plumbing. Or clothes that didn't leave me itchy, and dresses that hugged my body in all the right places, instead of hanging off me like a raincoat. Of course, I couldn't wait to see Lucy and Finn, even my sour-faced neighbour who chain smoked right under my bedroom window, which I always left open. But what I really looked forward to was food. Varied, unique concoctions of art that didn't leave me hungry immediately after.

As if taunting me, the scent of a savoury meal met my nostrils, grilled fish perhaps. There was this Japanese diner down the road from my apartment that made a mean Teriyaki grilled salmon. My mouth watered at the mere thought; even just rice was enough to have me salivating. I shook my head, as if I could shake away the thoughts. I was getting ahead of myself; I still had a month to go. It wasn't like I didn't appreciate the hospitality, I certainly did. But it would be nice to have variety, and choice, and freedom.

Lying my head against one of the rocks, I let the water come to my neck, my eyes closing. The warmth of the waters contrasted with the freezing temperatures just above the surface, and I reminded myself to look into hot springs when I returned home. In the meantime, though, I would appreciate this small privacy I was allowed, these quiet moments all to myself.

The tranquility would not last long, I knew that, but it was broken faster than I had anticipated. First the rapping of knuckles against my door, heavy and with obvious impatience. I knew who it was long before the screeching began.

"Phoebe!" Her voice was a banshee's cry cutting into the gale of the storm.

Fuck.

The door slammed open, her boots stomping across the floorboards as she slid to a halt before the back door.

"Is that…" Her voice wavered, glancing between the hulking wolf that eyed her warily, and where I sat in the pool.

"Hello, Eldrid. Lovely to see you again," I remarked, knowing full well my nonchalance would drive her insane.

"Things go that well with Ulfrik?" She feigned a gasp.

I groaned, rolling my eyes. "I'd rather go muck out the animal pens than have that discussion."

"That can be arranged," she beamed.

"Can I get dressed first?"

Eldrid pursed her lips, folded her arms, and leaned against the wall. At least she was letting me change before dragging me off to get covered in animal muck. I sighed, dragging myself from the warmth.

True to her word, Eldrid handed me a shovel and a wheelbarrow and put me to work in the frozen animal pens. They were easier to maneuver through than the fields, the animals had done half the work for me, stirring the ground into a muddy cesspool that I slipped and slid across like some poop-filled ice rink.

My muscles burned, and I had more blisters on my feet and hands than I cared to count. But by the time the sun was but a streak of gold on the horizon, I had finished. Even in the frigid wind, sweat coalesced on my forehead, beading across my skull. I'm sure I smelt awful, and the mere thought of sinking myself into the hot spring had me sighing with relief. I had one task left, and then freedom would be mine. At least, while Eldrid was preoccupied with the children.

Dodging the mounds of snow that had been shoveled into piles along the sides of the road, I pushed the cart along the length of the latticed fences. Nothing went to waste here, not even the poop, which I learned sometimes had a purpose other than fertilizer. I learnt that a few hours ago when one of the bakers came looking for a pile of cow dung to use to heat her oven. I cringed imagining the scent of animal feces wafting through my house. Some people seemed to feel the same way, because the area designated for animal fecal matter was situated far from the homes in a shack near where the lumber was stored.

As I stood there looking at the heaping mound of frozen poop, I couldn't help but think that the word shack was a bit generous, it was more like two wooden poles supporting a patchwork sail that did little more than keep out direct sunlight.

Heaving the wheelbarrow over the uneven ground, I tipped the contents onto the pile, before sliding it into place next to the half a dozen other wheelbarrows. It didn't make much sense to me, letting something made of wood sit open to the elements.

As voices cut through the clucking of the chickens in the coop behind me, an insatiable urge to find the owners overwhelmed the desire to retreat to my home to soak away my grime incrusted body. The nearest building reminded me of a barn, with its red-tinted walls and high ceiling, but it served as storage for excess supplies. I didn't have to step a foot inside to see the crates and barrels of preserved food and liquids stacked high within. I also didn't have to step inside to hear those voices clearly, even though it was obvious one of them was trying to keep it hush-hush.

I teetered at the edge of the doorway, hidden by a barrel of stacked poles as I peered into the door crack, trying to glimpse who argued in the dark.

"You think you can manage this?" asked a condescending voice that I was all too familiar with. I didn't need to catch sight of Ogden to know it was him who flitted in the shadows beyond the doorway.

His companion, however, was someone I was not familiar

with. I'd been here long enough to recognize a lot of the denizens of the Wolf Clan, if not by name then by voice or sight alone.

"Of course." His confidence was empowering, causing a smile to broaden on Ogden's face.

I shifted to get a better look of his companion, but it was useless. This man, who paced between the shadows and the lit torch in Ogden's hand, was shrouded by the garb of Ulfrik's guard. The leathers adorned with a howling wolf in ghostly white paint, the accompanying skull obscured his face so only his charcoal-smeared emerald eyes peered out into the gloom.

Something else stirred in the barn, and two more people, cloaked in dark hoods, emerged into the torchlight. One was clearly a woman, her figure outlined by a bodice and breasts that even a thick cloak failed to hide. She held hands with the man next to her, who was taller than the others in the barn, squaring his shoulders as he peered down at the guard and Ogden.

"We only get one shot," the man said. His voice was familiar, but I couldn't place it. He was an older gentleman, clear by the way he rolled his words on the tip of his tongue.

"We've been over this dozens of times," the woman groaned, placing her free hand on her companion's shoulder. I knew her voice, too, and part of me screamed Turid. But I couldn't see her face or her hair, and she kept her mouth shut after one look from Ogden.

"You realize one wrong move sends us all to our deaths," Ogden warned, his beady eyes narrowing.

The guard nodded. "I understand, everything is ready. The others are on board, we await your signal."

The guard reached out, clasping his arm with Ogden's. Something glimmered in the darkness, smeared across his arm like a patch of dirt. There was a mark there, faint in the flickering light, but sharp enough for me to make out the unmistakable shape of a feather. Bile rose in my throat, my head was heavy and my stomach queasy. This wasn't right, whatever was going on here. For the life of me I couldn't piece the information together, couldn't understand what I was bearing witness to. Whatever it was though, I felt compelled to tell someone, anyone.

As I inched backwards, my eyes locked on the people within, my back collided with something, sending planks of wood plummeting to the ground at my feet. My hands shot to my mouth, stifling the gasp that I knew was coming.

"Someone's here." Their heads whipped around to the doorway, the guard reaching for the sword at his hip.

Shit.

"You idiot, you left the door open," Ogden hissed.

They marched on the door, their eyes gleaming with a look I didn't want a translation behind. Somehow, I didn't think they were up for a chat, and with little regard for what was around me, I sent the remaining poles crashing to the ground as I made a run for it. I couldn't return the way I had come, if I did, they would have easily seen me, and something told me that Ogden wouldn't be too pleased to discover I was their snooper.

A covered alleyway ran parallel to the barn on the other side, returning me to civilization, to people, to witnesses. I was certain they hadn't seen me; my paranoid glances every now and then yielded no angry beady eyes following my retreat. I didn't rest until I was far enough into town that even if Ogden came across me, he couldn't pin the intrusion on me.

As I slowed to a walk, confusion lit the eyes of the few people who stopped to glance in my direction. My lungs burned, and my legs ached, and I had little doubt that the blisters on my feet were intact. With hands on my knees, I bent over in the middle of the road, desperate to still my beating heart and make sense of what I had heard.

What *did* I hear?

A pair of scuffed brown boots appeared in my view, and I followed them upwards to see black hair sticking out from beneath a yellow scarf that framed a pair of sapphire eyes.

"Not where I left you," Eldrid said, eyebrows raised.

"I-I just…" I stammered, not sure what to say, or even if she was the right person to say it to.

She held up a hand, silencing me. "I don't care what you're doing here, just tell me you finished cleaning the pens."

I nodded dumbly, my heart still racing.

"Good. Because you've been invited to dinner, again."

I froze. "With whom?"

A smirk brightened her face. "Our beloved king, of course."

Fuck. Or maybe not…if anyone needed to hear what I had just witnessed, it would be Ulfrik.

"Listen, I know something happened at the last dinner. But have no fear, you won't be alone this time, it's a sort of a politicians' dinner."

Ice settled in my veins, and it had nothing to do with the weather.

"Who else will be there, Eldrid?" It felt like a stone had settled deep in my stomach, my heart once again beat louder than a teenager who got their first drum kit for Christmas.

She thought for a moment, "Well…all the important members of the Wolf Clan. I've never been to one, but I imagine it would have Leif, Harvaldr, and Ogden, obviously."

She kept listing people that were going to be in attendance, people I had heard about or met randomly going about my chores, but I stopped caring the moment she mentioned Ogden. Something bad was going to happen, I was certain of it, and suddenly all I felt was a crushing weight on my shoulders. Whatever he was talking about in that barn, the plan he was desperate to keep secret, I knew it was going to happen tonight.

CHAPTER

TWENTY-TWO

Eldrid once again assisted with getting me ready. Clothing me in a fine woolen forest green dress embroidered with a silver thread at the hems, and a long-sleeved auburn overdress clasped above my breasts which were perked up by a cream laced bodice that for all intents and purposes had me looking like a medieval escort. That wasn't helped by her choice of rouge on my cheeks and a splash of crimson on my lips. The charcoal line she had drawn around my eyes accentuated the emerald depths, contrasting with my hair that was braided to below my ear, where it could wave freely across my shoulders. She seemed more proud of her work than last time. Although she made no mention of the previous outfit which sat in a basket by the front door with my other soiled laundry. It pained me to abandon it so, since it was a present from Ulfrik himself.

I needed a distraction, again. The silence stretching on and on was causing me to grind my teeth just to keep my anxiety in check. "You going to teach me what fork I'm supposed to use this time?"

She paused in her incessant fluffing of my hair. "Ah, yes…

well…you have to forgive me for that, I haven't been around another Traveler in so long, I forget simple things like cutlery etiquette would be foreign to you."

I rolled my eyes. "Forgive this peasant for her indiscretion."

"Okay, settle down! This is a formal dinner after all, with some pretty big names. First and foremost, though, we're going to have to fix your posture." She looked me up and down. "Sit in that chair over there like you would at dinner."

I did as she asked. Skoll stirred to life, following me into the front room as I took my place at the table. Eldrid's eyes widened in disbelief, chewing on her bottom lip as she debated how to say what she so desperately wanted to say.

"Yikes. Okay, first—shoulders back. Head high, arms tucked in, and for all that is holy please don't put your arms on the table." I groaned but did as she commanded. "Also, you don't sit that far back. I don't care how uncomfortable it is, but you sit on the edge." I adjusted myself again, and finally content with my posture she rifled through the drawer for cutlery. Arranging it around me as she pointed to each fork and spoon and knife, she told me which to touch first, which to touch last, and heaven forbid I didn't dab my lips gently with the napkin instead, as she so delicately put it: *smear my face like a barbarian.*

"Now, for the finishing touches." Digging in the bag that hung from her waist, she produced a dagger with a hilt that shined in the darkness gathering around us. A linen cloth was wrapped tightly around the blade, but I could tell it had been treated well. She passed it to me, a smile tugging at her lips.

"Did you make this?" My fingers dragged over the hilt, the ivory sheen mesmerizing.

"Yeah, with some help from the blacksmith, of course. Like I know anything about smelting." She scoffed. "My gift to you."

Unraveling the cloth revealed an iron blade with a running wolf etched into the blade itself. "This is…incredible, Eldrid…I can't take this." I didn't deserve this.

She snorted. "I won't be hearing any of that nonsense. I had this *made* for you."

There was no arguing with Eldrid, I knew that all too well. My eyes roamed over the delicate design, from the smooth hilt which fit perfectly in my palm to the blade which seemed almost like an extension of my hand.

"I carved it from an antler I found last spring," she said.

My heart melted. "This is amazing, Eldrid. Thank you."

"Of course. But wait!" Fishing through her bag once more she pulled out a leather belt, a matching scabbard secured at its side. "This is for you, too."

She fastened it around my waist before I could react, leaving me staring at it with a dumb expression on my face. As if sensing my confusion, she pointed to the scabbard where it sat against my left hip. "It fits in there."

The blade slid into the leather scabbard like a glove, the reddish-brown fitting perfectly complimenting the white and green and red of my outfit. I strode across the room, pausing before the mirror in my bedroom. She followed closely behind.

"What?" she asked, peering over my shoulder as I stared at my reflection in the mirror.

I shook my head, a replay of what I heard in that barn on constant repeat in my mind, bouncing around my skull like a tennis ball.

"It's nothing."

She smirked. "Nervous, huh?"

You could say that. "A little."

"Well, if it makes you feel better, Ulfrik asked me to chaperone the praell tonight."

Even though I supposed I was no longer considered one of the praell, it calmed me knowing Eldrid wouldn't be far.

"That does make me feel a little better." I offered her a smile.

"Okay, enough wasting time." Her eyes darted to where Skoll sat patiently by the front door. "Let's get going."

The weather here never ceased to keep me on my toes. The sky was clear, the firmament alive with shiny dots of green and blue, purple and white, but a darkness hovered on the horizon, a smear of ink against the twinkling lights. The wind was murder, as it had been for days, the cold biting of it permeated my flesh and sank into the very bone. Even as we walked past the smiling faces of content citizens, it amazed me that anyone could find joy in such a merciless atmosphere. Lucy and I always joked that Edinburgh, like London, was a sunless, drowned landscape that sucked the joy out of everything. But I would do anything to be back there under the grey of a Scottish sky. I'd long since fulfilled my Norwegian dream.

Ulfrik's home was abuzz with company. There were guards stationed every few feet, their charcoal smeared eyes hidden behind their wolf skull masks. Stableboys escorted horses from the house to the stables down the road, as the guests that had just arrived milled about in the courtyard, awaiting their king.

Eldrid and I took our spots in the back, hidden in the sea of visitors. A group of praell, noticeable by their muted yellow clothing and unadorned hair, caught sight of Eldrid and rushed to greet her. Bodil was among them, her tiny form drowning in a dress that I couldn't help but compare to a sack used for potatoes.

I found myself alone in a sea of people, awkwardly huddling beneath a rowan tree, whose name I knew only because of the significance it had for the Wolf Clan. The clusters of fruit that resembled scarlet blueberries and hung from the spindly branches were hard to forget. Not just for their looks, but for the warning attached. You only ate them if you were suffering from constipation.

The crowd stirred to life in the blink of an eye, and I followed their gaze to the front door where Ulfrik stood. Skoll trotted to his side, joining Hati there. With a dismissive wave the wolves disappeared into the house.

"Welcome, friends!" He beamed, ushering the crowd inside, and I caught sight of Eldrid and the other praell gathering around the doors, taking coats, and assisting others inside.

I followed the crowd within and Eldrid gave me a wink as she took my coat, hanging it among the dozen others on the wall. I was prepared to follow the hallway to the end, to the room where I had dined before with Ulfrik.

But the crowd wasn't going that direction, instead, they turned a corner on the left that I hadn't noticed tucked behind the coat rack, leading to the other side of the house. A pair of solid oak double doors halfway down the hallway opened to a high ceiling hall adorned with ancient oil canvases of scenes that meant nothing to me and mounted skulls of wolves. Some were exceptionally large, unnaturally so.

On the left side of the hall was a roaring hearth, on the right was two small doors that I was sure led to the kitchens. At the far end of the hall was a wall of glass that stretched to the wooden ceiling, revealing a winter wonderland beyond. The crowd dispersed before me, praell directing everyone to their seats at the wooden table that encompassed nearly the entire room. It had enough space to comfortably seat twenty or even thirty people, but tonight there were just over a dozen.

Ulfrik had taken his seat at the head of the table, a long backed solid chair adorned with a deep brown pelt that easily overshadowed the measly wooden chairs that surrounded the rest of the table. I knew what I would see, and yet I couldn't help but locking eyes with Ogden at the king's right-hand side. His eyes narrowed, but they did not reflect the slight tug of his lips, like he held a secret.

A sickening knot had settled in my stomach, an uneasiness that made it that much harder to drag my feet across the room to my seat. A praell led me to the empty seat on Ulfrik's left beside Leif. As I took my seat, he offered me a smile, which turned to a frown as he watched someone take the seat on my right. Harvaldr. He greeted me with a dismissive nod, his gaze drifting across the table to Ogden. That feeling in my gut worsened, and I couldn't help but fidget with the napkin in my lap.

I sat at the edge of my seat like Eldrid said, my shoulders back, head high, hands coiled in my lap.

Leif leaned over, whispering to me. "You look lovely tonight."

"Is that your way of saying I don't normally?" I taunted.

He grinned. "Still lively, I see."

Even the light banter couldn't extinguish the warning that sat in my subconscious. As everyone took their seats, Ulfrik stood, addressing the table.

"Welcome brothers and sisters, to the first official dinner of the Wolf Clan this year. I pray the gods bless us in our endeavors."

He sat, motioning to the praell that stood around the room between the many guards.

"Let us eat."

They disappeared behind those small doors behind me, emerging moments later with trays of food. Although it smelt delicious and looked even better, I had lost my appetite. This would serve me well, seeing as it was dainty and feminine and *proper* to have zero appetite. At least, that's what I remembered from my history classes, and one of the many reasons there was a stereotype amongst wealthy women to have fainting spells. Corsets and lack of food did not make a good combination.

A light conversation droned in the background, a somewhat comforting buzz to the clinking of glasses and cutlery on plates. The crackling in the hearth would normally distract me, calming the anxiety that sat in the background of my mind, buzzing around me like an irate mosquito.

Ogden seemed just as distracted as I, but I knew it wasn't for the same reasons. A man like that wouldn't know what anxiety was if it slapped him in the face. No, this man was fidgeting for another reason. His eyes darted from the untouched food on his plate, to the guards surrounding the room, to the double doors we had just walked through. He seemed to avoid the gaze of everyone at the table, including his king who was digging into the braised beef on his plate, oblivious to his Hand's shifty eyes.

I couldn't shake this feeling of dread. I followed his beady eyes to where they lingered behind me. With what I hoped was the most subtle of movements, I turned my head to my left. Harvaldr was deep in conversation with his companion, oblivious to anyone else around him. If he wasn't who Ogden was looking at, then whom?

There was a pattern here, and as I watched his eyes wander around the hall, I noticed it was deliberate. His gaze drew the same path around the room, and a few minutes of observing him made me realize it wasn't on his untouched plate, the guards, or the doors. It was on the lack of knives beside his plate, it was on the same six guards around the table, and it was on the row of sconces that led a path around the room to the roaring hearth and to the double doors we had walked through.

I wasn't insane, I couldn't be.

"Leif," I whispered, my heart beating wildly in my chest. I needed validation, I needed to warn someone.

He paused mid-bite, a shadow passing over his face as he observed mine. He leaned over. "What is it? Are you alright?"

"Something is wrong." My voice felt so quiet, like it wasn't my own.

"Perhaps you just need some fresh air, shall I call Eldrid?" His face was etched with concern, but for the wrong reasons.

"Listen Leif. Something is going on…something bad…" A praell interrupted us, filling our glasses with the hearty mead that had been warming our throats. And I realized, dulling our senses. The praell disappeared back to the kitchen, and I glanced around to confirm no one was focused on our conversation.

"There's no shame in being nervous, Phoebe. But we mustn't let it rule us," Leif said in a reassuring tone.

He wasn't going to listen unless I revealed everything, I steadied myself, my eyes never leaving Ogden. "Earlier today I was cleaning the animal pens, and I saw Ogden with three other people in the storage barn, they were talking about something… something they were going to do tonight…something *bad*."

Leif's mouth twisted. "And what do you think you heard?"

"I know it sounds ridiculous, but I've seen enough television to know what a mutiny sounds like." There, I said it.

He placed his glass on the table, sitting back, his gaze hardening. "That's a bold claim, Phoebe. I hope you realize what it is you are saying. Citizens are entitled to their discontent, to their opinions. Even someone like Ogden."

"Leif—"

He held up a hand, his gaze sweeping the room.

Maybe I was just paranoid, maybe I was trying to find any excuse I could to feed my distaste for this world that was forced upon me. But something still didn't sit right, no matter what Leif said. Of course, people were entitled to their opinions, and it was rather progressive that a society like this seemed to tolerate such a thing, but I was not immune to how quickly such things dissolved into chaos. It started with thoughts, then words, then shared feelings, and from there almost always became physical. It was human nature, and even though I had my doubts at times, I didn't dismiss the people of this world as human. After all, in some ways, they were just like me.

Leif stirred beside me; eyes wide as they searched the covered faces of the guards surrounding us. His hands disappeared beneath the table, and for a split second my heart stopped as I realized they gripped the hilt of a hidden knife secured to a leather band around his thigh.

"Leif?" I hissed.

"What's so interesting that we're whispering?" Ulfrik smirked, leaning closer.

"Fuck."

It was the only word that escaped Leif's lips as the entire room plunged into darkness, the stirring of footsteps in the darkness was all we could hear around us. Screams erupted in the hall, the crashing of plates, the scraping of chairs, and the sound of slicing and slashing filled the air. A moment later a sickly, sticky wetness spilled across the table, pooling around my fingers, soaking into the sleeves of my dress. That tangy, coppery scent that followed told me more than sight ever could. This was a coup.

TWENTY-THREE

Although darkness had engulfed the room, what little light from the moon outside pierced the floor to ceiling windows. Enough of the room became visible in a single second, betraying the contrast of a simple dinner moments before. Crimson pooled on the table, flecks sprinkled across the floor and walls, bodies slumped unmoving over plates of unfinished food.

Across the table from me Ogden made his move, a flash of light glinting from an unsheathed dagger in his hand as he pushed forward for Ulfrik. A scuffled had broken out around me, and in the briefest of moments where the moon was not covered by clouds, I could see Leif by my side. His hands were wrapped around wrists that held a bloody dagger inching closer and closer to his throat.

There was no thought, no second guessing, as I pulled the blade from my waist and struck the man in the throat. He gurgled, choking on his own blood, his grasp loosening as fell to his side, releasing Leif.

He hit the ground, unmoving, his eyes slowly closing. Moonlight shifted, revealing the hand that grasped the knife that nearly ended Leif's life. It was the same man from the barn, the one who promised Ogden he would fulfil his end of the bargain. The black ink of the feather was a stark contrast to his pale skin.

Grabbing Leif's hand, I shouted, "Ulfrik!"

He nodded dumbly, still in shock, but he understood what little I was able to say. It was written across my face, in my eyes, on my tongue. Ulfrik was in trouble. We struggled to get across the room, our feet slipping in the blood. Skirmishes had broken out, people fighting for their lives. But Leif knew what was at stake—if Ulfrik died, it was over.

Feet stampeded by us, bodies colliding against our own, but we paid them no heed. I followed blindly behind Leif, focusing on his golden hair in the darkness. I didn't know where we were headed, but I knew he led me from the hall, sneaking through one of the doors on the left. Whichever one we took didn't lead us into the kitchen. It led us into a dark corridor with a single door at the end. Leif nodded at me as we burst into the room, daggers drawn.

A single sconce was lit, casting ominous branched shadows across the room, illuminating a desk and two chairs within. Against the far wall—which took over an entire wall—were two shadows, struggling in the darkness. We could hear the grunting, see the sweat on their skin, and the glint of daggers suspended above throats. Ulfrik against Ogden.

"Ulfrik!" I cried out as Leif and I ran to help him.

The shadows shifted into the light, Ogden losing his grip as Ulfrik flung him across the desk. He slid across the wood, crumpling to the floor by the door. He shrugged it off, rising to his feet as two guards burst through the door. Their eyes darted between their king, and his Hand.

"Seize him!" Ulfrik seethed.

Leif and I stood behind our king, too stunned for words. Ulfrik's chest was heaving, blood dripping from a cut above his eye. His gaze was murderous, the shadows coalescing around him, giving him the illusion of an apostle of death.

"Guards!" he raged, pointing to Ogden. "Seize this traitor."

We held our breath as Ogden dusted himself off and pointed to the king. "Kill him."

The guards raised their swords, pointing in our direction.

"What is the meaning of this?" Ulfrik's hands balled into fists at his side, as two more guards burst into the room, closing off our only means of retreat.

"Your reign has come to an end, my lord," Ogden sneered, a vile smile lighting his traitorous face.

Ulfrik held his head high, peering down at Ogden from across the room. "You pathetic weasel, you think the Wolves would follow you?"

Ogden rolled his eyes. "Not me."

"Who, Harvaldr?" He chuckled.

He stood aside, letting the guards move forward. My gaze caught sight of something familiar, the knot in my stomach twisting. I knew one of those guards, and as he came closer, the light from that single sconce flickered, revealing the feather tattooed along his forearm. This was it, this was their plan, and I had done nothing to stop it.

"Does it matter? Such things mean nothing to the dead." As Ogden finished his sentence, the guards advanced, blood trickling across their blades and leather garb.

Ulfrik placed his arm in front of me, gathering me behind him. Tears welled in my eyes as I realized, he was going to fight them. Leif stirred beside us, and I watched as he pulled a dark ball from his bag, twirling it in his hands. Ulfrik glanced down at me, our eyes met for a single moment, and something stirred within me, a strange sensation followed by a voice.

Extinguish the light.

It startled me, having forgotten that such a thing was even possible. I had blocked it from my mind before in the throne room, putting it down to me being tired and scared and maybe just a little insane. But it was real, it had happened. I didn't know how, but right then, I was lucky it was still a thing.

I waited, counting the steps to the sconce on my left. I didn't have a plan at all, my eyes sweeping the room for some way to extinguish it, when I noticed a cup on the floor. Somehow it had survived Ogden's toss across the desk, and with most of the liquid still sitting within.

Taking a deep breath, I steadied myself. My heart roared in my ears, my palms sweaty, my legs shaky. Anxiety swelled as I repeated what I had to do over and over in my head, like a movie reel on repeat. *You can do this, Phoebe. It's just spilling a drink.* I could do this.

The guards closed in, left foot, right foot, three abreast at the tip of the desk. I dropped to the floor, scooping the cup up, the liquid sloshing inside. In one fell swoop I dashed to the wall, spraying the contents of the cup over the sconce. The moonlight lit the room as Leif gripped the ball in his hand and thrust it towards the advancing guards.

We plunged into pure darkness, a fine mist of ash enveloped us as a hand gripped mine, yanking me into the wall. Except, where that wall should have been it no longer was. I didn't have time to think about it as we spiraled downwards. The world became cold, damp; a mothy stench gripped the air around us, settling into our clothes and hair.

The grip on my hand tightened as I was dragged further into the depths of a lightless abyss. I didn't know who grabbed my hand, but I was certain it was Ulfrik or Leif. It was firm, but reassuring. The only noise in the shadows was the slapping of our shoes against stone and our panicked breathing.

We ran for so long in the darkness, I began to doubt even being awake. Without light, without being able to see, my world was an echo, and as the adrenaline faded, all I could focus on was the feeling of moistness within my shoes. The blisters that had only just healed were surely split welts by now. I didn't speak, I didn't slow down, even as my head spun, my legs ached, and I turned numb.

After a time, when I was almost certain I had forgotten what sight was, light sprouted around us. My companions slowed, our awkward jogs turning into an ambling walk as the tunnel we had been stuck in lit up. Fragments at first, shimmering spots across the stone wall, until the patches grew, consuming entire sets of bricks. They flickered, like fireflies, performing a chorus of waves that traveled the length of the tunnel far into the distance.

They illuminated Leif and Ulfrik, who still grasped my hand, in hues of red and gold and blue and green. Like Christmas lights they bathed everything around us in a subtle glow. It was oddly soothing, and eerie.

"What are these?" I breathed.

Ulfrik glanced over his shoulder at me, a shadow in those golden eyes. Leif saved him from having to speak.

"Legend says they are one of the *vaettir.*" His voice was flat, devoid of emotion. "A spirit that guides us."

"It's a damn bug," Ulfrik ground out.

Why did you say anything, Phoebe? They just lost everything, and that's the first thing you say? Fuck. Silence reined as we continued through the tunnel, the flickering lights doing little to illuminate the shadows that had gathered within us.

Somewhere ahead the stone sloped upwards, the tunnel widening into a rotunda of mossy stone held back by a dome of latticed wood. I had no doubt the structure was ancient, perhaps even predating the High Keep. We stood in the middle of the room, our eyes skyward, where the intertwining wood created an impenetrable grate to the world above. The breath of fresh air trickling downwards was a relief, and I drank as much as I could. Although I soon learned I wished I couldn't, as a breeze brought with it the scent of ash, and the sounds of those we had left behind.

The longer we stayed within the rotunda, the worse the sounds became. We could hear the pitter patter of panicked feet in the snow above, and the individual cries of men, women, and children. Whatever Ogden had planned, it didn't involve just Ulfrik, it involved the entire city, the entire clan.

Ulfrik dropped my hand, striding across the room to an archway in the fall wall. Leif darted in front of him, blocking the entrance.

"Move," the king growled.

Leif shook his head. "I'm sorry, my lord, I can't do that."

Ulfrik smashed his fist against the stone beside Leif's head, his voice dark. "I will not hide in the shadows while my people are being murdered."

The pained expression on Leif's face caused an ache in my heart. He didn't want to do this; he didn't want to stop the king from helping. But even I knew better.

"My lord, we both know if you make yourself known now, your body will be among the dead. You cannot help the Wolves if you do not draw breath."

The king's expression shifted from anger to pain, he knew Leif's words were true. Whatever was happening above would be far worse if he did not survive. While there was no body for Ogden to claim, the city was still his. Ulfrik backed away from his shaman, staring at the grate where the faintest of light from nearby sconces trickled in, mingling with puffs of snow.

Leif ran his hand through his hair. "Besides, if anyone is to blame, it is me."

Ulfrik whispered. "Why?"

Leif's eyes lingered on me. "She warned me, and I did not listen."

The king's head whipped around, his gaze boring into me. "You *knew*?" His hands balled into fists at his side, as he barely contained the rage that bubbled within.

I raised my hands. "I didn't know…not for certain…" Swallowing the lump in my throat, images of the faces of those at the table, and the praell that served us flashed in my mind.

Ulfrik closed the distance between us an instant, cornering me against a wall. "What did you know?"

The sounds of boots against the stone told me Leif stood somewhere behind the king, but like me he was hesitant to do anything. So, I had to, divulging the scene in the barn, the words I had overheard, Ogden's behaviour at dinner. Everything I thought it could mean. I left no detail out, no matter how minor. When I was done, Ulfrik's demeanor had softened, his clouded gaze far off as he retreated from me.

"I can't say I didn't suspect Ogden's disdain at my leadership, or that there were times where his loyalty was in question. But I didn't expect this." The king massaged his eyes, as if he could rub away the headache that no doubt was forming.

"What does Ogden want?"

Leif squinted up at the grate. "I have no doubt he and Harvaldr have conspired together, but neither of them wants the throne. Whatever they have planned was for the benefit of another."

Rubbing my arms to bring back the warmth, I stood by Leif's side. "Who?"

"One of the other kings," Ulfrik said.

Leif and I looked to our king, matching expressions of worry and fear on our faces.

"What do we do now?" I asked.

Leif glanced around the rotunda, his gaze lingering on the three archways on either end, as if trying to remember where they all led.

"We journey to the High Keep," Ulfrik said.

"Is it safe, to use these tunnels?" Although the wood and stone was in extraordinary shape, the idea of venturing once again into the darkness to only die by cave-in had my anxiety getting the best of me.

Leif nodded. "The knowledge of this undercity has been the burden of the line of shamans for centuries. Only we know of it."

I couldn't help but notice the carve marks on the stones. "What is this place?"

"The old world," Leif said, pointing to the etchings on the wall. There were no pictographs here, only runes carved into the stone, into the wood. "We're not sure who built it, but an entire world exists under the cities, connecting Forest, Cave, and Cliff to the High Keep. A labyrinth of twisting corridors of stone and wood, filled only with ghosts."

He led us to the far end of the rotunda, where an archway carved with runes of flickering bugs—vaettirs—illuminated it into a ring of blinking light.

"This path should lead us to the Conjunction, where we can take another path into the High Keep."

"*Should?*"

He shrugged. "I'm confident in my assessment."

Ulfrik scoffed. "Worst case scenario you complete the job Ogden set out to do."

Leif grimaced.

"We should get moving," I interrupted.

Leif led us down the tunnel, which was mercifully illuminated by the twinkling of the creatures perched on the walls. No one said a word, and it made it that much harder for me to stay quiet. I had so many questions. Why would the kings be fighting over the throne now, after it was won fairly in the arena? How long would it take to get to the Conjunction from here? What was the plan once we got to the High Keep? But I kept my mouth shut and focused instead on putting one foot in front of the other.

I cursed the fact that I was stuck with slippers on this unforgiving stone, and that the clothing I was in gave little freedom of movement. I felt like a damsel, heralded by her knights down a hall. I had done nothing. I could have saved all of them, I could have prevented this. But I hesitated, and innocent people died for it.

My fingers trembled, my heart beat loud and fierce, and slowly I realized I was fighting a losing battle. There was nothing I could do. Leif, Ulfrik, everyone else who has lived here, they were natural born warriors. They weren't put out by a broken strap, dry skin, or existential crises. They dealt with what they could and didn't bother to complain about it. I was soft and weak, and because of it the people I had come to care about were dead or dying. Eldrid, Bodil, Turid, the other praell whose names I couldn't even bother to remember. We had left them alone, to suffer whatever caused the screaming and shuffling above our heads.

"Phoebe?" Ulfrik's golden eyes swam as he regarded me. He reached out his hand, fingers collecting the fresh warm and salty tears that trailed across my cheeks.

I hadn't realized I had been sobbing. Lost in my own thoughts it didn't occur to me that anyone else was here with me, even though I could see them right in front of me. *There you go again, Phoebe, causing problems for others.*

"I could have saved all those people in the hall…" My voice broke.

His arms wrapped around me, drawing me in close, a hand gently stroking my back.

"There was nothing you could have done." His words were solemn, but I could tell he believed what he said was the truth.

Of course, there was nothing I could have done. Because I *am* nothing. The tears fell silently this time as I rested my face against his chest, my arms wrapping themselves around his back. My head swam, with images of those who sat eating beside us at the table, who had conversations filled with laughter and smiles with their friends, and the scent of that musky pine that Ulfrik always wore.

Leif's footsteps retreated, as his voice called from the dimly lit darkness ahead.

"We're here."

Pulling myself from his embrace, I offered Ulfrik a tight smile.

"We'll make this right, Phoebe. I swear to you."

I wanted to believe his words, but the more I thought about it, the harder it was to believe that the king could do anything now. After all, what could three people do? Taking a deep breath, I pushed it from my mind as we met up with Leif.

The tunnel once again opened into a spacious room of stonework held back by latticed wood. Runes were carved into every surface, but this room was very different from the rotunda. There were benches and chairs and tables and what I assumed used to be beds, spread throughout the entire room. In the middle sat a stone circle, and within, ash. People used to live here, and perhaps even died here.

Leif must have read my mind as he said. "Our entire

kingdom used to be Cave City, before the chieftains decided they wanted to differentiate between the Wolves and the Bears and the Eagles."

Ulfrik snorted. "It only served to divide us more."

Ignoring his king's remarks, Leif navigated his way through what was left of an entire civilization. The room was easily the size of six homes in the Forest City, and just like the rotunda, a trickle of moonlight and a sprinkle of snow drifted through grates on the ceiling.

"Where does this lead?" This archway was different, it didn't open into an endless tunnel, it opened into a thin rectangular room, a wall of impenetrable stone rose before us. There was no latticed wood, no grate in the ceiling, no evidence that this room served any purpose.

The gleam in Leif's eyes told me otherwise. His hands grazed the length of the stone, pressing against the individual bricks. *What is there, a special stone you press to reveal a fake wall?* I barely contained the snort, my hand covering my mouth in case Ulfrik or Leif glanced in my direction.

"There it is!" Leif exclaimed, and sure enough the moment his fingers pressed against the most normal of stone bricks, a grinding noise filled the air. A moment later a portion of the wall swung open, revealing another room within. "This way."

This room was made of wood, old and rustic, with nails jutting out of it. It was dusty, the air stale, and as the stone wall shut behind us with a click, I couldn't help but compare it to walking through the skeleton of a long dead monster. At the end of the room was another unassuming wall, but Leif didn't need to play with this one to see where the hidden button was. His fingers hooked underneath a part where the wood jutted out, but instead of pushing it open, he rasped his knuckles against the wood. There was an answering knock, and Leif didn't hesitate to push the wall in, revealing a pile of hay and a young man.

"Asger?" Ulfrik asked.

The man gasped, "My lord!"

Leif waved at them. "More important things are at hand than introductions. Tell me what you know, Asger."

His eyes briefly met mine before returning to Leif and the king. "Ogden and Harvaldr came through the gate moments ago with Eagle scouts."

"No…" Leif's eyes went wide, but Asger continued, addressing the high king.

"Arne controls the High Keep."

CHAPTER

TWENTY-FOUR

The muscles in the king's arms tensed, his jaw set tight.

Asger threw his hands out. "Wait! I know your instinct is to retake the keep, but those loyal to the Wolves have been rounded up and remanded in the dungeons."

While Leif pondered the information, Ulfrik spoke. "Do any of these tunnels lead to the depths of the High Keep?"

The shaman nodded. "Yes."

"Then we will save our people first and take the fight to Arne." His eyes glowed fiercely in the moonlight that flitted through the cracks of the wooden beams around us. I was certain we were in a barn somewhere.

"Asger, if any Wolves make it to the Conjunction, send them here." The young man nodded, and the door shut.

Retracing our steps to the main room, we took another archway. It led through another tunnel that plunged downwards in a spiral staircase into damp and moss and cold. At the very end of the staircase was a landing surrounded by stone. Leif fingered every brick, until one gave under his pressure, revealing a long room that was just wide enough for us to walk through single file.

219

Leif held a finger to his lips, and we peered out into the gloom. "We have company."

It was a mirage of sorts, a cloth that was just thin enough for us to make out shapes beyond it hung in front of us. A statue with locks that flowed in an invisible breeze just like its dress sat in front of the cloth. We sat huddled together, slowing our breathing, careful not to make a sound as footsteps echoed nearby.

Moments later a patrol of four guards walked by, my head swam and my breath became jagged as I begged for them not to see us. I didn't need to ask to know the feathers and beak masks meant they were Eagle Clan. Leif and Ulfrik didn't have a hint of panic in them, they were calm and precise, no doubt planning their next movements carefully. We waited for the guards to pass and turn a corner at the end of the corridor before we stepped out from under the cloth. Leif made a beeline for a doorway nearby, and a sigh of relief spread across us when it swung open on silent hinges.

Like the room below the earth, this one was long, and filled with tables, chairs, beds. Except unlike under the world, they were behind unyielding iron bars. There was a stirring in the shadows against the walls as people pressed forward, clamoring over one another as their frightened eyes beheld their king.

Leif and Ulfrik ran for the nearest cells, their hands gripping the men and women clad in wolf pelts and skull masks. Fiddling with the doors, the locks clanged loudly against the metal, but were proving to be invincible to anyone's efforts of sheer strength. We needed a key.

Running my hand along the walls, I followed them to the end of the room where a battered desk sat. It bowed under the weight of dozens of scrolls, sacks of coins, jewelry, and empty alcohol bottles. Rummaging through the drawers led to knick-knacks and mysterious stains that stank of liquor and, in one drawer, what I strongly suspected was vomit.

Then, as my hand shifted over a pile of soiled rags, I heard a clink. My heart raced as I threw the rags to the floor, sifting through them like a child in a candy bin. *I heard them; they were right there! Where were they?*

Just as I felt the creeping, overwhelming sensation of the walls crowding in around me, my heart beating so hard I thought it would stop, my fingers grazed something cold. Grasping at it, I pulled out a ring fitted with an assortment of iron keys. Soaring to my feet, I raced to the nearest cell, fidgeting with the key in the hole. By dumb luck—or the fact that every key was the same—the key turned, the latch clicked, and the lock opened. I ran to every lock of every cell, freeing the Wolf Clan to mutterings of praise and gratitude.

When the last person had escaped, Leif and Ulfrik brought them up to speed, gathering whatever information they didn't know, and placing the missing pieces into the puzzle. Letting the clan get reacquainted, I stood by the door, inching it open slowly to peer into the hall. Somewhere in the distance I could hear the guards returning.

"We don't have much time," I hissed.

Ulfrik raised his hand, and the nearly three dozen wolves quietened, forming a line behind their king. Leif peaked over my head, giving the all clear as we ran into the hall, disappearing behind the curtain as the first boot appeared around the corner.

Leif led us through corridors and passageways strewn with rubble and broken beams, jutting nails, dust, and stale air. We were silent, save for the sounds of our boots and shoes against stone and dirt.

Emerging within the large room, Ulfrik instructed everyone to spread out and rest. Leif waved Ulfrik and me to the room that opened into the barn. Standing before the wood, we held our breaths as we awaited the resounding knock. The wood creaked as the door swung open, and we were greeted by Asger. He offered us a smile, and stood aside, revealing a dozen Wolves.

"My lord!" they whispered, fear in their eyes and voices. Some had blood caked to their clothes or skin, or hair. Their eyes were wide, their skin pale. Whatever they had endured was echoed in the eyes of their king.

"Let's go," Leif said, ushering everyone including Asger into the large room.

Once everyone had settled down, Ulfrik went around the room, addressing everyone by name, and asking if they were alright.

"Where do we go now, my king?" asked a girl who wasn't much older than Bodil. She clutched her arm to her chest, where a bruise had spread across her wrist.

"Where *can* we go?" asked a frightened woman.

Good question. If Ogden and Harvaldr had taken the Forest City, and the Eagle clan controled the High Keep, where could we go? Even Ulfrik knew his people could not hide within the undercity for the rest of their lives, fearing every noise and light and shadow. That was not living.

A Wolf Clan guard spoke up, his voice cracking as he tried to disguise the immense pain he was in from a wound near his ribs. "My lord, if I may?"

Ulfrik nodded.

"When I was stationed at the Conjunction, I overheard members of the Bear Clan." He winced, a sharp intake of breath helping him to steady himself. "Bjorn may still be on your side."

The king chewed on this information, shadows crossing his face. The room fell into silence, all eyes on Ulfrik. Inhaling deeply, he looked to Leif, who gave him a solemn nod. I knew nothing about the Bear King, with his full beard and twin axes. There was no telling if he could be trusted, Ulfrik and Leif knew that. They only had the word of a single guard to go on, and that was simply what he had overheard. For all we knew, we were walking into a trap, into servitude or death.

"To Cave City."

CHAPTER

TWENTY-FIVE

There was an uneasiness in the air as the group meandered through the stone tunnels, wonder lit their faces as they beheld the blinking bugs. Whispers of prayers, and the word *vaettir* were repeated on their lips as they followed the tunnels south. Past the Conjunction, High Keep, the docks, and deep into the mountain.

We only stopped when we were assaulted by the freshest, coldest breeze. It was carried on a mournful gust that filled the tunnel like a vortex. We pushed onwards until we could see light shining from the end of the tunnel.

The tunnel widened, the very end tinged white by a fresh snowfall, and shadowed by towering stones that were too perfect to be natural. As we got nearer, the stones took the shape of obelisks, engraved with pictographs of bears and trees and people dancing.

"We're here," Leif said, leading us out into the open.

Standing on the edge of a cliff, we crowded close to one another to get a glimpse of the sprawling metropolis before us. Situated in a steep valley between two mountains was a city hewn from solid rock. Flickering sconces within told us there were people down there, going about their business as if everything was fine.

"Welcome to the Cave City," Leif said.

Murmuring arose in the crowd, and Ulfrik raised a hand, silencing them. With a flick of his wrist they followed Leif as he traversed a decrepit stairwell hewn into the side of the mountain. It was covered by towering trees, scraggly bushes, and giant boulders that I'm sure with the slightest earthquake would roll into the stairwell, crushing us.

The stairwell levelled out onto a rocky platform that, if you weren't certain what it was for, seemed bland and useless. Overgrown with weeds and loose stone, no one would think twice to glance back the way we had come. Even when I did, the stairwell was hidden from sight, as if it didn't exist at all.

Certain that we wouldn't be ambushed the moment we left the safety of the platform, Ulfrik pointed to a circular hole carved into the cliff at the other end.

"That is where we will find Bjorn." His voice was grave, but I could almost taste the hope in his tone.

As we neared the entrance we heard the shuffling of many feet and the clanging of metal. Within the blink of an eye, we were surrounded by men clad in armour, shoulders and backs suffocating under thick animal pelts, with skulls of sharp fangs casting shadows over faces smeared in blue paint. In their hands were grasped shiny axe heads over deep wooden handles.

They whooped and hollered, a chorus that drowned out the tiny frightened voice within my mind. It all faded in the blink of an eye too, into an eerie silence only broken by the wind as it heralded the footsteps of a single man. A man I had not seen in a long time.

Clad in leather pants and a split tunic painted with a bleeding bear's heart, held in place by metal pieces carved into bear heads, twin headed battle-axe secured in his right hand, was the king of Cave City.

His brilliant golden eyes sat shadowed behind bushy

eyebrows that framed the face of a true warrior. Ulfrik was muscular, but he was agile, built for speed—endurance. Like a wolf. Bjorn was the face of Canadian lumberjacks, Norwegian Vikings, or Mel Gibson as William Wallace. He was built like a truck, like a bear.

The man towered over everyone, peering down at us like ants. "The High King has graced me with his presence." His voice was deep, dark, and full of suspicion.

Leif fidgeted beside me, his gaze behind the Bear King. Ulfrik paid us little heed, his head held high as he spoke to who should have been his inferior.

"We have a problem, brother."

Bjorn smirked. "I should think so."

A vein bulged in the High King's neck. "I have been betrayed, and even now our dearest brother warms my seat with his treachery."

The Bear King nodded, but there was something he held back from saying. I could see it in the tensity of his muscles, the dismissive posture, in the gleam of those golden eyes.

"There is much to discuss, brother, but if you came here expecting my help, then you are mistaken."

Ulfrik's eyes narrowed as he took a few tentative steps forward. The guards raised their axes, closing in tighter around us.

"What is going on?" Ulfrik flexed his hand, preparing for a fight.

Leif stirred beside me, his hand on the knife at his waist. My hand drifted downward. If the High King and shaman were edgy, then I had every right to be as well. But the people who were caught up in this, the innocents that escaped with their lives, huddled behind us, certain that if a fight did break out, they would be slaughtered.

"I do not doubt that you are a beloved High King, loyal to the people and the crown. But I have my doubts about the results of the arena that brought you that title."

"You did not question my victory when I won it, or the decade after," Ulfrik ground out.

The Bear King ran the thumb of his free hand along one of the blades of his axe. "I believed you had won it fairly."

"And what has made you think I haven't?"

Bjorn's eyes glittered. "Arne."

"Our brother poisons your mind with fallacies to justify his illegitimacy," Ulfrik nearly spat, agitation clear on his face.

"Suppose they were lies, Ulfrik. But there is only one to settle this—"

"Oh no," Leif muttered beside me.

"I call upon the gods to witness the Besting."

The sharp intakes of breath around me told me everything I needed to know. This did not bode well for anyone. Leif moved in front of me, holding out a hand as if trying to usher me from view.

Bjorn stirred at the sight of me. "You have brought your mate as well, fantastic. The circle is complete then. You may take refuge this night in the Low Path." He nodded to a circle of smaller caves further down the cliffside.

It was not a request.

"It doesn't have to be this way, Bjorn," Ulfrik said.

I did not miss the hint of sadness that touched his features. He hardened his resolve, but whatever doubts he had dissolved when his eyes lingered on me once more.

"Prepare yourself, Ulfrik, for tomorrow, we fight."

Bjorn disappeared into that hole in the wall, his personal guards following after. Ulfrik made as if to follow, but the rest of the guards crowded around us. In the nicest way possible we were forced to march along the ledges of rock to a set of ten homes carved into the face of the rock. Every home was the same, adorned with a row of beds, couches, and basins of slowly trickling water.

As we were ushered into splitting up, the Wolves banded together quickly to give Ulfrik, Leif, and me a place to ourselves. The moment everyone was playing along, a man emerged from the darkness, rushing for Leif.

Leif turned just as a man wrapped his arms around him, his eyes wide.

"Leif!" he exclaimed with a shaky voice.

The shaman frowned, until recognition softened his face. "Father!"

I looked to Ulfrik with wide eyes, who beckoned me to take the seat opposite him at a table in the house. The father and son caught up, their voices lowering to murmurs every time a patrol walked past the entrance. It was clear that although they lived in the same city, they hadn't seen each other for a very long time.

Ulfrik tore his gaze away, his words gruff. "Are you okay?"

Was *I* okay? Part of me wanted to strangle him. He was branded a traitor, a cheater, and a liar, lost his home, his people, and at daybreak…I shook the thoughts from my head. My heart beat wildly, exhaustion tore at me as the empty fumes of adrenaline I had been riding all day dissipated.

"Are you?" I cringed at how snappy I sounded, but it elicited the most unusual response from him.

He chuckled.

"How can you laugh?" My voice was but a whisper.

Ulfrik leaned back in the chair. "I accept my fate, whatever it may be."

I felt disgusted. "How can you be so nonchalant about this? You could die tomorrow; your people could die."

There was sadness there. "I cannot hope to take on Arne without the support of Bjorn. If this is the only way to do so, then I accept."

"What is even going to happen?"

"We will fight, the chosen of the Bear versus the chosen of the Wolf."

"Chosen?"

His gaze blazed a trail from my hair, across my face, to my eyes. As if he was trying to drink in the sight of me, like he would never see me again.

"Ulfrik," I said.

Leaning forward with elbows on the table he kept his voice low. "The kings, their mates, and captain of their guard."

My heart skipped a beat, goosepimples crawling across my flesh. "I will have to fight?"

Ulfrik nodded. "I will fight Bjorn, you will fight his mate, and Kipp will stand instead as captain."

"I thought the kings had not officially chosen their mates." I was panicking, my eyes darting around the room like escape was an option. I knew it wasn't.

Ulfrik shrugged. "As far as I was aware, you were the only one. It seems things have changed drastically in the last few weeks."

My hands balled into fists. "I did not ask for this." I sounded pathetic, I knew that, but this wasn't the deal. I didn't agree to fight to the death to honor someone I had no intention of marrying.

Hurt flashed across his face like lightning. "And I wish it could not be so."

There was a shuffling of feet by the door as three guards armed with axes and torches appeared at the doorway. "We request shamans."

"What for?" Leif's father asked.

One of the guards fidgeted. "Frea's babe has come early."

Leif and his father stirred to action but paused at the doorway as Leif looked to his king. Ulfrik nodded, and with that they were off, leaving Ulfrik and me alone. The king leaned back in his chair, surveying the cupboards hewn from stone on the wall beside us.

"Are you hungry?"

His blasé attitude unnerved me, but my stomach replied in my stead. He took it as a 'yes,' rifling through the cupboards. Setting down a bowl and two cups on the table, he procured a jug of water from the fresh spring that ran through the rocks in the kitchen. It was like a chute, a primitive aqueduct carrying the water from somewhere nearby into every home. It was genius.

Pouring water into the cups, Ulfrik pulled a sack from a cupboard above the sink, taking his seat opposite me.

"Bjorn may be a little battle hungry, but he is not inhospitable."

Pulling on the strings, Ulfrik placed several plump red apples into the bowl between us.

"Are you sure those haven't been poisoned?"

"Doing things as tradition demands is a trait of the Bear King, he would never stoop so low."

"And yet he questions you winning the throne in a fair match."

Ulfrik grabbed one of the apples, twisting it in his palm. "Arne is cunning, devious, like a snake he fills your head with delusions. Bjorn doesn't trust him either, but he can't be seen as weak or taking sides without fulfilling his oath."

"And what is his oath?"

Footsteps sounded outside our door and our heads whipped around, watching as a patrol walked by, torches in hand. As their footsteps receded, Ulfrik cleared his throat.

"The Wolves have loyalty, the Eagles have cunning, and the Bears have strength. Each of us have our strengths and weaknesses."

"So, the bear clan are mediators?" Like Switzerland.

Ulfrik nodded. "The Wolves have always had a tenuous relationship with the Eagles, and although I cannot blame them for the animosity, it all stems from a single 'disagreement' more than a hundred years ago."

"Disagreement?" Somehow, I doubted it was something so simple.

Ulfrik rolled his eyes. "In that case, a Wolf did cheat in the arena."

I hated being right.

"Is Arne now using that to his advantage? To force a confrontation, to sow the seeds of mistrust among the Wolves and Bears."

A tight nod. "Now you know why we must fight tomorrow."

An uneasy silence stretched between us.

"So, what? The clans have been distinct and separated since then?" How can this kingdom operate thinking segregation would work? If they wanted their people to be united, then the clans really needed to be. There needed to be Wolves in the caves, and Bears on the cliffs, and Eagles in the forest.

"Sort of. The High King before me sought to reunite the clans, in a way, by creating the Conjunction. A space for them to mingle and realize there wasn't that much of a difference between us." I could tell he thought highly of the man who wore the crown before him, but it was obvious he held back a part of the story.

"And yet, in the Forest City it seems there are only Wolves."

His face twisted. "The Wolves are fiercely loyal, territorial even."

Not always.

"Except with Asger." Except with me. And Eldrid. My heart ached, hoping that she managed to escape, that it wasn't one of her screams we heard.

Ulfrik offered me a smile. "Asger was born Wolf."

My hand paused over the apples in the bowl, "Then why does he wear the feathers, the beak, the brand?" Even now my mind replayed the image of him taking refuge two houses down from us. He still wore the feathered cape, the beak secured by leather straps across his mouth, his chest adorned with the white paint of a screaming eagle.

"That is a complicated story that perhaps you should ask him yourself."

My mouth twisted. "I don't really know him."

"He remembers you, though."

I frowned.

"That day I rescued you from the lake, you took refuge in a stable by the wall. Asger worked in that stable, it was because of him that I found you in time."

It seemed I owed Ulfrik *and* Asger my life.

His eyes strayed to the bowl of red fruit. "You should eat. I know it's not much, but tomorrow you won't get a chance to." He bit into the apple in his hand, the sudden crunch waking me from the road in my mind I was becoming lost in.

"When does it start?"

He swallowed. "We gather at dawn."

I leaned back, my eyes drifting to the corner of the room where a stone hearth was alive with crackling flames. Although I had never been, these caves reminded me of the houses you'd see on travel brochures for Santorini, in Greece. It was a bucket list destination, and yet, under different circumstances, I felt like I would have preferred the cold yellowed stone of these caves in the mountains over the whitewashed rock of the Mediterranean. I'd never get the chance though. Even if Ulfrik survived, I didn't stand a chance. I had a whole two rounds of practice with Ulfrik, and I never came close to besting him. If living here had taught me anything, it was that these people were warriors. They stayed fit if not to fight, then for survival. My black belt in Karate would serve me little here.

Tears welled in my eyes and I tossed my head back in frustration.

"Phoebe."

His chair slid back, and he was by my side, palm held before me. I placed mine in his and he pulled me to my feet, embracing me. He was warm, firm, comforting, and I allowed myself this rare moment to just enjoy it. I didn't sob, I didn't choke, I sniffled as I wrapped my arms around him. I let myself enjoy that quiet moment under the mountain, just two people in the silence.

CHAPTER

TWENTY-SIX

We awoke to the warbling of birds in the trees outside the caves, their song heralding the arrival of dawn. The horizon was still dark, not even a tinge of twilight, and Ulfrik allowed me to bathe first. The hot water soothed my skin and aching muscles, but not the fluttering that anxiety brought on as it welled within me like a tsunami preparing to crash to shore. Nothing could relax me today, not the fire burning in the hearth, not the fresh air.

"What are these?"

I fingered the leather, admiring how beautiful—and deadly —it was. There were many different pieces, for the chest, shoulders, legs, and arms. My head swam as I imagined trying to dress myself without Eldrid's assistance. I should have paid more attention. But then again, none of her personal classes involved arming yourself for battle.

"The Wolves' ancestral fighting leathers." His eyes glittered as he spoke. Hidden memories danced behind those eyes. But that was a conversation for another day. That was, if we survived.

"Where did you get these?" Of everyone we had rescued, no

one carried bags or fancy armour like these. I couldn't imagine where they had come from. Certainly not the Bear Clan.

"Herleif procured them from the High Keep."

"Who?"

A smile tugged the edge of his lips. He must have realized that there wasn't any way for me to know who that was. "Leif's father."

The Shaman of the Bear Clan just walked into the Keep and took the High King's battle armour? "How did he get in and out of the Keep?"

"The same way we did—the tunnels."

Leif mentioned the shamans were the only ones with the knowledge of the undercity, the labyrinths that stretched beneath the earth. I always assumed he was Ulfrik's shaman because he was the last of his kind.

"I know it probably doesn't matter, but how did Leif become shaman to the High King?"

"For us, it certainly does matter. The shamans have their own ascension ritual, separate to the rest of society. Whereas the kings fight in the arena for their title, the shamans attune to the runestones. I couldn't tell you where they go, what happens. To someone like you and me, they appear to be in a deep sleep. When they awake however, a decision has clearly been made. When Harleif, Leif, and the other shamans came to, it had been decided. Whatever had happened, Leif had won. He secured his position as the Shaman to the Wolf Clan, and Shaman to the High King."

"There are more?" Leif always made it sound like he was the last of his kind.

Ulfrik nodded. "There aren't many, perhaps only ten spread throughout our kingdom. I can't imagine how many exist elsewhere."

The air vibrated around us, reverberating through my chest. Ulfrik's back straightened as we watched the barest of gold and red and blue twinkling on the horizon. Dawn was approaching, and the drums were our warning. Time was running out.

"We should prepare," he said.

Separating the piles of leather, he handed me one, giving me the privacy of the bedroom to change. I felt terrible for taking the bed last night, even more so since he'd been relegated to the couch. The last night before battle, and the High King was sleeping on a lumpy couch in the living room while a stranger took the bed. It was odd though that out of all the houses the Wolves were crammed into, Ulfrik and I were given the one with a single bed. It would have been more awkward had Leif returned during the night, but he had insisted on spending it with the Bear, helping her birth her first child. And although Leif didn't admit it, Ulfrik and I both knew he wanted time alone with his father.

There was no delaying it any longer, even as I stared at the pile in utter confusion. Stripping the beautiful dress Eldrid had laboured over, I let it crumple to the floor. I started with the pants and tunic, pulling them over aching muscles and skin that was stretched tighter than I was used to. I had lost a lot of weight since arriving here, but the plus side was that I had discovered muscles I didn't know I had. The belt Eldrid had made, with its scabbard that hid that deadly blade she had commissioned for me, fit perfectly through the holes in my pants, balancing delicately on my hips. The remaining pieces were where it became complicated. There was a vest, and miscellaneous pieces with their straps and clasps and buttons and layers. It was all too much, and all the while the drums beat a steady rhythm.

This was real, this was happening. My heart pounded in my chest, my fingers trembled as I tried to secure the clasps around my waist. I groaned in frustration, my eyes closing as I tossed my head back, seeking to control the emotions that boiled beneath the surface. Footsteps entered the room, and a soft voice spoke.

"Here, let me help," Ulfrik offered. His hands gently pushed mine away.

He was gentle and calm, placing the leathers on my shoulders, my forearms, my shins. Tightening the straps, securing the clasps, threading the laces through holes. When he was done, he lifted the ivory pelt from the table, securing it around my shoulders.

"You seem to know what you're doing," I said, more to break the silence than anything else, Ulfrik seemed to understand that.

"You'll be fine, you know that, right?" he said.

My eyes watered. "It's not me I'm worried about." Not entirely a lie, I was distraught that my choice was being taken away from me, that I might never get home now, my body would lay under the earth in this strange world. I worried for my brother, my best friend, for Ulfrik, for Leif, for Eldrid and Bodil, and all the other members of the Wolf Clan.

"This is not a fight to the death." His voice was tight.

I said what he avoided saying. "But people may die."

He nodded. "In war, there are always casualties. Whether that is death, or something else."

An urge welled within me, stronger than anything I could control. So, I didn't, letting my fingers rise, brushing gently against the king's cheek. His eyes blazed, a heat spreading across his cheeks, mirroring my own.

"I won't let you die," he said.

My heart stirred. "If we survive, I'll consider your proposal."

His answering smile melted my nerves, his body pressing against mine. If we had more time, if I had more time, maybe I could imagine a world where I lived—ruled—by Ulfrik's side. But we weren't afforded the luxury of privacy, footsteps outside the door pulled us apart from one another.

Leif strode into the house, carrying a bag that clinked every time he moved. Behind him was Kipp, the newly anointed Captain of the Wolf Clan guard.

"Finishing touches," he said, pulling out jars and vials to place on the table.

Mixing the powder of one jar with a vial of liquid, he created a thick, black paste. Murmuring words, almost like an incantation under his breath, he drew a line around Ulfrik's eyes, then Kipp's, then mine. They looked menacing, deadly, the golden of the

King's eyes and the bright blue of Kipp's were a stark contrast to the charcoal smear.

"As well as this." He pulled out three cloths that were delicately hiding something firm beneath and handed one to Ulfrik, to Kipp, and to me.

The cloth unravelled like it was wrapping paper and fell apart to reveal a shinning ivory skull of fangs. Ulfrik embraced his shaman, pulling away to tie the cloth over his mouth, securing the skull atop it. Kipp repeated the process with little issue. When it was my turn, my arms turned to spaghetti, and somehow, I had forgotten how to tie a knot.

"May I?" the king asked. My reply a simple nod.

Ulfrik held the cloth in his hands, pressing it gently against my mouth. Gathering my braided hair over my shoulders, my eyes met his as he tied it behind me, his fingers grazing the nape of my neck. Raising the mask of fangs to sit over the cloth, his fingers again trailed over my neck, slow and with purpose.

Could he see how it affected me? The hitch in my breath, the redness spreading across my cheeks, the warmth of my skin under his fingers. There was a hunger in his eyes, that I was ashamed to think matched my own.

"It is time," Leif said with a heavy voice.

A sliver of magenta highlighted the mountain, casting shadows as the sun rose.

"My lady?" Ulfrik said, offering his hand.

I placed mine in his. "My lord."

A healthy crowd had turned out. Men, women, and children of the Bear Clan gathered in their doorways, their murmurs on the wind an eerie reminder of what was about to happen. The Wolves followed us close behind, as the kings met in the valley below the caves. The decline was hard, the path hewn from the rock, trampled by centuries of foot traffic, was now coated in snow and ice, that quickly turned to slush beneath our boots.

There, in the darkness between the mountains, trickled a

ribbon of struggling water. It cut through a bed of pebbles that hugged the walls of the cliffs, creating a tunnel of shadows and frigid air.

What a place to die, I thought morbidly.

As we took our places on either side of the stream, a shaft of light brushed the side of the mountain, lighting the space around us. I was able to see the Bear King now, in all his glory—from the skull he wore over his head, the pelt draped across his shoulders and running down his back, to the brilliant blue paint slashed across his face like someone had dipped their fingertips into the bowl and slid it across his skin. He was more exposed than Ulfrik, arms bare, chest on full display. It seemed counterintuitive to me, giving someone so much access to your vital organs. But perhaps they knew something I didn't.

Bjorn strode forward, and Ulfrik mirrored him, the stream the only obstacle between the kings.

"Brother," they echoed.

Bjorn carried a sword whose hilt was fashioned into the shape of a wolf's head, and Ulfrik carried his brother's battle-axe. I hadn't noticed Ulfrik carrying the Bear King's weapon, and I certainly didn't know how or where Bjorn procured a sword that belonged to the Wolves. Their exchange was slow, careful, as if neither wanted to accidentally nick the other before their time. Something unspoken passed between them, in their golden eyes. I could feel the sorrow in the air, permeating off them like incense.

The kings motioned with their right hands, and the captains of their guards walked forward, facing one another. Kipp was smaller than his opponent, and younger. Years of experience was etched into the scars and hallowed eyes of the man behind the bear pelt. I didn't know Kipp, but if I had to bet anything, his inexperience would prove fatal, but he would last longer than I would.

"Captain," they echoed to one another. Kipp's voice shook, and my heart ached for him. He grew up in this world, such things would be normal to him, but I could imagine his thoughts probably echoed mine. *Why me?*

They exchanged long swords, the blades glinting in the filtering light of the newly awoken sun.

Leif whispered over my shoulder. "Address her as mate." He handed me a short sword; the blade deceptively light. "You present this to her, hilt first. And Phoebe?"

"Hmm?" was all I could muster.

"You'll do fine, just breathe. You are souls of fire; you do not break."

The kings motioned with their right hands, Ulfrik to me, and Bjorn to a woman who until now was hidden behind Leif's father. We strode forward, and with every step I took, I counted down the moment until my death. Standing before one another, eyes blazing as brightly as the hair on our heads, our voices rose at the same time.

"Mate."

Bjorn's mate was dressed like me. Her charcoal hair, tips dyed a faded red, was braided tightly against her head. Not as red as mine, but I suppose I now understood Leif's comment about 'souls of fire.' Her mouth was obscured by a cloth and bear skull, a pelt cascading across her shoulders, and thick leather pants and tunic left no skin open to the frigid air, or to my blade.

Even muffled under the cloth, her voice sounded so familiar. But I couldn't quite place it, I also didn't get the chance. A horn sounded nearby, startling me. The people who had joined us—Leif, Herleif, and Asger— retreated up the cliff, but their eyes focused on us. Bjorn, his captain, and his mate put distance between us, weapons gripped tightly.

A drumming, low and deep, echoed through the ravine. It was static, reverberating through my bones, setting goosebumps to rise across my arms. This was it. Ulfrik may well stand a chance, Kipp, too, if he got lucky, but me? I knew my fate; I didn't need to raise my sword against this woman to know she would best me.

You had a good run while it lasted.

All along the cliffs our observers, our witnesses, Bear and Wolf alike, peered down at us. They were blackened dots observing us, and part of me thought this was what it must be like for the tiny bugs in the vivarium at the zoo. It made my skin crawl, knowing my every move was watched, and judged.

Within a heartbeat, the drums stopped, and the kings began circling one another, keeping the stream between them. It wasn't deep enough to stop anyone from crossing, and from here I knew it would be a struggle to get over your ankle if you waded through. But it seemed to serve as a boundary, the defining part of this whole ordeal.

The crowd that haunted us from above was silent as the graves the losers would lie in when this was over. Ulfrik stopped, planting his feet into the ground. Bjorn smirked, hefting his mighty axe over his shoulder. A cry escaped his lips, one mirrored by the High King. They closed the distance between them, weapons raised, colliding into one another with the sound of scraping iron and struggling grunts.

I was stunned, locked in place. The kings traded blow for blow, their skills with their weapons plain for all to see. They were well-matched. A shadow twisted by my side, and Kipp darted past me, running to meet the sword of his opponent. They dodged left and right, Kipp one move ahead of the Bear captain. Bjorn's mate strode across the stream like it was nothing, twirling her sword in her hand like a toy.

Now, it was my turn.

There was little time to plan anything as her arm raised, sword glistening in the light. She charged, and it took everything in me to parry her blow. The vibration traveled from the blade, sending an eerie sensation rattling through my core. It made me feel sick, my anxiety sitting like a layer below my skin, ready to burst. My lungs worked overtime, trying to pump just enough oxygen into me that I didn't pass out. I was certain, however, that if I didn't pass out, I'd succumb to a panic attack instead.

I heard the cry, the clanging of iron, and then, the silence. The woman who stood across from me paused, her eyes on something behind me. Putting a few feet between us by backing up slowly, I turned to see what had drawn gasps from our audience on the cliffs above.

It was Kipp, pierced at the end of the long sword of the captain of the Bear Clan's sword. His face was twisted, blood dribbling from his mouth as he tried desperately to free himself from where the sword had punctured his chest. It was a fatal wound. I knew it, the captain knew it, and Kipp knew it. Yet he still tried, still struggled with blood-soaked hands to free himself. But his movements became jerky, uncoordinated, slower and slower. He wobbled on unsteady feet, teetering to the side before falling to his knees. He said something I couldn't hear, the captain nodding in response.

Ulfrik and Bjorn looked on, an unpleasantness across their faces. It was clear it was not the outcome they wanted, but it wasn't unexpected. The Bear captain bowed, pulling his sword free from Kipp's body. With a sickening sound, he fell sideways, the light draining from his eyes, his body limp. The captain removed himself from the ravine, heading back up the path to the audience above.

There was a moment of silence before the king's raised their weapons and went back to exchanging blows. If I could have watched, instead of participated, I would have been on the edge of my seat, my body tense as I prayed for Ulfrik's win. But I couldn't focus on him, not on the way his hair swished every time he raised his sword, the way his muscles bulged under his leather armour, or the intensity of his golden eyes, and the way he held himself.

I almost didn't evade her blow in time, my feet skidding on the rocks, my shoulders aching and forearms stinging. I couldn't afford the distraction, that was my fault. If I didn't want to end up like Kipp, there was no excuse for allowing Ulfrik to fill my mind like that.

My opponent retreated, long enough to let me find my feet.

My hands shook, the sword heavy in my sweaty palms. This wouldn't end, until one of us was dead—or dying. Steeling myself, I had come back to present just in time to jump back, avoiding the tip of her blade as it sliced through the air where I had just stood.

She grunted, the rocks beneath her feet shifting, sending her tumbling into the stream behind her. This was it, now or never, I would never get another chance. I charged for her before I could give myself enough time to think about what I was going to do. I knew myself too well to underestimate myself now.

She wasn't expecting it either, thrusting her sword forward. My body reacted faster than I could, sidestepping the blade to collide with her. We tumbled into the icy water, letting it pour over our faces as we scrambled over one another like children at a water park. We were clumsy, the rocks slippery. My back scraped the stones as she tried to grapple for height, but I struck out with my sword, the tip slicing into flesh.

She cried in agony, her grip loosening on me as she wrenched the sword from my hand, sending it clattering to the shore. I breathed deeply and, with my fist tightly clenched, rammed it into her stomach. She doubled over, a groan escaping her lips as I smacked the sword from her hand, sending it into the stream. She didn't expect any of this, and I certainly didn't either. There was no time for me to think it over. I counted every breath I took, and now I steeled myself as I bucked beneath her, sending her flying over me. As she was sprawled on her back, I gathered my legs beneath me, crawled across the rocks, and snatched her sword up.

I straddled her, her own sword against her throat.

"Do it!" she growled.

"I don't want to kill you," I exhaled, my body swaying from exertion.

"Do it, claim your victory."

I shook my head. "No."

Her free hand grasped my wrist, driving the blade harder

against her throat. Blood trickled across her exposed skin.

"No one else has to die."

Her eyes narrowed. "If a decade of karate didn't save me then I don't deserve to live."

My heart skipped a beat, spots clouded my vision as I realized who it was I fought, whose blood stained my hands.

"Lucy?" I gasped, my breathing erratic.

CHAPTER
TWENTY-SEVEN

Her brown eyes widened, as her shaking hand released my wrist to pull the mask from her face, tossing it to clatter against the rocks beside us. It was her; it was Lucy! My childhood friend, my best friend, the sole reason I was here, the sole reason I was fighting.

She was so different, yet still the same. The red dyed curly hair now faded to an almost pink, the beautiful brown eyes on impossibly smooth skin the shade of the night that had recently disappeared. It was her.

"Phoebe," her voice shook, her lips trembling.

I tossed the sword aside, gathering her into my arms, the façade fading as I burst into tears, not caring who saw or heard. I didn't care. Lucy was here, she was alive, she was well, and most importantly, we were together again.

"I thought I lost you," I wailed, my voice breaking as I pulled the mask from my face, letting it get lost among the rocks with her own.

"Fuck," she breathed, her grasp unyielding, wrapping around me like a boa constrictor.

There were voices rising around us, a mix of shock, concern, and an ounce of outrage. I ignored them all. Nothing existed for me outside this single moment in time, and the anxiety that had been building to boiling point faded away, replaced with a comforting blanket. It didn't matter what happened here on out for me, as long as Lucy was by my side.

I pulled back from her embrace, searching those eyes. "What happened?"

"God damn, I don't even know where to start. So much has happened since that hike, Phoebe." That was an understatement. "It doesn't even matter. I don't even care. I thought you died…" Her voice broke, a shadow crossed her face, replaying memories that she clearly would have preferred to forget. "When you fell off that cliff into the ravine, I was trying to find a way to get you. There was a cave, and stupid me thought 'Oh, hey a cave, maybe this leads down.' Down to you. But something happened. I don't even know, and next minute I was here, in a cave and this man clothed in a bear pelt with an actual bear by his side was just sitting there, staring at me."

I heard everything she said, repeated it over and over in my head, and even with my heart still racing and adrenaline pumping through my veins, all I could focus on was that Bjorn had a bear. *Focus on that later*, I reprimanded myself.

"Lucy…this entire time, you were right here, literally a stone's throw away. I was fighting to get back home. I was afraid you would die in the storm, or you'd get to the car and find that I wasn't there or lead a search team back for me. I was fighting to tell you I was still alive."

"I found the Bears, and you found the Wolves. What cruel twists and turns fate has given us."

I frowned, what a weird thing for her to say. Lucy wasn't the type of person to say things like that or believe in fate or that everything is planned. For her, if she wanted something, she believed she had to work for it.

My eyes glistened. "It doesn't matter, anyway, because now we can go home together."

Her face fell, muscles tensed, the shift in her demeanor had me pulling back to stare into the eyes that she kept hiding.

"Lucy?"

She took a deep breath. "I didn't think I'd have this discussion, Phoebe…I honestly didn't even think I'd ever see you again."

"What are you trying to say?"

Her gaze drifted to where Bjorn and Ulfrik stood, weapons hanging from their hands as they watched us, confusion marring their handsome sweat-beaded faces.

"I don't want to go home."

Fuck.

My world crumpled around me, caving in, suffocating. My mind repeated her words over and over: *I don't want to go home.* She didn't stutter, didn't hesitate, she was set in her decision long before I came into play.

"Lucy…" My voice felt so far away.

Rocks shifted under their boots as the kings joined us. Neither of them was sure what to make of the situation, hesitant to speak.

"We can discuss this later, there's more important things at hand." I wasn't going to argue, but I thought having my best friend stay behind in a world we knew nothing about was kind of important. At least to me it was.

Bjorn walked forward. "Explain, Yrsa."

Lucy hesitated, a weak smile on her tired face.

"*Yrsa?*" I whispered.

Ulfrik spoke. "It is common for Travelers to take a different name."

She smirked. "I'm surprised your name is still Phoebe, to be honest."

Eldrid also changed her name, assimilating within the culture so she wouldn't stand out. I couldn't imagine willingly naming myself anything else. I was Phoebe Wood, daughter of Jillian and Reginald Wood, sister of Finn.

Footsteps echoed around us, rocks clattering and dust billowing as Herleif and Leif joined us.

"What's going on?" Herleif asked, brows furrowed.

Bjorn cocked his head. "It would appear the mates know one another."

"Both with hair touched by fire, one with skin of snow, and the other with skin of ash." Ulfrik mused.

The coincidences were not lost on me.

"Regardless, finish it," Herleif said, nodding to me.

Finish it? Did he want me to kill my best friend? I didn't think death was the only outcome, I thought I only had to *best* her.

"I refuse," I said simply.

Lucy nodded, her chin raised in defiance. "Phoebe has won, I surrender."

Herleif shook his head. "That's not how this works, that's not how the Besting works."

Planting my feet into the ground, I stared him down. I didn't care that he was Bjorn's shaman, or Leif's father. I wasn't going to fight my best friend, and certainly not until death.

"Our laws exist for a reason, and we must abide by them."

"Why?" Lucy asked.

Herleif looked between her and the kings, an incredulous glint in his eyes. "It's not done. It has been this way for centuries. The true Besting, death may not be the desired outcome, but here amongst the stone, the winners must be clear."

I looked to the audience that had tripled in size since I had last looked up. They gathered down the paths now, blocking the sun and snow from view. It was them I addressed. There was only one way for them to understand what Lucy and I felt, and that was to speak their language.

"Must there always be blood shed? Your ancestors wanted to unite one another, under one banner, one home, one king. Yet here we are, fighting…for what? So we can fight some more." There was a shift through the audience as they looked to each other, Bears on one cliff, Wolves on the other. "Wolf, bear, eagle. Light skin, dark skin. Hair of fire, hair of ice, there is no difference between us. Except the ones we set ourselves. If you really want us to be one, united under one common goal, there need to be no Bears or Wolves or Eagles. There just needs to be an *us*."

Lucy strode forward, addressing the audience. Strands of her curly hair framed her high cheekbones, her eyes blazing behind the bright blue paint. As much as I hated admitting it, she looked like she belonged here, she looked like a warrior.

"What the mate of the Wolf King says is true. While we waste our time here, the Eagle King has taken the throne. We are so focused on honor, and doing what we think is right, we haven't considered that the Eagles haven't. Why are they not here?"

There was a scattered murmur amongst the Bears and Wolves, followed by an uncomfortable silence as eyes darted nervously between one another. The kings shared a furrowed brow, while the shamans whispered between one another. Leif caught my eye, giving me an apologetic twisting of his mouth.

Herleif waved his son away, addressing Lucy and me.

"It's a nice speech, but it changes nothing. The Besting demands a winner."

Lucy's eyes glowed with such intensity I was afraid she would burn him to a crisp. The blue paint splashed across her ebony skin only furthered her ferocity. Hidden somewhere deep down within me, a little voice crept to the surface. *She belongs here.*

"Fight me, then." She set her jaw; chin raised defiantly. I did not envy those who found themselves suffering from Lucy's stubbornness.

Herleif looked to his king, but Bjorn was clearly unwilling to go against his mate. His silence gave the shaman his answer, and Herleif was left staring her down. Ulfrik cleared his throat, drawing everyone's attention.

"I'm still High King, regardless who warms my throne." There was a pointed glance at Bjorn and Herleif. "Until Arne decides to join us in the Besting, he is a tyrant, a usurper, unworthy of the crown—*any* crown."

The sky darkened above us as snow trickled down from the heavens.

Bjorn smirked. "Then we bring the fight to the Eagle King."

The murmuring erupted into a cacophonous roar.

"My lord?" Herleif asked, eyebrows raised.

"What the mates say is true."

Herleif snorted. "My lord, they are *Travelers*! Their world is very different from ours; their people are different from ours. They don't value honor or strength or tradition. They defy it at every turn—"

The resounding slap of Bjorn's hand colliding with the shaman's face sent ripples of gasps through the audience. I stood in stunned silence, my eyes straying to Leif who stood with his head down. Herleif's mouth snapped shut, raising his head high as he tried to blink away the pain that formed a spreading reddish mark across his cheek.

"You forget your place sometimes," Bjorn remarked, eyebrows raised. "Ready the clan."

"Yes, my lord." Herleif's voice was tight, angry, but he acquitted.

Ulfrik looked to his brother, an unspoken understanding passing between them. The kings raised their weapons to the darkened sky. The crowd burst into clapping and screaming, vibrating the air around us.

"We march on the High Keep; we march on the Eagle king!" Ulfrik shouted.

CHAPTER

TWENTY-EIGHT

"I'm going to need a shrink after this," Lucy remarked, sharpening her short sword with a whetstone.

I snorted, adjusting the belt that sat on my too-thin hips. "Maybe I'll actually get treatment for my anxiety." I missed this, the jesting. But that voice in the darkness crept to the surface again, and with a whisper it shattered any pretense of us returning to normal. Lucy already said she wasn't returning home. A therapist, anxiety medications, none of that would do anything to fill the gaping hole of having lost my best friend.

"What's with the face?" she asked, wiping the blade with a damp cloth.

A sigh escaped before I could stop it. "We can joke about needing therapy and everything, but it doesn't matter, because in the end, I'm going home, and you're not."

"You know, you don't have to return home."

An uncomfortable silence settled between us as we polished our weapons and gear. This entire time I had worked for this, to return home—to Lucy and Finn. I hadn't considered anything else.

She placed a gloved hand on mine. "Just think on it."

I gave her a tight nod, my mind racing.

When Lucy and I emerged from the cave it was to an icy reception. The air was still sprinkled with fresh snow, and a heavy silence had fallen over the Cave City as people ran around preparing for war. Weapons were being gathered and sharpened, armour was being polished and fitted, food was being stored in piles, divvied up by diligent women and children with solemn expressions.

Lucy caught my eye. "Even the children have a role."

My mouth twisted. "You're okay with this?" I would never have thought my best friend—who squirmed uncomfortably at roadkill—would find solace in a world where children participated in war and slavery like it was normal.

Ulfrik stood at the entrance to the Bear King's personal residence, as officials and generals worked at a table laden with maps and weights and paperwork. Bjorn pushed the heavy stone weights carved into bears and wolves across the maps.

A man with a gruffy beard, braided and adorned with colored stones, approached the kings, his scarred hands carrying a massive battle-axe. His eyes narrowed, the white scar above his right brow in stark contrast to the blue paint splashed across his face like lightning.

I nudged Lucy gently. "Who's that?"

"Karhu, Hand of Bjorn."

I felt myself shrinking under his gaze. The disparity between him and Ogden was notable. This man was a hardened warrior, like his king, and he held himself with a surety that didn't scream *'pompous aristocrat.'* Part of me wondered what life—and the last few days—would have been like for Ulfrik if his Hand were more like this man.

The Hand addressed the two kings, leaning over the table to give his input. Everyone listened intently, hands on chins, eyes narrowed in thoughtfulness. It was clear this man knew what he was saying.

A shadow appeared at my shoulder, and we turned to see Leif beside us.

"I wondered where you two had run off to," he said.

Lucy smirked. "Just catching up."

"You know, Leif, there's been something on my mind." I stared him down.

He squirmed under my gaze. "Oh?"

"You knew of the Travelers that lived in the cities. Did you know of Lucy?"

Lucy turned to me. "There are others?"

"There are a few Travelers. Did I know anyone other than you on a personal level or what their names were or where they came from? No," Leif said pointedly.

"Likely story," I said, purposefully tinging my voice with suspicion.

He groaned. "It's not a conspiracy, Phoebe. I didn't know! You really think that if I discovered your best friend was the mate of Bjorn, I would have hidden that from you?"

My lips pursed. "I guess not."

Lucy snickered. "You have a knack for upsetting men, huh?"

I glowered at her.

A woman cradling a swaddled infant meandered through the crowd, stopping before us.

"Frea," Leif said with a smile, glancing at the sleeping babe in her hands. "How is he?"

"Alive, thanks to you." Her voice cracked. Whatever had happened that first night under the mountain when Leif was called away to assist his father, it must have been harrowing. Her skin was pale, eyes dull, any extra movement causing her to wince. But she gave a brave face to the world, or at the very least, in front of her king.

Leif's hand gently cupped the baby's head, his smile spreading. "Have you decided on a name?"

She sheepishly looked away. "I was thinking about naming him after you."

"Oh!" He was startled, his cheeks reddening. Composing

himself with a nervous throat clear and plastering the smile back on his face he retracted his hand from the baby's head. "I'm honored, truly. But perhaps the babe would be better suited to bear the name of his father."

Frea nodded sheepishly. "Yes, of course."

Leif laid a reassuring hand on her shoulder, squeezing gently. "Your boy will grow big and strong; he may not lead but he will command the respect of everyone."

"Who is the father?" I asked.

The shaman smirked. "The Hand of Bjorn."

We gathered within the Bear King's sprawling war room, decorated with skulls and bones and pelts. In the middle of the room was a massive stone table that cut it in half, adorned by a yellowed map of the city. As impressive as the room was, I couldn't tear my eyes from what hulked by the fireplace. Along the back wall, lying on a rug by the jumping flames of the hearth was a monstrous pile of fur that rose and fell with each breath.

"Is that…?" I swallowed.

"A bear," Lucy beamed.

Once the room had filled, Ulfrik looked at what meager forces had assembled around us, from the sprawling Bear Clan to the Wolves, to Asger who uncomfortably shifted from foot to foot. There weren't many, especially for a siege. Cunning and guile would win this, not raw strength, and I was beginning to feel disheartened. It was beginning to be like the Siege of Edinburgh—any of them—except we were the Scots fighting for freedom, and the Eagles were England, fighting for power.

That little voice whispered, *is it really a siege if the invaders have already won?*

"I won't lie to any of you, our chances of victory are low, but if we don't act against this indiscretion now, then our way of life as we know it is forfeit." Ulfrik's voice boomed across the room, stirring the bear to grunt in response.

A murmur arose, but Bjorn was quick to silence them. "I

would rather die trying, than give in to a fraud."

"The Wolves stand with their king!" cried someone in the back.

"Bears for Bjorn!" cried a member of the Bear clan.

Ulfrik and Bjorn raised their hands, silencing the crowd.

"On this day, we are not Wolves," Ulfrik started.

"And we are not Bears," Bjorn finished.

"This day," Ulfrik continued, "we are one."

The crowd erupted into claps and whoops, except the Hand of the Bear King.

"And the Eagle boy?" Karhu asked, eyeing him suspiciously.

There was an awkward silence as everyone's gaze turned to him. He shrank beneath the Bear Hand's simmering eyes.

"Asger can slip through unnoticed. He is a mere stableboy, a servant." Ulfrik looked to him. "Can you open the gates?"

Asger's mouth twisted. "The gates are almost barricaded, the walls patrolled."

He pointed on the map where the Keep gate and walls faced the Conjunction.

"A siege it is, then. The Conjunction is our only way," Ulfrik said.

There was an uncomfortable silence, the room felt smothering, a blanket of trepidation washing over everyone present.

"What about the Harbour?" Bjorn mused.

He shook his head. "We'd be slaughtered before we loosed an arrow."

It didn't make sense to me why the Harbour was even an option.

I whispered, "Why not just take the tunnels to the Keep?"

Leif leaned over. "The cities do not have a direct path to the Keep, below or above. The only way in or out is through the Conjunction. Or the Harbour."

Recalling the tunnels we had taken, it ran under or through the walls, and indeed it seemed as if the Conjunction was the central point of it all.

Ulfrik placed a heavy stone at the circular courtyard that

connected the cities and the Keep. "They'll have guards at the Conjunction, or at the very least, the gates."

Asger cleared his throat. "There were no guards at the Conjunction when I was there, they didn't care for it. It seemed like they cared more about controlling the Keep than anywhere else."

The kings exchanged a look, before Bjorn spoke. "They'll be reinforcing the gate, then."

"It'll be lambs to the slaughter," Karhu grunted.

"Not if we use a distraction," Leif interjected, a weird expression on his face.

The room swiveled, eyes on the shaman.

"Leif—" Ulfrik warned.

He held up his hands. "Hear me out."

Ulfrik waved his hand, urging him to speak quickly.

"What we need is a distraction."

Bjorn snorted. "You mean we need sacrifices."

"Not necessarily," Leif remarked.

Karhu splayed his hands against the table, leaning forward. Unnerved, Leif continued, side-eyeing me. "One of the first days this Traveler came here, she did something I wasn't entirely sure of. She gathered the snow into a shape. It was a strange, hideous thing that put me on edge. I'm willing to bet it will serve the same purpose for the guards at the gate."

Ulfrik frowned. "And that was?"

"A snowman, she called it."

Lucy leaned over, "*Really?*"

I shrugged helplessly. It never occurred to me when I built that sorry excuse for a snowman in the meadow that day, that Leif would remember it. Let alone that he felt uncomfortable by its mere presence.

"Show us," Bjorn said.

Turning on my heel, I strode from the cave, Lucy and Leif behind me. As the kings made to move, a voice broke over the sounds of the footsteps that followed us.

"Really, must we play games?" Herleif groaned, refusing to move from the table.

The room ignored him, following Lucy and me outside. Piles of fresh snow still clung to the ground. But that was not what I was after. Not even a minute of searching had me pulling the hardened day-old snow from under a windowsill, Lucy crouching by my side as we hastily built a snowman together.

Leif strode forward, a disappointed look on his face.

"There was something else you did."

Oh, right!

Searching the ground, I found several pebbles, and Lucy darted for two twigs that had fallen from a tree. Together we pressed them into the snowman, standing back to observe our creation.

There were scattered murmurings, but I didn't need to hear the words when the clans' thoughts were etched on their faces.

Lucy smirked. "Imagine these with blue and black paint."

Leif's eyes widened as he pulled a jar from the bag around his shoulder, swiping his hand inside of it to stain his fingertips. In one swoop he coated the eyes of the snowman in a charcoal strip.

Karhu folded his arms, leaning over to inspect it.

"Karhu?" Bjorn asked.

A slow smile spread across his face. "This could work."

There was an audible sigh of relief from Leif as the crowd gathered around the snowman like an idol.

"Phoebe…pinch me." Lucy said, holding back her laughter. I had to admit it was incredulous to consider that something as simple as this could help turn the tide in a war. But it worked for the Trojans, did it not?

The group gathered back around the table, all eyes on the High King. The flickering light of the hearth struggled to surge past the hulking bear that slumbered in front of it, casting wicked shadows along the walls and faces of those present.

Leif pointed to the Conjunction and the gate of the High Keep. "If we build the snowmen here and here and have our main forces sit here, we can send a smaller team through the tunnels."

"Why can't we assault the Keep with all our forces in the tunnels?" Herleif asked.

Ulfrik shook his head. "Because the guards would lock down the keep, blockading us until reinforcements from the Cliff City arrived. That Keep is made for being able to shut sections off at a time, and Arne knows that."

"Yes…we'll need the bulk of our forces in the Conjunction to bide time," Bjorn said, leaning over the map.

Karhu nodded. "I'll get to work on logistics."

There was a moment of silence, as everyone considered what had been decided so quickly.

"It's settled then. We take the Conjunction with a team designated for the distractions, while a small group infiltrates the Keep," Ulfrik said. "Let us break for now, rest, and recuperate. If you are not summoned to my chambers later then you are free to assume you are not on the team infiltrating the Keep."

Voices filled the room as people began to leave. Those whose voices were needed to decide who went where staggered around the table.

A hand tapped my shoulder as I turned to leave, my gaze meeting the swirling golden eyes of the High King.

"Could I steal you for a moment?"

I looked to where Lucy stood, her head cocked questioningly.

"Sure," I said, my hand waving Lucy along. She stayed for but a moment longer, until her attention was drawn to Bjorn who had appeared by her side.

We sat at the edge of a cliff; the stars shone brightly above, as if they cared not for the clouds that hugged the mountainsides. The snow had stopped, and now only a cold breeze kissed our cheeks. It was serene, quiet, intimate, and a fluttering sensation filled me.

"We've barely had time alone." Ulfrik wouldn't meet my gaze, his eyes lost in the sparkling firmament above.

I made a noise, not trusting myself to speak.

"You're unhappy."

I nodded.

"Why?"

It would seem odd to him; I couldn't fault such a reaction. After all, how could I be unhappy when everything I could ever want was at my disposal. Food, warmth, friends, family—there was so much more to life in this world that Lucy had fallen in love with. Even Eldrid had said so. There's only so much you could have been or done back home. What would I do if I returned without Lucy? I already knew the answer to that: nothing. I would be an empty shell that occupied my brother's couch until the day I died.

With my eyes downcast, I spoke in a voice that barely felt like my own. "Before I came here, I had lost someone dear to me. I had no hopes, no dreams, life was a blur of just existing. Lucy plucked me from the darkness, and then we came here. At first, I thought once again I'd be stuck in an endless loop of existence, with nothing to hope or dream for." I turned to him, the wind catching loose tendrils of my hair to fly across my cheeks. "But you've shown me that there is something to look forward to here, I suddenly have hopes and I suddenly have dreams and I don't know what to do."

"So much can change in a day, in an hour, in a single moment. Lives are lost and gained, and the world keeps turning, oblivious."

"Time is a cruel mistress," I murmured in response.

Ulfrik reached out to brush a strand of my hair from my cheek, tucking it behind my ear. The warmth of his skin against mine sent a shiver down my spine.

"You will always have a home here," he said.

Was he prepared to let me go? To return me to my people, to my time.

"Thank you," I muttered, my throat thick as I tried not to cry.

"I want you to consider my offer." He referred to the proposal, and the butterflies in my stomach fluttered. "You don't need to give me an answer now, I only ask you to consider it."

What did it matter? If this worked, I'd return home in less than a month without my best friend, and if it didn't, I wouldn't get to return home at all.

"You're on your third proposal, my lord," I teased, my voice oddly calm considering I could feel my pulse in every inch of me. I couldn't believe I was considering this. But if I was stuck here for the rest of my life, I knew I'd have to let these feelings I had been hiding in the blackened abyss of my heart float unhindered to the surface. It would be easy to fall in love with him, too easy. "If we survive this, I'll marry you." I hid my eyes from him, focusing on the snow that drifted from the cliff we sat on into the ravine below.

Ulfrik shifted, placing his arm around me as I rested my head against his shoulder, willing myself to stifle the flow of tears that burned trails across my cheeks.

He nuzzled the top of my head with his cheek. "I hope we survive this."

You know what, Ulfrik?

"Me, too."

CHAPTER

TWENTY-NINE

At the first sign of dawn, we emerged from the caves, forming a slow procession marching up the ridge to the tunnels. The only sound to accompany us into the darkness of the undercity was the scuffing of our boots on the stones. Torches were lit as we descended into the bowels of the world.

It always unnerved me to be underground, the howling echoes of things in the distance, the flickering at the edge of your vision that you weren't sure was real. Here and now, it reminded me of the time I accompanied my brother into the hidden world beneath the cobbled streets of Edinburgh. A promise was a promise, and a twentieth birthday present to him turned into hours of panic attacks for me. I couldn't help grimacing in remembrance. It couldn't have been every day paramedics were called to the vaults because someone's anxiety decided it wanted center stage.

Whispers met our ears as we emerged into the main room adjacent to the Conjunction. No light twinkled above, there was no sound but the howling of the wind, it was almost as if we sat in the bones of a civilization beneath a city of ghosts.

The group split up, taking up the room as Leif once again went through what everyone's orders were. With tight nods in response, we filed out into the adjacent room, emerging into the straw-choked loft of the stables. Asger led the way, pretending as if he had just returned from a long day's work. He was convincing, his hair slick with perspiration, his skin held a reddish hue. If I had to hazard a guess, I would wager that Asger wasn't fond of tight spaces.

The twittering call of a songbird met our ears, and those of us who were sitting amongst the piles of hay emerged down the ladder. We skulked through the darkness, leaving the comfort of the flickering torches behind in the undercity.

Asger awaited us, his eyes scanning the parapets above. Nothing moved, except the flags waving from the battlement. Ulfrik glowered beside me, and my eyes followed his. They weren't the same flags that were flown when I first arrived. These were pure darkness, plastered with an eagle of solid gold screeching towards the sky.

"How *dare* he," Bjorn spat.

Lucy rested her hand against the Bear King's shoulder, his eyes glittering when they met hers. She was the tallest in our group of friends, since elementary school, but even now her five-foot-nine frame was dwarfed by that of her king—her *mate*.

A pain shot through my chest, reminding me what I now had to lose. Before I knew she was here, death wasn't that bad of an option. I didn't know if she would be there waiting for me when I returned, or if she had perished in that blizzard. Now I knew, though, now I had a choice, and I was deathly afraid of making the wrong choice and losing it all.

Quelling the anxiety that welled within my chest, I fought for control, my hands shaking. That was an issue, if I survived, and dwelling on it would only serve as a distraction, fuel for the flame of my impending death. Anxiety would do that to you, bore a hole somewhere deep within, and no matter what you do to fill it, it would eat it up like a black hole. Food, TV shows, weighted blankets, cups of warm tea—it was a crutch, a band-aid. Those days, weeks, *months* spent in a daze on my brother's sofa reignited those feelings. If I lost Lucy, it would be just like losing my mother.

"Phoebe," Lucy whispered.

Of course, there were tears in my eyes, and I angrily tried to wipe them away without smearing the black paint that covered my eyes. She offered me a sad smile, but it meant very little. She didn't know that it was her, not our situation, that had me in tears.

"I'm fine," I insisted, pushing through the crowd to put distance between us. If I stayed, she would have bullied the reason for my watery eyes from me, and that was not a conversation I was ready to have.

Somehow, I had found myself beside Leif. He patted my shoulder. "Are you ready?"

To build snowmen? "Sure."

Leif started calling names from those who loitered nearby, directing them to the piles of snow that had been shoveled under windowsills, in darkened corners, and against the walls. Members of the Bear and Wolf clans worked side by side, rolling snow into snowmen in painful silence. Every odd sound had us freezing on the spot, frantically searching the parapets and gates, afraid at any moment that our movement would be discovered.

Every now and then I caught sight of Lucy and Bjorn, working in tandem to create dozens of snowmen in the time it took Leif and me to build four. He wasn't as adept at crafting mounds of snow, but neither were many of the others. It didn't matter though, we needed them as a distraction, nothing more. I couldn't fault them anyhow, they had no idea what it was they were building, and in the frigid air of a darkened morning before dawn, it was hard to see what we were doing, too.

There was no way to be sure that time had passed, the sky never changed, nor did the frigid wind that blew through the Conjunction. But the snowman army was slowly taking form. All around the market area, where there once sat stalls, now supported the haphazardly balanced frames of stacked balls of snow.

Taking a moment to breath, I surveyed all that we had done in what felt like a short time. There were dozens upon dozens, possibly nearing a hundred. I couldn't decide if I wanted to laugh or cry. Balancing between the absurdity and overwhelming brilliance of such a plan, I was beginning to feel optimistic. But something was missing.

"I need some sticks or something," I said.

Leif's mouth twisted. "I don't think it's wise you go alone."

A shadow loomed over us as the Hand of the Bear King said, "I'll accompany her."

It was clear the shaman didn't like such an arrangement, but he waved us off, returning to the snowman who kept collapsing beneath his hands. The hulking Hand followed me as I scoured the nearby alleyway between two stone buildings. A row of canvas was stretched between them, blocking any light from trickling below. It was much warmer here, as if the cloth managed to ease the bite of the winter chill.

There was an abundance of stones and sticks and strips of cloth lying about, as if the workers used this area to sweep debris away from the main square.

"These will work!" I bent to gather the sticks in my arms, as a snap reverberated through the alleyway.

The sticks fell from my hands when my eyes met a young man, dressed in leathers painted with a screeching golden eagle. He stared at us, dumbfounded, caught in the middle of unzipping his pants. He was frozen in shock, his eyes widening as he realized who we were.

Karhu was the first to break the fear that had gripped us, his voice deep and without remorse. "Kill him."

The man bolted.

Fumbling with the dagger at my waist, I followed in Karhu's footsteps. He was far ahead of me, the struggling shouts of the Eagle Clan man shattering the dense cloud of silence we had been working in.

He disappeared around the corner of the building, with Karhu hot on his trail. I could hear the shuffling of feet, the scratching of stone, and as I rounded the corner my heart stopped. The man slid to a stop; his lips wrapped around the mouth of a curved horn. With his last breath, and Karhu's dagger at his throat, the man sent a bellow through the air. A heart-seizing moment passed before an answering horn sounded on the other side of the wall.

"Well, if they didn't know we were here before, they do now." Karhu reached down, ripping the horn from the dead man's hand, shattering it against the stone wall.

I winced.

"We should go," Karhu said.

As soon as we exited the alleyway, Ulfrik and Bjorn were in our faces. Leif, Herleif, Lucy, and Asger ran up behind them, the rest of the Wolves and Bears stood nervously nearby. I couldn't bring myself to meet anyone's gaze.

"What happened?" Bjorn hefted his battle-axe over his shoulder.

Karhu strode forward, his eyes darting left and right. "We encountered a scout."

Bjorn made as if to say something, but he paused, a frown marring his battle-ready face. A whistling filled the air, and a second later one of the Bear Clan members beside Ulfrik fell to the ground. A white feathered arrow protruded from his chest, his eyes losing their light.

"Run," Karhu growled, whirling in the direction the arrow had come from.

The Conjunction erupted into chaos as every man and woman ran for cover.

"The wall!" screamed a man near me.

Following his petrified gaze to the parapets, I watched in horror as shadows coalesced atop it. One, two, three—I lost count as they darkened its surface, slowly taking shape. I saw the gloved fingers clutched around wooden bows, the metal tips of arrows glinting in the flickering lights of torches that came alive around them. Their arms drew back and, as one, loosed dozens—if not hundreds—of arrows to rain down upon us.

Bodies fell around me, and in the chaos all I could see was death. I called out to them, to Lucy and Leif and Ulfrik, but my voice was lost in the screams.

Karhu yelled out nearby, directing groups of warriors armed with bows to begin firing back. Splattered in blood, with an arrow protruding from his thigh, Karhu had inserted himself into a stall, using the snowmen in front as cushion for the arrows that rained down on him.

"Hold!" he screeched over the mayhem.

And indeed, we were holding. But people were still dying, far more people adorned with wolf pelts and bear masks than those plastered in feathers fell. The white snow was smeared with ribbons of crimson.

As I skirted the corpse of a Wolf Clan woman, an arm shot out, pulling me under the awning of a nearby building. It wasn't just any building, it was the stables, and it wasn't just any arm, it was Ulfrik.

I drank in the sight of him, my shaking hands running across his long ebony hair. Blood was splattered across his face and neck, but it wasn't his. Shadows moved behind him as Leif, Lucy, and Bjorn emerged from the darkness. They bore similar expressions of horror on their tired faces, but no one was injured.

"Are you hurt?" Ulfrik breathed a sigh of relief as I shook my head.

Someone screamed outside, followed by a thud. I swallowed that sickly bile that sat at the back of my throat.

"What now?" Lucy asked.

Bjorn's face hardened. "The plan remains the same."

"But all those people…" I whispered, my breathing ragged, adrenaline still coursing through my veins.

Ulfrik's expression turned grave. "They knew what their purpose was. Hold the line, hold the attention, and death may be the result. But if their sacrifice leads to our reclaiming the

Keep, then it would be a well-deserved death."

"May the gods grant them mercy," Leif said, bowing his head.

We exchanged glances, but said nothing, as one by one we climbed the ladder to the loft. Swinging the hidden wall open we piled inside, leaving the lambs to the slaughter.

Although the echoes of our footsteps resounded through the stone tunnels, every now and then we could hear shouting. Where we were now ran parallel to the chaos outside, but Leif was adamant we take a more direct approach. The tunnels of the undercity did not just empty into the dungeon, but also led to the library, king's bedchamber, and the throne room.

As we climbed spiraling staircases hewn of stone in the darkness, my heart had yet to cease its hammering. My hands balled into fists at every sound, anything to remind me of the innocents who had been left to fate.

A warm hand rested itself on my shoulder, and even in the gloom I could just make out the shape of Ulfrik. I was certain he was offering me a smile of reassurance, and I was glad for the darkness, because I could not reciprocate it.

I never understood the concept of war, of killing one another because our beliefs differed. But that was the problem—most wars were not fought because the common man didn't believe in what his neighbour believed in. It was because their kings and emperors, czars and warlords had a staunch belief that could not be swayed. That was how it has always been and, I was afraid, would always be. Lucy had always joked that if women ruled the world, there would never be wars. If we didn't like the policies of our peers, we would simply ignore them—shun them—like catty high school cliques. Sometimes I wondered how true that would be, and perhaps whether our world would be better off. Then again, I tend not to believe my musings, after all, I argued the world would be at its most peaceful if dogs ruled it instead.

"We're here." Leif's whisper cut through the silence, and for a moment I struggled to believe he had said anything. I'd been so wrapped up in my own thoughts he could've been talking this entire time and I would have been none the wiser.

There was a struggle as his hands searched for the hidden door in the darkness. Ulfrik, Bjorn, and Lucy crowded around me as it swung open silently, revealing another tunnel. Except this one was different, the walls were thinner, a coating of thick dust lay on the floor where it had seeped through the tiny cracks around us. It wasn't just dust that managed to find its way in here, light permeated the tunnel in pinpoint beams.

As we stood beneath the shifting dust and light, voices sounded above us, crisp and clear as day. My companions froze in their tracks, staring upwards. Shadows passed by, the sound of footsteps receding.

"Did I say you could leave?" growled someone.

Ulfrik, Bjorn, and Leif tensed, shifting forward to get a look at who spoke. From their posture and scowls, it could only have been one person.

"I have better things to do than play your games, Arne," a man replied.

I froze, my face no doubt mirroring my companions who huddled in the dust beside me. The Eagle King stood directly above us. This must be the throne room, the room where I first met Ulfrik.

There was a snapping of fingers, and two heavyset boots sounded to either side of us as the mystery man cried out. "What is the meaning of this?"

"You have no time for games, and I have no time for weak-minded fools."

We could hear the man struggling in the grasp of what had to be Arne's personal guards as he was dragged before the Eagle King.

"I will not ask you again, Harvaldr."

His response was heralded by a light chuckle. "No."

You could almost hear the smirk in the usurper's voice. "You would lead an insurrection, but you would not take part in assimilating the people you were so desperate to help?"

"Is that what you call this? *Assimilation*? You told me my people would finally have a true leader, that they would be safe and happy. All I saw were innocent women and children being slaughtered in the streets." Harvaldr muttered.

"In war, there will always be casualties," Arne replied casually.

"Women and *children*, Arne. You promised me, Ogden promised me, that they would be safe! No true king would condone the lives of innocents."

There was a creaking above us, as if Arne was adjusting himself on the throne. "Ogden?"

"My lord," came the curt, snide reply of a man who was enjoying this exchange.

Ulfrik exhaled angrily and I pressed my hand into his.

"Kill him."

We looked between each other as Ogden strode forward. The undeniable sound of a sword being pulled free of its scabbard met our ears, that horrid metallic sound, before it was replaced by an equally horrible sound: metal piercing flesh. There was a thud directly above us, followed instantly by the foul coppery scent of blood as crimson drops made their way through a crack, pooling at my feet. I bit my tongue, swallowing to convince myself that vomiting wasn't the best option right now.

"Get him out of my sight," Arne spat.

The sound of Harvaldr's body being dragged across the top of our tunnel disappeared into the distance. There was a moment of silence, broken suddenly by the man who had no qualms about killing children.

"Where are my *brothers*?" The last word laced with venom.

Ogden snorted. "It seems they thought taking the Conjunction would give them the Keep."

There was a hollow laugh. "Fools."

"What is your command, my lord?"

"Drain the keep, I want the Conjunction taken. Reinforcements should arrive soon from the Cliff City. This pathetic attempt at reclamation will be silenced soon enough."

"Yes, my lord."

"And Ogden?"

"My lord?"

"Kill anyone who stands in our way."

Footsteps receded, and Bjorn waved his hand, pointing down the tunnel. Retreating into the stairwell, we were smothered by darkness once more. Once Leif was sure we were safe, he dared to speak, although it was barely above a whisper.

"What do we do, my lord?"

The kings bowed their heads in thoughtfulness, but this was time wasted that we could not afford. I knew that, and I was sure everyone else did, too.

"If we let Ogden alert the guards, everyone in the Conjunction will die," Lucy said.

I interjected, "Where else do these tunnels lead?"

Leif spoke from the darkness, his voice suspicious as if not sure where I was leading this to. "The closest exit is the king's bedchambers."

That gave me an idea. "Can we ambush him?"

Ulfrik squeezed my hand. "He has to pass my chambers to the stairwell that leads to the guard's quarters."

"Then let's catch us a traitor," I said.

CHAPTER

THIRTY

We darted down the stairwell to the landing below. A tunnel arched off into the darkness, narrow and dank, it led us to a faux wall of wood. As the door creaked open, we found ourselves in an alcove tucked beneath a trapdoor. When slid open, it revealed the planks of the underside of the High King's bed.

"This entire time, an assassin could have been hiding in plain sight," Ulfrik remarked, tossing a raised brow in Leif's direction.

Ignoring his king, Leif flattened himself, crawling on his stomach to emerge from the underside of the bed. We followed suit, hugging the side of the bed as we peered around the empty, cold, and dark bedroom. The thick curtains had been drawn, leaving only a sliver of the sky beyond the balcony. The sun would be rising now, the horizon aflame.

Boots, scuffing the stone with little care for the history that was squashed beneath their feet, sounded just beyond the solid oak door, reinforced with metal plating. Rushing to the door, we filed behind it, waiting. Ulfrik, Bjorn, and Leif had their weapons tightly clenched in their hands, the glint of the swords and axes was mildly distracting. Lucy gripped my hand, her short sword in the other.

As the boots neared the door, Bjorn leaned forward, twisting the knob, letting it creak open just enough for us to have a peek of what lay beyond.

"What the…" remarked someone on the other side.

The boots halted, gathering around the door.

"Probably just ghosts," someone else replied.

There was an answering snort. "What are you lot? Sniveling praell? Check it out." That was the voice we were waiting for. Ogden.

"There's no way they could have made it into the Keep," was the reply.

"And yet, my dungeon is empty," Ogden growled.

His dungeon? I hoped the others caught the distinction in verbiage. Perhaps Arne was not the plan for High King after all, he was merely a pawn.

There was a shuffling of feet as the door swung open, hiding us behind it. Through the crack in the hinges, we watched as four shadows passed inside. We held our breathe, willing them to come closer. But then, nothing. The footsteps began to retreat, the shadows passing by the hinges.

Shit, they were leaving!

There was no forethought in what I did as I raised the dagger Eldrid had gifted me and flung it across the room. It collided with a mirror hanging above the dresser, shattering it into a thousand tiny fragments. The room filled with the sound of broken glass clattering against the wooden floor, followed by the unsheathing of weapons. Men filed into the room, two, three, four, six.

"Now!" Ulfrik yelled, emerging from behind the door.

The others followed, their swords and axes clanging against the Eagle Clan. Feathers scattered, showering us in fluff and blood splatter. Men fell to the floor and as we emerged victorious, we faced the doorway.

"I wondered when you would show yourself, and here I

thought you had left, cowering into the Old Wood with your tail between your legs," Ogden sneered. "Too bad your efforts are in vain, even now your friends' blood paints the streets red, much like your whore's hair."

Ulfrik pulled back his arm and hurled the sword towards Ogden. In the blink of an eye, a shield appeared from the side, held by an Eagle Clan member in full battle gear. The sword bounced harmlessly to the ground, furthering the glint in the former Hand's eyes.

"Only another example of why you're not fit to call yourself *High King*," he snickered. "But now, I tire of you. You've had your chance for fun, and now, it's time to join the rest of your clan."

"It's your clan, too!" Leif growled.

Ogden snorted. "Not anymore." A horn bellowed in the distance, somewhere far below. "And for you, not much longer."

The man holding the shield strode towards the entrance of the room. Until now, we stood there, silent, waiting, listening, unsure of which breath would be our last. I looked at my best friend, my heart dropping as I watched her trail after Bjorn. He blazed across the threshold, colliding with the shield bearer, sending them both crumbling to the floor. Ulfrik raced after him, shoving Lucy out of the way as another shield bearer, waiting just out of sight, raised his axe. I cried out, my voice lost in the commotion. She was seconds from losing her head, and now the man who saved her life, the man who had saved mine, was staring death in the face.

Leif charged through the throng, jumping over Bjorn where he had wrestled his shield bearer to the ground. The shaman collided with Ogden, sending them both tumbling to the hard stone floor.

I watched as my friends struggled, holding the line that stopped the men and women at the Conjunction from being hopelessly outnumbered. I had to do something, anything. It was now or never, Phoebe. But my hand grasped my scabbard, and I stared empty handed at the chaos that unfolded before me. My dagger lay somewhere in the darkness on the other side of the room.

Lucy's cry snapped me back to the throng, to what really mattered. A glint caught my attention, on the stones between Bjorn and Ulfrik, who still traded blows with their respective shield bearers. Not giving myself the time to think it through, like always, I darted forward, scooping up Ulfrik's sword, and spun around, slicing it through the air.

A gurgle escaped from the lips of a man wearing the beak of an eagle. His sword clattered to the floor as he collapsed, blood spurting from the gash in his neck. A familiar whistling noise rushed past me, and I heard a thud that was distinctly not the noise of it hitting wood or stone.

"Phoebe!" Lucy called to me, her voice cracking.

My friend clutched her arm, an arrow protruding from her bicep.

"Lucy…" I gathered her against my chest, watching as two men armed with bows and arrows advanced from down the corridor.

They charged at us, arrows flying through the narrow corridor, separating us from our friends. Ulfrik, Bjorn, and Leif were pinned in the king's chamber. The sounds of swords clashing and men grunting with every hit filled the air. I didn't know if they saw us or were even aware that archers stood on the other end of the corridor. My back collided with a table sitting against the wall, adorned with ceramic bowls of bright red apples.

Taking this opportunity, the archers advanced, rounding the corner. Pulling their arms back, they stared us down. Flipping the table onto its side, I yanked on Lucy's good arm, dragging her to the floor. The bowls smashed on the stone, shards scattering as far as the apples rolled. Arrows pierced the wood, and I thanked whatever god was on our side that just the tip of them emerged on the other side.

Lucy clutched her arm close to her chest, a crimson ribbon snaking its way down her skin, tears lighting her eyes in the flickering sconce light. We were stuck.

"Well, that didn't go the way I thought it would," she chuckled, a forced sound that laced the blood beneath my skin with toxicity. I couldn't lose her, not again.

"Y-you'll be fine." Curse my stammer.

She rolled her eyes. "Of course, I'll be fine, it's just a flesh wound!"

I couldn't find it in me to laugh like she could, but I offered her a weak smile.

A shadow crossed over her face as arrows struck the table, the tips mere inches from our backs and heads.

"What?" I knew that look, when she bit her lip in thought, her eyes losing focus as a mishapen plan took place. "I know that look, Lucy."

"We're pinned down." Her eyes were distant.

"Clearly," I grunted, flinching as another arrow pierced the table, grazing the nape of my neck.

"Tell me a joke." That earned her a more sincere smile.

"Ulfrik proposed to me." She gasped in a pathetic attempt to disguise the wince. "And I told him, if we survived this, I'd accept his proposal."

We could hear the cries of Ulfrik and Bjorn, and even though I knew they were nearby, it sounded like they were far away.

"Well, looks like you're about to save a lot of money." Lucy attempted to giggle, but the sound that came from her was not more than a pained huff.

I snorted. The day we graduated high school, Lucy, dangling from the arm of her boyfriend of a year, loudly declared weddings were a sham, and she'd happily get married in a tent strung across a bog.

Her hand grasped mine, fingers entwined.

"Phoebe, I love you." My heart broke.

"I love you, Lucy."

She would not wait here to die; I knew what went through the head of my best friend, ever since elementary school. We weren't surrendering, we were two peas in a pod. My free hand, shaking and slick with sweat, grasped the sword I had taken from Ulfrik. Lucy raised hers in kind.

"On the count of three?" she asked.

I nodded.

"One," I said.

My heart hammered beneath my chest.

"Two," she said.

Her lip quivered.

"Three," we said in tandem.

Rising from the table riddled with arrows, swords raised, we charged. The two archers paused, their puzzlement replaced instantly by sickening smirks. Raising their bows with mock slowness, arrows knocked, elbows bent, they waited.

I roared, matching that of Lucy's war cry. Together we charged them, knowing this was it, this was the end. I prayed that our sacrifice served as a distraction, allowing the kings to free themselves.

A lithe swordsman, silky golden hair flowing behind him, sliced downwards into the archer's bow wielding hands. Severed from their weapons, the men drew back in shock, blood curdling screams were the only replies as Leif's sword rose once more and slit their throats. Crimson dribbled forth, coating the pristine ivory feathers of their mantles.

My heart soared. Lucy and I ran to him, our faces expressing our gratitude and disbelief. We weren't dying, at least not yet. He had saved us. We were so close, only feet away, when the corner peeled away, revealing a shadow standing behind Leif. In the flickering light of the dying sconces, beady eyes peered into the gloom.

My heart seized as Ogden's sword slid into Leif's belly.

"Leif!" I screeched.

A shadow passed over me as a familiar warrior bounded past me like a raging bull, colliding with Ogden. His hand pulling the sword from Leif's abdomen as he was smashed against the wall. Karhu growled, his forearm pinning the former Hand's neck against the chipped stone.

I slid across the stone at his feet, scooping Leif into my arms. He was still conscious, his eyes closed as he fought the pain. Blood pooled around his stomach, dripping onto the stone beneath us. My hands shook from a mixture of adrenaline and anxiety as I bit into the sleeve of my tunic, ripping off a section that I folded over and over before pressing it firmly against the wound.

Leif groaned but placed his hand over mine, his head rolling in my lap. Karhu turned to us, the blue paint splashed across his face was smeared with sweat and blood.

"How did you get to us?" Lucy asked.

The same thought passed my mind. I thought it was over, that we had lost. We were pinned, surrounded, and yet at the eleventh hour not only did Leif come to our aid, but Karhu as well.

He gave us a smug look, the first time I'd seen him do anything resembling a smile.

Lucy frowned, "That horn…was that you?"

He nodded just beyond where we stood, towards Asger, who wielded a sword against a guard's throat, demanding he surrender. Ulfrik and Bjorn emerged from the bedchamber, wiping the blood of the shield bearers onto their pant legs. Ulfrik's eyes darted to mine, and Bjorn's to Lucy. Filled with visible relief, their expressions changed as they beheld Leif fighting to stay conscious in my lap.

"Leif." Ulfrik knelt beside me, taking Leif's free hand in his. Ulfrik's other hand wrapped around me, gripping my shoulder with reassurance. He was happy to see me alive, he didn't need to say it, I felt it.

"Remember when we were kids," Leif coughed, eyes squinting with every move he made, "You said battle shamans were a ridiculous notion, they would be useless in battle."

Ulfrik breathed deeply, fighting his emotions as he jested, "Clearly I was right."

Leif laughed, his body heaving as he fought the pain. "Next time, I'll have to listen to you."

The Wolf King glowered. "Next time, I'll put you in charge of the stables." Their gazes lingered on the stableboy binding several of the guards that had been spared with thick rope.

"Pathetic."

With rage swelling in me, I stared down Ogden, still pinned to the wall beside me.

"Enough!" growled Karhu.

Ulfrik released his shaman's hand, rising to meet the Bear King.

"Arne is close," Ulfrik said, staring down the hall.

Bjorn wiped the blood from his face, spitting at the shield bearer's corpse. "Let's go."

"But…Leif…"

The High King's fingers grazed the top of my hair, where the braid still clung to my head for dear life.

I cradled Leif close, afraid that if I let him go, he would be gone forever. Like Lucy, like Finn. I didn't realize it in the beginning, but Leif had become like a brother to me.

Ulfrik whistled at two Wolf Clan members standing nearby. They stood at attention, blood staining their pelts with dirt and ash. Whatever had happened that led to them taking the Keep, it was clear they had seen more than they bargained for.

"He doesn't die, you hear me?" The Wolf King knew how ridiculous his command was, the position it put these simple soldiers in. Emotions were running high, and this was as expressive as Ulfrik dared to get. He had to hold it together, he had to save face. Like a good soldier, like a good king.

Kneeling beside me, they reached for him, but I pulled back.

"I'm a nurse, I can help him!" My voice cracked, and I hated the tears that gathered.

They paused, looking to Ulfrik. He eyed me a moment before kneeling beside me, resting a hand on my shoulder.

"They can help him, too." My gaze met his, and I could see the sincerity in them. Of course, they could. I didn't doubt his own people, but surely, I could do more to help him than they could.

"Ulfrik—"

He shook his head. "I'm not letting you out of my sight. Let them take him." His eyes twinkled, and for the briefest moment, I could see fear swirling in those depths. Not fear for Leif, but fear for *me*.

"Just…make sure to keep pressure on the wound," I murmured, not entirely convinced they could do any better than me.

They gathered him in their arms, Leif's hands holding back the crimson wave. He offered us small smiles, replaced moments later by searing agony as they carried him away. The Wolves and Bears who had survived whatever chaos ensued outside gathered around us, looking to their kings for direction.

Ulfrik turned to the crowd. "Down this hall awaits the traitor who pit brother against brother, father against son, sisters against sisters, and mothers against daughters. Such an affront to our way of life cannot be tolerated."

"There is no way out of the throne room. Hold this hall to the very last man," Bjorn said, hefting his battle-axe over his shoulder. Ogden squirmed nearby, fighting for a breath.

The kings looked to Karhu. Nodding he said, "I have this covered, go."

The Wolves and Bears hollered, their battle cries shattering the air as Ulfrik, Bjorn, Lucy, and I made our way to the throne room. The double doors were wide open, the hairs on the back of my neck stood on end. It didn't seem right, something was wrong. An eerie silence drifted just beyond those doors, and the kings strode forward, without a care in the world. Lucy and I darted after them.

THIRTY-ONE

The throne room was just as I remembered it. A raised dais at the far end supported three towering chairs of stone illuminated by roaring hearths, torches, and braziers spread throughout. Sitting with shoulders back, head raised high, in the very center of the dais, was the Eagle King. He greeted us with a venomous smirk, his hand beckoning us closer.

"So, the washed-up kings and the sluts of the Bear and Wolf clan have finally shown themselves." His sneer was toxic, setting a pit deep in my stomach.

"It's over, Arne," Bjorn said.

"Oh no, dear brother. It has only begun."

A horrible screech filled the air, and doors snapped shut behind us. Beams of iron were locked into place by two guards, clothed in ebony cloaks, faces obscured by bone white bird skulls. The beaks, razor-sharp, glinted in the light. When the light shifted, I understood why, the tips were made of iron.

Noises drifted in from the hall, muffled by the heavy, near-impenetrable doors. Ulfrik and Bjorn struggled between the guards that advanced from behind us, and Arne who taunted them from the throne.

"Come, brothers, let us play." He twirled a spear in his hand, eyeing down the kings.

Ulfrik and Bjorn turned to us, the unspoken questions plain as day across their faces.

Holding my sword in front of me, I said, "We got this."

Lucy joined my side, sword held aloft, ready to jump as soon as they made a move. With great effort, the kings left their mates to deal with their errant brother. I couldn't afford to watch them as the closest guard swung at me, his sword slicing through the air a hair's breadth from my face. Lucy cried out, running forward to push back the second guard. Their swords clashed with a frightening clang, loud enough to break me and make me realize I needed to be present.

It would have been so easy, and preferred, to slip away into that zone I did when I had little care for the world around me. But right there, right then, I couldn't afford that. It wasn't just my life on the line, it was Lucy's, and Ulfrik's, and Bjorn's, and all those in the hall beyond those iron-beamed doors.

The guard charged me again, a wicked glint in his eyes as the sword came within a mere inch of skewering me. He was fast, and far more skilled than I. That wasn't a particular thing to boast about, however, seeing as he probably trained for this very moment his entire life. I should have tried to have more training sessions with Ulfrik and paid attention to every detail.

A glint of silver sliced through the sleeve of my blouse, leaving it flapping like a broken bird's wing. Fuck. *Focus, Phoebe!* I could pity myself later. The reprimanding, however, was enough for the guard to sweep his leg under my feet, sending me crashing to the cold stone floor.

Lucy hollered over the chaos. "Tricks, Phoebe! God damn it, girl!"

Tricks? The realization hit me like a truck. I might not have been any good at swordplay or archery or anything else the people in this world had spent their entire lives practicing, but I was good at one thing they weren't.

Ten years of karate don't fail me now!

"Shit!" Lucy cried, blocking a blow that staggered her backwards.

The guard hovered over me, and although only his eyes were visible, I could sense the smirk hiding beneath that iron-tipped beak. Straddling my waist, he had me pinned, sword dangerously close to my throat. Red was all I could see, all I could feel, all I could breathe. It engulfed me, an anger so absolute, so primal, that as I let it course through my veins I wondered if this was truly me, or something else.

I didn't know if this was how my ancestor's felt when they were staring down the end. They always said it was like a light at the end of the tunnel, maybe even darkness. But all I saw was crimson, like the tendrils of my hair that had broken free of my braid. This was it, the last chance I'd ever get.

Tricks, Phoebe.

There was one technique that I was so fond of, that our sensei dubbed it my *signature move*. It didn't serve me very well after that, but until he had brought attention to it, I had a near perfect record of wins against my fellow students.

Striking out with my left hand, I grasped the Eagle guard's wrist. His attention whirled, fixating on removing my feeble grasp. That was all I needed, as I struck out with my right hand, balled into a fist. It collided with the underside of the guard's jaw. Grunting, he collapsed atop me, unconscious.

Slithering out from beneath a man who weighed almost twice as much as I did, my breathing was ragged and my vision spotty, as I turned to watch Lucy's sword wrenched from her hand. It slid across the floor, the guard raising his sword for the final blow. Scooping the unconscious guard's sword up, I charged at the man who held my best friend's life in his grubby hands. Aimed low, my sword pierced through the gap in his leather armor, slicing through tunic and flesh. Blood coated my hands, the sword lodged deep in what I could only presume was bone, as the man teetered forward and collapsed.

As he writhed in agony, his legs were splayed in opposite

directions, and panic etched on his face like a tattoo. I couldn't help but wince, it wasn't what I intended at all. Such a slow, cruel death, and in that moment all I could think was that if this had happened back in my time there was a chance he would survive. But he would be maimed, disabled, because as I followed the blade to where it protruded from his spine, I knew I had severed his spinal cord. He would be a paraplegic, now. *If he survived.*

Lucy strode forward, wrenching his sword from him. With a face void of emotion, she slid the blade under his neck, and yanked it forward, cutting his throat. Tossing the sword on the ground she staggered forward, enveloping me in a weak hug, panting.

I didn't have the energy to process what had happened, the adrenaline holding my anxiety at bay. The only thoughts that rumbled through my head were that I was alive, and Lucy was alive, and right now that was enough. Until the clang of metal and frustrated grunts met our ears.

We turned to face our kings, slick with sweat and dirt and blood, pressing the advantage against a king that was weaker and slower than them. They had Arne cornered, his spear held before him as he struck out against the advancing kings. I didn't know how many blows had been traded, but the advantage was not with the Eagle King. Ulfrik lashed out with his sword, snapping Arne's spear in half, the iron-tip clattering to the stone at their feet.

"You may have bested me, brothers. But your friends have not."

Bjorn took a step forward, knuckles bone-white where they gripped his battle-axe. "I have had enough of your games."

"So have your compatriots, who lay dead and dying, broken and forgotten, just beyond the doors."

The throne room lapsed into an uneasy silence, there was no sound from beyond those doors. No grunts, or cries, or fighting. Just emptiness, as if a battle had never been waged. The silence did not last, however, shattered within a single heartbeat with the most unexpected sound just beyond those solid doors.

There was no mistaking what it was, as a long, mournful howl drifted through the slivers of wood.

Lucy and I exchanged furrowed brows, my heart skipping a beat, as we looked to the iron-beamed doors. As one, we darted across the hall, skidding to a halt. We worked together to lift the beams, letting them drop to the floor with a heavy thud.

Heaving with sore, tired muscles, we dragged the creaking doors open, revealing chaos just outside. Chaos, and a most familiar face. Clad in a tattered dress, leather vest, and wielding an axe and shield, was a woman I was beyond grateful to see. Her charcoal smeared eyes widened in relief as they beheld me. She strode into the room, surveying what she had fought to reach.

"Eldrid." The awe in my voice was palpable, and for the briefest of moments I wondered if I had snapped, and she was a figment of my imagination.

Behind her skulked two monstrous wolves, lips curled back, revealing yellowed fangs, muzzles coated in blood. Hati and Skoll strolled forward, snarls emanating from deep within their throats.

Eldrid smirked. "Fancy meeting you here."

"It seems you were wrong," Ulfrik remarked to his brother, who stared with unconcealed rage at the intrusion.

Eldrid pointed her sword at the Eagle King. "We have your surrounded, false king. Surrender, and we may yet show you mercy."

Boots marched in tandem across the stone as dozens of women garnished in wolf pelts, eyes smeared charcoal, shields and swords in hand, filled the room.

"Shieldmaidens," Lucy said. "Impressive."

Eldrid threw her a wink before embracing me. "You look good in armour."

I offered her a weak smile. Maybe I did, but I couldn't imagine it that way. To me, armour only signified death, and I'd had my fair share of it.

"Will you surrender peacefully?" Ulfrik asked, towering over the Eagle King sprawled across the ground.

A smile tugged at the edges of his lips, golden eyes ablaze in the flickering brazier light.

"No."

"It's over," Bjorn said.

Arne shook his head, the feathers on his shoulders bristling. "My dear brothers, it has only begun."

An acrid smell met my nostrils, potent enough I was worried it would singe the hairs inside. Stifling a gag, my face puckered, eyes squinting as they watered.

Bjorn's eyes rose to the rafters, where smoke began to manifest, deep black and foul, it spread along the ceiling like a miasma.

"I would run if I were you." Arne sat up, eyeing down everyone in the room. With a flourish, he pulled a stone from beneath his robes. It was in every sense, identical—albeit smaller—to the runestone that had brought me here. Three-sided and carved in red runes, they had an eerie glow to them.

"No…" Ulfrik growled. "You wouldn't."

"What is it?" Bjorn's gaze jumped from Arne to Ulfrik.

Arne held it aloft for all to see. "The catalyst."

"Do you have any idea what that thing is capable of?" Ulfrik seethed, rushing forward to grab Arne by the collar of his ripped shirt.

"If I cannot have this Keep, neither can you." His maniacal laughter filled the room, spreading fast like the smoke that now clung to the rafters.

Ulfrik dropped his brother to the cold stone floor, spinning around with Bjorn on his heels. The shieldmaidens darted from the room as fast as their bulky shields let them, Eldrid directing them through the castle. Ulfrik grasped my hand as he ran by, and I watched Bjorn do the same to Lucy.

The smoke was billowing from the throne room, so rapidly that it had filled the hallway now in a smothering blanket of impenetrable darkness. We hit every table, every chair, every corpse. No matter where we went, the smoke was ahead of us, blinding us, choking us.

Ulfrik's grip was absolute, and through the tears stinging my eyes, blurring my vision, I couldn't help but look to him. This man who saved me time and time again, went against the wishes of his own people, and put his life repeatedly on the line with little thought for himself…my heart ached and soared, unsure of what emotion to give in to.

It doesn't matter if you give into the warmth of him if you die here.

Something soft brushed against my leg, and I stared into the amber eyes of Skoll. On the other side, hugging close to Ulfrik, was Hati. They followed us closely, steering us around splintered wood and broken stone.

We spiraled from floor to floor, stairwell to stairwell, every new hall and corridor was choked in an absolute abyss. If not for Ulfrik's hand, and the near constant coughing around me, I would have thought I was all alone. I gave his hand a squeeze, and he answered with one in return. I was grateful for everything he had done, even if it didn't show, even if I didn't express it in my words or actions. There was a light at the end of this tunnel, though. Even choked by ash and soot and crumbling stone and cracking wood. I had made him a promise.

Entire sections of wall peeled away, falling mere inches from us. Exposed nails, sharpened stone, fractured wood lashed out. I felt it tear at my clothes, at my skin, blood trickling and pooling beneath my armor.

"We're almost there," Ulfrik shouted above the chaos.

There was a brightness in the gloom ahead, sunlight or torchlight I did not know. But there was light, and the halls and corridors we ran through widened. I knew this room, remembered it. Leif had brought me through it that very first day when I was remanded as a praell of the Wolf King. Through the darkness, I could just make out the tables and benches, but where there used to be men relaxing with mugs of ale in one hand while tending to oiling their leathers and sharpening their swords in another, there was only rubble and ruin. Ulfrik was right, we were almost out.

He pulled me to the side, up against a lopsided table, as he shouted at the Bears and Wolves, and even Eagles, to run and keep running. He was staying behind to ensure everyone escaped. The horrid sounds of the foundation being consumed by fire was all I could focus on over the roaring of my own heartbeat.

There was a sickening crackle and my eyes strayed above. A beam splintered, and as Skoll darted ahead of me, the beam collapsed, hitting me in the back. I fell, my grip on Ulfrik severed, my body hitting the sharp stone with a sickening thud.

"Ulfrik!" I cried into the plume, my heart racing as I struggled to remove my leg from beneath the beam.

He was instantly at my side.

"My leg," I breathed, smoke choking my lungs.

Grunting, the Wolf King struggled to remove the beam where it had me pinned. His eyes were frantic in the gloom, his muscles bulging, coated in sweat.

The room was deserted, his people safe. Except for me, and except for him.

"Leave me." I couldn't let his people be leaderless, not for my sake.

He scoffed. "If I did that you wouldn't keep your promise to me."

His words were said with jest, but my heart ached.

"Darn, y-you caught me." I winced as agony tore through my leg and lower back. I didn't know if anything was broken, but I could just make out the movement of my wiggling toes in my boots.

"Phoebe." He looked me in the eyes.

"Ulfrik."

He swallowed nervously, but I could just make out the twinkle in his eye.

"I love you."

I wanted to hesitate, to question the feelings that flitted about within me. The emotions that roiled just beneath the surface. But I knew what they were, what they had been all along. There was no reason to deny it any longer, no reason to question it. I knew exactly how I felt.

"I love you, too."

He held my head in his lap, his fingers brushing the tendrils of hair from my face as smoke billowed. His head bent to mine, and I awaited eagerly for the kiss that I knew was coming. Except, it didn't, as a shadow blocked the light coming in from the entryway.

"Isn't that sweet," remarked a familiar voice, the voice of the stoic Bear King.

Lucy skidded into view, her king at her side. "You two can do this later—outside."

Together, the three of them knelt beside me, and with their combined might, heaved the beam from atop me to clatter against the stone. The entire ceiling began to bend, stone and dust and splinters raining down around us. Lucy and Bjorn cried for us to run, casting nervous glances back to make sure we were able to follow. I knew Lucy too well, if I was going to fall, so would she, and I refused to let that happen.

Ulfrik seemed to have the same idea, beckoning me to hurry as I struggled to stand. He tossed my arm over his shoulder, coaxing me to move. White hot agony, like a bolt of electricity, shot up my leg into my backside.

"I can't," my voice broke, and with every step I attempted to take my legs threatened to crumple beneath me. The pain was nearly unbearable, tears streaming across my cheeks as I tried in vain to take my first step.

Ulfrik said not a word as he bent, one hand against my upper back, as he scooped me into his arms, darting towards the entryway. As he carried me across the threshold, the frame bowed, snapping in two, as the Keep crumbled around us. Dust and smoke and ash and fire and snow filled the air.

The fog lifted in time for us to survey the damage. Wailing and scattered cries of agony scratched the back of my mind. I was acutely aware I was witnessing the death of something precious. An impenetrable monument to their people, their culture, their way of life was gone now, a pile of rubble slipping from a shell—a skeleton—that was now worthless.

Eldrid and the shieldmaidens had abandoned their weapons, tending to the wounded in the courtyard. Bear, Wolf, Eagle, it did not matter who you were, all were given food and drink and medicine. Or so I thought. Asger stood sheepishly to the side, and it was clear he felt out of place. Who could blame him? His king betrayed him, and he was forced to turn his sword on his own. There was animosity here, among the survivors. Some wolves and bears had turned against any of the surviving eagles, labeling them traitors, outcasts. Shouting and name calling exploded onto bouts of fistfights, that instantly dissolved into groups hunting down, isolating, and ganging up on those who were mistakenly on the wrong side of the battle. I understood their disdain, their anger, but it was misplaced. Even I knew not every Eagle Clan member was at fault or responsible, sometimes we did what we did, even if it was wrong, just to survive. You could not fault human behavior, especially in times of war.

Hefting me close to his chest, Ulfrik climbed the stairway leading atop the wall. Setting me down, Ulfrik stood surveying the masses. Lucy waltzed forward, throwing my arm around her shoulders, keeping me upright. Ulfrik addressed the languishing crowd from atop the parapets. Their faces were a mixture of exhaustion and languishing fear. "Today, our people have suffered through treason and death. Our world, our way of life, will never be the same. But make no mistake, we will never surrender. We will grow from this."

Bjorn walked forward, patting his brother on the back. "A wise person once told us that we are not that different. Bear, Wolf, Eagle. And if we truly want to be united, then we must do so as one clan."

Murmurings buzzed on the breeze as the crowd questioned what their kings were getting at. My heart soared realizing that Ulfrik and Bjorn had agreed with me.

"We should not let our differences define us, but our similarities," Ulfrik said. "From this day forward, we are not three clans, we are one."

Beside him, Bjorn, Lucy, and I, stood in mute wonder, at

our king, at our home. The stoic previous king of the Bear Clan brought his hands together, his clapping causing the sea of people to join in, the cacophony vibrating the air around us.

"We are one!" someone shouted. A call that rose among all those in the courtyard. Thousands of voices rising into the air. "We are one, we are one, we are one!"

CHAPTER

THIRTY-TWO

Among those scattered under the awnings of the courtyard, there was a single person I had to see. My limp was pronounced, but not so much that I couldn't convince the others to let me hobble across the yard on my own, or at the very least, with a makeshift cane that resembled a simple stick. Ulfrik would have had more to say about it if he wasn't instantly assaulted by questions and concerns.

I didn't get far before a crowd began to form. Men, women, and children emerged from hiding to sift through the remains of the once illustrious city. Men pried fallen beams and heavy stones from doorways and alleyways, women collected blankets and medicine, while children picked unspoiled food from the rubble. Whatever could be salvaged was dragged through the smoldering ruins to a pile in the center of the crowd. Here, the injured and elderly helped sort them.

But it was there, amongst the smoke that snaked towards a greying sky, that I noticed a peculiar shadow darting between the buildings. This shadow hung back from the prying eyes, hesitating at the far edge of a crowd, the hood over their head being pulled taut against their face. Slowly, I picked my way through the rubble, my eyes never leaving the shadow as it too began to pick its way towards an alley on the other side of the crowd. For every step it took, I took two. I seemed to have completely forgotten the pain in my leg, or the pronounced limp it produced. For me, the only thing that existed was whoever was skulking around the people I cared about. I wished—*begged*, to be wrong. Maybe this person was simply frightened, or still trying to come to terms with what had happened. I could understand that. But something about the way this person held themselves, clutching their cloak close to their body, avoiding eye contact with everyone they passed—something was wrong.

I closed the distance between us when my quarry tripped over a beam that cut an alleyway in half, allowing me to get close enough to see the stitching on their dark green cloak. They suspected nothing. We were in a delicate dance, but only one of us knew it. Until a jolt of pain like a lightning bolt ran up the length of my leg and into my back causing me to cry out. I bit back the cry, hoping it wasn't too late, even though I knew it was. The shadow froze, like a deer in headlights, turning to face me in that small alley.

My blood chilled in my very veins. The space somehow got smaller, the walls caving in on me. There was no mistaking the mottled skin on the left side of her face that hugged her jaw and snaked down her neck beneath the dark green cloak. All I saw was red, like a bull at a rodeo. She had survived.

"*You*," I hissed.

Turid's eyes widened, recognition immediately replaced by an unmistakable sense of fear. Tears gathered in her eyes, and she bolted.

"Turid!" I screeched after her, my mind moving faster than my legs allowed me to.

Pain erupted in my foot, my calf, my knee, and I buckled, crashing to the ground. But I didn't give myself even a moment to catch my breath, for the pain to register, as I scrambled back to my feet and raced after her the best I could. But the pain was blinding, and I knew the further I pushed myself, the more damage I was doing. But I couldn't—*wouldn't*, let her escape. Too many people had lost their friends, their families, their loved ones, and her conspiring led to their anguish.

I didn't even pay attention to my surroundings. The world flew past, with its stonework and wooden beams, snapping flags in the breeze, and simmering fires. All I saw in the chaos was that green cloak, and somehow, I managed to keep just enough pace for her to fail to escape me at every turn. Until the tight alleys disappeared, and I found myself thrust into a courtyard of manicured bushes and cobbled stone.

It was then I realized where I was. The wooden slats over the windows of the building she had disappeared into, the towering walls that hid it from the outside…and my gaze immediately sought out the sprawling stone mansion to my right, with its now decapitated statues and blood-stained grand staircase. This was where I had fled, past the horses in the stable, along the wall to that hole that led out into the surrounding forest. She was trying to escape.

Hobbling across the slick cobble stone towards the stables, I followed her behind the hedges, hugging the wall. There in the wall a grate lay open beside a hole, where a dark green cloak and a booted foot disappeared just as I freed myself from the branches that clung to me, slowing me down. Kneeling beside the entry, I allowed myself a moment to breathe, before peering into the abyss. On the other side sat an expanse of snow before a gently swaying evergreen forest.

Movement caught my eye, and I watched as Turid gathered herself to her feet, not bothering to shake the snow and dirt that clung to her hems before making a beeline towards the trees.

"Turid!" I hissed after her. Bending down, I gathered my hems, ready to make after her.

But instantly I felt hands grip my shoulders. I didn't bother to stare up at whoever held me, I dug my hands into the dirt, my anger silent on my tongue as the grip tightened and pulled me back from the hole.

I stared up with pure hatred for whoever had the audacity to stop me, and immediately simmered at the sadness in the eyes that stared down at me.

"Eldrid...*why?*" My voice broke.

She shook her head, kneeling beside me in the dirt. Together we watched the dark green cloak disappear within the trees, the forest swallowing her whole.

"It's not worth it."

I brushed her hand off me, my eyes still on the tree line. "She doesn't deserve to leave, Eldrid—"

"She will face judgement, Phoebe. The gods will see to that." And even as she said it, in the distance a wolf howled, joined by another and another.

My gaze narrowed, but I couldn't make out anything. "What's going on?"

"The hunt begins," Eldrid said, standing to her feet. "Let us return, someone is looking for you."

Eldrid had insisted on throwing my arm around her shoulders, helping support me back through the streets towards what remained of the High Keep. Not a word passed between us, and although I could feel she was tense, I knew she believed what she had said. Turid would not escape lightly out there in the wilderness.

I shuddered remembering that voice on the wind, the cold that bit into my skin, and the icy water that filled my lungs.

"Are you okay?" Eldrid's voice broke through the memory that haunted me.

I offered her a tight smile. "Yeah."

We finally made it back to the courtyard of the Keep, where people continued to clean and cook and gather supplies.

"So, who was looking for—" I didn't finish the sentence as my eyes caught sight of a golden-haired man lying on a bundle of hay and furs.

His eyes were shut tight, and a shieldmaiden stood beside him, gently dabbing a washcloth against his forehead. I unhooked myself from Eldrid, limping towards him. The shieldmaiden looked up at me, before returning to wiping the sweat from his brow.

"I'll take over," I said.

The shieldmaiden regarded me a moment, hesitant to leave.

"Please, get some rest." I encouraged. She nodded and disappeared into the crowd.

I grasped Leif's hand in mine. He was weak, his skin pallid, but he was conscious. He struggled against the morning light in his eyes. "You survived."

"I could say the same to you." His chest was bare to the frigid air, a tight bandage around his waist, a light pink stain as a single dot.

"Does it hurt?" Of course, it did, but in the healthcare industry you were always taught to talk to a patient, even if it was to state the obvious. The easiest way to do that was to ask a question, because people preferred answering questions in times of pain than holding a conversation on their own.

He smirked, seeing through what I was trying to do.

"A little bit, yourself?" He eyed the cane I used to hold myself upright.

I shrugged. "Not even a flesh wound."

A comfortable silence settled between us. There was something he held back saying, however, a shadow across his face that was impossible to hide or decipher.

"Have you decided, yet?"

I frowned. "What?"

He watched as the sun's rays pierced the cloud of smoke that rose from the ruins of the High Keep. "To stay or to go."

My eyes strayed to the man who now was approaching with trepidation. He paused, discerning the atmosphere between us. Skoll and Hati sat at his heel, looking up lovingly into the eyes of their pack leader. Lucy and Bjorn were close behind, hand in hand. Everyone was here, everyone was nearby. Eldrid and Asger flitted by within earshot, no doubt sensing the abrupt change in our demeanors.

Releasing Leif's hand, I turned to Ulfrik. Fear, worry, doubt, all flashed behind those tired golden eyes. His hands were warm when I grasped them, his lips lifting at the sides as I offered him a smile.

"A promise is a promise," I said.

We were safe, we had survived.

His eyes widened, but there was doubt still in those depths. "Do not think you must do this because you promised, Phoebe."

I smirked. "Oh no, Ulfrik. I do this because I want to."

"Are you sure?"

I nodded.

The courtyard had lapsed into a silence as those who could stand or walk came closer within earshot. They waited, the tension in the air so thick you could cut it with a knife.

Ulfrik kneeled, holding my hands. His eyes searched mine, his voice strong. "Phoebe, will you marry me?"

"Yes."

There was no hesitation, no second thought, no anxiety, or niggling voice in the back of my head. I was sure. Not just because I had faced down death and admitted my feelings to him. It was because I truly loved this man.

As we embraced one another, Ulfrik pulled me close, twirling me in his arms as our eyes met. I had longed for this moment, leaning into him as he did the same. Our lips met one another, soft and gentle at first. It advanced quickly, becoming urgent, passionate. When finally, we broke apart, a raucous applause greeted us, as the unified people of this world shouted their approval. Lucy and Bjorn, Eldrid and Asger, Leif, even Hati and Skoll and the giant bear I hadn't seen since the Cliff City, stood around us, excitement palpable in the air. In the distance, an eagle soared high over the smoldering ruins.

I had everything here, and so long as they stayed by my side, it was all I could ever need. Whatever the future may bring, we would face it head-on, together.

acknowledgements

Firstly, I would like to thank my mother and sister for their unrelenting support of my dreams. From my very first project and everything in between, they have always been there for me, cheering me on.

Secondly, I'd like to thank my friends and reading team who provided many hours and days of their lives to make my projects the best they could be.

And last but not least, I'd like to thank my consort, who was enthusiastically by my side throughout everything.

about the author

Currently residing in Los Angeles, Toni was raised in Australia and Japan. She spends her free time worshipping her two cats, who she can't disprove aren't vengeful deities. Hobbies include avoiding reality such as: reading, writing, playing video games, and watching the same five television shows as background noise. Featured in several anthologies, you can keep up with her works at *www.tonimobley.com*.